Sons of Liberty

*Book IV
of the Royal Sorceress series*

ALSO BY CHRISTOPHER G. NUTTALL

The Mind's Eye

Royal Sorceress series
The Royal Sorceress
The Great Game
Necropolis

Bookworm series
Bookworm
Bookworm II: The Very Ugly Duckling
Bookworm III: The Best Laid Plans
Bookworm IV: Full Circle

DIZZY SPELLS SERIES
A LIFE LESS ORDINARY

Inverse Shadows Universe
Sufficiently Advanced Technology

Sons of Liberty

Book IV
of the Royal Sorceress series

Christopher G. Nuttall

Elsewhen Press

To Aisha and Eric

Prologue

Written for publication in *The Times*, London, 1831. Article suppressed at the request of His Majesty's Government.

INVASION!

It has just been reported that the French, having somehow escaped our doughty sailors in the Grand Fleet, have landed a major army on the shores of our beloved country! French soldiers have been reported at Dover, Hastings, Eastbourne and Brighton! French ships have been reported ravaging the south coast and trading fire with the batteries defending Southampton and Portsmouth! French airships have reportedly attacked defensive positions in Tunbridge Wells! The treachery of the French Tyrant-King in launching such an invasion will not go unpunished!

Addressing the Members of Parliament in joint session with the Lords, LORD LIVERPOOL, HIS MAJESTY'S PRIME MINISTER, informed them that British troops are already being dispatched to Surrey, where they will push the dastardly French back through Sussex and Kent into the sea! The DUKE OF INDIA has resigned his former post and taken command of the army! Our sailors are already moving the Channel Fleet to block all lines of retreat, despite shifty and cowardly attacks mounted by French submarines! And the Royal Sorcerers Corps, Britain's great strength, is moving to support the counter-attack, led by the formidable LADY GWENDOLYN CRICHTON!

His Majesty asks that every true Englishman do his duty to keep the French from crushing our troops, invading our cities and ravishing our women!

The Lord Mayor and Governor-General of London has issued a proclamation to the citizens of his city.

Martial Law is now in effect! All members of the regulars, the militias and the trained bands are to report for duty immediately, where they will be issued with weapons. All able-bodied men who are not already serving or in vital positions are to make themselves known to the Area

Wardens, who will assign them to positions building up the defences. All women and children are to remain in their homes, unless ordered to do otherwise by the Area Wardens. Anyone found on the streets without permission risks arrest and possible detention.

Martial Law is now in effect! Do not share rumours, lies or other stories that might cause panic and upset. Do not discuss your work, or your husband's work, with anyone. The person you talk to might be a French spy! Something you consider to be harmless might be very dangerous indeed, if told to the wrong person. All citizens are warned to keep their eyes open for signs of French spies or sympathisers! Call the Area Warden AT ONCE if you suspect someone is aiding the French!

Martial Law is now in effect! All members of the London Police Force have been armed and ordered to enforce the curfew. Members of the lower classes are warned that anyone caught looting, rioting or otherwise taking advantage of the invasion will be shot on the spot.

Do not panic! Do not despair! Do not listen to false rumourmongers! The French will be repelled from our walls and shoved back into the waters, where they will drown!

God Save The King!

Chapter One

he French are coming," Major Carrington Shaw whispered, hoarsely. "I can *smell* them."

Gwen gave him a sharp look. Shaw had been assigned to her – and Merlin, the sorcerous combat team – at very short notice, *too* short notice. He was handsome enough, she supposed, but his bombastic attitude made her suspect that he'd bought his commission, rather than earning it through talent. And the looks he gave her, from time to time, suggested that he was one of the men who thought women shouldn't be anywhere near battlefields, no matter how much magic they had.

"Stay down," she hissed. She could feel the French presence too, tiny sparks of magic from the south-east that flickered through the ether. The French had to have committed most of their combat sorcerers to the invasion, despite the risk of setting their sorcerous research back fifty years and opening themselves to a counter-invasion. If they took Great Britain, they'd practically win the war outright. "We need to take them by surprise."

She felt sweat running down her back as the sound of distant gunfire grew louder. The French had successfully occupied a line running from Dover to Brighton, she'd been told as the Royal Sorcerers Corps hurried to join the defence line, but they wouldn't stay there for long. Landing on British soil, after decoying the Channel Fleet out of position, had been a daring stroke, yet the Royal Navy was already moving to block both their reinforcements and their line of retreat. The French had no choice but to advance on London as quickly as they could, living off the land.

And good luck with that, she thought nastily. The

government had worked hard to move as much as it could out of the threatened area, although countless small farmers had refused to uproot themselves to an uncertain fate. *There aren't enough stables between here and London to keep even a small army going for more than a few days.*

Her lips twitched, then she sobered, recalling the horrific scenes as the sorcerers had disembarked from the trains at Dorking. Hundreds of women and children, the former terrified; the latter crying, had been herded onto trains heading north. No one knew if they *could* be fed, when they reached their destination, or even where their final destination was going to be. It was quite likely that most of them would never see their homes again, not if the rumours from the occupied zone were true. And most of the menfolk had been pressed into helping to dig trenches and build barricades ...

"They'll be coming to Dorking," Major Shaw breathed. "There's nowhere else they can go."

Gwen felt another flicker of irritation, which she swiftly suppressed. If Major Shaw had been in combat before, she would have eaten her hat. There was no shortage of officers with experience in India, Africa and North America, but they were needed elsewhere. Shaw might have been assigned to her because the Duke of India, an experienced military man, thought it would keep him out of the way. There was no room for an inexperienced officer when Britain herself was at stake.

"They have to," she agreed, glancing at him. His long fingers were playing with his goatee, nervously. "Capturing the rail lines into London will allow them to block us from moving our forces back to defend the city."

She smiled at his astonished look – she might as well have been speaking French – and turned back to watch for advancing enemies, feeling his eyes boring into her back. Major Shaw wouldn't expect a *woman* to understand the basics of logistics, let alone military operations ... but Gwen had been studying them ever since Master Thomas had died, leaving her as the Royal Sorceress. She'd always feared this moment would come, the day she had to lead the Royal Sorcerers Corps into battle. And the hell of it was that no one would blame her – publicly – if she backed off and allowed Sir James Braddock to take command.

But they'd whisper about it privately, she reminded herself, firmly. A man who turned his back on the enemy would be called a coward, loudly and clearly, but women weren't expected to be *brave*. There were no women in the red-coated infantry readying their defensive positions, no female sailors manning the decks as the Royal Navy advanced into the channel … just her, the lone sorceress on the battlefield. *No one would ever take me seriously again.*

She ran her hand through her sweaty blonde hair, silently grateful she'd cut it so short. Long hair might be a mark of distinction among the quality – she knew girls who had hair so long it dragged on the floor – but it would have got in her way, if she'd had to fight. The outfit she'd inherited from Master Thomas was hot and stuffy, yet she knew she couldn't change it for anything, not now. At least she wasn't trying to fight in a dress. She had a sudden mental image of herself crouching in the woods, wearing a long green dress, and snickered at the thought. She'd look thoroughly absurd.

Major Shaw coughed. "Something funny, My Lady?"

"Just a stray thought," Gwen said. She closed her eyes for a long moment, reaching out with her other senses. The flickers of magic were growing stronger. "They're nearly here."

A cavalryman rode up from behind, his red uniform glinting in the sunlight. "Message from His Grace, the Duke of India," he barked. "The French are advancing towards your position! The hussars are moving up to support you!"

"Thank you," Gwen said, curtly. She almost laughed at the cavalryman's double-take when he realised she was a woman. "Tell the hussars to remain behind the trenches until we scatter the magicians."

Major Shaw glanced at her, sharply. "They'll lose the chance to hit the Frenchmen before they scatter."

Gwen glared back, allowing her anger to show. "They'll be slaughtered if they have to face magicians," she snapped. She looked up at the cavalryman. "Take my orders to their commander!"

"Yes, My Lady," the cavalryman boomed. He'd clearly

realised who she was, who she had to be. "It shall be done!"

He cantered away, just as the French magicians came into view. Four men, flying through the skies like birds. No, not quite; two of them were Movers, providing the motive power, while the other two were Blazers, watching for targets on the ground. One of them sent a pulse of magic crackling downwards as she watched, although she was unsure what he'd seen as there was no one further southeast than her force. Maybe he'd just spotted a rabbit and blasted the poor animal, just to be on the safe side. Or to add to their rations. Gwen was sure the French magicians ate well – they needed to be well-fed to use their magic – but even they had to be feeling the pinch. The French Navy couldn't hope to keep them supplied.

"I see them," Major Shaw breathed. He snapped his rifle into firing position. "I can take them."

"Don't shoot," Gwen snapped. She had no doubt Major Shaw could *hit* the Frenchmen – he was an aristocrat, probably used to going shooting every Sunday – but she had a feeling it would be useless. The enemy magicians were protected by their magic. "Let them get closer."

"They're coming too close," Major Shaw hissed. "They'll see us."

He pulled the trigger. The gun barked. It was a good shot, part of Gwen's mind noted; he would have hit his target if the enemy magician hadn't been protected. But all it had done was reveal their position to the enemy. Gwen swore, using words she'd picked up from some of the soldiers, and launched herself into the air. The French Blazers targeted her, streams of magic crackling over her shields; she smiled, then reached out with her own magic, yanking the Blazer away from his comrade. He plummeted towards the ground, screaming in terror.

The Mover hurled himself forward, his magic grappling with Gwen's and trying to crush her in her own shields. He was powerful, she noted, as she hit the ground and bounced; certainly more powerful with his single talent than she was with her multiple talents. But he wasn't prepared for her. She used her own magic to create a blinding flash of light, disorienting him long enough for her to charge the ground below him with magic. Seconds later, it exploded inside his protective shields. They snapped out of existence, allowing her to burn his head to ash. There was no point in taking chances with a magician.

Strong man, she thought. She wasn't sure *she* could have held her shields in place, if she'd been blinded. The shock alone would have weakened her. *A shame he was on the wrong side*.

She glanced up as she felt another spike of magic, then slammed her shields into place as a pair of French Movers charged her, their magic picking up trees, rocks and soil, hurling them towards her. The instinctive response was to hurl herself upwards, out of the way, but she knew that would be a mistake. One Mover would be enough to pull her out of the sky; two would be enough to rip her apart, if they caught her between them. Gritting her teeth, she summoned a wave of fire and threw it back at them, trusting in her power to shield herself from their makeshift weapons. Her head began to ache as ... *things* ... pounded into her shields, but she held firm. The torrent of projectiles disintegrated into dust, then came to a halt. One of the Frenchmen was starting to choke.

Idiot, she thought, coldly. *Breathing smoke isn't wise.*

Bracing herself, she ran forward, magic spilling out in front of her. She caught hold of one of the Frenchmen and hurled him into the air as hard as she could. It wouldn't kill him, not when he could fly under his own power, but it would make him a target for the other British magicians. The other turned to face her, slamming a punch of force right into her shields. If she hadn't been protected, it would have shattered her. As it was, it picked her up and hurled her right across the battlefield. She landed hard and bounced ...

Cursing, she stumbled to her feet as the Frenchman approached, his face twisted with bitter anger. She wondered, dully, if he recognised her, then decided it hardly mattered. Save perhaps for Lord Mycroft, there was no one whom the French wanted dead more. Her ears were ringing – she thought she might have damaged them, somehow – but she gathered all the magic she could to her, gritting her teeth in anger as she realised it was pitifully low. She could taste blood in her mouth, feel it trickling down her neck ... The

Frenchman lifted his arm, ready to slam her one final time …

…And was sent careening into the air as Sir James slammed into him, his magic smashing right into the Frenchman's protections. He caught himself and hung in midair, glaring down at his new foe. Gwen forced herself to summon another spark of magic, then nodded to Sir James. The Mover yanked on the Frenchman's shields, pulling them open long enough for Gwen to hit the Frenchman with a pulse of magic. His body and power disintegrated in the same instant, leaving pieces of blood and gore to fall over the battlefield. Gwen stumbled to her knees almost as soon as the enemy died. Darkness flickered at the corner of her eyes, threatening to pull her down. She hadn't pushed herself so hard since the Swing.

Where I nearly died, she reminded herself, as she heard the sound of running footsteps. *And I would have died, if Jack hadn't saved me from Master Thomas.*

"Drink this," Sir James said. He pushed a canteen against her lips. Gwen sipped, tasting water and a hint of whiskey. "Do you want to withdraw?"

Gwen scowled at him. Sir James didn't have to worry about being thought a weak and feeble woman, even if she *did* have the heart and stomach of a man. She couldn't leave, not without undermining her position so badly she knew she'd never recover. Besides, if the French took London, she'd be doomed anyway. They'd hardly take the risk of letting her live. Indeed, given what she'd heard from Jack and the treacherous Sir Charles Bellingham, she was privately resolved to kill herself rather than allow the French to take her prisoner. She had a very good idea what they'd do to her.

"No," she said, forcing herself to stand upright. The water helped, although she knew she was badly drained. "Where are the others?"

"Holding the line," Sir James said. There was a hint of amused reproof in his tone. "You did well, but you *are* part of a team."

Gwen felt her cheeks heat. *Merlin* was a team, but she wasn't part of it. *Sir James* took magicians with different talents and worked them into a whole; she had all the talents, yet preferred to work on her own. But she couldn't afford to work on her own in wartime. She needed to learn to fit into a team.

"I know," she said, finally. If only there had been more time to practice! But it had been scant days between her return from Russia and the outbreak of war. "And ..."

She broke off as she felt another spike of magic. A trio of Frenchmen were running towards them, surrounded by hideous monsters. Gwen had to admire their skill, but not their common sense. The illusions were striking, too striking, to be real. It would have been more effective, she noted as Sir James wrapped them both in a protective shield, if they'd created a vision of French soldiers charging their position. A soldier on the battlefield might well have thought that illusion was reality.

"Blazers," Sir James said, as the illusions snapped out of existence. His shield began to glow as the Frenchmen bombarded it with magic. "And not particularly well-trained ones either."

Gwen nodded, then reached out with her magic and caught hold of all three Frenchmen, hurling them up and into the air. Unlike the Movers, Blazers couldn't fly under their own power. They'd fall to the ground and die, when gravity reasserted itself. She let go of them, wondering absently just where they'd land. Maybe they'd come down right on top of the Frenchman in command.

"I need to link up with the others," Sir James said. "Do you want to come with me?"

Gwen shook her head. "I need to find out what's going on," she said. In all the excitement, she'd lost track of the overall battle. Now there was no immediate threat, she might have to find Major Shaw and get an overall report. "I'll catch up with you."

She half-expected Sir James to insist she come with him, but he said nothing and merely marched off to the southeast. Gwen felt an odd stab of envy, then reached for her magic and tested it, gingerly. She still had enough to be dangerous, she reassured herself, if she needed to fight. Bracing herself, she pulled her magic around her and rose off the ground and into the air. Her ears were still muffled – she made a mental note to check with a Healer, after the fighting was done – but she could hear the sound of artillery fire. There was no way to be sure, but it seemed to be growing closer.

It was hard to see anything clearly. The battlefield was swathed in smoke. Flames were rising from the nearby woodland, suggesting that someone was trying to burn out the defenders. Explosions flickered and flared where shells landed. A burning airship drifted into view, her crew fighting desperately to keep her in the air even though it was futile; she hit the ground and exploded into a massive fireball. Gwen couldn't help feeling a flicker of contempt. Both sides had plenty of reason to know, by now, that airships just couldn't survive anywhere near Blazers ...

And the Hussars were mounting a charge against the French lines.

She felt her heart drop into her boots as the charge picked up speed. The French were battered, yes, but they weren't *broken*. As she watched, they formed a square and greeted the hussars with canisters of grapeshot. Gwen tried to think of something – anything – she could do, but there was nothing. The Hussars were brave men. They didn't break, they didn't run, but it hardly mattered. The last of them fell from his horse and died well before reaching the French lines.

I gave them no orders, Gwen thought, as she dropped down towards her command tent. *Who sent them out to die?*

"Lady Gwen," Major Shaw said. He sounded impossibly cheerful. Beside him, a pair of staff officers, wearing fancy uniforms, were smoking. "I ..."

Gwen cut him off. "The hussars are dead," she snapped. The urge to tear him apart rose up within her. Two hundred men, most of them aristocrats, were dead. "What have you done?"

"I saw an opportunity and I took it," Major Shaw said. He didn't sound apologetic. "I did what I thought needed to be done."

"Tell me," Gwen ordered, lacing her voice with Charm. "What were you thinking?"

"I did what you would have done, if you were not hampered by your sex," Major Shaw said, sounding rather perplexed. He didn't seem bright enough, Gwen noted, to realise he was being Charmed. His cronies made no attempt to hide their amusement. "One must take decisive action on the battlefield ..."

The disobedient fool, Gwen thought. Her temper snapped. The hussars had been thrown into battle and slaughtered, *pointlessly*. There was nothing wrong with taking decisive action, but the moment had been wrong. And he had felt he could disobey her because she was a woman ...?

She reached out with her magic, with the talent she'd discovered in Russia, and caught hold of his mind. "Stay here," she snarled. He let out an odd little gasp, as if she'd pricked him with a pin. "Sit down. Issue no further orders. Keep your mouth shut!"

Major Shaw sat down, his entire body shaking with ... *something*. Gwen barely noticed, just as she barely noticed the two cronies who were backing away from her. She had to fight to keep from ripping his mind to shreds. It would have been so easy ...

Instead, she turned and walked back to the war.

Chapter Two

ondon felt ... *eerie*.

Raechel Slater-Standish walked slowly down Pall Mall, feeling alone in the middle of a teeming city. The streets, normally full to bursting with cabs, carts and thousands upon thousands of hawkers, traders and pedestrians, were deserted. She couldn't help feeling as if the entire population had just vanished, stolen away in the middle of the night, even though she knew it was absurd. The Lord Mayor had warned the population to stay indoors and keep out of the way, particularly if the French laid siege to the city. She sensed, more than saw, hidden eyes peeking at her as she picked up speed. They had to be wondering who she was and why she was out on the streets. No young woman should be out and about with the French breathing down their necks.

I have a pass, she thought, feeling the sheaf of papers in her bag. *And somewhere to go.*

She shivered, despite herself. Her aunt had never really grasped just how many times Raechel had slipped out of the house. She'd ordered the maids to keep a sharp eye on the young mistress, after all, and the maids were *everywhere*. And yet, Raechel knew she'd never really gone into Greater London, beyond the bright lights and safety of the richest part of the city. There were footpads out there, men who would steal from a young woman – or do worse, if they thought the girl had no one who would avenge her. But she'd seen worse in Russia, she reminded herself. The undead had almost killed her ...

A horse cantered up beside her, the mounted policeman looking down at her with cold suspicious eyes. Raechel felt a flicker of surprise, then told herself not to be stupid. She *looked* respectable – the dress she wore marked her out as middle-class, rather than the finery she normally wore – but she shouldn't be on the streets at all. The policeman had no reason to believe she wasn't anything more than a merchant's daughter.

"Your papers, Miss," he said.

Raechel produced one of the pieces of paper she'd been given, after her brief interview with a government official, and held it out to the policeman. His eyes went very wide – the permit authorised her to go anywhere, save for the red zones surrounding the city – and he passed it back hastily, as if he feared it would burn him. Raechel gave him a cheeky smile, then folded the paper up and put it back in her bag. He doffed his hat to her and cantered off.

It could have been worse, she thought, as she watched the policeman ride off into the distance. *He could have tried to insist on escorting me to my destination.*

She shook her head as she turned the corner and headed down, past a long line of houses she knew to be both expensive and exclusive, even though they were relatively small. Her uncle had often bemoaned the simple fact that even *he* couldn't afford more than one, despite his great wealth and political standing. Raechel had pointed out, rather dryly, that there weren't enough of them to go around, driving the price upwards sharply. Her uncle hadn't been impressed. He'd merely ordered her to go back to learning ladylike arts while waiting for a suitable husband.

Her lips quirked at the thought. Her uncle's idea of what made a suitable husband would be nothing like hers. And if he'd known just how far she'd gone, in some of the hidden clubs for younger members of the aristocracy, he'd have disowned her on the spot ... unless, of course, keeping the money from her father's legacy was more important to him. It probably was. Ambassador Standish needed money and connections to promote himself in the corridors of power.

She stopped outside a simple black door and hesitated, feeling – again – unseen eyes peering at her. Lady Gwen had told her that she'd put Raechel's name forward for training, but warned her that it was going to be hard, very hard. Being a secret government agent was *always* hard, particularly if one happened to have spent the first eighteen years of one's life as a spoilt brat. Raechel hadn't liked the implication, but she had to admit that Lady Gwen had a point. Sneaking out for furtive kisses – and more – wasn't anything like as dangerous as fighting the undead in Russia.

And you wanted to make something of yourself, she told herself. It would be easy to wait until her father's legacy passed to her, then spend the rest of her life partying, but she wanted something more. *This is the way forward.*

Taking a breath, she stepped forward and tapped on the door.

There was a long pause, then the door swung open of its own accord. The corridor beyond, illuminated by gaslights hanging from the walls, was empty. A chill ran down her spine as she recalled all the stories of haunted houses, where vengeful ghosts lay in wait for their prey ... and then she shook her head, firmly. A magician could easily have opened the door for her, even from a distance. Moments later, she felt a gentle force tugging at her, inviting her inside. She could have turned and run, but instead she walked forward, into the house. The door closed behind her as soon as she was inside. Ahead of her, another door gaped open invitingly. Raechel scowled – did they really need all the theatrics – and then walked onwards, through the door. The room was empty, save for a young woman standing against the far wall. Raechel felt an odd tingle at the back of her mind as the young woman looked up at her.

They studied each other in silence for a long moment. The woman was older than Raechel, she thought, probably at least twenty-five. Her face was very pale, a natural paleness Raechel knew she'd never be able to emulate, no matter how much cream and dust she piled on her face. It was framed by short dark hair that gave her an impish look, although the way she held herself suggested she was used to much longer hair. And while she wore a simple white dress, Raechel had no doubt the woman was from the aristocracy. No commoner could hope to maintain that sort of poise.

"You are wrong, I'm afraid," the woman said. She spoke in the genteel tones of the aristocracy, just like Lady

Standish, but there was a hint of amusement in her voice that Raechel's aunt would never have allowed herself. "I was not born to the aristocracy."

Raechel stared at her in shock. How the hell had she ...?

Understanding clicked. "Get out of my mind!"

The woman – the Talker – smiled. "Learn how to stop me," she challenged. "Anyone can, with enough effort."

Raechel glared at her, then tried to recall Gwen's lessons. She wasn't given to contemplation, not like her aunt. It was hard to organise her thoughts, then shield them against questing probes from a Talker. Every time she thought she had it, she felt that accursed tingle at the back of her mind ...

"We will need to work on that," the Talker said. "Tell me about yourself."

"I have a better idea," Raechel said, sullenly. The damned woman could at least have told Raechel her *name*. "Why don't *you* tell me about myself?"

"As you wish," the Talker said. "My name is Irene, by the way."

She paused, closing her eyes thoughtfully. "Your name is Raechel Slater, or so you think of yourself. Officially, as the ward of Lord Standish, you are Raechel Slater-Standish. You are eighteen pushing eighty" – her lips curved into a thin smile – "and have been rebelling against your aunt for the last two years, mainly by going to dubious parties and having sexual relationships with junior scions of the aristocracy. The danger of finding yourself pregnant never really occurred to you, as your paramours promised to pull out before it was too late and they lost control. Which, incidentally, is not a reliable method of birth control."

Raechel blushed, furiously. Memories rose unbidden to the forefront of her mind. Young men, handsome enough to make her heart flutter, rakish enough that she *knew* her aunt would never approve of them ... some good at giving her pleasure, some only interested in themselves. And Irene, if that was her real name, had seen everything in her mind ...

She cringed in embarrassment, but Irene went on.

"You went to Russia because your guardians feared to leave you in London alone," she continued. "There you met the Royal Sorceress, who was posing as your maid at the time; Lady Gwen set you straight and convinced you that you could be something more than just another brainless beauty. You requested a post at the Royal College. Lady Gwen promised to ensure an introduction, instead, to the covert branch of British Intelligence. After a brief interview, you were given an address and told to come here. To me."

Raechel nodded, shortly.

"You are impulsive," Irene concluded. "There is no doubt that you are smart, but you are often driven forward by your emotions rather than common sense. You were very lucky indeed not to wind up pregnant, which would have been hard to explain to your guardians, not least because you wouldn't be sure just who'd fathered the brat. Lady Gwen was capable of playing your maid long enough to get to Russia and carry out her mission. Can you do the same?"

"Yes," Raechel said.

Irene gave her a long look. "Very well," she said, finally. "You will be trained. *I* will train you. If at any moment you want to leave you may do so, but there will be no second chance to shine. You can stay in London with your money and look for a suitable husband."

"I'd rather die," Raechel said, surprising herself.

"That may be an option," Irene warned. "Covert work is *never* played by the rules. An agent who gets into deep trouble may wind up dead, or worse. And very few people will know how you died and why."

"I understand," Raechel said.

Irene nodded. "You will do everything, and I mean *everything*, I tell you to do," she added, sternly. "Again, if you want to leave you may leave …"

"But there will be no second chance," Raechel said, irritated. She was no maid who needed the same orders repeated time and time again before she understood, no rake who needed to be told *no* twice before he backed off. "I understand."

"Good," Irene said. She reached around the back of her neck and undid her dress. It fell to the ground, pooling around her feet. Raechel stared, then looked away, hastily, from her naked body. "Undress."

"*What?*"

"Undress," Irene repeated. There was no give in her voice. "Undress or leave."

Raechel hesitated. She had never been naked in front of anyone, save for her maids, since she was a very young girl. Even her liaisons at the club had involved nothing more than hauling up her dress to allow her paramours entry. To be naked in front of someone on the same social level as herself was wrong, against everything she'd been taught. Even her husband shouldn't be allowed to look at her naked body. And yet ...

Gritting her teeth, she unbuttoned the dress and allowed it to fall to the ground. The undershirt followed, allowing her breasts to bobble free. They were larger than Irene's, she noted with a flicker of vindictive glee. The older women who talked about thinness clearly hadn't realised just how much men enjoyed large breasts, although *that* was wanton behaviour and not ladylike. She hesitated before removing her drawers, but Irene was relentless. Slowly, she pushed the underclothes down to her feet and stepped out of them, leaving her clothes on the floor. She found it hard to repress a giggle. She was naked!

Irene studied her carefully, her eyes examining every trace of Raechel's body. Raechel looked back, noting with some amusement that Irene shaved *everywhere*. It was a sign of wanton behaviour, she recalled being told by one of the maids. Only lower-class women shaved everywhere. And yet, she'd considered doing it for herself in pursuit of pleasure. If she hadn't been sure the maids would have told her aunt ...

"Men like it that way," Irene said, shortly.

Raechel coloured, again. "Stop reading my mind."

"Learn how to keep me out," Irene repeated. "You think I'm the only mind-reader you're likely to encounter?"

"No," Raechel said. Gwen had been worried about a French Talker, hadn't she? "But it's hard ..."

"Try being an opera singer sometime," Irene said. "You'll find it much harder than you think."

"I can't sing to save my life," Raechel said. Was Irene an opera singer? It would make excellent cover for her activities, wouldn't it? "Do I have to learn?"

"If you have the talent, you might as well make use of it," Irene pointed out. She reached out and poked at Raechel's arms, then gently turned her around. "Do you know how to fire a gun? Fight to defend yourself?"

Raechel snorted. "I fought in Russia," she said, "but no one ever taught me how to fight."

"I will," Irene said. "Come with me."

She turned and walked out of the door. Raechel followed, feeling cool air drifting against her naked skin. Downwards, deeper into the house, a man was standing, watching both women with cold eyes. Raechel yelped and covered herself hastily, stumbling backwards in shock and horror. No man had entered her bedchamber, not even her father or the butler. The thought of them seeing her naked …

"Come on," Irene said. She seemed unbothered by the man's presence. "And keep your hands by your side."

Raechel glared at her, seriously considering simply recovering her dress and running for her life. To expose herself so blatantly to a man's gaze … it just wasn't done. And yet, Irene seemed completely unconcerned. Had she exposed herself – or worse – in the course of her duties? She might well have done …

Stubbornly, Raechel forced her legs to move and follow Irene down the corridor, even though the man was staring at her. Irene gave her a mischievous smile as they reached another door, then led the way inside. Raechel sagged in relief as soon as the door was closed behind her. She was shaking, either in embarrassment or rage. Angrily, she banished the feeling and looked around. The room was crammed with wardrobes, just like the ones she used at home.

"You'll go through worse," Irene said, bluntly. "Trust me on this. The sooner you abandon society's conventions, the better."

"Oh," Raechel said. She found it hard not to snap at the older woman. "And have you done that yourself?"

"The rules are different, depending on where you go and what role you play," Irene said, wryly. Her lips crinkled with amusement. "A French noblewoman, for example, has far more freedom than a British noblewoman. She will often have affairs with other noblemen, although she will be careful not to fall pregnant. Her husband, of course, will feel the same way. But a British noblewoman who is caught having an affair will be disgraced and banished to the country, if she's lucky. You have heard of the marriage of Lady Seymour Dorothy Fleming and Sir Richard Worsley?"

"Yes," Raechel said. Her aunt had been a young girl during the whole affair and spoke of it often, normally when rebuking Raechel for not being perfectly ladylike. "It's one of the great cautionary tales."

"And so it is," Irene said. She cleared her throat. "The average British nobleman will have no hesitation in setting up a mistress, but he will react badly to any thought his wife is enjoying the same liberty. Learn the rules of any given place before you break them."

Raechel swallowed. Did her uncle have a mistress? She found it hard to imagine her stuffed shirt of an uncle doing anything of the sort, but she had to admit it was possible. And her aunt wouldn't say a word, even if she *knew* ... she'd probably be glad that her husband was slaking his lusts somewhere else. A proper woman was not supposed to admit the existence of sexual pleasure, let alone feel it for herself ...

"Quite right," Irene agreed.

I'm going to learn how to block you if it's the last damned thing I do, Raechel thought, grimly.

"Good," Irene said. "Work on it. You'll have plenty of time to practice."

She opened a large wardrobe, revealing dozens of different outfits. Raechel stared; there was a dress that wouldn't be out of place in the palace, a milkmaid's outfit, a working class dress that had been patched several times ... and, beyond them, a handful of masculine outfits ranging from a military uniform to an elegant suit and jacket.

"Tell me," Irene said. "Why did I order you to undress?"

Raechel felt her cheeks burning, yet again. "To show me what I would have to do."

"Partly," Irene said. She tapped her finger on her chest, between her breasts. "And partly to strip you of your identity. What you wear" – she waved a hand at the outfits – "will give you a new identity. Wearing a disguise is not just about putting on a silly outfit, but assuming a whole new identity. You must not act out of character or you will be discovered."

She produced a maid's outfit and held it up. "A maid is always respectful to her employers," she added. "She is never cheeky, never rude; whatever happens, she never raises her eyes or fights back. A maid may be slapped – or worse – by her mistress and she has to take it. She cannot fight back."

Raechel swallowed. She was no stranger to her aunt's hand, but the thought of allowing someone else to strike her …

"Precisely," Irene said. "You have to play the role convincingly, if you want to succeed."

She smiled. "Still want to play?"

Raechel hesitated, then nodded.

Chapter Three

"What I would like to know," Lord Mycroft said coolly, "is just what happened to Major Shaw."

Gwen groaned, inwardly. It felt like only bare hours had passed since the French offensive had been broken, since the French had been forced back to enclaves surrounding Dover and Brighton, since she had been recalled to London. At least Sir James could handle matters, if the RSC needed to get involved. The vast majority of the French magicians had been killed in the Battle of Dorking.

"He got a number of good men killed," she said. Her tired mind hadn't quite processed why she'd been called to the Diogenes Club, rather than Lord Mycroft's office. Clearly, she was in trouble for *something*. "I told him to sit down and shut up."

"You broke him," Lord Mycroft said. "Rumours are *already* spreading."

His voice hardened. "I ask again, Lady Gwen," he said. "What did you do to him?"

Gwen gritted her teeth as she turned to stare out of the window, towards the spires of the Britannic School. It was hard, so hard, to keep her temper in check. Lord Mycroft had been one of her strongest supporters, right from the start. He didn't deserve to have her screaming at him, as if he was in the wrong. And yet, the nasty part of her mind wondered if he *was* in the wrong.

"I have a report here from the doctors," Lord Mycroft added. "Major Shaw has been crying and shaking uncontrollably for the last five hours. The entire command staff saw him blubbering like a little boy. I dare say that rumours have already reached his family, having grown vastly out of proportion. It will not be long before they start demanding punishment."

"I am no daughter to be slapped, nor wife to be rebuked," Gwen snarled. She fought hard to control herself. Life would be so much simpler if she'd been born a man. "That ... oaf disobeyed orders in the middle of a battle and got a great many good men killed!"

"You are a servant of the Crown," Lord Mycroft said, sternly. "And I ask *again*, for the *final* time, what did you do to him?"

Gwen sagged. "I discovered that I could ... *influence* ... someone if I combined Charm and Talking," she said, slowly. Master Thomas had controlled *her*, back during the Swing. The memory of no longer being in control of her own body was terrifying. "I didn't realise just how bad an effect it would have on Major Shaw."

Lord Mycroft looked up. "And you were going to mention this *when*?"

"I first managed to get it to work in Russia," Gwen said. "There was a Russian soldier I managed to ... to redirect. I was going to discuss it privately with you when I had the opportunity."

And that, she knew, was a lie. She'd left quite a few details out of her report, fearing what would happen if the truth emerged. Charmers were already feared and hated for their power, yet a strong-minded man could avoid being Charmed. Her power – her *new* power – was much harder to defeat. If people were scared of Charm, what would they make of a power that could *control* someone? And a power possessed by only one person.

"I see," Lord Mycroft said. "And you had no idea of the side effects?"

Gwen shook her head. She hadn't noticed any when Master Thomas had controlled *her*, although she'd been too busy trying to fight to survive. And the Russian soldier ... she felt a sudden stab of guilt. Had *he* been in trouble because of her? He'd only been doing his duty, not getting in her way ...

"No, My Lord," she said. "I didn't expect him to do more than obey me."

She clenched her fists in helpless rage. Major Shaw would have thought, right up until the moment Gwen returned from Russia, that he'd be working with Sir James. He would never have dared to disobey Sir James, let alone take matters into his own hands. Maybe he *did* have reason to question the competence of a woman on the battlefield, but she'd fought during the Swing and in Russia …

"He disobeyed orders," she added. "And he got a number of men killed."

"So you said," Lord Mycroft said. "And you would be right. The Duke of India is not happy with him."

Gwen felt a flicker of vindictive glee. The Duke of India was not known for tolerating incompetents, no matter their connections. Shaw would probably have been summarily removed from his post, perhaps even shot for incompetence in the face of the enemy. And no one would have dared quibble with *his* opinion. Britain's most famous professional soldier brooked no interference with his command.

"But your actions have caused this government a political problem," Lord Mycroft added, grimly. "Quite apart from the fact you kept this new … talent … a secret" – Gwen winced at his tone – "you also broke the mind of a well-connected young man. Even if he recovers, Lady Gwen, it is going to cause a great many problems."

Gwen sighed, looking back at the school. She'd wanted to go there, once upon a time, despite the horror stories she'd heard from her elder brother. There were even *women* at the school, the daughters of Indian or African rulers mingling with the British aristocrats who would one day rule their countries. She could have gone …

… But her mother had refused to even *consider* the possibility.

"I was the commanding officer," she said, tiredly. She looked back at Lord Mycroft, willing him to understand. "He shouldn't have disobeyed."

"That is not in dispute," Lord Mycroft said. His tone softened, slightly. "I understand precisely how you feel, Lady Gwen, but his family will be furious. And it will tie in to the concerns about having a woman – a *young* woman – in command of the Royal Sorcerers Corps. There was a strong feeling that you shouldn't serve as the tactical commanding officer, whatever post you held."

"Master Thomas didn't have such problems," Gwen snarled.

"Master Thomas was nearly ninety years old, with experience that stretched all the way back to the Seven Years War," Lord Mycroft pointed out. "He fought in the American Revolution, the War of 1800 and various conflicts in India. There was never any doubt about his ability to do the job."

Gwen nodded, conceding the point. Even in his last year of life, when he'd taken her on as an apprentice, Master Thomas had been a very dangerous man. He'd been in his position for so long that he'd known where *all* the bodies were buried. It was unlikely that anyone could have dislodged him, if anyone had dared to try. Even the *King* had known better than to push the old man.

"You are nineteen years old, more or less," Lord Mycroft added. "You have been in your post for less than a year and your experience of military command in the field is non-existent. And you had almost no experience of *anything* before you were pushed into the role of Royal Sorceress. Sir James says good things about your skills as a lone warrior, but questions your ability to fight as part of a team."

I was kept at home, Gwen thought, bitterly. *Mother hated the thought of letting me go into the great outdoors.*

"There are plenty of good reasons for people to question you, Lady Gwen," Lord Mycroft added. "And while some of them have to do with your sex, which is beyond your control, there are plenty that don't."

Gwen took a breath. "How exactly am I supposed to gain experience," she asked, "when I am denied the only way to gain experience?"

"I believe Major Shaw might have asked himself the same question," Lord Mycroft said, sardonically. "And you know how *that* turned out."

He cleared his throat. "It has been decided, by myself and the Prime Minister, that your talents would serve us better elsewhere," he added. "And it so happens we have a task that may well allow you to gain the experience you need."

Gwen scowled. "You're sending me into exile."

"In a manner of speaking," Lord Mycroft said. "But the task is *quite* genuine."

He paused. "Do you recall Sir Simon Muybridge?"

"Yes," Gwen said, surprised. She forced herself to recall the middle-aged sorcerer. He'd missed the Swing – he'd been in Ireland at the time – and she hadn't really had time to form an impression of him. But Master Thomas wouldn't have promoted him if he hadn't felt the Blazer could handle the job. "We met briefly, two weeks after the Swing. He was on his way to America to take over as Sorcerer Commanding."

"He's dead," Lord Mycroft said, shortly. "And so is all but one of the trained sorcerers assigned to America."

Gwen stared at him. "Dead?"

"Poisoned," Lord Mycroft said. "Sir Simon made the mistake of hosting a dinner for the sorcerers under his command, before they were deployed to Amherst to meet the expected French invasion. A cook poisoned the soup, according to the reports; Sir Simon and the other sorcerers died in quite considerable pain. The lone Healer assigned to New York was apparently at the Viceregal Palace, unable to make it back in time. Only one sorcerer survived the poisoning."

"Oh," Gwen said. She bit down the urge to say a very unladylike word. "We have no sorcerers in the Americas at all, save for him?"

"There are a handful of untrained sorcerers," Lord Mycroft said. "Thomas Rochester, His Majesty's Viceroy, has used emergency powers to conscript them. However, they *are* untrained. They need a training officer, now."

He scowled, his jowls wobbling angrily. "I *warned* the Viceroy of the dangers!"

Gwen blinked. "Dangers?"

"The cook was a black slave," Lord Mycroft said. "A fine cook, by all accounts; he belonged to Sir Simon personally. And one fine day, with every combat sorcerer in America sitting down to dine, he dumps poison in the soup and runs for his life. He might even make it to French territory before he gets caught!"

"I see," Gwen said.

She gritted her teeth in understanding. The French had abolished slavery in their territory years ago, after the War of 1800. They'd even started treating coloured men and women as equals, realising the dangers of trying to build an empire in lands where the white man was outnumbered fifty to one. And they'd been using their treatment of coloured people as a recruiting tool for years. How could she blame a slave for snatching at the golden ring of freedom, despite the risks …?

Her blood ran cold. "There are thousands of slaves in the Americas."

"More like hundreds of thousands, perhaps a million," Lord Mycroft said, curtly. "And a large number of them will be men of military age. The plantations are watched closely, but it would be very hard to stop a slave rebellion in the south before it spread out of control – or the French arrived to arm the slaves and add them to their forces. A rebellion that erupted under our nose would make it much harder to hold on to the south, let alone push the French back into Mexico."

He sighed. "That isn't the only problem," he added. "The American Tories have been making enemies, while the American Whigs are largely powerless. Poor Americans are wondering if the slaves will take their work, such as it is, while wealthier Americans chafe against the industrial restrictions. Oh, it was a mistake to condone slavery, even if it *did* win us the support of powerful men. I fear we will wind up paying for that sin in due course.

"The Viceroy has inherited a snake pit, Lady Gwen, and it's likely to get worse before it gets better. Any proposals for reform get shot down by the Tories before they can reach London, which adds strength to more radical groups who want to make another bid for independence, using the war as a distraction. And any plans to cut the import of slaves or bring the slave-owners to heel run into other problems. The last thing the government needs, right now, is a power struggle in New York."

Gwen frowned. "The slave-owners aren't going to join the French, are they?"

"I do not know," Lord Mycroft said. "On the face of it, they would have to be insane to join the French, knowing that the French would probably free the slaves. But on the other hand, they might believe that the French would betray the slaves, just like Lord Dunmore did after the war came to an end. They may feel they can hang on to their power despite abandoning the crown.

"But the radical groups are likely to cause trouble too," he added. "They are no friends to slavery, Lady Gwen, but they will have interests in common."

"I see," Gwen said. "What do they actually *want*?"

Lord Mycroft smiled. "Depends who you ask," he said. "There are a number of different demands, ranging from universal suffrage and a united American Parliament to outright independence from the British Crown. General Howe may have intended to keep the Americans divided, when he arranged the post-war government, but it has caused a number of unintended problems. In particular, the Tories are organised at a level the Whigs simply cannot hope to match."

"Which causes frustration," Gwen said.

"And frustration leads to violence," Lord Mycroft agreed. "His Majesty has agreed, secretly, to back a bill granting the Americans a Parliament of their own. Certain powers will still be reserved to the Crown, naturally, but the Americans will be in a much better position to sort themselves out."

"That will not please the Tories," Gwen predicted.

"No, it won't," Lord Mycroft said. "The timing will be particularly poor. These concessions will be made as a last resort, which will make us look weak. I'm having to leave the exact *moment* this bill is announced to the Viceroy too. He's surrounded by Tories, so his timing may be very poor indeed."

He shook his head. "But the prospect of a French invasion may get a few heads focused on *important* matters," he added. "And now we come to *your* task."

"Training sorcerers," Gwen said.

"As far as anyone else knows, that's *precisely* what you will be doing," Lord Mycroft said, simply. "You'd hardly be the first officer sent to the Americas while matters cooled down here. Major Shaw's family can be soothed, if necessary. Unofficially, I want you and Irene to monitor the situation in America and advise the Viceroy. You'll have several sets of orders when you depart, Lady Gwen. Use whichever one seems best for you and burn the others."

"I understand," Gwen said. A thought struck her and she paused. "Irene … has taken on an apprentice."

"Then that apprentice will have to go to America too," Lord Mycroft said.

He sighed. "You know it won't be long before the French footholds in Britain are crushed, if they're fool enough to fight to the last," he said. "But overall, losing America could cause us a great many problems. The French embarrassed us when they managed to land on our soil, Lady Gwen; they made us look weak. Their raiding squadrons are already hammering our shipping too. We cannot afford many more such embarrassments."

"I won't let you down," Gwen assured him. "When do you want me to leave?"

"We're organising a convoy of ships to depart in seven days, depending on how the naval war goes," Lord Mycroft said. "That should include a number of troopships, providing reinforcements to General Paget. Yes, *that* Paget."

Gwen hid her amusement. General Henry Paget had run off with his second wife while married to his first. The whole affair had been a major scandal at the time, she recalled; her mother had chatted about it constantly. General Paget's first wife's family had not only demanded a divorce, they'd clawed back the dowry and a major payment from General Paget's family in exchange for not chasing him through the courts. If the General hadn't been competent, he would probably have been dismissed from the army. As it was, with polite society unwilling to tolerate his presence, he and the second wife had been dispatched to America.

"You should have enough time to organise matters so the RSC can cope with your absence," Lord Mycroft added. "I suggest you leave Sir James in command, again."

"Understood," Gwen said. "Can I take other sorcerers with me?"

"I advise against it," Lord Mycroft said. "We may well need them here, to cope with future French raids – and raiding the French ourselves. I understand you need more experienced sorcerers in America" – he held up a hand before she could say a word – "but we don't have many to spare. Losing Britain would be the end of the world."

Gwen nodded. The Royal Navy could retreat to America or India, but what would it find when it arrived? A colony willing to fight to recover the motherland, or a rebellious society intent on shaping a future for itself, free of any obligation to a distant government? And the French would not be gentle, either. The terms they imposed to end the war would cripple Britain, once and for all.

"I know," she said, finally. "I won't let you down."

"I suggest you have a long rest, then see to your daughter," Lord Mycroft added. "I'll have papers sent to you at Cavendish Hall. You'll have a chance to read them before you depart."

His voice hardened, again. "You may be asked precisely what happened to Major Shaw," he warned. "Just tell them that he had an unusually bad reaction to Charm."

Gwen nodded, once. "I understand what is at stake," she said. "I'll keep my mouth shut."

Chapter Four

 tragic business, simply tragic," Lady Mary Crichton said. "I would have considered young Carrington to be a potential husband for you."

Gwen fought hard not to roll her eyes. She might get along better with her mother these days, but she never ceased to be amazed at her mother's ability to dismiss unwanted or unwelcome facts. There was no way *Gwen* would have considered marrying Carrington Shaw, even if he *hadn't* tried to usurp her authority. They would not have made a suitable couple.

"Men are hardly interested in courting me, mother," she said, sipping her tea. "I have not received any proposals, let alone expressions of *interest*."

"You did have Sir Charles," Lady Mary pointed out. "He *was* interested in you."

Gwen felt her cheeks heat. "Sir Charles murdered his best friend and was planning to betray Britain to the French," she said, tartly. She'd allowed him to distract her during the investigation, she recalled. It could have ended very badly. "I don't think it would have made for a happy marriage."

"Marriages are not meant to be *happy*," Lady Mary said. "They're meant for linking families and wealth together and for producing children."

"I want something more, *mother*," Gwen said. She hated to admit it, but she knew it was unlikely she'd ever marry. What sort of man would want to marry a sorceress? The only men likely to be interested were ones who thought that marrying her would be their ticket to wealth and power. They'd be very disappointed if they tried. "And I already have a child."

She looked around. "Where *is* Olivia?"

"The maids are currently bathing her," Lady Mary said. "I was planning to take her to the Windsor Ball tonight."

Gwen frowned. "I trust you will not let them make fun of her," she said. "It would be a shame if I had to do something about it."

"Fear not, they know she has close kin," Lady Mary said, briskly. "And this ball might be her best chance at making a good match."

"You are *not* to push her into anything," Gwen said. "To all intents and purposes, she *is* my daughter."

"She's adopted," Lady Mary pointed out. "Do you not want a child of your own?"

Gwen hesitated. In truth, she wasn't sure. If she'd been born without magic, she would probably have been married off as soon as she turned sixteen, married to someone her parents chose. They wouldn't have sold her to a monster, she thought, but they wouldn't have put her happiness at the top of the agenda. By now, she might well have had a child or two, maybe more. She knew girls who were her age, perhaps even younger, who'd already given birth to two or three children. And others who had died in childbirth.

"I don't know, mother," she confessed. "But I have no husband. I believe a husband should come first."

"I will keep an eye out for you," Lady Mary said. "But Master Thomas's will has confused the issue."

Gwen felt a hot flash of triumph. Master Thomas hadn't just apprenticed her; he'd practically adopted her. It had been a formality, just to ensure he could be alone with Gwen without causing scandal, but it had separated her from her biological family. And when he'd died, she'd inherited his wealth as a free woman, rather than a daughter. Whatever happened, that wealth was *hers*.

"I am sure no one would mind if you were to say you were acting as my representative," Gwen said. "But I don't think you would find many suitors."

"Lord Mycroft is unmarried," Lady Mary mused. "And he would appreciate you ..."

Gwen giggled. "He's a danger to shipping!"

"Regardless, he comes from a good family," Lady Mary

said. "I could approach him on your behalf."

"No, thank you," Gwen said, quickly. The thought of copulating with a man who was not only forty years her senior, but fat enough to pass for a beached whale was alarming. And he'd never look her in the eyes again if her mother went to him to open negotiations. "I would prefer someone closer to my age."

She shook her head. There was no way she could handle the duties of a housewife, particularly one of her social class, and those of the Royal Sorceress. And she couldn't step down, either. Master Thomas had made sure a Master Magician had to lead the Royal Sorcerers Corps, if only to keep the bickering among lesser magicians to a dull roar. Gwen was, quite literally, the only one for the job. Even Sir James, as resourceful and talented as he was, couldn't handle it indefinitely.

"Most young men of your age are already married or betrothed," Lady Mary pointed out. "I could find a widower, but the youngest I can think of right now is ten years older than you."

"Perhaps I'll meet someone in America," Gwen offered.

Lady Mary looked horrified. Gwen didn't bother to conceal her amusement. American peers – and merchants who had yet to be ennobled – had been marrying British peers, buying their way into the aristocracy. It hadn't been an entirely successful arrangement, from what she'd heard, but it had given a number of older families a new lease on life. *And* she couldn't deny that strengthening ties between Britain and America was hardly a bad idea.

"One would hope not," Lady Mary said. "How could anyone be *sure* of his breeding?"

Gwen opened her mouth to say something else, but closed it when she heard the door opening behind her. Turning, she saw Olivia being escorted into the room by one of the maids. Her adopted daughter looked uncomfortable in a long green dress that suited her blonde hair; indeed, Gwen couldn't help thinking that Olivia simply didn't look *natural* in such a dress, no matter what the maids did. But then, Olivia had been on the streets for most of her life …

Being a captive in Russia probably didn't help, Gwen

thought, as she rose. There were dull shadows in Olivia's blue eyes, recollections of horrors that no girl should have to see. But, as Jack had pointed out so long ago, many of the horrors deemed too horrific for girls to see were *happening* to girls. *And she wanted to kill herself not too long ago.*

"Olivia," she said. She gave her adopted daughter a tight hug. "How are you feeling?"

"Clean," Olivia said. Her accent held traces of the streets, despite the best elocution teachers money could buy. "They scrubbed every last inch of me."

"And make sure you don't get that dress dirty before tonight," Lady Mary said, aiming a pointed gaze at the grandfather clock. "We have to be on our way in less than three hours."

"I'm sure she'll be fine, mother," Gwen said. She had horrific memories of being forced to dress herself time and time again, just to please her mother. Lady Mary was practically a force of nature in the dressing room. "And she might have to leave in a hurry, anyway."

Olivia looked up, alarmed. "They might need me?"

"I don't think so," Gwen said, reassuringly. Lord Mycroft had talked about keeping Olivia's necromantic talents in reserve, just in case the battle went badly, but Gwen doubted she'd be needed. The last report she'd read had stated that the French enclaves were under constant attack, wearing the French down piece by piece. "But you might need an excuse to slip out."

"Gwen," Lady Mary said.

She rose, stiffly. "I shall be in my rooms, readying myself," she added. "It is imperative she does not dirty her clothes. A number of young men are coming to the ball."

Gwen watched her go, then looked at Olivia. "You do look nice in that dress."

"I feel like a mark," Olivia grunted. She snorted in a very unladylike manner. "Do you know how much the jewellery alone is worth? And how easy it would be for me to lose it?"

"Watch yourself," Gwen advised. The exact truth behind Olivia's family roots – or lack of them – had been carefully buried, but it didn't take much to start tongues wagging in polite society. "You don't want a bad reputation now."

Olivia snorted, ruder this time. "Do you think any of the toffs will want to marry *me*?"

Gwen shrugged. "Do you want to marry *them*?"

"No," Olivia said. "But your mother insists that I need a good match."

"There's no need for you to have any sort of match," Gwen said. She pushed Olivia towards one of the chairs, then sat down facing her. "But if you want to get married, this is the way to go about it."

Olivia's face darkened. She rarely spoke of her time on the streets, but Gwen had heard enough – from Jack, from Lucy, from Irene – to make a number of guesses about what life must have been like for Olivia, even if she *had* spent most of her time wearing male clothes and pretending to be a boy. It was quite possible that Olivia would *never* want to marry, or would have to have a very awkward conversation with her partner before they tied the knot.

"Leave it for the moment," she said, sitting back. "There's a more important matter to discuss."

"You're leaving," Olivia said.

Gwen blinked in surprise. "How ...?"

"Your mother was saying that you did something bad," Olivia said. "And that you would have to leave the country for a time."

"I'm afraid so," Gwen said. Now she'd had a wash and a long sleep, she couldn't help feeling a little ashamed of what she'd done. There had been other options. "And I can't take you with me."

Olivia looked down at the wooden flooring. "You're going to leave me here with *her*?"

"She won't harm you," Gwen reassured her. Lady Mary had to be *very* daunting, particularly to someone of no aristocratic blood. "And ... and you might be needed."

"I won't raise the dead again," Olivia said. She looked up, meeting Gwen's eyes. "Whatever happens, I won't raise the dead. You didn't hear the whispers."

"I heard enough," Gwen said. "And I won't force you to do anything."

She shook her head. The people who had argued, a year ago, that Olivia should be put to death might have had a point, given what had happened in Russia. Reports from St Petersburg were vague, and the French weren't sharing what they knew, but British Intelligence believed there was a civil war underway. There was no way to know how many Russians had joined the ranks of the undead, or how many had survived the destruction of Moscow. Russia was cold enough to preserve undead bodies for years.

"They will," Olivia whispered. "And I'll kill myself before I let a Charmer get his hooks into me again."

"You won't have to," Gwen said. She hoped devoutly that she was right. "The French have been beaten, I think."

Olivia nodded, slowly. "When will you be home?"

"I don't know," Gwen admitted. Training a group of sorcerers could take months, if not years. But she doubted she'd have that long. The French armies in North America presumably knew that the invasion of Britain had failed. "At least a year, perhaps longer."

Olivia's face fell. "Are you sure?"

"I can send for you, once I know the lie of the land," Gwen offered. She had no idea if Lord Mycroft would let Olivia go, but she could convince him that Olivia was unlikely to raise the dead on command. "Or I could try to get you into the Britannic School."

"No, thank you," Olivia said. "It's hard enough trying to cipher on my own."

Gwen smiled. Young women were normally educated at home, at least among the aristocracy. *She'd* certainly been home-schooled. For Olivia, who had never learnt to read and write until she'd come to Cavendish Hall, trying to learn with a pack of aristocratic girls would be torture. It would be hard to blame her for trying to escape the school.

"As you wish," she said. She sighed, looking at Olivia's dress. "I would take you for a walk, but mother *does* carry on so."

Olivia smirked. "We could go anyway."

Gwen shook her head. "I have to head back to Cavendish Hall," she said. "I just wanted to see you again, before I leave. There may be no time once the preparations start in earnest."

"I understand," Olivia said, reluctantly. "Just … just ask

your mother to stop nagging me about the dreams."

"I will," Gwen said. Olivia had started to have nightmares almost as soon as she'd been rescued, nightmares which had rapidly worsened to the point where she either tried hard not to sleep or woke up screaming. "And I love you."

She gave the younger girl another hug, then spoke briefly to Lady Mary before hurrying back out to the carriage. Traffic in and out of London had dropped off sharply over the past few days, save for carts bringing food and drink into the city in case of a siege. Gwen had no doubt that it would pick up soon, once the last of the French enclaves were crushed, but for the moment it only took thirty minutes to drive from her father's mansion to Cavendish Hall.

"Lady Gwen," the guard said. He tipped his hat to her as she stepped through the gates and started the walk up to the mansion. "Doctor Norwell asked you to speak with him as soon as you returned."

"I see," Gwen said.

She walked up the driveway and through the main doors. Cavendish Hall was almost empty; the sorcerers had been sent to the war, the researchers and support staff had been moved north to Oxford ... she was mildly surprised that Doctor Norwell hadn't gone too. But he had always insisted on making sure proper records were kept. He'd claimed to have served the RSC since before Master Thomas had become the Royal Sorcerer and, judging from his looks, Gwen was inclined to believe him. He was definitely old enough to be her grandfather.

"Lady Gwen," Doctor Norwell said, as she stepped into the library. "I trust your daughter is well?"

"Well enough," Gwen said, glancing around before sitting down in one of the comfortable armchairs. "They made a terrible mess in here, doctor."

Her lips thinned. The library was one of her favourite rooms, but it no longer *looked* like a library. The books had been stripped from the shelves and transported out of the city, even though she knew that ninety percent of them were nothing more than nonsense. Writing down magic spells was pointless – magic simply didn't work like that – but hardly anyone outside the RSC or the government knew it. Conmen had been selling books of 'magic' to gullible idiots for years, then pocketing the cash and vanishing before the buyers realised that none of the spells actually *worked*.

"The books needed to be safeguarded," Doctor Norwell said. He had a fussily precise voice, one that practically *reeked* of the aristocracy. "Lady Gwen, I received the final report from Healer Lucy."

Gwen took the sheet of paper and scanned it, rapidly. Lucy was blunt, as always; Major Shaw's condition had yet to improve, no matter what she did. He verged between bawling like a child to shouting at his sister, almost managing to hit her twice before he'd been tied to the bed. His self-control was completely gone. It was impossible, Lucy had concluded, to get any sense out of him. Or to put any sort of timetable on his recovery.

"My fault," Gwen said.

"I'm afraid so," Doctor Norwell said. "Do you have anything you want to add to the report?"

"No," Gwen said, reluctantly. She didn't know *what* he thought of the whole affair. Doctor Norwell was no magician, but he'd been around magic long enough to know how it worked. And he'd been close to Master Thomas. He might well deduce the truth, no matter what she did. "We'll keep an eye on him, won't we?"

"He'll end up in one of the bedlams, if he doesn't get locked away in the attic," Doctor Norwell said, levelly. "There is no sign of improvement."

Gwen shuddered. She'd seen the bedlams – and she'd practically been locked away herself, although she'd had much more freedom than any madwoman. If there was something she could do ... but there wasn't. She doubted going to see him would make things any better ... his family would probably want more than exile for her, when it sank in. They'd want her dead.

And there's no way to fix the damage, she thought. *I didn't even mean to hurt him!*

"Pay for his treatment," Gwen ordered, finally. It was the least she could do. And she'd never notice the loss. "I'll arrange for a bank draft to cover the costs."

"As you wish, My Lady," Doctor Norwell said.

"Send a message to Merlin," Gwen added, standing. "Once he's no longer needed at the front, Sir James is to make his way back here. I need to speak to him."

"I believe Merlin is tasked to support the final assault on Dover," Doctor Norwell said, thoughtfully. "The assault is planned for dawn tomorrow."

"That will give me time to prepare," Gwen said. She doubted the French would hold out for long; they had literally nowhere to go. And with farmers sniping at any Frenchman who got separated from his unit, they had good reason to consider surrender to the regulars. "Let me know when he's on his way here."

"Of course, My Lady," Doctor Norwell said. "But I would be surprised if he were here in less than a couple of days."

"It's all right," Gwen assured him. She needed time to read the remainder of the files before she made any plans, although she knew better than to stick to them. Everything in the files might well be out of date. "I can wait."

Chapter Five

ou're still walking like a girl," Irene said, sharply. "Stand *upright*, damn you."

Raechel obeyed, gritting her teeth. As daring as she'd considered herself, male clothing had always been *verboten*. Wearing trousers had been unthinkable, even after the Trouser Brigade had made a habit of wearing trousers in public places. But they were still openly feminine, merely wearing male clothing. *She* was pretending to be a man.

"I'm not used to walking like this," she snapped. Three days of being an apprentice had taught her more than she'd ever imagined, but she knew she had a very long way to go. "I've never worn male clothing in my life!"

"Having your breasts bound probably doesn't help," Irene said. She gave Raechel a considering look as the younger girl stood upright, holding her head in the air. "A pity your face is so pretty, really. It's quite noticeable."

"Thank you," Raechel said, sourly. "Is there anything I can do about that?"

"Wear a cap and look sullen," Irene said. She smirked as she produced a dirty cloth cap and placed it neatly on Raechel's head. It barely fitted over her hair. Irene had made her tie it up into a tight bun, when Raechel had refused to cut it. "You'll be taken for a young boy."

Raechel scowled as she stared into the mirror. Loose brown trousers and a grey shirt – both looking as though they'd seen better days – made her look odd, although she didn't *think* she could really pass for a man. Even with the truss pushing her breasts against her skin, she could still see where they should be. The cap might give her face a masculine cast – and a hint of makeup added flecks of stubble – but she didn't feel convincing. She looked like a little girl dressed in her father's clothes.

"You already know what you are," Irene said, artfully. "Another woman might spot you, but the male mind will take its cues from your clothing. They'll see you as a young lad on the streets."

"Oh," Raechel muttered.

She glared at the mind-reader. She'd spent at least two hours a day learning to meditate, the first step in blocking Irene out of her mind, but her defences tended to lapse as soon as she stopped concentrating on them. Mastering the art of keeping her mind closed while doing something else was taking forever. And then, Irene had warned, she would have to learn the art of *lying* with her mind. A probing Talker might be suspicious if he or she encountered a mental shield.

"You're not doing badly," Irene assured her. "But you have to keep walking like a man."

Raechel sighed, but did as she was told. It wasn't easy to walk straight upright – swaying her hips would make her look unnatural, Irene had warned – let alone look Irene straight in the eye. Young women weren't supposed to make eye contact with men, particularly young unmarried men; they were meant to keep their eyes lowered demurely, while sneaking peeks when they thought they weren't being watched. She hadn't realised just how many habits had been hammered into her, from the moment of her birth, until Irene had pointed them out, one by one. They'd become second nature very quickly.

"The trick is to remember to *think* like a man," Irene added, as she donned her own clothing and posed in front of the mirror. "Men recognise a pecking order, a hierarchy; they will cling to their place in the hierarchy even when it no longer suits them. That's why you get wealthy merchants deferring to lords, even though the merchants could buy and sell the lords out of pocket change. They still think of themselves as inferior."

Raechel blinked. "Why?"

Irene shrugged. "Men like knowing where they stand," she said. She smirked. "And there are quite a few men who are very good at sending dominant signals to other men. They're the ones you have to watch, when you meet them. They can be quite dangerous.

"At the same time, men can be possessive of far more than their wives," she added. "A man will be possessive of his job, so he'll bitterly resent a superior coming in and telling him what to do, even if the superior is *right*. Men stake out their territory and guard it very carefully, even if it costs them dearly. I recall one opera director who lost his job because he wouldn't give his patrons any say in what actually *happened*."

"He sounds like an idiot," Raechel observed.

"Oh no," Irene said. "He was very good at his job. But he also thought of the job as *his*."

She shrugged, again. "Given our clothing," she said, "what do you think we are?"

Raechel looked back in the mirror. "Newsboys," she said, finally. It was the only thing she could think of. "Is that right?"

"Workers," Irene said. "We look like workers released from the defences."

She turned to the door. "Come on," she said. "Let's go outside."

Raechel's mouth dropped open. "We're going out?"

"It's the only way to test your progress," Irene said, briskly. "Just recall all the rules and pitch your voice low. But don't try to overdo it."

Because that just sounds unnatural, Raechel thought. The trick to acting, Irene had explained, was not to *overact*. Her first attempts to talk in a male voice had been laughable; she'd tried to talk like her uncle, an upper-class twit if ever there was one. *I can't afford to sound like I'm acting.*

She felt … oddly exposed the minute they walked out the door. The streets were no longer empty; hundreds of men and women were milling about, drinking toasts and cheering the gallant soldiers who'd returned from the war. Irene had told her, earlier, that the king had addressed the crowds personally, telling them that the first and greatest battle had already been won. But the war itself was far from over. The French had been knocked back, yet they hadn't been knocked out.

It seemed impossible to believe that the crowds surrounding her couldn't see through her clothing, couldn't pick out her femininity ... and yet, no one seemed to notice. Irene led the way through the streets, buying a newspaper from one of the running newsboys as she passed before picking up a bag of apples from one of the stores. Raechel started to relax into her clothing, concentrating on putting forward the right image even as she studied the men as they walked up and down the streets.

"They don't seem to be paying any attention to us," she murmured, as they turned down a side street. She wrinkled her nose at the foul smell that suddenly surrounded them. "Why not?"

"Why should they?" Irene asked. "You're a man, as far as they're concerned."

She was right, Raechel realised. The next street held dozens of women, wearing dresses that left absolutely nothing to the imagination, and calling out to passers-by. Raechel felt herself blush at some of their cruder suggestions, even though she doubted they were physically possible. How could anyone *do* that for a living? She tried to imagine what it must be like to work as a prostitute and shuddered. It had to be an horrific life.

A young woman, only a year or two older than Raechel herself, jumped in front of her. "Wet your whistle for you, governor? And then dip your wick?"

Raechel couldn't help herself. She recoiled in shock. The woman's dress was torn, revealing the tops of her breasts; her face was covered in so much paint that it looked profoundly unnatural. She swayed forward, her lips clearly ready for a kiss ...

"No, thank you," Raechel managed. She barely remembered to deepen her voice before it was too late. "I have a wife."

"Ah, your wife won't know," the woman said. Her lips gaped open. Raechel noticed that some of her teeth were missing. "And I do things no wife would do."

Raechel forced herself to walk around the woman and onwards, to where Irene was waiting patiently. The whore called something rude after Raechel – she was grateful she didn't know what the words *meant* – but didn't make any attempt to follow her. Irene gave her a sidelong look when Raechel caught up with her, then led her onwards. Raechel didn't dare turn to look behind her. She was sure the entire crowd was staring at her.

"You handled that well," Irene said, once they were safely out of earshot. "There was no way you could let her take you into an alley, of course."

"Of course not," Raechel agreed, casting a sidelong glance into one of the alleyways. There were dark shapes there, half-hidden in the darkness. "She would have done it in there?"

"She'll be an expert," Irene said, flatly. "A young man your age? It wouldn't take her long to satisfy him with her mouth. Or if he'd wanted something more, her pimp would have been happy to escort the happy couple into a room."

Raechel swallowed hard to keep from throwing up. Her *mouth*?

Irene shot her a concerned look, then led her through a handful of streets and back to Pall Mall. A line of policemen were walking past, keeping a sharp eye on the revellers as they started to dance and sing. Raechel held herself steady as one of the policemen gave her a sharp look, then walked on without saying a word. Had he seen through the disguise? Or had he merely thought she didn't look wealthy enough to be on the street? She had no way to tell.

"You didn't do badly," she said, as they stepped into the house and closed the door. "That whore could have broken your guise, but you handled her well."

Raechel swallowed, again. "How can anyone live like that?"

"They rarely have a choice," Irene said, flatly. She turned to look at Raechel, who cringed back under her stare. "That woman was probably born into a poor family, too poor to afford a dowry to attract a good husband. They might have sold her to a pimp or married her off to someone who expected her to turn tricks for him on the streets. Whatever she earns, she'll give to the pimp or he'll beat her. And, when she's too old to attract customers, she'll be left to die on the streets or sold to one of the darker brothels. No one will care if she dies there, as long as the customers are satisfied."

"But there are charities," Raechel protested. "Aren't there? My aunt is proud of her good works ..."

Irene lifted her eyebrows. "How pleased were *you* when your aunt judged you?"

"I wasn't," Raechel said. "But whores ..."

"People like your aunt expect everyone to behave in a certain manner," Irene said. There was a hint of anger in her tone, although it didn't seem to be aimed at Raechel. "Young girls are expected to be seen and not heard, to marry decent men and bring up decent children. Those who trespass against those unspoken rules are treated as though they *deserve* everything they get, even though they may have had no choice. I imagine your aunt makes it clear to those she *helps* that they are fallen women, that they are forever tainted, that they deserve nothing from her. And I have no doubt she expects them to fall to their knees in gratitude in front of her."

Raechel could believe it. Her aunt had been given to maddening lectures, particularly when some young girl had done something – anything – that had made eyebrows rise in cool disapproval. She knew plenty of girls who had been married off quickly – too quickly – and others who had been sent to the country, where they were effectively isolated from polite society. And they'd been aristocrats.

"The charities do very little effective to *help*," Irene added. "They simply don't understand the problems facing someone – anyone – born into such conditions. How can they? It is completely alien to their experience."

She shook her head. "Get into your poor-woman's dress," she added. "We're going out again."

Raechel stared. "Can't we ...?"

"No, we can't," Irene said, cutting her off. "Get your dress on. I need to have a word or two with Ivan."

There was no point in arguing, Raechel realised. Gritting her teeth, she walked back into the dressing room, dropped the male outfit on the floor and pulled the poor woman's dress over her head. It wasn't bad, really; it made her look like a shopkeeper's daughter. She gathered herself, trying to imagine how such a girl would think. Irene *definitely* had a major advantage, she had to admit. She didn't have to *guess* how someone thought about their life.

She would be poor but honest, Raechel thought. Her mother would work too, just to keep the shop running; Raechel the Shop Girl would have inherited that attitude, even as she hoped for a decent match. Her mother had hammered numbers into her head until she was a better accountant than her father or brother. She might smile shyly at the boys, but she'd never dream of disgracing her family by going further. And she wouldn't be a fainting flower from the aristocracy. She wouldn't even *see* an aristocrat.

"Very good," Irene said, stepping into the room. "You look just about right."

Raechel frowned. "Just about?"

"Let your hair down," Irene said. "Really, a wig would be far more practical."

"I would prefer to keep my hair long," Raechel said, stiffly. She understood Irene's point, but she rather liked her red locks. "And besides, what happens if someone pulls on it?"

"That's why you secure it in place," Irene said. She undressed rapidly, then donned her own dress. "Have you defined yourself?"

"Raechel the Shop Girl," Raechel said, and ran through a brief description as she let her hair down. "Good enough?"

"Good enough," Irene said. She checked her appearance in the mirror, then inspected Raechel minutely. "Let's go."

"We could practice with pistols, instead," Raechel said. "Or you could show me some more tricks with the knife …"

"You'll have plenty of time for both onboard ship," Irene said. "You *do* remember we're going to America, right?"

Raechel shuddered. She'd never been on a ship, but she'd heard stories. "We can't take an airship? We took an airship to Russia."

"That was over land," Irene pointed out, tartly. She led the way out of the room. "Travelling to America would be over the cold grey Atlantic Ocean. An accident would dump us in the water and we'd drown."

"If we survived the fall," Raechel pointed out.

"Better not to take chances," Irene said. "Even with Lady

Gwen along, survival would become rather doubtful."

She smiled, then opened the door and walked onto the streets. Raechel followed, feeling slightly more natural in the simple dress. The crowds were growing larger as the day wore on, hundreds of thousands of men and women celebrating the defeat of the French. But, this time, she could sense eyes glancing in her direction. Countless young men were looking at them as they walked past.

I'm decently dressed, she thought, shocked. No one had stared at her so blatantly when she'd been on the streets before, even when she'd been heading to the club. *They shouldn't be looking at me.*

But they were. She forced herself to keep walking, remembering that she was nothing more than a shop girl out for an evening stroll with her friend. This time, Irene kept them well away from the alleyways, perhaps fearing what would happen if they walked into the darkness. Raechel couldn't help feeling relieved as the day slowly turned into evening and the crowds got louder and louder. It wasn't the sort of place Raechel the Shop Girl would go, she was sure. She'd have headed back home long ago.

The crowd drew apart, suddenly. Raechel blinked in surprise as she recognised Lady Gotham, striding up the road as if she owned the city. She was followed by a tired-looking maid, who was carrying so many boxes that she looked to be on the verge of falling over and dropping everything. The maid stopped for a moment, just to catch her breath and Lady Gotham whirled around, beginning a long tirade on the subject of lazy servants who didn't know what was good for them. Raechel felt a flicker of sympathy for the poor girl. The crowds were staring as she was berated in public.

"Come on," Irene hissed.

They were midway down the next street when she heard a handful of men behind them, laughing and joking together. She tensed as they were suddenly surrounded, then gasped in shock as she felt a hand squeezing her buttock. Before she could stop herself, she whirled round and slapped the man right across the face. His comrades laughed loudly and hurried onwards, a couple of them waving cheerfully as they passed. Even the man she'd slapped was laughing.

Raechel glared at them, suddenly understanding *just* how the whores felt. She was practically alone, without the protection of clothes that marked her as a member of the aristocracy … if they'd wanted to do worse to her, she couldn't have stopped them. She felt naked, yet soiled, her skin itching where he'd touched her. Raechel the Shop Girl wouldn't have dared tell anyone, either. Her father might have blamed *her* for her fall from grace.

"You'll have to learn to cope with worse," Irene muttered. "Trust me on this."

"I want a bath," Raechel muttered back.

"Once we get home," Irene told her. "Do you want to back out now?"

"No," Raechel said, firmly. What was left for her in London? Her aunt would be back in her home soon enough, bullying the servants and trying to run Raechel's life. "I'll keep going."

"Very good," Irene said. "But believe me, you *will* encounter worse."

Chapter Six

ir James Braddock, My Lady," Doctor Norwell said.

Gwen looked up from her desk as Sir James was shown into the room. He wore his combat tunic, rather than his normal suit and tie; she wondered, absently, just who he was trying to impress. Sir James was a married man, she knew, but he and his wife had surprisingly little contact, even for members of the aristocracy. It was quite possible he had a mistress or two on the side.

Or he just wanted to see what would happen in London, she thought, rising. She'd heard stories of giant street parties, where all the normal rules seemed to have gone out the window and men and women had danced together without supervision. *All the nice girls love a uniform.*

"Welcome back," she said, holding out a hand. "And congratulations on your victory."

"It was the Duke's victory, not mine," Sir James assured her. He shook her hand with none of the hesitation most men would show. "Dover surrendered, once we had the enclave sealed off and under constant shellfire. The frogs preferred to march into camps rather than face our people."

Gwen nodded as she waved him to a chair, then sat back down behind her desk. The stories of what farmers had done to lone Frenchmen had only grown more bloodcurdling in the last couple of days, ranging from Frenchmen being brutally murdered to Frenchmen being castrated and crucified. Not that she blamed them, not really. The stories of what had happened to British men and women, caught behind the lines, were equally unpleasant, while the French had inflicted vast damage on the farmland. It was going to be a nightmare for the refugees, she knew. The government was unlikely to commit much money to help rebuild after the war.

That would smack too much of bloody socialism, she thought. Lord Liverpool was one of the most tight-fisted Prime Ministers in recent history, a man who begrudged every last penny in the budget. *Who wants to help farmers?*

"There were nine deaths in all, among the corps," Sir James added. "Their bodies have already been shipped back to their families for burial."

"We'll have to hold a service for them, afterwards," Gwen said. She wondered, absently, if she'd be in Britain for the end of the war. America might consume her attention for the next few years. "Their families have been compensated?"

"They'll have the payments sent to them, I believe," Sir James assured her. "I don't think they'll lack for anything."

"Very good," Gwen said. She cleared her throat as she sat upright. "I'm going to America for the next few months, perhaps longer."

Sir James nodded. He didn't look surprised. It had been meant to be a secret, but someone in the government must have blabbed, either to impress his family or to make connections with Major Shaw's family. Or maybe Lord Mycroft had quietly authorised the release of the information, just to make it clear that Gwen *was* facing some punishment. It would help keep Major Shaw's family quiet.

And he probably got a lot of blue bloods killed when the Hussars attacked, she thought, darkly. *Would their families not have something to say about that*?

"You will hold the position of Royal Sorcerer, in my absence," Gwen continued. Sir James hadn't done a bad job, while she'd been in Russia, although there had been relatively little to do. Everyone had been preparing for the war. "I'm not sure what use the government will make of the sorcerers, but I imagine you'll make yourself useful."

"I'm sure we'll find something to do," Sir James agreed. "A descent on their coastlines would definitely give the French something to worry about."

Gwen scowled. The French had a far more powerful army than Britain; indeed, their build-up of ironclads, merchant shipping, airships and submarines had been a major concern over the last few years. Britain's navy was far stronger, but two-thirds of it were scattered all over the globe. If the French managed to gain even a limited superiority in the English Channel for a week, their army would almost certainly crush Britain's defences and take London.

But they gave it their best shot, she thought. *And we won.*

"Landing on their coastline would mean facing their army on its territory," she said. "Is that something we dare to risk?"

"If we don't, the war stalemates, like every other war we've fought with the French since the Seven Years War," Sir James countered. "And neither side will be closer to total victory."

"True," Gwen said. Lord Mycroft and the Duke of Iron would decide Britain's future steps, once the American situation was stabilised. "Are you willing to take on the role?"

"I don't anticipate immediate problems," Sir James said. "Do you?"

"Not while there's a war on," Gwen said. She met his eyes. "Afterwards … try to be diplomatic."

Sir James nodded, curtly. "Thank you," he said. "When do I actually take command?"

"Tomorrow morning," Gwen said. She'd been tempted to lumber him with all the paperwork, but it was *her* job. "I should have everything straightened out by then, I think."

"Very good," Sir James said.

"There isn't anything new," Gwen added. Sir James was already familiar with the duties of a Royal Sorcerer. "The new recruits for training should be arriving next week, unless they get diverted because of the war; make sure they're trained as quickly as possible. They're going to be needed."

"Understood," Sir James said.

He paused. "And Major Shaw?"

"Has not recovered," Gwen said, flatly. She felt another stab of guilt, mingled with bitter frustration. If the idiot had had the sense to follow orders … "He's under observation in the ward."

"I thought he could be kept under control," Sir James said. "But he saw the war as a chance to win glory."

Gwen scowled, remembering the battle. Crawling in the mud was hardly ladylike, but it had kept her alive. If a French sniper had managed to catch sight of her, she might have died before she knew she was under attack. She *had* tried to keep her magic around her in a protective shroud, but she knew it wasn't easy ... she shook her head. If that was glory, Major Shaw was welcome to it.

"I'm sure there would have been plenty of opportunities to get himself heroically killed elsewhere," she said. She had to fight down a sneer. "All he did was get a great many other men killed, for nothing."

"I know," Sir James said. "But he didn't have the experience to know better."

"And he thought I didn't know what to do," Gwen added. She sighed. Major Shaw had *wanted* to believe it was time to send in the Hussars. "Idiot."

She looked back down at her papers, no longer feeling in the right frame of mind to read them. She *did* have a secretary, thankfully, but there were just too many matters that had to be handled by the Royal Sorceress personally. Sir James would have to cope with them, while she was gone ... in the certain knowledge that the various departmental heads would feel free to ask Gwen to reverse any decisions after she returned. No doubt she'd have a whole pile of petitions to read and answer when she came back.

"I'll formally transfer authority tomorrow morning," she said, rising. "Thank you for coming."

Sir James looked surprised at her sudden dismissal, but merely rose to his feet and strode out of the room. Gwen watched him go, torn between envy and a bitterness that had grown increasingly common over the last year. She could catch a murderer, a murderer who had also been a traitor and a spy; she could face a maddened undead monster in Russia and win ... and yet, she wasn't considered a suitable replacement for Master Thomas. It wasn't just that she was a girl too, although that was a convenient excuse. Ideally, she would have had years with Master Thomas, learning the ropes as well as where the skeletons were buried, before she took the job.

Jack would have had those years, she thought, sourly.

Master Thomas had thought highly of his young protégée. Hell, if he'd stayed loyal, Gwen doubted she would ever have been called to the colours herself. *He could have stayed in the corps and made changes from the inside.*

She shook her head as she opened the hidden door and made her way down the secret staircase. A year of butting heads with the bureaucracy – and the various vested interests that made up the Royal College – had taught her that change, true change, came slowly. And if she hadn't managed to find two new talents, the Royal College wouldn't have changed anything like as much as it had. The old men – and they were old men – in charge hated the thought of *anything* changing.

And Master Thomas could keep them in line, she thought, as she reached the hidden exit in the lower basement. *They don't take me so seriously.*

Leaning against the wall, she reached out with her mind, testing to make sure no one was there to see her when she opened the door. She had no idea why Master Thomas had converted the servant corridors into secret passages, but she had to admit they made it easy to get around the vast building without being detected. Only Doctor Norwell and Lord Mycroft knew they even *existed*, although she suspected that some of the aristocratic magicians had guessed. Servant passages were meant to keep the servants out of sight, away from their betters. She opened the door, stepped through into the corridor, and closed it hastily behind her. The Healer Ward was just down the corridor.

"Lady Gwen," Lucy said, as Gwen stepped through the door. "You are well?"

"Well enough," Gwen said. Lucy might be used to irritating men, but Gwen doubted the Healer could do anything to cure her *real* problem. "Is he still in the ward?"

"I'm afraid so," Lucy said. "Even *feeding* him has been a bit of a problem."

Gwen nodded, then walked down the corridor. There weren't many patients in the ward, not when it normally took only a few minutes for the Healers to work their magic. Indeed, the only real problem was the *shortage* of Healers. They were a rare breed, apparently, and every Healer they'd found had been female. Luckily, the prospect of being healed was enough to convince men to visit a female Healer. Male doctors might as well have been butchers for all the good they could do.

Major Shaw was sleeping in a metal chair, straps wrapped around his wrists and ankles. He looked normal at first, Gwen thought, until she saw his eyes. They were twitching backwards and forwards under the eyelids, as if they were on the verge of popping out of his head. She took a step forward, unsure what – if anything – she should do. If there was a way to cure his mind through magic, Lucy would have found it by now.

"You inflicted a great deal of harm," Lucy said, quietly. "Did you know ...?"

"No," Gwen said. "I ..."

Major Shaw jerked awake, his blue eyes flickering from side to side before focusing on Gwen. He opened his mouth and screamed, a high-pitched sound that was so loud Gwen stumbled backwards, covering her ears. Lucy pointed a finger towards the door; Gwen nodded and hurried back out of the ward. Behind her, the screams continued to echo until one of the orderlies slammed the heavy door closed.

Gwen cursed under her breath, feeling yet another stab of guilt. Charmers had been known to cause mental breakdowns, when their victim was unable to hide from reality any longer, but such breakdowns rarely lasted long. Even a weak-willed man could come to terms with what had happened to him, if he tried. But Major Shaw seemed to have been completely broken, perhaps for the rest of his life. He had been an arrogant bastard who'd got over a hundred good men killed ...

... *And yet he doesn't deserve to be broken*, Gwen thought, bitterly. It was her fault. In hindsight, there were plenty of other options she could have used. But in her frustration and anger she'd made a mistake. *And now he has to pay the price.*

She wandered slowly back up to her office, glancing into the empty training rooms as she passed. The training cadre had done a good job of stripping the building of everything necessary to train young magicians, although most of the equipment would be easy to replace. Her lips quirked; no one on the outside would believe it, if they saw the room. It was commonly believed that magicians needed staffs, wands and potions made from fancy ingredients to do their work …

A thought struck her and she scowled. Jack, no doubt, had taught the French *precisely* how to construct their own training facility.

Not that it would have been that hard, once they stopped thinking of magicians as demons, she thought, coldly. *The basic principles of magic aren't hard to deduce, even without a teacher.*

"Lady Gwen," Doctor Norwell called, when she walked past his office. It was right next to hers, one of Master Thomas's arrangements she'd never bothered to change. "There are two of Lord Mycroft's men here to see you. They're waiting in the visitors' room."

Gwen frowned in puzzlement. Lord Mycroft had sent her an immense stack of files to read, but nothing else. She hadn't been expecting to see him until shortly before her departure, still three days away. But something might have come up. Shaking her head, she walked down the corridor and peered into the visitors' room. Two young men were seated on the sofa, wearing the bland suit and ties of government servants. There was something odd about their faces.

"Lady Gwen," the first man said, rising to his feet. "May I say what a great pleasure it is to meet the Royal Sorceress face to face?"

Gwen felt her eyes narrow. *That* was hardly a common form of address. She looked at both men, puzzled. There was definitely something odd about them …

Understanding clicked. "Irene?"

The young man smirked. "Got you that time," he – she – said. There was a hint of cockney in her voice. "How do we look?"

"Raechel," Gwen said, looking at the other figure. Now she *knew* who she was looking at, it was easy to see the subtle clues that the person wasn't remotely masculine. "You look … different."

"I wasn't expecting to fool you for long," Irene said, as she sat back on the sofa. "But you wouldn't have looked twice at us if you'd met us on the streets."

"Probably not," Gwen conceded. She knew better than to dismiss civil servants as unimportant, but they were still very much part of the background. "How is Raechel coming along?"

"I'm right here," Raechel said.

"She is doing better than I expected when playing a female role," Irene said, ignoring her in favour of Gwen. "She's still having some problems playing a male role, I'm afraid. That generally takes longer to learn."

Gwen nodded. It had taken her time to learn to walk and act like a man, even though too many people knew she was a woman for her to try to pretend otherwise. But then, men *did* tend to react better to people they *thought* were other men. The more masculine she looked, the better the reception.

"She's also quite intelligent, if unfocused and untrained," Irene added. "She definitely has the right attitude for this sort of work, although she might have done better if she'd been raised in a lower-class household. Her tolerance for the simple brutalities of life is alarmingly low."

"Noted," Gwen said. She would have to sit down with Raechel, once they were on the ship, and talk about her progress. Right now, there were other matters to worry about. "Do you have her covered?"

Irene nodded. "Officially, Lady Standish is still in a madhouse," she said. "Russia certainly did a great deal of damage to her mind, I'm afraid. Raechel Slater-Standish will therefore have the distinct honour of accompanying Lady Irene Darlington" – she waved a lazy hand at her chest – "to the Americas. Lady Irene will serve as chaperone during this long affair, as she is a distant relation of Lady Standish."

"Very good," Gwen said. "And Lord Standish?"

"Has given his approval," Irene said. "He does not want the burden of a young ward when he has no shortage of work in the Foreign Office."

Gwen smiled in approval. If a young lady could not be chaperoned by her mother, for whatever reason, it was not uncommon for a more distant female relative to take on the burden of escorting and protecting the girl. She had no doubt there *was* a Lady Irene Darlington somewhere in the tangled web of families that made up polite society, although she might be surprised by what was being done in her name. Lord Mycroft had quite a few false identities floating around, just waiting for the moment to use them.

"I could just have stayed in London," Raechel pointed out. "It's going to look as though I'm in trouble, isn't it?"

"Hardly anyone in America will care," Irene assured her. "And besides, who could possibly blame Lord Standish for wanting to keep you out of danger?"

"He took me to Russia," Raechel snapped.

"It wasn't meant to be dangerous," Gwen reminded her. In truth, she doubted Lord Standish had been offered a choice. "Still, if you don't want to go ..."

"I do," Raechel said.

"Then meet us at the ship, as planned," Gwen ordered. "And make sure you have enough to occupy yourself for three weeks. It's going to be a long voyage."

"Don't worry," Irene said. She smiled, rather unpleasantly. "I'll keep her occupied."

Chapter Seven

"I hope you have a pleasant voyage, Lady Gwen," Lord Mycroft said, as the carriage rolled to a halt. "And that you reach New York safely."

Gwen nodded, unable to keep from feeling a little nervous. She'd been on boats before, but she'd never sailed on the ocean. An airship would have been nicer, she was sure, yet she understood why they couldn't take the risk. The chances of surviving an accident at sea were far greater than surviving an airship crash.

"I won't let you down," she promised him. "And thank you for driving me down to the docks."

Lord Mycroft gave her a flicker of a smile. "I can't stay," he said. He held out a hand, which she shook firmly. "But I do wish you every success."

Gwen reached out and drew back the curtains. The driver had taken them through the two checkpoints, right up to the docks themselves. HMS *Duke of India* rose up in front of her, her masts towering up towards the sky. Steam rose from her smoke stack, reminding Gwen that the ship was both a sailing ship and a steamship. Beyond her, four other troopships floated, the troops having been loaded aboard last night. She shuddered, thinking of the cramped conditions the common soldiers would have to endure. Their horses wouldn't have a good time of it either.

"Thank you," she said, as she opened the door. "I'll see you soon."

She dropped neatly to the ground and walked towards the gangplank. The docks were far up the river, just in case the French tried a repeat of the Dutch raid on the Medway, but the ship was rising up and down slowly anyway. She nodded to the soldier on guard at the bottom of the gangplank, then forced herself to walk up onto the ship. It felt odd beneath her feet, even though she was used to flying through the air. She hoped, desperately, that she wouldn't fall seasick. The last thing she wanted was to spend the voyage in her cabin, praying desperately for calm seas.

"Lady Gwen, I believe," a voice said, as she reached the top of the gangplank. "I am Captain Bligh. Welcome aboard."

Gwen nodded. She'd read his file. Captain Archibald Bligh had a reputation for being a harsh taskmaster – his hard face, scarred and pitted by years in the service, certainly supported it – but there were few seamen more competent. No wonder the Royal Navy had given him command of one of the largest hybrid vessels in the fleet. Behind him, a pair of men stood, both wearing army uniforms. She couldn't help thinking that they could easily have passed for Major Shaw's twins, although the leader was supposed to be more experienced and competent. She'd read his file too.

"Thank you, Captain," she said. "It's a pleasure to be here."

"We will be sailing with the evening tide," Bligh informed her. "Colonel Jackson will escort you to your cabin, if you don't mind. Once we are underway, I will be hosting a small dinner in the officers' mess. I trust you will be attending?"

"Of course," Gwen said. She might find herself seasick, but she could wait to make her excuses until she *knew* she was unable to attend. "Where do you want me?"

"I would prefer that you stayed in your cabin until we are firmly underway, My Lady," Captain Bligh said. He sounded firm, but there was a faint undercurrent of concern in his words. "The crew have much work to do."

"I understand," Gwen said. She doubted she'd be happy with a handful of inexperienced landlubbers running around too. "I'll wait until I'm called."

Captain Bligh looked relieved. "Your luggage has already been stowed away," he informed her. "Colonel?"

Gwen studied Colonel Jackson as he stepped forward, his comrade saluting sharply and then strolling away. Up close, she had to admit that Jackson didn't look *that* much like

Major Shaw, although they did have some features in common. Jackson *definitely* had more experience, she noted, judging from the campaign ribbons on his chest. And he wouldn't have been put in command of the reinforcements if there had been doubts about his competence.

"It's a great pleasure to meet you, My Lady," Colonel Jackson said. He didn't offer to shake hands, but Gwen wasn't surprised or offended. Men weren't *supposed* to shake hands with women, after all. "I was hoping to hear about your time in Russia personally."

"It was an adventure," Gwen agreed. She wasn't sure she wanted to talk about it, but she doubted she had a choice. Jackson hadn't been in London during the Swing. If he encountered the undead, he was likely to underestimate them badly. "The Tsar went mad."

She allowed Jackson to lead her down a ladder and along a long wood-panelled corridor until they reached her cabin. Inside, there was no light, save for a single oil lantern hanging from the ceiling. Gwen hesitated, then generated a light globe of her own, wondering just how Jackson would respond to it. His eyes went wide in surprise, but otherwise he showed no reaction at all. He'd probably seen a great deal of magic during his time in the army.

"It's one of the largest cabins on the ship," Jackson said, apologetically. "But I'm afraid there are no portholes …"

"It doesn't matter," Gwen assured him. The semi-ironclad's designers hadn't dared include windows, knowing they would be nothing more than cracks in the ship's armour. "There's enough room for me."

"Captain Bligh says we can probably go up on deck once the ship is underway," Jackson assured her. "I'd go mad if I had to stay in this pokey cabin for more than a few hours."

Gwen looked around. The cabin wasn't particularly large, but it was clean, although a faint smell she didn't care to identify hung in the air. A chamberpot hung from one of the bulkheads, beside a bucket of clean water. Bathing was going to be difficult, even though she could use magic to heat the water. One of her trunks sat on the deck, the others – as Captain Bligh had said – would be stowed away in the hold. She hoped she wouldn't need anything from them. Three weeks, perhaps longer ... she could endure. She'd endured worse.

"I should be fine," she said. She cocked her head, wondering if he was flirting with her. It showed incredible nerve, if he was. Even if she hadn't had magic, she was several rungs higher up the social ladder than him. "Is there anything else I should know?"

"Anything you want washed can be put outside your cabin, where it will be cleaned by the crew," Jackson said. "You didn't bring a maid?"

"No," Gwen said. Martha had been reluctant to risk setting foot onboard ship, so Gwen hadn't pushed the matter. It wasn't as if she needed assistance to get dressed during the voyage. Besides, space was limited on the vessel. "I don't need one."

"Lady Olivier has two maids with her," Jackson said. "I'm sure she would let you borrow one, if you changed your mind."

Gwen shrugged. "Who else is onboard ship?"

"So far? Forty-odd passengers, ranging from you to a handful of traders heading to the Americas," Jackson said. "The remainder should be onboard before the tide."

"One would hope so," Gwen said. She looked at the bed, meaningfully. "I'll get a nap now, if you don't mind. I'd like to be awake when we leave harbour."

"I'll knock on your door to wake you," Jackson assured her. "Until then, goodbye."

He bowed, then hurried out the door. Gwen smiled ruefully to herself – she had a feeling she was going to be seeing a great deal of Jackson, even before they reached New York – and then turned to her trunk. The lock had been carefully designed to be impossible to open without magic; carefully, she unlocked the trunk and opened it. A handful of files rested on top of a mound of books and clothes. She couldn't help thinking that, by the end of the voyage, she and the other passengers were going to be *very* smelly.

Maybe I should have brought a maid after all, she thought. It had really been nothing but stubborn pride that had kept her from ordering Martha to accompany her or simply finding another maid. Officers might have batmen, servants who attended to their needs on campaign ... there was no reason why she couldn't have a maid. *But it would have added yet another complication to my life.*

Sighing, she took one of the files, sat down on the bed and began to read it. Lord Mycroft's agent, whoever he was, had done his best to unpick the complex relationships that made up the Viceregal Court, despite a social scene that made London look simple. America was clearly a *very* odd place. Some of the most powerful men and women in the colonies wouldn't be considered high on the social ladder in London, even though some of them possessed more land than any Duke in Britain. The networks of patronage, she was starting to suspect, worked differently. Matters weren't helped by a number of American aristocrats giving themselves titles to which they had no right.

It felt like hours before a dull quiver ran through the ship. Jackson banged on the door seconds later, although he didn't come into her cabin. Gwen wished, suddenly, that she could go up on deck, but Captain Bligh's word was law when his ship was at sea. Putting down the file, she lay on the bed and felt the sensations running through the ship, trying to understand just what was happening. Distant voices shouted out unintelligible commands, followed by more odd movements. A steady thumping noise echoed through the ship. The vessel was clearly leaving harbour.

"Lady Gwen," Jackson called, tapping the door again. "Do you want to come up to the deck?"

Gwen sat upright, swung her legs over the bed and walked to the door. The deck felt odd under her feet, but she didn't feel sick. Jackson was waiting on the other side of the door, beaming from ear to ear. It struck her, suddenly, that he'd been nervous that someone higher-ranking would be appointed to the convoy. He'd have lost his first chance at an independent command.

"Keep one hand on the railing until you have your sea legs," Jackson advised. "The motions will get worse when we get out into the open sea."

"Thank you," Gwen said. She could fly, if necessary, although she knew there was no way she could make it from Britain to America. Getting from Oxford to London during the Swing had almost killed her. "How do we get onto the deck?"

"This way," Jackson said. "We have to stay out of the way."

They clambered up a wooden staircase and onto a battlement-like structure. A handful of other passengers were already there – Gwen smiled as she recognised Irene and Raechel – watched by a couple of sailors. They didn't seem happy to be near the passengers, Gwen noted, even though Raechel wasn't the only beautiful girl among them. But then, if she recalled correctly, sailors thought that a woman onboard ship was bad luck. She snorted at the thought – how could colonies be established without women? – and then turned her attention to London. The remainder of the city was slipping into the distance at incredible speed.

"The *Duke of India* is one of the fastest ships in the fleet," Jackson commented. He stood next to her, just a *little* closer than was companionable. "The voyage to America will be completed in record time."

Gwen nodded, unwilling to look away from the city as it shrank in the distance. The deck was beginning to heave under her feet now, the ship rising and falling as she cleaved her way through increasingly choppy water. She turned her attention to the forts lining the river banks – the French would be in for a nasty surprise, if they ever dared to raid the Thames – and smiled coldly as she saw a pair of sorcerers hanging in the air above them. London – and England – would be safe while she was gone.

"Tell me something," Jackson said. The air was growing colder, even though it was midsummer. A number of passengers were already heading back below decks, as if it would be warmer under cover. "What do you do when you're not the Royal Sorceress?"

"I'm always the Royal Sorceress," Gwen said. She'd had no end of invitations to balls of one kind or another, but she'd declined most of them. The only one she'd gone to had been with Sir Charles and that had ended badly. "I don't get time off."

Jackson gave her an odd look. "There's no one you can leave in charge, even for a few short hours?"

Gwen shook her head, wordlessly. A man could take time off without it being held against him, but a woman taking time off was considered a sign of weakness. A holiday? There was no way she could take leave without creating the impression that the Royal Sorcerers Corps could get along just fine without her. Who knew what the departmental heads would get up to, if she wasn't keeping a sharp eye on them? It was hard enough leaving Sir James in command while she headed to America …

"That's not right," Jackson said. "You need time to relax."

"Duty comes first," Gwen said. "And magic problems can be disastrous if they're allowed to blossom out of control."

"Then take the opportunity to enjoy this voyage and relax," Jackson said. "That's what I'm going to do."

Gwen nodded. The last report from America had made it clear that Franco-Spanish forces were mustering in New Orleans, their northernmost outpost. It wouldn't be long before the enemy advanced north, into territory dominated by slave plantations … plantations worked by slaves who would no doubt turn on their masters the moment the French made their appearance. And without magical support, the defenders would be badly hampered. She had very little time to relax …

… But, at the same time, there was nothing she could do until she reached New York.

"I will," she said. He'd moved a step or two closer to her while she'd been thinking. "And maybe I'll find something else to do."

"Take up chess," Jackson advised. "It's good for the mind."

They stood together until a sailor appeared and informed them that Captain Bligh was waiting for them in the officers' mess. Jackson grinned at her, then led the way down to the giant compartment, which was illuminated by dozens of brightly burning lanterns. Irene and Raechel were already there, wearing simple clothes, but quite a few of the other passengers were missing. Seasickness had caught up with them already.

"Make sure you eat at least one piece of fruit a day," Jackson muttered, claiming the seat next to her. "You'll need it to stay healthy."

Gwen nodded, then looked at the Captain. He was carving a large piece of beef personally, while another officer in military uniform ladled out potatoes, vegetables and gravy. Gwen wondered, absently, just how it had been cooked so quickly. Magic? It was possible, she supposed, although she doubted a Blazer would waste his time cooking when there were far more important tasks to be done. Pushing the thought aside, she made a mental note to eat as much as she could. Later meals were unlikely to be anything like as good.

"Please, start eating," Captain Bligh said, once everyone had been served. "I'm afraid the others will not be joining us for dinner."

"Seasickness," Jackson muttered.

"Quite," Captain Bligh agreed. He raised his voice, slightly, as his passengers began to tuck in. "We will be rounding Dover this evening and hopefully linking up with the remainder of the convoy off the Lizard tomorrow morning, then setting sail for New York. As you are no doubt aware, that will be the last *certain* chance to mail a letter back to Britain. We *may* – I say again, we *may* – meet up with a mail packet during the voyage, but that is not guaranteed."

Gwen nodded. The Royal Navy wanted to put Talkers on all of its ships, but there simply weren't enough to go round. She was surprised, though, that *this* convoy had no Talker ... unless they expected *her* to play that role. But Lord Mycroft knew she couldn't push a message very far. Nor could Irene, for that matter. Her talents lent themselves to mind-reading, not sending messages.

"If you want to send a message, please give it to the purser before we meet the remainder of the convoy," Captain Bligh added. He paused. "There are also some other matters we need to discuss."

And he wants us to eat and listen, Gwen thought. *His own food is growing cold.*

"The sailors have jobs to do," Captain Bligh warned. "Please do not interrupt them while they are working, or enter their quarters without permission. I will not hesitate to put anyone – and I mean *anyone* – caught bothering the sailors in irons until we arrive in New York."

Gwen wondered, inwardly, if he was bluffing. The passengers included aristocrats and senior military officers. Captain Bligh might have boundless authority during the voyage, but there would be consequences if he mistreated any of his passengers. Who knew which way the Admiralty would jump?

Particularly with Lord Nelson so keen to curry favour, she thought, grimly. It might have been better for him if he'd died as a young man, rather than remain in his post until he had become a national embarrassment. *He might overrule Bligh even though he understands the importance of discipline at sea.*

"We will get you to New York safely," Bligh concluded. "Until then, please enjoy your dinner."

Chapter Eight

aechel sat on the deck, in the cabin she shared with Irene, meditating.

It was hard, very hard, to keep her thoughts from wandering. She was not a naturally contemplative person – she wanted to be *doing something* – and focusing her mind didn't come easily to her. And the harder she tried, the harder it became to keep her thoughts under strict control. Forming a mental shield was one thing, but holding it in place was quite another.

Gwen had an unfair advantage, she thought, feeling a flicker of envy. *She had to learn to keep her magic under control from a very early age.*

She felt a tingle at the back of her mind and hardened her shield, holding it firmly in place as Irene probed her thoughts. Constant practice had made it easier for her to sense when her thoughts were being read, but it was still hard to keep Irene out. Raechel's emotions leaked from behind the shield, bringing memories with them. Irene, in a reflective mood, had compared mind-reading to looking up items in an encyclopaedia. One thought led rapidly to another, which led to a whole string of memories. And false memories, she'd insisted, rarely had the *taste* of real memories.

"You're doing better," Irene said. "What were you doing with Captain Parker?"

Raechel clamped down on her thoughts, hard. The question had unleashed a flurry of memories – the airship captain kissing her, his hands stroking her breasts, Gwen bursting in on them – all of which would be read by Irene if she didn't keep them under control. She felt the tingle grow stronger, but somehow managed to keep her thoughts behind the shield. A second later, the tingle receded.

"That's a dirty trick," she muttered.

"It's amazing what an innocent question can do," Irene pointed out, tartly. "And this is the perfect opportunity to work on your shields."

Raechel nodded, reluctantly. After the brief excitement of rounding the Lizard and meeting up with the rest of the convoy, the days had started to blur together as soon as dry land was over the horizon. It was easy to believe that the convoy was all that remained of the world, that there was nothing beyond the horizon. How had Columbus managed it, she asked herself, as he'd cruised further and further into the unknown? There had been no way to *know* there was a great continent on the other side of the ocean.

"They knew the world was round," Irene said. "They just thought they'd run into India if they kept going west."

Raechel flushed. "Do you *have* to keep reading my thoughts?"

"You need to keep a shield in place at all times," Irene told her. "There's no way you can learn to master *lying* with your thoughts until you can keep an intruder out of your mind."

"I know," Raechel said. She rubbed her temple, wondering why she felt so tired. It wasn't as if she'd done much, apart from a daily walk around the deck. "But it doesn't seem to work for long."

"You haven't mastered the art of keeping the shield in place," Irene said. "It's a matter of schooling your thoughts to keep moving in the same direction. Right now, even a minor Talker would be able to tell if you were lying, even if he couldn't read your thoughts."

Raechel sighed. "How do we even *know* there will be a Talker watching me?"

Irene pointed a long finger at her. "Imagine yourself a government minister – or an underground mastermind," she said. "Would you pass on the opportunity to watch your people for disloyalty?"

"But people will be nervous if they know their minds are going to be read," Raechel pointed out. "Wouldn't that skew the results?"

"Not really," Irene said. "A person might be nervous about having his thoughts read, but it wouldn't read out as disloyalty."

Raechel shuddered. She didn't think she wanted to work anywhere there was a prospect of having her thoughts read, but she had a feeling it was already too late. Did her uncle have his thoughts read regularly? Or were mental probes reserved for the lower-ranking officials in his department? Irene had told her, time and time again, that the best secret agents weren't the ones who strolled around as though they owned the place, but the ones who passed unnoticed. But Raechel had already learnt that lesson from Gwen. Who would have imagined that the Royal Sorceress would pretend to be a maid?

The thought cheered her up, slightly. Practicing meditation was boring, but dressing up was fun, once she'd got over her first reaction. The trick, Irene had said, was never to lose sight of who you were pretending to be. It was hard, particularly when she posed as a lower-class woman, but she thought she was getting the hang of it. Passing as a man was far harder.

"Back to work," Irene said, briskly. "We've got another three hours before dinner, so we may as well make the most of them."

Raechel groaned. "You don't have more to tell me?"

"I have *plenty* to tell you," Irene said. She smirked. "Consider it an incentive to learn how to hold a shield in place."

The next two hours passed slowly, too slowly. Irene's probes grew stronger as Raechel learnt how to make a tougher shield, her questions becoming more intrusive in the hopes of provoking an emotional reaction. Raechel couldn't help wondering just what Irene had done, in the service of the British Crown, that had inspired some of the nastier questions. Raechel knew full well that she was hardly the ideal aristocratic daughter, let alone ward, but there were some lines she had never even *considered* crossing.

"You're doing better," Irene said. This time, Raechel kept the shield in place until she felt the questing probe. "It's a pity you didn't start earlier, but your family has no history of magic."

Raechel nodded, curtly. Aristocratic women – with a single exception – were expected to suppress their magic. As far as the outside world was concerned, *Gwen* was the sole female aristocrat with magic. In truth, Irene had pointed out, quite a few families quietly encouraged their daughters to develop their talents, intending to use them to enhance the family's position. It was always an interesting guessing game, Raechel had learnt from her aunt, to try and deduce which particular daughter might have a hint of magic.

Irene cleared her throat. "We may as well get ready for dinner," she added. Raechel knew, perfectly well, that she didn't mean getting *dressed*. "What do you make of young Fredrick?"

"He's a nice young man," Raechel protested, careful to keep her mental shields firmly in place. Fredrick Hauser, the First Mate, had sat next to her at dinner every night for the last ten days. His conversation wasn't that interesting, she had to admit, but he was easy on the eye. "What about him?"

"He's interested in you," Irene said.

Raechel snorted. She'd known that without needing to read his mind. She just wasn't sure what to make of it. Fredrick was too young, really, to understand the thrill of a quick affair, unlike Captain Parker. Her cheeks heated at the memory. Captain Parker would have understood that the affair would have to come to an end, almost as soon as it had begun. Fredrick might not grasp that until it was too late to avoid a scandal.

"He *is* of aristocratic blood," she said, dryly. The Hauser Family wasn't anything like as powerful as the Slater or Standish Families, but they were very definitely blue bloods with ties to the House of Hanover. "Aren't you supposed to be chaperoning me?"

"This squadron has secret orders," Irene said, ignoring the question. "Orders that were not revealed to me, during my briefing. I want you to convince him to tell you what those orders are."

Raechel gave her a sharp look. "Should we be trying to find out?"

"Anything someone feels like keeping a secret is worth knowing," Irene said. She smiled, rather sardonically. "And besides, it's a good test of your talents."

"Oh," Raechel said. "Is that *all*?"

Irene shrugged. "Anything we do here, onboard ship, can be contained, if something goes badly wrong," she said. "Lady Gwen will help, if necessary. Her orders would supersede Bligh's if magic was involved. Later, when we are in New York, it will be much harder to prevent disaster. Your cover might be blown completely."

"I don't have a cover," Raechel protested.

"Yes, you do," Irene said. She pointed a long finger at Raechel's face. "You are the daughter of Lord Slater and the ward of Lord Standish, a pretty young heiress with nothing but wool between her ears. You have no experience of the ways of the world, no awareness of life outside your home and no understanding of men. *That* is what they expect you to be, Raechel, and that is the impression you are going to cultivate. People always talk much more openly when they think they can't be understood."

Raechel scowled. "Is there no way I can be like Lady Gwen?"

"If you want to dominate the social scene by sheer force of personality, backed up by money, I suppose you could," Irene snapped. "But if you want to get something *useful* done, it's better to be underestimated. A naïve young ingénue is so much more attractive to a man than a foul-mouthed woman who shows off her intelligence to all and sundry."

"Fine," Raechel said. "I'll do what I can."

She was almost relieved, an hour later, when the dinner bell rang and they made their way up to the officers' mess. Gwen was already there, chatting to a young military officer about Russia and the Mad Tsar; she nodded politely to Raechel and Irene, then returned to her conversion. Raechel couldn't help wondering if Colonel Jackson was flirting with Gwen, even though she was the Royal Sorceress. They had certainly spent a great deal of time playing chess in the passengers' lounge.

"Lady Raechel," Fredrick said. He rose to pull a chair out for her. "I trust the day has gone well?"

"I have been sewing," Raechel lied. Her mother – and then

her aunt – had tried to insist that she learnt how to sew, on the grounds it was a ladylike skill, but she hadn't had the patience to master it. "My chaperone has been feeling a little under the weather."

She didn't miss the flicker of interest in Fredrick's eyes; she'd been careful to look for it. He was really too young to mask his emotions well, even though he *had* been a serving naval officer since he'd turned thirteen. The Royal Navy might allow aristocrats to purchase commissions, but even the scions of the richest and most powerful families had to start out as midshipmen. Lord Nelson had insisted on it, when he'd become First Lord of the Admiralty, and no one had the power to overrule him. The young men had to learn the basics before climbing to higher ranks.

And Fredrick wants a ship of his own, Raechel thought. He was young, but a good recommendation from his commander – and aristocratic backers – would put him in an excellent position to win command of one of the new ironclads. Or even a sailing ship, although she wouldn't last five minutes against an ironclad. *Maybe that's why he's interested in me.*

Dinner was a quiet affair, as she'd expected; Captain Bligh led prayers, then chatted quietly to one of the military officers while eating. The food had grown progressively duller over the last few days, although Irene had insisted that Raechel had to eat properly just so she could do her exercises in her cabin. Raechel doubted she would ever be a strong woman – Irene had told her that there were farmers' wives who were stronger than artillerymen – but she would have a surprise or two for anyone who tried to grab her. Concealing a knife in a dress was easier than it seemed.

"I need to go back to the cabin," Irene said, when the main course was finished. "Take care to hurry back as soon as you can."

Or don't, Raechel thought. Technically, Irene was meant to be with her every time she set foot out of the cabin. There was no hope of a private conversation with Fredrick as long as Irene was nearby. But now … Irene had left, just as she'd promised. *I'm on my own.*

She chatted to Fredrick, feeling her heart starting to pound in her chest. It had been easy enough to signal interest to

Captain Parker, but Fredrick? She had no idea what he would make of any signals she sent, particularly while they were in the dining compartment. And he might want to go too far … it was funny, part of her mind reflected, just how easy it had been to allow Parker to seduce her, back when there had been nothing at stake. Or she'd *thought* there was nothing. Gwen had snapped her out of it in more ways than one.

"I need to take a walk," she said, as the dinner came to an end. "Would you care to accompany me?"

"It would be my pleasure," Fredrick said. He held out a hand and Raechel took it, feeling oddly guilty. "Shall we walk the deck?"

Darkness was falling over the convoy as they walked onto the deck, broken only by lights mounted at each end of the vessel. Overhead, the stars were starting to come out, twinkling merrily in the dark sky. Fredrick had told her that sailors could navigate by the stars, but Raechel found it hard to believe. She'd never been encouraged to study astronomy when she'd been a little girl.

She looked at Fredrick, standing next to her, and felt another pang of guilt. But she knew what she had to do. "I'm not looking forward to New York," she said, as a conversational opener. "It's nothing like London, is it?"

"It's very different in many ways," Fredrick said. He hadn't let go of her hand. "What do you want to do when you're there?"

"I'll probably be kept in the house," Raechel said. "Lady Irene took me as a favour to my family, but she doesn't have any obligations beyond escorting me to New York. I don't know anyone there."

"You know me," Fredrick said. "I should be around."

Raechel looked at him. "I thought the convoy was going back to Britain," she said. "Isn't it?"

"The freighters will be, once the next set of escorts is assembled," Fredrick said. They reached the railing and stared into the darkness. Faint lights bobbled in the distance, marking the position of the other ships. "I'm not so sure about the warships, or the troopships. We were told to assume that we would be spending a year on station."

Raechel glanced at him. "Is that normal?"

"I spent two years in the West Indies, once I was commissioned," Fredrick said. "There weren't any steamships on station, not back then. We sailed around the Caribbean, chasing pirates and smugglers while keeping a sharp eye on the French. One of my commanding officers even insisted on surveying the waters around Cuba, in preparation for the war."

"That must have been grim," Raechel said.

"It was," Fredrick said. "The weather was hot and moist, disease spread rapidly ... going on shore leave was a good way to wind up on medical leave. And most of the planters wouldn't give us the time of day. I think they were deeply involved with the smuggling trade."

Raechel frowned, unsure how to proceed. "What do *you* think will happen in New York?"

Fredrick smiled. "I don't know for sure," he said. He wrapped an arm around her, very gently. "We could die tomorrow, you know."

"I hope not," Raechel said. She leant into his arm as cold air blew across the water. "What do you *think* will happen?"

"The real problem with moving troops and supplies around America is the sheer *size* of the territory," Fredrick said. "There's a railway between New York and Amherst, but it isn't large enough to cope with military supplies. I think we'll be moving the troopships south, after we've had a chance to rest and exercise the horses. Amherst isn't the closest place to the French, but it has the best seaport."

He paused, his arm tightening slightly. "Unless Colonel Jackson wants to try to land near New Orleans," he added. "The French must have similar problems of their own."

"I see," Raechel said.

She looked up at him and found him looking back at her. He was learning forward, very slightly ... it would have been easy to draw back, but instead she allowed him to bring his lips to hers and kiss her. Irene had been right, she realised, as the kiss deepened. Once she'd grown used to male company, it was easy to let herself kiss other men. His breathing quickened, deep in his throat, as he pulled her into a tight embrace, his hands running down her back. He was inexperienced, part of her mind noted. His touch was rougher than it needed to be.

And how far, she asked herself, *does he expect to go?*

She felt ... cold. There was none of the thrill of doing something she *knew* would horrify her aunt, there was none of the delight of doing something that would upset society ... even the prospect of being caught by a wandering sailor didn't excite her. She could feel his excitement, pressed against her body, but ...

Fredrick let go of her and jumped backwards. "My Lady..."

Raechel turned sharply, then felt a wave of *Déjà Vu*. Gwen was standing there, looking ... *shocked*.

"Return to your duties," Gwen ordered, coolly. It wasn't her job to issue orders onboard ship, but Fredrick didn't look as though he wanted to dispute it with her. "Raechel, come with me."

Chapter Nine

wen fought hard to keep her anger under control, but it was difficult. She'd expected better, somehow, after Raechel had matured in Russia. She wasn't the girl Gwen had plucked from the arms of Captain Parker, her dress around her waist and his hands on her breasts, not any longer. And yet, Gwen had caught her with the First Mate! Didn't Raechel have a lick of sense?

"Tell me," she said, once they were in her cabin with the door firmly closed. "What were you thinking?"

Raechel met her eyes. "I was thinking that I was doing as I was told!"

Gwen blinked. "By Irene?"

"Yes," Raechel said. "She wanted me to see what I could coax Fredrick into telling me."

"I see," Gwen said, finally. Unfortunately, she believed Raechel. Seducing someone to learn his secrets was precisely what Irene did, among other things. "And did she tell you the dangers?"

"I'm not going to get pregnant," Raechel protested. "*You* warned me about that, didn't you?"

"Your reputation will also be dented," Gwen pointed out. "And that could harm you in the future."

Raechel glared at her. "And what if I decide I don't care?"

"You do not have the luxury of putting your reputation aside," Gwen said. *She* could do it, if she had any ladylike reputation left after dressing as a man and doing a man's job. Raechel, without magic and the ward of a powerful family, had far less freedom. "And what would it do to *him*?"

She sighed, feeling her head start to pound. "What will

you say to him when he asks you to marry him? Or when his family goes to your uncle and asks for your hand in marriage?"

"I will say *no*," Raechel said. "Does it matter what we do together?"

"It might," Gwen said. "What happens if he tells *everyone* what you did together?"

She ground her teeth in irritation. A man could have a dozen lovers, if he wished; he could go to a brothel, lure the maid into bed or even keep a mistress. No one would care, even if he had a whole secret family of bastard children. But a woman? A woman had to guard her chastity – and then her virtue – with care, knowing that one slip would mean disgrace and utter ruination. Fredrick Hauser would be believed, she was sure, because Lord Standish's enemies would *want* to believe him. And Raechel's life would come to an end.

"I don't think he would," Raechel said.

"Men have done stupid things before," Gwen pointed out. How many problems had she had to solve, as Royal Sorceress, that started with one of her magicians doing something stupid that involved a woman? "If he wound up so angry, so hurt, he might lash out at you without thinking about the consequences to himself."

If indeed there were any consequences, she added, silently.

"Captain Parker understood," Raechel said, sullenly.

"Captain Parker was at least a decade older than you," Gwen said, remembering the airship captain. She had no idea what had happened to him, after they returned from Russia. "I don't think the First Mate is more than a year or two older than you."

She shook her head. "It's madness."

"Irene told me to do it," Raechel said. "And I *did* learn something useful ..."

Gwen snorted. "Useful to *whom*?"

Raechel glared. "And *you* have been talking to Colonel Jackson!"

It took all of the mental discipline Gwen had mastered, over a year of dealing with men who thought she was too young or too female for her job, to keep from slapping

Raechel as hard as she could. How *dare* she? She liked talking to Jackson, but she wasn't inclined to see him as a potential husband.

"Colonel Jackson and I," she said with icy calm, "have not been alone together. I have not been to his cabin and he has not been to mine. We have never put ourselves in a compromising position. You, on the other hand, were seen leaving with Fredrick by everyone at the dinner table! They will believe, I am sure, that you and he *did* compromise yourselves."

"I'm going to have a word with Irene," she added, before Raechel could think of a cutting response. "And you are going to stay here until I do."

Raechel nodded, shortly. Gwen eyed her for a long moment, hoping that Raechel would have the common sense to do as she was told, then turned and stalked out of the cabin. It wasn't a long walk to the cabin Irene and Raechel shared, but Gwen dawdled, deliberately, to get her temper under control. Irene could probably sense her anger from the other side of the ship, if she happened to be letting her talent run wild. She'd probably want to keep an eye on Raechel and Fredrick from a distance.

She tapped sharply on the door, then opened it. Irene was sitting at her desk, reading one of the innumerable files Gwen had passed to her. She looked up as Gwen entered, her eyebrows rising in silent inquiry. Gwen felt a touch on the outskirts of her mental defences, a questing tendril trying to sneak into her mind. She pushed back, tightening her defences, as she closed the door. Irene should know better than to try to read her mind.

"She was kissing Fredrick when I found her," she said, without preamble. Irene would know what she was talking about. "Did you put her up to it?"

"She needed to practice," Irene said, flatly. There was no hint of guilt in her voice. "Did you have a few words with the young man?"

"I told him to go back to his duties," Gwen said. She kept her anger firmly under control, knowing that it would damage her shields if she allowed it to run free. "What were you *thinking*?"

"I was thinking that Raechel needed to practice," Irene said. She rose, slowly. "Or did you imagine that she would be able to remain ... unsoiled by the gritty realities of the job?"

Gwen glared at her. "And her *reputation*?"

"Doomed," Irene said. "I imagine it won't be long before her reputation is tainted, no matter what happens. She can either marry and live a blameless life or work for the Crown. If the latter, people will start to question her sooner rather than later."

"You were tainted from the start," Gwen snapped. It wasn't fair, but she was past caring. "I don't think *she's* tainted ..."

"She surrendered her virginity two years ago, shortly after she entered the care of her aunt and uncle," Irene said, coolly. "Since then, she has had sex with five other men, all members of her outlandish club. She has also gone very close to crossing the line with a number of other men and two women. Her reputation has only survived, I suspect, because of her uncle's power. Very few people would dare to whisper about his family without real proof."

Her eyes narrowed. "Or do you feel that lower-class women are tainted from birth?"

Gwen recoiled, honestly shocked. She'd known that Raechel had a taste for male company – it had been obvious from the first day they'd met – but she hadn't realised just how far Raechel had gone. She had to have been mad. A pregnancy would have been utterly disastrous, proof that she'd jumped well over the line. Even if she'd been raped, after being beaten into submission, she would have been blamed. Far too many men believed it was impossible to rape a virtuous woman.

"I didn't know," she stammered, finally.

"Of course not," Irene said. "You didn't *want* to know."

She cleared her throat. "I repeat my earlier question," she said. "Do you feel that lower-class women are tainted from birth?"

"No," Gwen said. She wasn't entirely sure where Irene came from, but she rather doubted Irene had been born an aristocrat. Singing on the stage was a profession that was firmly closed to anyone above the middle classes. "But Raechel ..."

"Needs to understand just what she's getting into before it's too late," Irene said, firmly. "Or what's getting into her, for that matter."

Gwen blushed. "You are *not* to order her to have sex with anyone. Or to use her wiles to manipulate people."

Irene quirked her eyebrows. "You mean, not to do what women have been doing since time out of mind?"

"Explain," Gwen ordered.

"You know as well as I do that men have all the power in the family," Irene said. She shrugged, meaningfully. "Raechel needs to learn this too. What little power women have is only theirs as long as the men are prepared to allow it. There are very few legal protections for women – and if they don't have powerful families who are prepared to back them up, they're in trouble. Women have been learning to manipulate men since Adam and Eve. It's the only way to protect themselves."

"Perhaps, if women weren't so vindictive to their fellow women, they would find it easier," Gwen snarled.

"But a woman who stands outside convention is a threat to her fellow women," Irene said, tartly. Her face shadowed for a long moment. "You know what happened in Bohemia, Lady Gwen."

"You were lucky to escape with your life," Gwen said, quietly. "Raechel isn't like you, Irene."

"She is," Irene said. "She's inexperienced, true. She hasn't learnt the calculated ruthlessness of a woman born to the lower classes. And, until now, she didn't have a cause to play for. But she is very much like me as a young girl."

She looked down at the deck. "You have to learn to use whatever assets you have to best advantage," she added. "And you stop feeling guilty after you comprehend, deep inside, just how quickly you can be discarded."

Gwen closed her eyes for a long moment, then sighed. "Do you expect her to give up her identity?"

"She may have to, eventually," Irene said. "Lady Raechel Slater-Standish isn't exactly a public figure, but if she's always present when something interesting happens ..."

"I see," Gwen said.

"I told her that she could leave at any moment, if she wanted to back out," Irene added. "And so far she's stayed, despite learning some uncomfortable truths. I think that says something about her, doesn't it? You and Raechel have quite a bit in common."

That, Gwen knew, was true. She'd wanted to use her talents, truly use them; Raechel, too, wanted to do something *meaningful* with her life. And there were very few options available to a woman, particularly one without magic. Raechel would find herself nothing more than a high-ranking wife, just like her aunt, if she married and stayed in London. Hell, she might not even be allowed to accompany her husband overseas, if she married a diplomat or a soldier. Lady Standish hadn't accompanied her husband until the final fatal trip.

And I bet she regrets that now, Gwen thought. Lady Standish had been a harsh mistress to her maids, including Gwen. It had been a taste of life as a servant and Gwen hadn't liked it at all. *She's still in that bloody bedlam.*

"Very well," she said, finally. "But you are not to push her into *anything*."

"I understand," Irene said. "Please send her back here when you can."

***

Raechel made sure to tighten her mental shields as she stepped into her cabin, although she was too conflicted for them to do much good. Part of her was embarrassed beyond words at being interrupted by Gwen, part of her was silently relieved that they'd been caught before they went too far. How bad would things have been, she asked herself, if they'd gone further before they'd been caught? And would the entire ship know before breakfast?

"I owe you an apology," Irene said, once the door was closed and locked. "And something of an explanation."

She took a breath. "My parents were lower middle-class merchants; my father a refugee who fled Germany as a young man, my mother the youngest daughter of a poor family in

Glasgow. Father was a talented singer and taught me how to sing, although we were too poor to hire tutors. I was a *good* singer, so good that I often sang solos outside church for Christmas and Easter. A passing impresario noticed me, followed me home and extended an invitation to join the opera."

Raechel frowned. She had the odd feeling that Irene had deliberately left something out.

"I was excited, very excited, when I first entered the theatre," Irene continued. "There was little hope for me elsewhere, you see. Father had insisted that I learn to read, write and do sums, which put me ahead of most of the young men who might otherwise have asked for my hand. Young girls weren't meant to be educated. I'm still not sure how father managed to pay for the lessons. But it was enough that I wanted more from life. The glamour and glitter of the stage sounded better than life managing a tiny shop."

"Like me," Raechel said.

Irene nodded. "It didn't take me long to realise that I had to … *work* … for my roles," she said, bitterly. "A casting agent wouldn't take me on unless I … *worked* … for him. I felt filthy, afterwards, even though it led directly to my first major role. It was a great success, yet I still had to … *work* … to be sure of constantly remaining in the limelight. I was both a star and a prisoner. The only way for me to maintain some shred of independence and dignity was to learn to manipulate the men who controlled the stage. I rapidly learnt the value of information, particularly information that no one else had. It didn't take me long to add blackmail to my skills.

"In hindsight, my talents were already starting to develop. But I didn't know that at the time.

"Five years after I started, I gained enough independence and wealth that I was being noticed on a wider stage," she added. "We were travelling Europe at the time, you see. There I met a … nobleman who flattered me, promising that he would make me his lady. It was enough to convince me to live with him for several months."

Raechel's eyes narrowed. "You couldn't read his thoughts?"

"Only emotions, at the time," Irene said. "And I think he

genuinely believed what he was saying, to be honest. His father wasn't expected to die soon. He thought he had time to convince his family to accept me. It wasn't as though I wasn't qualified for the post. But his father died and his sisters, who had never liked me, convinced him that he needed a wife from a better family. He wanted to keep me as a mistress, but I decided it would be better to flee his territory before I suffered a small accident."

She snorted. "The stress pushed my talents up a notch," she added. "I fled to London, half-mad, and found a place to hide. The bastard hired detectives to follow me, one of whom was alarmingly good. Luckily, I had a few allies of my own by then. I faked a marriage and vanished, leaving a mocking note for the nobleman. He thought I had good reason to keep everything a secret too now, so he called off his dogs."

"But you didn't get married," Raechel said. "How did you fake it?"

"I had some help," Irene said. "Suffice it to say that, shortly afterwards, I was recruited by British Intelligence."

She smirked. "And the nobleman in question was killed by the French, a few years later," she added. "I believe his wife was killed too."

Raechel frowned, unsure what to say. How much of the story was actually true?

"All of it," Irene said. Raechel flushed and slammed her shields back into place. "I've left out a few details, but the basic outline is accurate."

She looked up, meeting Raechel's eyes. "I have done a great many things I'm not proud of," she added. "And they were *necessary*. You'll have to … lower yourself to do the same, if you want to survive in this world. Trying to sweet talk Fredrick is barely the icing on the cake."

"It wasn't easy," Raechel said. "And we were interrupted…"

"Maybe you can pick it up again later," Irene said. "If you still want to, that is …"

Raechel flushed. Irene's advice had covered a multitude of subjects that her aunt would have flatly denied existed, if Raechel had had the nerve to ask. She hadn't even *thought* about some of the different ways to please a man, or herself, until Irene had mentioned them. Now, it was clear that Irene had *done* them herself. It had been the only way to survive and prosper in her world.

"There's something else I should tell you," Irene warned. She held up a dainty hand. "Do you know Geoffrey Norton, Barrister-at-law?"

"No," Raechel said. The name was unfamiliar. Besides, she'd never been encouraged to have any dealings with lawyers. "Who is he?"

"A friend," Irene said. "A stout, sturdy Englishman. Works for the Royal College. He loves me, more deeply and truly than he knows. I like him too, more than I care to admit. But if he knew what I'd done, even after I came to work for the Crown, he'd be revolted."

"Men have married widows before," Raechel pointed out.

"Everyone knows that widows are *respectable*," Irene said. "Men can be quite funny about certain matters."

"I know," Raechel said.

"If you want to keep learning, you may find yourself cut off from polite society forever," Irene warned. "Really, you need a whole new identity, one you can discard at will."

"Polite society isn't *polite*," Raechel said, automatically. The thought of being permanently separated from her aunt and uncle wasn't a bad one. "And I'm not going to stop now."

Chapter Ten

do wonder just why the French committed so many magicians to the invasion," Colonel Jackson said, as he moved his knight forward. "Didn't they know they risked terrible losses?"

"I dare say they thought they didn't have a choice," Gwen said. She frowned, stroking her chin contemplatively. Jackson was a *good* player, better than her. "Victory in the Battle of Dorking would have allowed them to make peace on excellent terms."

"Perhaps," Colonel Jackson said. He watched as she moved a pawn forward, then pushed his bishop across the board, opening up a whole new angle of attack. "But we would have worn them down, regardless."

He looked up. "Unless you have other secret weapons hidden in Cavendish Hall?"

Gwen shrugged. *Olivia* probably counted as a secret weapon, although there wouldn't be many dead bodies around for her to animate. The French understood the dangers of leaving corpses lying around as well as the British. But then, the government might have been secretly collecting and storing dead bodies, just in case. They'd done worse during the Swing.

"The French are a lion," she said, as she moved her own knight back. "We're a whale. Each one is supreme in its own environment, but unable to come to grips with the other."

"Interesting concept," Jackson said. He seemed more inclined to give thought to her words than most of the men she met. "Do you think ...?"

He broke off as a voice echoed through the hull. "Man for action," it bellowed. "Man for action!"

Gwen rose, feeling a trickle of alarm running down her spine. There had always been a danger of encountering a French squadron on the voyage, although Captain Bligh had taken pains to reassure the more nervous passengers that the French would be hard-pressed to *find* the convoy, let alone muster the force to attack it. Gwen gritted her teeth as she glanced around for Irene and Raechel, then remembered that they were still in their cabin, reading files and discussing their plans for New York. A handful of crewmen rushed past the door, their leader bellowing orders as they passed. Gwen glanced at Jackson, then headed to the ladder. She had to know what was going on.

"My men aren't equipped for fighting at sea," Jackson muttered, as he followed her. Gwen was silently grateful she was wearing trousers rather than a dress. "They'll be sitting ducks if a French squadron gets into gunnery range."

You should be with them, Gwen thought. She wasn't surprised that Jackson had chosen to sail on *Duke of India*, rather than one of the cramped troopships, but it wasn't a decision she could support. *And you might be needed there.*

Captain Bligh turned to look at her as she led the way onto the bridge. "Get off my bridge," he snapped. "A battle is about to take place."

"She's a sorceress," Jackson pointed out, before Gwen could say a word. "She might be very useful."

The Captain eyed him darkly, then nodded. "Seven French warships, heading right towards us," he ordered. "Some bastard must have given them our projected course."

Or they had a magician looking for us, Gwen thought. It wouldn't be easy, locating a convoy of ships in the middle of the ocean, but the French might have managed to do it. *Or they might just have had an immense stroke of luck.*

She peered into the distance, watching as the French ships came into view. They had to have been spotted from the mast, she realised; the lookout would have seen them long before they were visible to anyone on deck. The ships looked nasty, she thought, although they didn't look to be purpose-built steamships. No doubt the French had hazarded most of their iron warships on crossing the English Channel.

Which makes sense, she told herself. *Outfitting an ironclad for crossing the ocean is far harder than building ships to cross the water to England.*

"Sailing ships," Jackson commented. "Your guns should be able to make mincemeat out of them, Captain."

"They'll have a layer of armour," Bligh countered. "A lucky shot could be fatal for us – or for them."

He turned to bark orders to his crew. The squadron was separating into two formations; the warships proceeding onwards to meet the foe, the freighters and troopships hanging back. It puzzled Gwen until she realised that, if the engagement went badly, the other ships would have a chance to scatter before the French chased them down. A handful of them might even make it to New York.

"They're forming a line," Jackson whispered. "I think they expect a passing engagement with us, then a chance at the freighters."

Gwen nodded. The French would probably find sinking the warships very satisfying, but if they had any sense they'd concentrate on the freighters. Blocking reinforcements to America would make life easier for their armies, particularly when the great offensive finally started ... if it hadn't started already. Being so badly out of touch disconcerted her more than she cared to admit. A flash of light flickered on one of the French warships, followed by a great gout of water splashing up far too close to the lead British ship ...

"They're taking aim," Jackson said.

"I'm going out there," Gwen said. A throbbing eagerness was running through the crew – she could sense they were looking forward to coming to grips with their enemy – but she knew an engagement could be disastrous. Losing a single troopship would cost the lives of thousands of men. "Tell the gunners not to shoot at me."

Jackson gave her a sharp look and nodded curtly. Gwen glanced at Captain Bligh, who was passing orders to the signallers, then hurried out of the hatch and pulled her magic around her, lifting off into the air. She heard someone cry out behind her, but there was no time to turn and look. The chances of survival if she landed in the cold water were minimal. She rose higher, searching for her targets. The French ships were running up a string of flags, led by their king's arms. She had no idea what the others meant.

Wooden ships, she thought slowly, as she studied her targets. They weren't quite wooden – Bligh had been right, there was a layer of armour covering their hulls – but their masts were wooden and there was no sign of a steam engine. The warships were completely dependent on the wind to get around, which was hardly a major problem. Bligh had told her, during one of the innumerable boring dinners, that warship steam engines were nowhere near completely reliable. *Duke of India* would run the risk of losing power in the middle of the ocean without her sails. *But the French have no steam engines.*

A shot cracked past her, coming from the lead French warship. She glanced down in surprise and saw a man standing on the deck, holding a sniper rifle. One of the men who shot at sailors on the rigging, she thought, remembering some of Fredrick Hauser's war stories from the Caribbean. It had been clear, from the way he'd said it, that the sailors regarded such snipers as deadly enemies. Other enemy sailors might be picked up and taken prisoner, after a battle, but the snipers would be killed if they were identified. The French would do the same to any snipers *they* caught.

She formed a fireball in her hand, then threw it down towards the French ship. The Frenchman jumped backwards in shock. He'd expected a Mover, she realised, as she hurled another fireball. He might not have realised she was a girl, let alone realised that she was the Royal Sorceress. But he'd know now, she was sure; she launched a third fireball into the French rigging, watching from high overhead as flames licked through the canvas, sending the lookout falling to the deck. Gwen almost reached out with her magic to slow his fall, or to catch him, before remembering that he was the enemy. The battle was not yet won.

More bullets cracked around her, bouncing off her magic. The other French ships were firing now, aiming their heavy guns at the squadron while the soldiers on their decks were trying to shoot Gwen out of the sky. Gritting her teeth, she shot a series of fireballs in all directions, trying to set fire to the remainder of the enemy fleet. Their sails caught fire, one by one; she watched, grimly, as the flames spread down the mast and onto the wooden decks. And then one of the ships exploded with staggering force.

Must have caught something explosive, she thought, numbly. Bligh had warned her that fire was a deadly enemy onboard ship, particularly when there were barrels of gunpowder lying around. Did ships still use barrels of gunpowder? She couldn't recall. But Bligh was certainly old enough to remember the days when gunpowder was used to launch solid iron balls towards the enemy. *I* ...

Something *flashed* through the air towards her. She ducked, dropping down instinctively, as a chunk of iron almost slammed into her magic. A Frenchman stood on the deck, pointing a finger at her. Gwen had almost no time to react before a wave of magic crashed into her, tearing apart the power holding her in the air. She threw back a fireball desperately, then let go of her grip on the air and plummeted down, breaking free of the Frenchman's magic. A Mover. They had a Mover onboard ship. She caught herself before she hit the water, then hurled another fireball into the French ship, pushing as much power as she could into the blow. Flames licked over the side of the vessel, seconds before the main mast came tumbling down to the deck. Seconds later, it exploded, followed rapidly by another ship.

Gwen braced herself, expecting to see the French magician flying into the air, but saw nothing. An untrained Mover then, she noted absently as she rose higher, watching for other magicians. The French squadron lay in ruins, the four remaining ships burning brightly as flames tore through their hulls. Their crews were hastily scrambling into boats or jumping into the cold water, preferring to brave the Atlantic than die with their ships. Gwen felt magic billowing up within her, itching to lash out at the Frenchmen, but she forced it down with an effort. The French weren't a threat any longer. How could they be?

And I'm the only known Master Magician, she thought numbly. Master Thomas had insisted that they were special, but she hadn't really believed it, not deep inside. But he'd been right, she knew now. She might lack the raw power of Sir James, or the skill of Irene Adler, but she was far more versatile than either of them. *Look what I did to the French.*

She watched the last French warship explode into a billowing fireball, then turned and flew back to the *Duke of India*. Captain Bligh had halted and started to deploy boats, ready to pick up any of the Frenchmen who felt like being taken prisoner. Gwen wondered, absently, just what would happen to them, once they reached New York. A spell in a POW camp until the end of the war, perhaps, or a prisoner exchange with the French? Either one was possible.

The crewmen on deck started to cheer as soon as she dropped down and landed neatly on the giant ship. Gwen smiled, wondering when they'd stopped seeing her as bad luck. Maybe after she'd beaten the French so decisively ... oddly, the thought made her scowl. It had been the most one-sided victory in history for ... for at least living memory. Even the slaughter of the Spanish warships escorting the vast treasure fleet, back in 1802, hadn't been quite so lopsided. Lord Nelson had crushed the Spanish, but he'd lost two ships of his own in the battle.

"My Lady Gwen," Jackson said, as she walked back to the bridge. "That was very well done."

"Thank you," Gwen said. Just for a second, she told herself, she could bathe in honest praise from a man. Jackson didn't seem scared, or intimidated, or convinced she was out to steal his glory. But then, they *were* at sea. The cynical part of her mind argued that it would be a different story on land. "What are we going to do with the prisoners?"

"If they give their word not to cause trouble, we'll treat them decently," Jackson assured her, firmly. "And if they do cause trouble ..."

He mimed cutting his throat with one hand. Gwen understood, then turned to look at the Frenchmen as they were hauled out of the water. They looked stunned ... stunned or angry; some made the sign of the cross in Gwen's direction as they were patted down for weapons and anything that could be sold in New York. Gwen would have felt pity, if she hadn't known what the French would have done to her – and to every other magician, before their king had realised he needed them. The French magical program would be far more advanced if they hadn't wasted thirty years killing every magician who appeared in France or Spain.

Blame the Pope, she thought, darkly. *And now the Pope is a French tool.*

"Lady Gwen," Captain Bligh said, as they stepped onto the bridge. "Thank you."

"You're welcome," Gwen said. "Did we lose anyone?"

"No, fortunately," Bligh said. "You sank them all before they had a chance to get the range."

"Definitely *very* well done," Jackson said.

Gwen yawned suddenly, hastily covering her mouth in a reaction her mother had drilled into her. Young women did not yawn in public. It simply wasn't done. Doing so much magic, so quickly, had drained her. Maybe it wasn't quite as bad as the Battle of Dorking or the desperate struggle to escape Moscow, but quite bad enough.

"I need some rest," she said. "I'll try to see you tonight for dinner."

"Please allow me to escort you to your cabin," Jackson said.

Gwen nodded – all of a sudden, she was too tired to argue – and clambered down the ladder onto the lower deck. A pair of sailors waved cheerfully at her as they walked past, staring at her in awe. It made a change, she decided, from having them watching her as though they expected her to start turning people into frogs, left right and centre. Didn't they *know* magicians *couldn't* turn people into frogs?

Of course they don't, her own thoughts mocked her. *Very few people know what magic can do.*

"Here you are," Jackson said. "Are you going to be all right?"

"I just need to sleep," Gwen assured him. "Using so much magic at once is costly."

Jackson nodded. "Do you want me to stay with you for a while?"

Gwen hesitated. The hell of it was that she was tempted. Jackson could stay with her while she slept … but the price would be too high. Far too high. No matter what they did – or didn't do – rumour would destroy both of them.

"No, thank you," she said. "I'll see you tonight."

She stepped through the door, closing it behind her, then collapsed on the bed.

***

"So tell me," Irene said, as they returned to their cabin. "What do you make of our Frenchman?"

Raechel frowned. The French officer was the highest-ranking Frenchman to be pulled from the water, save for a warship captain who'd been so badly hurt that he'd breathed his last almost as soon as he'd been hauled into a rowboat. She had to admit he was a handsome man – she knew from her trip to Russia that the French were not inhuman monsters – but the resentment on his face was almost palpable. Losing was bad enough, she knew, yet losing so badly had to be humiliating.

Almost as humiliating as being berated in front of a crowd, Raechel thought. Irene had told her to study the Frenchman closely, without speaking to him. *Or worse, perhaps. What will happen to him when he gets home?*

She took a moment to gather her thoughts. "A nobleman," she said, finally. "But not a *noble* man."

Irene lifted her eyebrows. "What makes you say that?"

"He was plucked from the water, where he would have surely drowned," Raechel said. Irene might tell her she was wrong, but she wouldn't mock her. "He should be grateful that we bothered to pick up prisoners. And yet, he's fuming with rage."

"Being beaten by a young girl probably helped," Irene said. She sounded amused, rather than annoyed. "Do you think he can be trusted?"

"I don't think so," Raechel said. It was a test, of course. The obvious answer was that *no* Frenchman could be trusted, but somehow she doubted Irene would accept *that* answer. "He doesn't act like a man who'll keep his word."

"Most men hate the thought of losing everything," Irene agreed. She smiled as she lay back on the bed. "Being a prisoner won't make him feel very happy."

Raechel scowled. "It's more than that," she said. "I'd bet he used influence to jump ahead, but now his career is in ruins."

"You'd win that bet," Irene said. "Right now, our French captive is considering the virtues of suicide – or an attempt to kill Gwen. He doesn't care about the other captives."

"But …" Raechel swallowed and started again. Irene had made it clear that prisoners who caused trouble were rapidly executed, even prisoners of noble blood. If the Frenchman no longer cared about his fellow Frenchmen. "We need to stop him!"

"He'll be under guard," Irene assured her. "And I would be surprised if he works up the nerve to go after Gwen. He's torn between hatred and a deeply frustrating fear."

Irene smiled. "She does have that effect on people, doesn't she?"

Chapter Eleven

and Ho!”

Gwen looked up from the chessboard, then joined the flurry of passengers as they made their way up to the deck. The remainder of the voyage had been uneventful, but the combination of French prisoners and reduced rations had been wearing down the passengers long before New York came into sight. She couldn't help feeling relieved as she scrambled onto the deck and peered westwards. A handful of towers rose up in the distance, dominating the skyline. Hundreds of ships were heading in and out of the harbour, ranging from giant warships and ocean-going freighters to tiny fishing and patrol boats.

"It's impressive," Jackson said, coming up behind her. "Welcome to the new world."

Gwen listened with half an ear as he pointed out a handful of landmarks. A giant pair of statues – the Brothers Howe – were perched on an island, watching benignly as ships made their way to and from New York. Beyond them, dozens of fortresses, bristling with guns and surrounded by troops. New York had been taken with ease, she recalled, when the Americans had rebelled against the British Crown. The same factors that made the city so prosperous – and so important to the empire – rendered it vulnerable when its owners lost control of the seas. If the French tried a landing in New York, she was sure, they'd regret it long before a single soldier splashed ashore.

"Manhattan is effectively an island," Jackson added. "They don't have room to spread out."

"Just like London," Gwen said. "But with larger buildings."

She shook her head in awe. An apartment in Mayfair or Pall Mall could be hideously expensive, even if it was nothing more than a handful of rooms. But there was never any shortage of people willing to pay for such a prized location, so close to the centre of the British Government. Manhattan would be just as important, she thought, but the Americans had built towering apartment blocks to house visitors to the city. No one would ever get planning permission to build anything like it in the heart of London. There was no style to the buildings, she noted as the ship finally approached the dock, but the Americans didn't seem to care.

"I'll see you soon, I hope," Jackson said, holding out a hand. "I have to get the men offloaded, then report to the General. We'll probably be back on the ships within a day or two."

Gwen blinked in surprise, then shook his hand firmly. "Good luck," she said. Getting the troops to the borders would be far quicker if they stayed on the water, despite the risk of French raiders. "Maybe I'll see you later."

She watched him go, then shook her head as the ship came to a halt. The voyage had grown boring very quickly, despite the brief excitement when the French had attacked, but now she felt almost tired. And yet, she knew she couldn't delay, not even long enough for a wash and a change of clothes. They were four days overdue, after having been out of contact for over three weeks. God alone knew what might have happened along the borders, or in New York itself. She turned and walked down to the gangplank, which was being tied firmly to the jetty. No doubt she wasn't the only passenger relieved to be finally off the boat.

"Your luggage will be sent after you, Lady Gwen," Fredrick Hauser said. He didn't look too put out by the coming separation from Raechel, Gwen noted, although he could just be hiding his feelings well. She didn't want to know what Raechel and he had said to one another after she'd caught them together. "And we thank you for sailing with us."

"It was a pleasure," Gwen lied. Maybe she hadn't got seasick, unlike some of the other passengers, but she'd been *very* bored. "Please give my regards to your captain."

"I will, My Lady," Fredrick said. He gestured towards a horse-drawn brougham waiting at the bottom of the gangplank. A young man in a black suit was standing next to it, looking up at the ship. "Your carriage awaits you."

Gwen nodded, then walked down the gangplank. The young man straightened up when she reached dry land, then opened the carriage door. Gwen climbed inside; he closed the door, then scrambled up behind the horses as Gwen pulled back the curtains. She wanted to see New York, rather than hiding in the coach. The carriage jerked into motion as the driver cracked the whip, rocking backwards and forwards as it headed into the city. Gwen stared out of the window as they left the docks. New York was *teeming* with life.

The natives were *large*, she realised; the average man looked *bigger* than his London counterpart, his clothes far more colourful than anyone outside the landed aristocracy or the military. She wondered, for a moment, if they were all rich, before deciding it was impossible. They couldn't *all* be wealthy, could they? No, it was just the fashion. She shook her head – it would never catch on in London – and then started as a line of black men came into view, carrying boxes down towards the docks. They were hardly the first black men she'd seen – there was a fashion for black servants in London – but there were so many of them! And there were red-skinned men and women walking around too.

There have to be more people in this island than there are in London, she thought, as the coach turned onto a long street leading north. The smell of horse manure was growing stronger, a problem that blighted London too. *Or maybe fewer people but more concentrated in a smaller space.*

She forced herself to keep watching as the carriage headed down the street. New York *throbbed* with life, unlike so many British cities. There was a strange energy in the air that delighted and frightened her at the same time. Even now, with war breathing down their necks, the citizens seemed more animated than anyone she'd seen in London, at least outside the ballrooms. She couldn't help noticing that young women seemed unaccompanied, even the ones who were clearly upper-class. Their dresses were so tight in the right places that they would have shocked London society to the core. Gwen found herself thinking that Raechel would probably *love* New York.

The carriage came to a halt outside a large palace, set within high stone walls. Gwen admired it as the driver chatted briefly to the guards; the palace looked rather like an aristocratic mansion in Britain, but smaller. She puzzled over it for a long moment before recalling that land was in short supply on Manhattan. The palace was probably as large as it could be without causing massive disruption. She pushed the thought aside as the carriage lurched back into motion, heading through the gate and up to the main doors. A young woman was already standing there, wearing a long pink dress.

"Welcome to Howe Palace, My Lady," the driver said, as he opened the door and invited Gwen to step out. "I will collect your luggage and transport it to the Sorcerers' Hall."

"Thank you," Gwen said.

She tipped the driver, then turned her attention to the young woman. It was easy to recognise her from the files: Lady Arielle Franklin-Rochester, the Viceroy's fifteen-year-old niece. She was already a beauty, Gwen had to admit, although there was something oddly forward in the way she wore her dress. Her long dark hair hung down to the small of her back.

"My Lady," Arielle murmured. Her voice was strangely-accented, as if she wasn't quite used to talking like an aristocrat. "Welcome to Howe Palace. My uncle is waiting for you, but if you would like some time to freshen up first …?"

"Please," Gwen said.

Arielle led her into the building. Gwen glanced around with interest, unable to escape the impression that whoever had designed the palace had wanted a monument to British triumphs in the war. A large painting of the scene when George Washington had surrendered to General Howe dominated the inner chamber, surrounded by smaller pen-portraits of notable British officers and administrators who'd served in the war. She couldn't help thinking that there was really too much dignity in the painting of Washington, for a man who had ended his life on the scaffold. But then, even

General Howe had admitted that Washington would have been a great man, if he'd had a chance to learn his trade.

She turned her attention back to Arielle as the younger girl showed her a washroom. Gwen stepped inside gratefully and splashed water on her face, silently relieved that the girl had stayed outside. The Viceroy's wife had died years ago, she recalled; it wasn't unusual for a man in his position to arrange for a female relative to run his household, even if she was surprisingly young. But then, family came first. *And* it would give Arielle a chance at finding a match among the best men in American society. Gwen straightened up, checked her appearance in the mirror, then walked back through the door. Arielle was patiently waiting for her.

She must be used to women taking longer to use the facilities, Gwen thought, wryly. One distinct advantage of the male clothes she wore was that they were easy to get on at speed, without assistance. There were girls she knew back home who literally could not get dressed without help from the maids, a kind of learnt helplessness that made her sick. *I don't know why their mothers let them get away with it.*

"My uncle is waiting in his study," Arielle said. She led the way up the stairs, then stopped outside the door. "I hope I will have a chance to speak with you later, Lady Gwen."

"I hope so too," Gwen said. She *would* like to talk to Arielle, if only because she might have noticed problems that would have escaped her uncle. "And thank you."

"It was no trouble," Arielle said, as she opened the door. "I should be thanking you for insisting on a lack of ceremony."

Gwen smirked. The next viceroy, when he was appointed, would have five whole *days* of ceremonies before he formally replaced the current viceroy. Thankfully, Lord Mycroft had made certain that there wouldn't be a welcoming ceremony for *her*. She knew hundreds of aristocratic women who would be offended, if the entire palace staff wasn't assembled to bow and scrape in front of them, but she'd always hated such affairs. Far too many people knew her as a devil-child.

"My Lady Gwen," Thomas Rochester said. He shook her hand without noticeable hesitation, then motioned her to a comfortable chair. "Welcome to America."

"Thank you, Your Excellency," Gwen said. She sat, resting her hands in her lap. "It's good to be here."

She studied the viceroy with some interest. His Excellency Thomas Rochester, Marquess of Swanhaven, Viceroy of British North America, looked surprisingly healthy, compared to some of the other aristocrats she'd met. He would be in his early forties, according to the files, but he definitely looked as though he could go on campaign at a moment's notice. If she recalled correctly, he *had* gone campaigning in the hinterlands several times during his first four years as Viceroy. His dark hair was cropped close to his scalp, his face had the bruised look of someone who'd been in too many fistfights for his own good ...

Not a handsome man, she decided, finally. *But very definitely a formidable one.*

"I will have tea and cakes served, momentarily," Rochester said. "My servants are already preparing a small repast for us."

"Thank you," Gwen said, fighting down a flicker of impatience. She'd never enjoyed meaningless social formalities. "I was given to understand that the situation was urgent ..."

Rochester's face darkened. "Losing all of our sorcerers, bar one, in a single day was a mighty blow against us," he said. "So far, we have had very little trouble along the line, but I imagine that will change shortly."

He waved a hand towards the map mounted on the office wall. Gwen turned to study it, noting the red outline of British North America ranging from the icy wastelands of the Canadian North to the lower reaches of Florida. Beyond it, great swathes of territory were green for the Franco-Spanish Empire or blue for Russia. She'd heard that the Russian settlements in Alaska had declared themselves independent, in the wake of the Tsar's madness and death, but very little had come of it. Russia had too many problems to do something about the rebels.

"The map lies, Lady Gwen," Rochester warned. He stood and drew a line with his finger, roughly a hundred miles to the west of New York. "We don't control half of the territory we formally claim."

Gwen frowned. "Who does?"

Rochester snorted. "Whoever is there," he said. "Beyond the mountains, we have hundreds of illicit settlements, ranging from runaway slave villages to the remains of the rebels we crushed back in 1777. And there is no shortage of Indian settlements too ... many of our frontier villages trade with the hidden colonies, despite laws against any contact. They think we can't stop them and the hell of it is that they're right."

He shrugged. "The French have the same problem, of course," he added. "There are great swathes of territory they don't control."

Gwen nodded, slowly. It wasn't a problem she'd expected, but in hindsight it should have been obvious. America was *vast*. And while Britain had been governed, reasonably consistently, for over a thousand years, America had barely been settled for over two *hundred*. The British Empire might be greater than Alexander's had ever been, but it had never been fully charted.

She turned as she heard the door opening behind her, to see a dark-skinned woman carrying a large silver tea tray. There had to be some white blood in her, Gwen reasoned; her skin was a rich chocolate brown, rather than black. The maid put the tray down on the table, curtseyed politely to Rochester and then backed out of the room. Her movements showed no trace of emotion at all.

And if she wants to poison us, Gwen thought, *she has plenty of opportunity.*

"I'm planning to hold a ball tomorrow night," Rochester said, as he poured the tea. "I trust you will be attending?"

Gwen blinked in surprise, distracted from her worries. "A ball? There's a war on!"

"Yes, there is," Rochester said. "We need to make a show of confidence, Lady Gwen. A ball – a succession of balls – will help keep the Tories loyal and convince the Whigs that attempting to work outside the system is futile. I dare not show weakness on the eve of a continent-wide war."

He smiled. "And besides, quite a few people want to meet *you*," he added. "They've heard a great many tales about your career."

"All untrue," Gwen hazarded. If she'd done half the things she knew she was credited with doing, thanks to the stories growing in the telling, she would probably have taken over the government by now. She shook her head, dismissing the thought. "Your Excellency ... how do you know your maids can be trusted?"

"She was ... *tested* ... by a Talker," Rochester said. "They were *all* tested for loyalty. I believe they know better than to betray me."

Gwen eyed him, doubtfully. Having one's mind read tended to cause resentment, even in someone who'd been wholeheartedly loyal beforehand. It was a gross invasion of privacy ... and, somehow, she doubted the servants had been given much choice. Hell, the servants might have mastered the art of *lying* to a mind-reader. The mental discipline they needed to tolerate slights – and worse – from their masters would lend itself well to fooling an overconfident magician.

I should ask Irene to watch for trouble, she thought. It was a shame that Irene couldn't come with her, but they weren't officially travelling together. *She'll have ample opportunity at the ball.*

"I hope you're right," she said, out loud. "Do you expect trouble?"

"Unfortunately," Rochester said. "I *always* expect trouble."

He sighed. "I got this job, Lady Gwen, because I was married to an American and half my family is American," he added. "Or so I was told."

Gwen nodded. "It makes sense," she said. It was how Lord Mycroft – and aristocrats in general – thought. Family ties were more important than paper contracts. "And you've kept the ship of state on an even keel."

"Barely," Rochester said. "The last war we fought with the French was useful, in that it helped the colonials to come to terms with the outcome of their revolution. And it also answered one of their grievances, the presence of a papist majority in Quebec. But now ... there are too many different factions, being pulled in too many ways. The French might weaken one of the factions so badly that the entire edifice will topple into chaos."

"The slave owners," Gwen guessed.

"Correct," Rochester said. He took a gulp of his tea with no apparent ill effects. "They're among the strongest supporters of the Crown, but they're detested by a number of other factions."

Gwen sighed, then took a sip of her tea. She'd sense poison, wouldn't she? Sensitivity was the least-understood of the talents, but she *did* have a sense for danger. Unless the poison was only lethal in large doses …

"And then there's the industrialists," Rochester continued. "They don't care about politics, but they want to build up America's industry. It's turning into a right little snake pit."

"I see," Gwen said. She knew she should be heading to the Sorcerers' Hall, but she needed to hear what was going on. A man like Rochester would be happy to explain things to her, in great and probably unnecessary detail. "Who else is there?"

Chapter Twelve

hy, little Raechel," an annoyingly loud woman brayed, as Raechel led the way into the house. "You are as pretty as I was led to believe!"

Raechel gritted her teeth in annoyance. Irene had told her that *someone* would be escorting them for the first couple of days, introducing them to everyone who was anyone, but did it have to be someone so *annoying*? Her voice was shrill enough to give Raechel a headache within seconds, while her fat belly wobbled like a tub of lard. The dress she wore was no doubt expensive enough to keep a seamstress's family dressed for years, but it couldn't disguise her bulk.

"Lady Sofia, I presume," Irene said. If she felt any annoyance or dismay herself, Raechel couldn't see it on her face. "It's good to meet you in person, rather than exchanging brief messages."

"I met Lady Raechel's father during a brief visit to the colonies," Lady Sofia bellowed, heedless of any possible hurt her words might cause. "It is a very great honour to assist in introducing his daughter to the *ton*."

"That was why I looked you up, when I knew we would be coming," Irene said. Raechel wanted to glare – Irene was *flattering* the mad cow – but she knew better than to allow her annoyance to become *too* obvious. "Her father spoke often of you."

"I'm pleased he remembered me," Lady Sofia said. She was talking so loudly that Raechel wouldn't have been surprised to hear complaints from the other end of the island. "He really *was* a remarkable man."

She looked at Raechel, her eyes running up and down

Raechel's dress. "But your dress, my dear, simply will not do," she added, her eyes starting to water with fake tears. "You cannot attend the Viceroy's ball in such an outfit. I'll have my dressmaker sent round to ensure you look your best for the young men. *Why*! There are dozens of young unattached men who will be attending the ball. The entire *ton* is talking about who the Viceroy's boy will marry!"

Her voice deepened. "He's half-American on his mother's side, the poor thing," she added, her tone suggesting that there were few worse fates for a young man. "But he *is* a Franklin and Franklin was always loyal to the Crown."

Raechel blinked. *Benjamin* Franklin had never been particularly loyal, according to the files, even before the Americans had rebelled. But then she remembered his illegitimate son, who had definitely been a loyalist. The files had suggested that the only reason *Benjamin* Franklin hadn't been hanged alongside Washington had been the intervention of *William* Franklin, who'd probably relished the chance to make his father indebted to him. Raechel could understand that impulse all too well.

"I'm sure we will be the talk of the town," Irene said, pleasantly. Raechel ground her teeth in frustration. They still hadn't managed to leave the lobby! "It will be interesting to see how the social scene differs from London."

"Oh, you *must* tell us what is currently in fashion," Lady Sofia said. She clapped her hands, loudly, and a maid appeared. "Have tea served in the drawing room, chop-chop!"

"Yes, My Lady," the maid said. Raechel felt a stab of sympathy. She looked young, too young. And there was a nasty bruise on her pale cheek. "Would your guests like to refresh themselves first?"

"I think we would," Irene said, before Lady Sofia could say a word. "We'll see you in the drawing room?"

"Of course, of course," Lady Sofia brayed. "I've ordered the very finest in cakes for you."

She waddled off, snapping orders to the maid. Raechel glanced at Irene, then followed her into the washroom. Her reflection in the mirror looked tired, very tired. Lady Sofia had a point about the dress – she'd donned an old one, knowing that she'd be driving through New York – but really, she needed at least nine hours sleep before facing anyone. And who did Lady Sofia think she was, anyway?

"We need someone who can introduce us to society," Irene said, curtly. "Lady Sofia fitted the bill."

Raechel washed her face then glared at her reflection. "If that … loud cow is the one who introduces us," she muttered, "we'll be the most hated people in the colonies within the week."

"She has connections," Irene pointed out. "And you should know it."

"Yeah," Raechel said. Someone as annoying as Lady Sofia wouldn't have been welcome in polite society without *very* good connections. "And did she really know my father?"

"They could have met, while Lord Slater was in America," Irene said. "Lady Sofia has been here for the last decade, ever since leaving London."

"She probably got kicked out," Raechel said. "She's not going to be sleeping here, is she?"

"I doubt it," Irene said. "I paid enough to get this house to ourselves."

Her voice hardened. "And be careful what you say," she added. "A woman like *her* will remember any rudeness for many years to come."

She led the way back out of the washroom and down into the drawing room. An immense sweet table stood against one wall, groaning under the weight of pastries and cream cakes, while a smaller table held a silver kettle and a jug of milk. Raechel wanted to shake her head in disbelief at the display, wondering just how many guests Lady Sofia had invited. A display of wealth was one thing, but offering so many cakes that couldn't possibly be eaten …

Lady Sofia must be rich, she thought, as she took a comfortable seat. A woman who was both wealthy – and in control of her wealth – and well-connected would be welcome anywhere. She felt a stab of bitter resentment, before reminding herself she didn't *know* about Sofia's life. *Or her husband must not care about how much his wife spends.*

"You must tell me what is in fashion at the moment," Lady

Sofia said, passing Raechel a plate piled high with cakes. "We hear so little from London."

"I believe long dresses have come back into fashion," Irene said. "And economy is the watchword, with the war underway."

Raechel was impressed that she managed to say that with a straight face. No one had told polite society that *economy* was the watchword, not with hemlines so low they scraped the floor and caused no end of incidents. A single aristocratic dress from a fashionable dressmaker cost enough to keep an entire regiment of soldiers in boots and shoes, if her calculations were even remotely accurate. And, judging by her table, Lady Sofia didn't even know the meaning of the word.

Raechel took a bite from one of the cream cakes and winced at the sweetness. The cake had to be at least half sugar, she decided, as she washed it down hastily with tea. Many of the scones were coated in sugar too ... the sheer expense in wasted food had to be considerable. Maybe the maids would sneak a few home, Raechel thought. Better that than the pastries going to waste.

"Always a good thing," Lady Sofia said. "Some of the dresses worn at balls these days are *quite* scandalous. My, you can even see the young lady's ankles! It causes the heart to race and poor decisions to be made."

"My mother would have agreed," Irene said, casually. "Who else will we be meeting at the ball?"

Lady Sofia was a frightful bore, Raechel decided after nearly two uncomfortable hours in the drawing room, but she *was* a treasure trove of information. She knew every last scandal, every last social mistake, that had been committed in the last decade and she was more than happy to share. Some of the people she talked about had been mentioned in the files – particularly General Paget – but others were new. Raechel didn't know Lord Jackson or Lord Tarleton, yet they were clearly important. And *definitely* politically active.

"Lord Tarleton is a very old Tory," Lady Sofia commented. "His wife is a dreadful harridan, while his son is definitely inching towards the Whigs. I fear for his seat in the Lords when the old man passes away. His son is really too old to be kept at his father's beck and call."

Raechel found it hard to sympathise – she'd been at her *aunt's* beck and call – although she understood how the young man must feel to be trapped permanently in his father's shadow, unable to do anything of consequence until the old man died. Surely the young man could have gone to sea or joined the army, if he wanted something to do with his life. But Lady Sofia seemed to think that Lord Tarleton wanted his son by his side at all times.

"I'm sure I shall enjoy meeting them," Irene said. She finished her last pastry – Raechel had no idea where she'd put them – and rose to her feet. "I'm afraid my charge really does need her sleep, My Lady. Would you excuse me while I put her to bed?"

"Of course," Lady Sofia said. "We can talk *beaus* when you return."

Raechel swallowed the words that came to mind as she rose to her feet and followed Irene up the stairs, into a small bedchamber. It was *much* smaller than the one she'd enjoyed in London, at least when she'd been living outside the city limits, but vastly superior to the cabin on the ship. The bed had been made up neatly for her, while her trunks had been placed on the floor. She was surprised the maids hadn't already started unpacking.

"She is a useful source of information," Irene said, once the door was closed. "And all of this is very interesting to know."

"If you say so," Raechel said. She glanced through a side door and smiled in relief as she saw the bath. She'd washed on the ship, but she still felt grimy. A proper bath would be wonderful. "You're not going to let her marry me off, are you?"

"Of course not," Irene said, dryly. "Your guardians would be *most* upset."

She shook her head. "Have a bath, if you wish, and then have a long nap," she ordered, firmly. "I'll keep her talking longer, if I can. She's very happy to talk to me."

"I noticed," Raechel said. "Why?"

"Because you *are* a rich heiress and the person who introduces you to your future husband will be sure to reap a vast reward," Irene said. "Lady Sofia has every incentive to overlook any ... odd ... behaviour from you."

"Oh," Raechel said.

Irene gave her a smile, then turned and walked out of the door. Raechel cursed under her breath – the longer she spent with Lady Sofia, the stronger the urge to just say something that would get her tossed out of polite society once and for all – and then turned and walked into the bathroom. It was perfect, complete with hot and cold running water. She hadn't expected such luxury in New York ...

And you are here to perform a job, she reminded herself, as she filled the bath and undressed rapidly. *And putting up with Lady Sofia is part of it.*

***

There was, by law, a Sorcerers' Hall in every British city, Gwen knew. They tended to be mid-sized buildings, places where magicians could register, train their talents and spend time with other magicians. During her time as Royal Sorceress, Gwen had expanded the facilities in Britain itself to cope with an influx of lower-class magicians and add Healing wards to the buildings. The older magicians had grumbled, but doing some good for the surrounding population had gone a long way towards repairing the damage caused by the deliberate extermination of so many lower-class magicians. But whoever had designed the New York Hall clearly hadn't heard of her improvements.

She scowled as she took in the brooding building. It looked like a fortress, one of the gothic mansions from the trashy romance novels some of the younger girls passed around when they thought their elders weren't looking, the ones with handsome heroes and ugly villains who always ran, when they realised their plans were foiled. There were no guards outside, unlike Cavendish Hall, but the doors were firmly closed. Clearly, the sole remaining sorcerer in the Americas had shut up shop.

Gritting her teeth, she strode over to the door and tapped, firmly. There was no answer, although she doubted she'd get one. Bracing herself, she reached out with her magic and unlocked the door, allowing it to swing open. Inside, the corridors were dark and shadowy; dust billowed in the air as if no one had entered for years. She summoned her power and created a ball of light, sending it ahead of her to illuminate the darkened corridors. Like Cavendish Hall, the corridors were lined with portraits of magicians who'd fallen in the line of duty. She couldn't help noticing that several places had obviously been cleared for new portraits.

A voice quavered out of the darkness, echoing down the corridor. "Who's there?"

Gwen frowned. "Lady Gwen, Royal Sorceress," she called back, reaching out with her magic. Someone was sitting in the far room, surrounded by a haze of magic. She heard something clinking in the darkness as she walked forward and gathered her magic around her in a protective shroud. If it was an ambush of some kind, she'd trigger it the moment she walked into the room. "I've been sent to help."

"Help," the voice said. It – he – sounded sodden. "You're here to help!"

"Yes, I am," Gwen said. She cast the light ahead of her as she stepped into the far room. A middle-aged man was sitting at a table, surrounded by a pile of bottles. Judging from the sight, he'd been drinking steadily for hours, perhaps days. Gwen was morbidly impressed that he hadn't collapsed completely. "And you are?"

The man giggled. "Captain Harry Wayne, Blazer," he said. It was hard to be sure, but his accent was a strange mix of British and American. "Not that there's anyone left to command, My Lady."

Gwen stalked over to the windows and pulled open the slats, allowing light to shine into the room. Wayne groaned, shielding his eyes, as she turned back to get a good look at him for the first time. He wasn't exactly ugly, but his face was flushed and covered in dark stubble, while his uniform was torn and stained. She cursed herself for not having paid more attention to the New York Hall before going to Russia. Clearly, things had been getting out of hand long before the mass poisoning.

"We'll find others," Gwen said. "What happened to the servants?"

"Hanged, My Lady," Wayne said. He giggled again, lifting a bottle in an ironic toast. "They all danced in the air as their necks broke, save the traitor. Bastard fled so quickly we couldn't catch him."

Gwen closed her eyes for a long moment. "Put down the bottle," she said, firmly. "Go have a shave, a bath and then get into a clean uniform."

"You're a lot more bossy than Master Thomas," Wayne said. He held the bottle in front of his lips, mocking her. "Do you know what he said to me?"

"No," Gwen said. If Master Thomas and Wayne had exchanged words, and she knew it was possible, they hadn't made it into the file. "What did he say?"

"He said I should drink myself to death," Wayne pronounced, as if it were the punchline to a joke. He lifted the bottle to his lips and took a swig. "Who am I to defy the Royal Sorcerer?"

Gwen reached out with her magic, yanked the bottle out of his hand and smashed it against the wall. "You can drink yourself to death later," she snapped. Wayne half-stood, magic flickering around his hand, but she held her ground. Showing weakness was never a good idea. "Right now, you are to go shave, wash and get into a clean uniform – *after* showing me the records room."

Wayne glowered at her. "And if I refuse?"

I could make you, Gwen thought. She forced the instinct out of her mind before she could make the same mistake for the second time. *I need you ...*

"You will be shipped back to England to answer for your dereliction of duty," Gwen said, instead. "It's been over a month since the remaining sorcerers were killed. It was your job to recruit others from the registry and put them to work. What do you imagine the Duke of India will say when he hears about it?"

Her voice hardened. "Or I could just kill you out of hand," she added, coldly. "We are in a state of war. No one will object if I execute you for dereliction of duty in the face of the enemy."

She felt a pang of guilt at his shocked expression, which she ruthlessly suppressed. Wayne couldn't have done much, not without a training cadre, but at least he could have *tried*. Save for the handful of Talkers scattered around the continent, she and Wayne were the only trained British magicians for thousands of miles. A strong man in his position could have accomplished much.

And the Viceroy clearly didn't realise just how bad things had become, she thought. The irony chilled her. Master Thomas had fought hard for a degree of independence for the Royal Sorcerers Corps, but it had come back to bite them hard. *He could have done something if he'd had the time ...*

She shook her head as Wayne rose to his feet. "The French aren't going to wait for much longer," she warned. "And we don't have much time."

"Yes, My Lady," Wayne said, unsteadily. "I'll find you the records now, if you wish."

And then start arranging for new servants, Gwen added, silently. She'd need to ask Irene to vet them, once the servants were lined up ... despite the risks. Another French agent might just get her as well as the other magicians. *There's far too much at stake.*

Chapter Thirteen

his is all we have?"

"All the ones within easy reach, My Lady," Wayne said. A wash and a change of clothes had done wonders for him, but he still looked like a man who'd bitten into something sour. "I left purebred Americans off the list because they're unreliable."

Gwen eyed him, darkly. "Unreliable?"

"Yes, My Lady," Wayne said. "The generation that endured the war knew better than to raise a hand against the government. Losing a third of New York to fires that were set by the retreating rebels taught them the dangers of trusting radicals. But the current generation is less inclined to accept the *status quo*. We caught a pair of the most promising magicians at a meeting of radicals, only three months ago."

Gwen rubbed her tired eyes. "You don't think they'd fight to defend their home?"

"I'm *sure* they would fight to defend their home," Wayne said. "I'm just concerned about who they would consider the *enemy*."

"I see," Gwen said. She looked down at the list, again. "So we have seven magicians; three Blazers, two Movers, a Sensitive and a Changer."

"I'd be concerned about the Sensitive," Wayne said. "According to the reports, he keeps losing at cards."

Gwen scowled. No *genuine* Sensitive should *ever* have lost at cards, not when they could read someone's emotions as easily as a Talker. Maybe it wasn't the same kind of magic, but the end results were the same. The Sensitive had to be a fake or otherwise crippled. Either way, he was useless.

"There may be some women," she said. "Are there none?"

"They have not registered, My Lady," Wayne said. He gave her a considering look. "My Lady, the colonials are rarely *kind* to magicians. Even after Master Thomas visited the colonies twenty years ago, it was rare for a colonial magician to openly reveal himself. Too many of the settlements are strongly religious."

Gwen winced. As embarrassing as it was, there *had* been witch-hunts – genuine witch-hunts – in Scotland and Ireland; hell, some magical children in *England* had been killed, even though the Royal College would have happily taken them as foundlings. She knew just how lucky she'd been to escape such a fate, after her powers had manifested. If her parents had been a little less decent, she would have ended her days in the farms – or simply suffered an accident. No, she could understand why someone with magic might keep it to himself, despite the law. There was too great a chance of being murdered by his neighbours.

"Then we work with what we have," she said. She'd have to send a message to Lord Mycroft, asking for what little he could spare. "Can you recruit some servants?"

"I can," Wayne said. "But how can they be trusted?"

"We can have them scanned by a Talker," Gwen said. She didn't want to bring Irene into play too soon, but she doubted she had a choice. "Or we can look for people who don't have a motive to betray us."

She scowled as she recalled the half-caste maid. The French had a huge advantage when it came to recruiting, simply because they treated men of all colours as equals. Hell, slavery had officially been banned in their colonies, although the work-peonage system wasn't really much better. All they had to do was offer the promise of freedom and they'd have hundreds of thousands willing to come to work for them.

"We can try," Wayne said. He paused. "There *are* women from England who have come to the Americas in search of husbands. I can recruit a few washerwomen and suchlike from amongst them."

Gwen blinked. "Husbands?"

"The frontier is constantly expanding, My Lady," Wayne

said. "And there is a significant shortage of women."

"Very well," Gwen said. It wasn't ideal, but it would have to do. "The Viceroy's Ball is tomorrow night, unfortunately. Send messages to the magicians, reminding them of their duty as registered sorcerers and inviting them to the hall. That gives us a day to get this place cleaned up, emptied of alcohol and rendered safe for habitation."

Wayne gave her an appalled look. "No alcohol?"

"It's bad for magic, as you well know," Gwen said, primly. Besides, it was going to be hard enough to train the magicians without alcohol being involved. "And we really need to train them up as fast as possible."

"Yes, My Lady," Wayne said. "I'll send the messages now."

Gwen eyed his back as he shuffled out of the room. Throwing open the windows and lighting a dozen lanterns had transformed the hall, but it still needed a thorough clean before it was suitable, let alone impressive. She rather doubted any of the new recruits would be happy if they saw the hall in a messy state, let alone willing to fight for the country. Rising to her feet, she walked out of the door and up the stairs to the bedrooms. The doors had been pinned open, revealing that beds remained unmade and personal possessions left lying where they'd fallen. It was just something else that should have been handled before she arrived ...

She walked into the master bedroom and sighed. Sir Young, the senior magician, looked to have gone out for an evening stroll, rather than to his death. His books were still on the desk, covered by a thin layer of dust. She picked up one of them and frowned as she read the title: *Magic And Murder*. She'd read it herself, months ago. The author would have been darkly amused, she thought, to know that his book had made it across the Atlantic, although it was unlikely he'd ever get any royalties.

A drawing lay under the book, showing a young woman standing upright, two toddlers holding her hands. Sir Young's wife and children, Gwen recalled; the file had stated that the wife had been too sickly to accompany her husband to his final post. Lord Mycroft would have seen to informing them of his death, Gwen was sure; she wondered, vaguely, how they'd taken it. Death in combat was one thing, but to die at the hands of a treacherous cook was quite another. There was something sordid about it.

Poor woman, Gwen thought. Sir Young would have a few thousand in the funds, if she was any judge, but who knew if it would go straight to his wife? It all depended on the marital contract. *Surely she won't be left completely destitute?*

She made a note to add an inquiry to her message to Lord Mycroft, then headed down the corridor to the library. It was smaller than Cavendish Hall's library, but crammed with more books. Not all of them, she noted with some amusement, were official textbooks. It looked as though the magicians had bought dozens of cheap books and added them to the collection, presumably after reading them first. Gwen picked up one of them and rolled her eyes at the title. There were times when she felt the inventor of the printing press had a great deal to answer for.

Wayne came up the stairs as she walked out of the library, his face flushed. "I've sent messages to the magicians and to the women," he said. "We should start getting answers soon enough."

"Very good," Gwen said. "Right now, I want to box up everything that was left behind by the dead magicians. We'll ship it back to their heirs, if they had heirs."

"Yes, My Lady," Wayne said. "I'll fetch boxes from the cellar."

Gwen watched him hurrying back down the stairs, feeling suddenly very tired and old. Back in Cavendish Hall, Doctor Norwell and the cleaning staff had handled all such matters, on the rare occasions when a resident magician had died in the line of duty. The only dead magician she'd had to deal with personally had been Master Thomas, after the Swing. She'd wanted to go through his possessions, hoping against hope that there would be some answers hidden amongst them. But there had been nothing.

His secrets died with him, she thought. There had been five Master Magicians – seven, perhaps, if one counted an unnamed girl in Russia and the Saint of Grimsby – and Gwen was the only one still alive. *If he told Jack what he knew, before Jack turned on him, Jack never had a chance to share his secrets with me.*

She shook her head when she heard Wayne muttering under his breath as he carried a handful of boxes back up the stairs. It would be better, far better, to keep a man like Wayne busy, too busy to start thinking about alcohol – or that he was taking orders from a teenage girl. She just didn't have *time* to handle an argument. Slapping him down would only make matters far worse, in the future. She *needed* him.

And this is his only chance to redeem himself, she told herself. *He won't waste it.*

Hoping desperately that she was right, she took one of the boxes and went to work.

***

In all honesty, Raechel had almost forgotten what it was like to sleep in a proper bed, let alone just relax completely. The bed was sinfully comfortable, the room was cosy enough to make her drowsy even if she hadn't already been tired and, after the bath, her body felt warm and relaxed. She hadn't bothered to get dressed, even into a dressing gown, before climbing under the sheets and closing her eyes.

She was awakened by a sharp tap on the door. "Raechel," Irene called. "It's time to get up, if you don't mind."

Raechel sat upright, convinced that Irene was right next to her. It took her long bemused seconds to recall that they were in New York – and that Irene was on the other side of the door. Not that it mattered, she reminded herself as she slapped her mental shields into place. Irene could probably read her thoughts from outside the wooden door.

"I'm awake," she said, as she climbed out of bed. "Can I have a moment to get dressed?"

"Come downstairs when you're ready," Irene ordered. "We're going to be going out later, so make sure you have your trousers and shirt handy."

Raechel groaned – that meant male guise, she was sure – but pulled a robe over her head before opening the door and heading down the stairs. A smell rose up to greet her as she reached the bottom and peered into the kitchen. Irene was standing behind the stove, stirring something in a large pot. It smelt of meat, potatoes and carrots.

"Raechel," Irene said, without looking round. "Do you know how to cook?"

"No," Raechel said. "Do I *need* to know?"

"It can be a very useful skill," Irene said, dryly. She jabbed a finger at a small wooden table, barely large enough for two diners. Raechel took the hint and sat down. "Girls of your social class are rarely taught *anything* practical, beyond simpering at men and ordering the maids around."

"They're useful skills," Raechel protested, without heat. She was growing used to Irene's snide remarks, if only because she had to admit the older woman was right. "You spent far too long teaching me how to simper yourself."

"They leave you dependent on others," Irene pointed out. She didn't bother to rise to the bait, merely ladled a little stew into a bowl and placed it in front of Raechel. "Through extreme carelessness, I have failed – alas, me – to hire staff for our lodgings. A truly *terrible* oversight."

Raechel frowned. Hadn't there been a maid in the house earlier? She must work for Lady Sofia, the poor girl. "Won't that look a little odd?"

"It will look a *lot* odd," Irene said. "I'll be hiring a handful of servants tomorrow morning, of course, but I thought we could fend for ourselves tonight. Servants have eyes and ears, as you well know, and they may not have our best interests in mind."

"Joy," Raechel said. She took the spoon Irene held out to her and tasted the stew. It was surprisingly nice, although a little bland. "Can't we cope without them?"

"Not without causing too many eyebrows to rise," Irene said. "It's lucky that no one, save for Lady Sofia, has visited us yet."

She sat down, facing Raechel. "What were your first impressions of Lady Sofia?"

Raechel scowled. "A bore."

Irene nodded. "Do you feel that's accurate?"

"She *was* boring," Raechel said. The mere memory of the oversweet cakes and pastries made her teeth hurt. "But she did know a lot of the good gossip."

"She knew everything," Irene said. "Or she certainly believed she did."

"She was telling the truth?" Raechel asked. "Or what she thought was the truth?"

"There's no difference, unfortunately, when mind-reading is concerned," Irene said. "Lady Sofia never actually lied to us, not intentionally. How much of what she said is actually *true* ... well, we'll find that out when we attend the ball, tomorrow. Lady Sofia was good enough to drop off our invitations before she left."

"Finally," Raechel muttered.

Irene gave her a sharp look. "You find her so appalling?"

"She's a ruder version of my aunt," Raechel said, bluntly. There was no point in trying to lie to Irene. "If she wasn't wealthy and well-connected she wouldn't be welcome anywhere."

"She's the way she is because she's scared she'll lose everything," Irene said. There was no condemnation in her voice, merely quiet understanding. "Her husband is very much a hen-pecked man, yet he uprooted her from London and brought her to America when his job moved overseas. She had to fight her way into a whole new social scene from scratch. If she goes back to London, she fears everyone will have forgotten her."

"Not a chance," Raechel muttered.

"Perhaps not," Irene said. She cocked her head. "But just because someone is annoying doesn't mean you should hate them."

Raechel scowled, resentfully. Her mother had been a distant presence in her life, but her aunt had spent years trying to control her, to shape her into a compliant little girl who would marry well and make the family proud. Lady Sofia was far too much like her aunt for Raechel ever to *like* her. The overbearing friendliness could easily turn to disdain in a heartbeat, shoving her unfortunate victim right out of polite society ...

"Your shields are leaking," Irene warned her. "Trying to understand someone is often more productive than mindless hatred."

Raechel felt her temper snap. "I would be more understanding," she said, "if people like her were more understanding to people like me."

Her aunt would have exploded at her tone. Irene merely looked amused.

"She *is* trying to do you a favour, by her lights," Irene said. "And that isn't something to take lightly."

She rose. "Get your street clothes on," she added. "We're going for a walk."

Raechel scowled at her back as Irene led the way up the stairs, not bothering to try to hide her resentment. Irene must have picked up on her feelings, but said nothing as she walked into her bedroom and closed the door. Male guise gave her a sense of freedom, she'd admitted once, that Raechel didn't share. But Irene was small enough, she knew, to pass for a man easily, unless someone forced her to undress.

Or put his hand in her pants, she thought, as she donned her street clothes. *But that isn't likely to happen, is it?*

She hurried back downstairs and met Irene waiting behind the door, looking like a surprisingly dapper young man. Irene looked Raechel up and down, nodded curtly in approval and led the way out onto the streets. It was still warm, even though the sun was beginning its long fall towards the horizon. Irene picked a route at random and Raechel followed her, trying desperately to memorise landmarks as she moved. Some of Irene's more practical lessons had concentrated on finding her way back home, after wandering through a random part of the city.

They didn't attract any attention, she noted to her relief; indeed, they blended in surprisingly well. The Americans came in all shapes, sizes and colours; she couldn't help noticing that the darker the skin, the more attention they received from other men. Being black had to be a social handicap, she realised, even though she'd found her uncle's butler – Romulus – to be a very smart man, as well as a deep-cover agent. There was a strange tension in the air that was so thick she could practically cut it with a knife.

And the women are hurrying off the streets as night falls, she thought. For the first time, she understood why Irene liked wearing male clothing. *That's not a good sign.*

"Too many separate bars," Irene muttered, as darkness fell over the city. "Do you know what that means?"

Raechel shook her head. She would never have been allowed in a working man's bar in her *old* life. The men were drinking sullenly, pouring the beer down their throats as if it were water. They didn't *seem* cheerful.

"Too many different groups, too little integration," Irene commented. She kept her voice very low, although there was no one in earshot. "Every group has its own bar. Do you know what that means?"

"No," Raechel said. The crew on the ship hadn't been allowed in the officer's mess, but that wasn't the same … was it? "I don't."

"Too much dislike and hatred among different groups," Irene said. She turned to lead the way back to the house. "If they can't even drink together at the end of a long day, they'll find it easy to believe the others are all having special advantages, while *they're* being put down and exploited. And that's going to end badly."

Chapter Fourteen

he Honourable Lady Gwendolyn Crichton," the announcer said, his voice echoing through the ballroom. "Royal Sorceress of Great Britain and her Empire."

Gwen kept her face fixed in a polite smile as she descended the stairwell into the ballroom, grimly aware of hundreds of people staring at her. She'd made the decision to wear her suit, rather than a fancy gown, even though it would shock the gathered crowd. But she needed them to think of her as a man, or something as close to masculine as possible, rather than a young girl.

It was a large ballroom, she noted as her gaze swept the chamber, looking for names and faces she'd seen mentioned in the files. Nearly two hundred men and women had arrived ahead of her, the younger ones moving smoothly around the ballroom floor while their elders were standing along the wall, talking quietly in small groups. The real business of government would be done in private rooms, Gwen knew; the ball itself acted as an informal place to meet and relax before and after the private negotiations. She caught sight of the Viceroy, holding court near the foot of the stairs, and strode towards him.

The dance music changed, becoming something lighter as more couples flowed onto the floor, watched by prowling chaperones. Gwen couldn't help noticing that, while the young men wore suits and ties, the young women wore dresses that would have attracted *very* astringent comments back in Britain. The American noblewomen seemed less concerned about displaying the shape of their bodies, or the tops of their breasts; one dark-haired girl who danced past was wearing a skirt that didn't fall past her knees. Gwen dreaded to imagine what the society matrons in Britain would have said about her, if they didn't have a collective heart attack on the spot. The older noblewomen didn't seem so concerned about what the younger ones wore, even the chaperones.

They're rebelling, Gwen thought. *They're wearing those clothes to say they don't care about our social conventions.*

She shook her head grimly. After Jack – and Raechel – she wasn't naïve enough to believe that the genteel surface of the *ton* was anything more than a facade, but most rebellious urges were satisfied out of sight and mind of the social matrons. Raechel's club had been shocking, yet it had been hidden away in a side street, officially ignored by those in power. But here, the signs of open resistance and rebellion were all around her. It boded ill for the future.

"Lady Gwen," Rochester said. The Viceroy wore a resplendent uniform that made him look like a senior officer, right down to the sword on his belt. His cronies, the men surrounding him, looked hardly less magnificent. "Thank you for coming."

"Thank you for inviting me," Gwen said. It wasn't entirely truthful, but she was starting to think that she'd learn a great deal by attending the ball. "This is very much like London."

"Isn't it just?" The Viceroy said. He motioned her forward, pitching his voice so low that Gwen could barely hear him. "We'll be talking a great deal over the next few days, I shouldn't wonder, so I'd like you to take this opportunity to relax and mingle. We have to make a show of confidence."

"I understand," Gwen said. She'd found the time to read a couple of broadsheets while working at the Sorcerers' Hall, which – just like their British counterparts – had a nasty habit of reporting rumours as fact. "Rumours are spreading wildly."

"True," Rochester said. "Let us see who we have here."

He nodded to a number of men as they gathered together, allowing their wives and children to seek the fun of the dance hall. Gwen listened, silently grateful for her mother's lessons, as the Viceroy pointed out the movers and shakers of the American political scene. She wasn't surprised, not really, to discover that a number of Whigs had been invited to the ball, along with the loyalist Tories. As in Britain, families were rarely solidly Whig or Tory. The oldest families had always bet on both sides in any political dispute.

"And this is my son, Bruce," Rochester concluded. "My wife's greatest gift to me."

Gwen frowned, inwardly, as Bruce gave her an uninterested look. He was a year or two older than herself, she recalled, but it was clear that he lacked his father's skills. Rochester was a talented soldier and a gifted administrator; *Bruce* had simply never had the chance to make anything of himself. Gwen would have been sorry for him, if he'd been a woman, but as a man he had ample opportunity to make a life for himself out of his father's shadow. Going to sea would definitely make a man of him. The howling seas didn't care if a man was the highest of aristocrats or the lowest of commoners.

He was handsome enough, she supposed, but his face lacked character. His brown hair was long, framing a face that bore no hint of struggle or wisdom. Indeed, there was a hint of powder on his face, a French fashion that had never really caught on in Britain. Gwen couldn't help mentally comparing Bruce Rochester to Sir Charles and finding him lacking in all respects. Sir Charles might have been a traitor, a murderer and a cad, but no one could say he'd been lacking in character.

"I say, Your Excellency," a loud voice barked. "When are you going to do something about the slaves?"

Gwen turned. A florid-faced man was standing behind the Viceroy, holding a large glass of wine in one hand. Gwen would be willing to bet good money that it wasn't his first, judging from his flushed face. Behind him, a young man was looking embarrassed. His son, she guessed, resisting the urge to shoot him a look of sympathy. David and she might have been lucky with their father, but some fathers were just hideously embarrassing.

The Viceroy took it in stride. "Lord Boone," he said. "What do you propose I do about the slaves?"

"Treacherous literature has been found in the slave houses,

again," Lord Boone proclaimed, his voice echoing through the room. "We had to hang a dozen bucks just to make sure it didn't spread, what?"

"It's really very simple," another man said. He oozed his way into the group, a hint of malicious amusement crossing his face. "The slaves want to be free. And can you blame them?"

"We take care of them," Lord Boone thundered. "They shouldn't be learning to *read*!"

He turned to the Viceroy. "Your Excellency, we need additional troops to watch the slaves," he said. He didn't seem to be capable of speaking quietly. "The French have been peddling their lies again!"

"They are not lying," the second man said. He tapped the side of his chin meaningfully. "I would wager a thousand pounds that your slaves want to be free."

Lord Boone rounded on him. "The African is unable to even *feed* himself without help from his betters," he snarled. "Freedom? They wouldn't know what to *do* with freedom!"

Gwen rather doubted that it was true. Romulus had been a very smart man, held back by the colour of his skin. The slaves might know nothing of the world beyond their plantations, but she didn't blame them for wanting to try to be free. God knew she'd wanted to be free of her parents too … and there had been times when she'd been able to delude herself that she wasn't their property, something a slave would never be able to forgot.

"Mark my words," Lord Boone snarled. "They'll all be dead in a year after they are freed!"

"No doubt," the Viceroy agreed. "Bruce, why don't you take Lady Gwen onto the dance floor" – the two men stared at her in shock, as if they'd only just realised she was a girl – "while I discuss this matter in private."

"Yes, father," Bruce said. Even his voice was curiously flat, Gwen noted. He held out a hand to Gwen. "If you'll do me the honour, Lady Gwen?"

Gwen would have preferred not to dance, but she suspected she didn't have a choice. Taking his arm, she allowed him to lead her onto the floor and around the room, moving in tune with the music. He *was* a surprisingly good dancer, she noted, although that shouldn't really be a surprise. Dancing was so much a part of the aristocratic tradition that children learnt how to dance from the moment they could walk upright.

"No one really cares about the slaves," he said, quietly. "There are factions here – the freemen – who would prefer to just ship them to the French."

"And other factions that will fight to keep them," Gwen guessed, coldly. She closed her eyes in pain. Slaves were property. The anti-slavery campaigners in Britain had been unable to convince Parliament to ban the slave trade, if only because of its economic importance. If nothing else, compensating the slaveowners for their human merchandise would be a major drain on the empire's resources. "Why?"

"No one likes change," Bruce said. He looked up, meeting her eyes for the first time. "I understand you were in London during the Swing?"

"I was," Gwen said, curtly. She didn't want to talk about it, but a good relationship with the Viceroy's son was essential. "It was ... bad."

"But the poor rose up and held London for several days," Bruce said. There was a hint of genuine animation in his voice. "It must have been quite *something*!"

"It was nightmarish," Gwen said. She didn't want to *think* about rebels ravaging London – or what Master Thomas had done in a desperate attempt to stop them. "Thousands of people died in the fighting. Even now, the city has not recovered."

"They won, though," Bruce added. "Didn't they?"

Gwen shrugged. The government had made a number of concessions, after the Swing, but how much had life really changed? Universal suffrage and secret ballots hadn't made *that* much of a difference, had it? Sure, there were commoner magicians in the Royal Sorcerers Corps and a few more politicians of humble origins, but really ... life had largely gone on as it had before the Swing.

And other things didn't change at all, she thought, darkly. *Women are still the property of their families, slaves are still slaves, servants are still beaten and abused by their masters ...*

"I heard a great deal about Jack," Bruce said. "Was he

really a hero?"

"He died saving Britain from the French," Gwen lied. It was the official line, afterwards, and there was an immense statue outside Charing Cross to prove it. "He may have been misguided, but he was a true hero."

She cursed inwardly. Jack might have died stopping the undead – although it had been Olivia who'd stopped them permanently – but the full truth had been carefully buried. Blaming the necromantic outbreak on the French was safer than admitting that the British Government had unleashed the monsters in hopes of bringing the rebellion to a speedy close.

Bruce lifted his eyebrows. "Misguided?"

"Jack felt – deeply – the plight of the poor," Gwen said. She still had nightmares about some of the harsh truths he'd shown her, that dreadful night. "He blamed the aristocracy for keeping the poor in such conditions. But I don't think he had any real plan to shift from occupying London to actually taking control of the country and governing it. He couldn't take power for himself, let alone pass power to the poor."

"I see," Bruce said.

Gwen eyed him, darkly. "Why are you so interested in the Swing?"

"We heard stories, but there was very little *reliable*," Bruce said. "I didn't know what to believe."

"Jack was a good man and he was a bad man," Gwen said. Jack had spared her life, when he could have cut her throat with ease, and shown her the darkness underpinning the aristocratic world. But he'd also killed dozens of men personally and organised an uprising that had killed thousands more. *"That* is something you can believe."

She felt an odd flicker of sympathy for Bruce. His father was the Viceroy, true, but it wasn't a position that would pass down to Rochester's son when he died. Bruce would inherit a title – and lands as well, unless she was much mistaken – yet it wouldn't compare to the authority wielded by his father. He was in the odd position of being linked to power, but unable to claim it for himself. Even David had a stronger position than Bruce.

Bruce sighed. "Do you think the Swing was doomed from the start?"

Gwen's eyes narrowed. "I don't know," she said, finally. She assumed Jack had had a plan to deal with the regiments outside the city, but she had no idea what it might have been. Had he thought the regiments would mutiny? "I do know that it caused a great deal of damage."

"But it achieved some of its aims," Bruce countered. "Didn't it?"

"I suppose," Gwen said. "But ..."

She broke off as she saw Raechel and Irene appear at the top of the stairs. Raechel wore a long green dress that flattered her body, her red curls falling down in ringlets until they brushed her shoulders. Beside her, Irene looked older, although Gwen would have been hard-pressed to say *how*. It was something in the way she held herself, Gwen decided, after a long moment. Irene was in her late twenties, yet she walked like an older woman. It was easy to believe she was clinging desperately to what little beauty she had left.

"Lady Irene Darlington and Lady Raechel Slater-Standish," the announcer called.

Gwen couldn't help noticing that, in her own way, Raechel drew as much attention as Gwen herself. Older women eyed her calculatingly, while young men stared and young woman fumed. Raechel wasn't just beautiful, Gwen knew; she was heir to a quite considerable fortune. The man who married her would become instantly wealthy, no matter what the marriage contract said. No one would expect Raechel to deny her husband the use of her money.

And it's more than just wealth, Gwen thought, as she turned back to Bruce. *It's access to some of the very highest levels of society.*

"I understand you were with her on the voyage," Bruce said, as the music changed into a slow waltz. "Was she as boring as she looks?"

Gwen blinked in surprise. She hadn't expected *that* reaction. Bruce was unmarried. Gwen would have bet half her fortune that Rochester had told his son to try to woo Raechel, pointing out that it was a chance to catapult the family up the social ladder. And yet, Bruce wasn't interested? How could he not be interested? Even if he had a taste for the intimate company of men ... well, he'd hardly be the first of that kind to have a marriage that looked perfect, at least from the outside.

"We had little in common," Gwen said. As far as anyone outside the government was concerned, she and Raechel were nothing more than acquaintances. "She had to leave England for a while, the poor girl."

"Ah," Bruce said. "And my father seems to wish to speak with you."

He led Gwen off the dance floor, over to where the Viceroy was standing. Rochester looked irked, Gwen decided, although he was making a determined attempt to hide it. Being caught between two factions couldn't be fun, she knew; she'd certainly been forced to hammer out compromises in Cavendish Hall. And there was much more at stake in America.

"Bruce will chaperone us," he muttered, as he led the way to a private room. "Don't want too many tongues wagging, do we?"

Gwen concealed her amusement with an effort. Rochester was at least three times her age, perhaps older. The thought of his son chaperoning *him* was just absurd, although maybe the rules were a little different in America. If the women had more freedom, perhaps a man could serve as a chaperone. It wouldn't be the strangest thing she'd seen in her career.

She nodded, shortly, once the door was closed. "Problems with the slaves?"

"The French are trying to incite them to rise against us," Rochester said. "Hardly a new problem, but all the worse when we don't have the troops to spare to guard the slave plantations. Giving them all to the French would solve one problem at the risk of creating several new problems."

"Yes, Your Excellency," Gwen said.

"Lord Bristol is a Son," Rochester added. He nodded towards the man who'd countered Lord Boone's rant about the slaves. "I'd bet my life on it."

Gwen looked up. "A Son?"

"The Sons of Liberty," Rochester said. "We thought we'd bested them after the Battle of New York, but they've recently begun to resurface. They want to separate America from the British Crown, even though it would be disastrous, if they can't get a joint parliament of their own. And to think they have a handful of MPs in London!"

"America is a big place, father," Bruce said. "And London is very far away."

Rochester snorted. "Anarchists, the lot of them," he said. "Do they have any idea what will happen if they do manage to cut the links between America and the motherland? The French will invade!"

"A long period of civil war would be equally disastrous," Gwen mused. "It hasn't been *that* long since the Young Pretender tried to claim the throne."

"Exactly," Rochester said. "There are too many seditionist factions, Lady Gwen. Any step I take to favour one of them, or even to impose a settlement, will anger the others."

He sighed. "Take Lady Gwen back to the dance floor," he added, glancing at Bruce. "She has a busy day ahead of her tomorrow."

"I have a report for you," Gwen said.

"Right now, we have to look confident," the Viceroy said, cutting her off. "A display of weakness now would be disastrous."

Chapter Fifteen

'm not going to be far away," Irene had said, just before they'd descended the steps into the ballroom. "But you need to move on your own."

Raechel had nodded in agreement. Irene would be her chaperone, as far as anyone knew; a chaperone who took her duties so seriously that Raechel had good reason to want to stay as far from her as possible. No one would question Raechel spending hours on the dance floor, moaning and groaning about Irene's intrusiveness, or Irene herself quietly making the rounds of the older women. They'd assume Irene would have the final say in any developing relationship and, if things were what they seemed, they would have been right.

She walked down the stairs slowly, taking the time to survey the ballroom. Her mother – and later her aunt – had compared formal balls to battlegrounds and, as absurd as it seemed, she had a point. The interactions between the great and the good – women as well as men – shaped politics. A decision taken during a meeting between two aristocrats, nominal enemies, could resolve a problem or end a pointless feud. The American ballroom was smaller than she'd expected, but in every other respect it was identical to the ballrooms she recalled in London, right down to the young folk enjoying themselves while the older folk talked politics.

"Lady Raechel," Lady Sofia said. She swept out of the crowd, wearing a long white dress that failed to hide her bulk. "You're looking good!"

"Thank you, My Lady," Raechel said. In truth, the dress was naughty enough to give her a thrill, when she'd worn it for the first time. Even now, looking at hundreds of far more revealing dresses, she couldn't help feeling that she was dancing along the line. "It is a pleasure to be here."

"Of course it is," Lady Sofia said, her smile growing wider. She took Raechel's arm and pulled her forwards. "Let me introduce you to some friends of mine."

"I believe Raechel would prefer to speak freely," Irene said, briskly. Her tone was friendly, but there was an underlying warning that Raechel had no trouble hearing. "You can introduce me to your friends first."

"Of course, of course," Lady Sofia said. "Raechel will stay in view, won't you?"

"Of course, My Lady," Raechel said, bobbing a curtsey. Perhaps it was wrong of her to be amused, but Irene had been quite rude … and Lady Sofia had no choice, but to take it. "I'll be sure to stay on the dance floor."

"See that you do," Irene said, sternly.

Raechel nodded. She'd thought she was learning how to disguise herself, but Irene took the art to a whole new level. She didn't look *that* different – Lady Sofia probably saw no real difference – yet she conveyed an impression of age and authority that would cow a dowager duchess. *No one* would dispute Irene's right to assert her authority over her charge – and *everyone* would understand Raechel wanting to escape her. A chaperone, particularly one charged with escorting a wealthy heiress, was a power in her own right.

She smiled at the young men as Lady Sofia led Irene towards the wall, where a number of older women were gathered, chatting quietly amongst themselves. A young man, barely two or three years older than her, detached himself from the crowd and came towards her. He was definitely handsome, Raechel decided, although there was a nasty scar on his right cheek, suggesting he'd fought in a duel at some point. She'd heard that American nobility preferred swords to pistols when it came to settling matters of honour. It made no sense to her.

"Lady Raechel," he said, with a smile. "Would you care to dance with me?"

"It would be my pleasure," Raechel said, lowering her gaze demurely. The young man wore a suit and tie, but the way he wore it suggested he was more used to a uniform. A soldier in the regulars, perhaps, or a militia officer? "I haven't danced for months."

She allowed him to lead her onto the ballroom floor and guide her through the steps of an unfamiliar dance, listening carefully as he chatted about his career. Rupert Vincent – he didn't give her his name until they were halfway through the dance – was a militiaman, as she'd guessed. New York's defences needed bolstering, he explained, and the young noblemen had responded by forming the militia. They drilled every day in fancy uniforms, preparing to repel the French.

"You must be a pretty sight," Raechel said, trying to sound admiring. "Does everyone wear fancy uniforms?"

"Only the officers," Rupert said. "The common soldiers can't afford uniforms for themselves, you see. So we give them a basic uniform ..."

The dance came to an end. Raechel half-expected Rupert to try to keep her for the next dance – there didn't seem to be any dance cards in the Viceregal Palace – but another young man jumped in and asked her to dance with him instead. Raechel smiled at Rupert, who didn't look pleased, then allowed the second man to guide her onto the floor. Polite society – or whatever passed for it in America – would understand. If she showed too much interest in one young man, it would be seen as the start of a developing relationship.

Good thing I'm not here to marry, she thought, as the second dance came to an end. *I'd be spoilt for choice.*

The third dancer turned out to be a merchant, although he wasn't clear on who actually owned the family business. Unlike the other two, he was refreshingly honest about what he wanted from her; respectability and an end to the industrial restrictions enacted by the British Crown. Raechel had heard that certain types of manufacturing were only permitted within Britain itself, but she had never considered the implications. Losing Britain wouldn't just tear the heart out of the empire, it would cripple whatever was left.

"Right now, costs for all kinds of machinery are high because they have to be made in Britain and shipped over here," Christopher Wiggins explained. "Just shipping something over the ocean is a major pain. And then there're the import duties. The Tories get fat, everyone else gets thin."

"And no one tries to make machinery over here," Raechel mused. She doubted her guardians would have considered Christopher Wiggins as a potential husband, not for one second, even though he and his family were clearly wealthy. "Not at all?"

"Of course not," a cross voice said. She looked up to see a grim-faced young man carrying a glass in one hand. "My father gets richer through denying the right to build factories than he would by building factories."

Raechel frowned. "And you are?"

"Hamish Tarleton, My Lady," the young man said, in a tone that would probably have been taken as a direct challenge back in Britain. He wanted to humiliate Wiggins, Raechel suspected, either by daring him into a duel or putting him in a spot where he couldn't defend Raechel. Either one would be disastrous. "My father is a member of the Viceroy's Council."

"My *uncle* is a member of the Privy Council," Raechel said, pitching her voice to suggest she was bored. If she was lucky, it would defuse the situation before things became unpleasant. "What do you think of the industrial restrictions?"

"My father favours the farmers and slaveowners," Hamish said. He snorted rudely. "I don't think the old man realises the problems lying in store."

"He doesn't see the shortage of gunpowder as a problem," Rupert said, coming back into the group. "I think we may run short if we have to fight a major battle."

"It's all those bloody Germans," Hamish said. "No one really trusts them."

Raechel leant forward. "The Germans?"

"Germans fleeing the French and Russians," Rupert said. He shrugged. "The Viceroy was kind enough to allow them to settle, if they took an oath to the crown, but they don't fit in very well. They only speak German, they don't know our laws ... half of them might even be working for the French. What's going to happen to America if the German population keeps growing?"

"There won't be an America left," Hamish grunted. "We need to kick the bastards into shape or into the water."

Raechel kept her face impassive as the conversation darkened, slowly putting the pieces together. The Viceroy had convinced London to accept a large number of German refugees after the French started to clamp down on the tiny German states. It was a way to boost the white population, he'd said, and he might have been right. But he'd also alienated the original settlers of America, who saw the influx of Germans as a potential threat. There were, apparently, a number of towns that were so strongly germanised they might as well be in Germany.

Divide and rule, Raechel thought. There was enough seditionist sentiment within the group surrounding her to create a major problem. *The Viceroy might have thought he could balance the Germans against the Americans.*

She shook her head, inwardly, and kept listening. If the group surrounding her, which included young women as well as young men, was representative, there were hundreds, perhaps thousands, of seditionists in New York alone. And if the same was true in the rest of America, Viceroy Rochester was sitting on a tinderbox. Rupert, the militia officer, might not be shooting in the right direction, when the fighting finally started. There was a very nasty sense of simmering anger in the air.

"The Tories can count on the slaveowners for support," a young man said. He hadn't introduced himself, which suggested he was already married. "They won't change as long as they have their votes."

"The slaves are a major problem," Christopher Wiggins said. "What's to stop the slaveowners from training their slaves to do *everything* done by white men?"

"Or from taking over the farms," an older man added. "That's what happened in Ancient Rome."

Raechel blinked, then turned as she felt someone poke her in the side with an elbow. A young woman was standing there, with jet-black hair and an impish smile that reminded Raechel – helplessly – of Irene. The impression was so strong that she glanced over to the wall, where Irene was holding court, just to make sure she was still there. But the newcomer was definitely younger, with none of Irene's experience or cynical view of the world. The dress she wore was low-cut enough to make Raechel blush. Being topless in a secret club was one thing, but in public?

"You have quite a formidable chaperone," the girl said. She stuck out a hand. "I'm Jane, by the way."

"I'm Raechel," Raechel said. "She's a very *controlling* chaperone."

Jane gave her a sympathetic look. "What got you sent over here?"

Raechel frowned. "What makes you say that?"

"Oh, come on," Jane said. She smiled. "I looked you up in *Who's Who*. The daughter of Lord Slater, his sole heir ... you shouldn't be here unless London was too hot for you. My mother got into trouble and that's why *I'm* over here."

"You don't sound angry about it," Raechel observed.

"I've met enough Londoners to know I don't want to live there," Jane said, seriously. "My mother was pushed into a marriage she didn't want, with a man she didn't love, because of money. And it wasn't even *her* money. Here ... I can reject a man, if I don't want him."

She smiled. "And you haven't answered *my* question."

Good thing we talked about this ahead of time, Raechel thought. *Someone was bound to ask, sooner or later ...*

Jane eyed her, expectantly. Raechel wished, just for a moment, that she had even a fraction of Irene's power. Jane had to have an ulterior motive for asking, but what? And who, if anyone, had put her up to it? Her mother? Her brother? One of the society matrons surrounding Irene?

"I had a major fight with my aunt," Raechel said, finally. It was true enough; she'd *often* had fights with her aunt. "There was a ... scene ... at a house and a great deal of very expensive soothing was required. My uncle decided it would be better if I spent the rest of my minority in America."

"A minority at your age," Jane said. "That must *sting*."

Raechel nodded, curtly. A common-born woman enjoyed far more freedom than any noblewoman, even though she was sure – thanks to Irene – that many of those women would have happily changed places and accepted life in a gilded cage. Raechel's parents were dead, but she was still obliged to consult her guardians on everything until she turned twenty-five and gained her freedom. By then, she was sure, her uncle would have married her off to some doddering old fool who'd waste her father's money on wine, women and song.

"Can't go anywhere without her," she said, nodding sharply in Irene's direction. "Can't even use the facilities without her hanging around."

"Pooh," Jane said. "Sounds like you've had some really rotten luck."

She leant forward. "But you're in America now," she added, lowering her voice. "And there are people who will take your side."

"Lady Raechel," Hamish said, breaking away from the original group and coming to join them. "Would you care for another dance?"

"I'll see you again," Jane said, cheerfully. "I'm sure you'll be visiting my house sooner or later."

"You probably will," Hamish said, as he pulled Raechel back onto the dance floor. "Her mother knows everyone in town."

Raechel nodded, slowly. "Does anyone here really care about London?"

Hamish gave her a considering look. "In what way?"

"Jane was saying her mother was exiled from London," Raechel said. "But that doesn't seem to be a problem here."

"You might be surprised at just how many people have come here after being kicked out of London," Hamish muttered. He glanced from side to side, then nodded to a tall man wearing a military uniform instead of a suit and tie. "That's General Paget, the bigamist. He couldn't stay in London, but no one cares about that here. And over there is Lady Parkinson, who was tried and convicted of criminal conversation. Over here, no one cares."

Raechel frowned. "She had an adulterous affair?"

"No one cares, not here," Hamish said. "This country is a land for fresh starts, not for continuing old grudges from England."

"A fresh start," Raechel mused. "I think I'd like that."

Hamish laughed. "Could you give up your wealth?"

Raechel shrugged. It wasn't *her* wealth and never *would* be her wealth, unless she managed to avoid being married off until she turned twenty-five. Now, with the British Government owing her a favour, maybe she could escape such a fate … but even so, it would cause problems. If she died young … she wasn't quite sure what would happen in that case. It wasn't as if anyone would respect *her* post-mortem wishes.

She pushed her morbid thoughts to one side as other young men came to dance with her, chatting briefly about themselves while she listened. Hamish wasn't the only one who thought America was a land for fresh starts, she discovered; quite a few Americans – even ones with ties to England – felt the same way. And most of them wanted to remove slavery from the shores of America before it brought the colonies crashing down.

It was almost a relief, she decided, when Irene finally pulled her off the dance floor. She said a hasty set of goodbyes, then obediently followed Irene through a maze of corridors and out of the rear of the building, where the carriages were waiting. Lady Sofia had loaned them a driver as well as a handful of servants, although Irene had warned her not to say anything where the driver could hear them. Lady Sofia might not be spying on them for the French, she'd added, but that didn't mean she wouldn't use anything her agent overheard against them.

"Not a bad introductory ball," Irene said, as the carriage drove back to the house. "I trust you had a good time?"

They exchanged stilted conversation until they returned home, where the driver was dismissed and they walked into the living room. The servants had lit a fire, but – as Irene had ordered – withdrawn for the night. Raechel was no stranger to servants living in her home, yet the building was really too small to keep an effective distance between them …

"You didn't drink," Irene said. "Well done."

Raechel nodded, not trusting herself to speak. Irene had flatly forbidden her from taking even a sip of alcohol, even though several of the young ladies had been gulping wine down in a startlingly unladylike manner. Strong drink loosened the tongue, she'd warned; Raechel knew, from experience, that she was correct. A young lady could get into trouble if she drank too much …

"The youngsters" – it felt odd to say that about people who were roughly the same age as herself – "don't feel much sympathy for the Crown," she said. "The more Americanised they are, the less sympathy they have."

"True," Irene said. She looked up, suddenly. "I'll tell you something interesting, too. A couple of the young people chatting to you had *very* good mental shields."

Raechel blinked. "Like mine?"

"Better than yours," Irene said. She smirked. "I wonder what they have to hide."

"Perhaps they just don't like having their thoughts ransacked," Raechel pointed out, tartly.

"Perhaps they don't," Irene agreed. "But that raises the issue of just *who* taught them how to shield their thoughts."

"The French?"

"Could be," Irene said. "You need a Talker to teach you how to shield your thoughts. And it really needs a *powerful* Talker."

Raechel shuddered.

"Trouble is very definitely brewing, Raechel," Irene warned. "And the sooner we get to the bottom of it, the better. Right now, if we go to war, I don't know what side half the people in that ballroom are going to be on."

"And if half of them turn traitor," Raechel finished, "the war will not go our way."

Chapter Sixteen

t was a relief, Gwen decided as she climbed out of bed, that Wayne had been able to find a handful of servants for the Sorcerers' Hall. She'd always made certain to bathe and have a good breakfast at Cavendish Hall, a habit she'd picked up from Master Thomas before his death, a habit she'd had problems keeping during the trip to Russia. Merely having the various rooms cleaned and tidied for the coming sorcerers made the building look a great deal more welcoming. She ate her breakfast slowly, then read the report Irene had written once she'd left the ball. It didn't make pleasant reading.

The Sons of Liberty are growing stronger, she thought. *And they have at least one Talker on their side.*

She scowled as she sipped her tea. She'd kept her mental shields firmly in place while she was at the ball, but she hadn't sensed any intrusion. It meant nothing, though. Very few Talkers would take the risk of trying to probe her thoughts, knowing that she would probably be able to sense their magic and take steps. And she didn't have anything like the power necessary to sense deceit, if the deceiver had even the slightest fragment of self-control.

"My Lady," Wayne said. He walked through the door, looking surprisingly alert for a man who'd been halfway to permanent drunkenness a day ago. "The new magicians are ready to begin training."

Gwen rose, picking up her top hat and walking cane. Master Thomas had set the style, back in London and she'd kept it. The idea of fighting while wearing a dress … she smiled at the thought, then dismissed it. Quite apart from the simple fact that she would be unable to command respect, she'd run the risk of someone looking up her leggings when she went flying through the air. She glanced at Wayne – he'd donned a standard sorcerer's outfit, a cross between a military uniform and a respectable suit – and then led the way out into the training ground. She couldn't help feeling a flicker of dismay at the sight before her. Six men stood there, two looking resentful and out of place in the uniforms they'd been issued. The remaining four seemed to be better at hiding their feelings.

"Under the Sorcerous Act of 1790, all registered magicians can be conscripted into the Royal Sorcerers Corps," Gwen said, flatly. It had never been done before, she knew; very few magicians turned down the chance to serve their country *and* collect a very high wage. "With our recent losses, I have been forced to conscript you six into the Corps. I know none of you signed up for this, but the country needs you."

She took a breath. "You will be paid the standard salary, plus a regimental combat bonus," she added, after a moment. The last thing she needed was half of them deserting. "If you don't decide to stay, after the war is over, you will also be paid a completion bonus."

"That's very well," one of the magicians said. "But will we get our jobs back?"

Gwen took a moment to gather herself. It was rare for her to be interrupted by a trainee magician, certainly not at Cavendish Hall. But the magician – she assumed he was Timothy O'Rourke, judging by the Irish accent – had carved out a life for himself as a sailor, despite the magic that would have made him much more. A Blazer could be a truly dangerous threat, as she'd taught the French sailors. She understood why he might not want to leave.

"If you want your old jobs back, you will get them," she promised. If the war was won, the Viceroy would see to it personally. "If not, we will make other provision for you."

She took a moment to study the six magicians. Harry and Vernon Jameson were brothers, both Movers. She'd wondered if they were twins, when she'd seen the file, but further reading had confirmed that Harry was older by three years. Even so, they didn't look that different; they had black hair, muscular frames and identical smiles. Beside them,

Marcellus Grams and Colin Shepherd looked very different; Grams looked like a businessman, complete with gold-rimmed spectacles, while Shepherd looked like a postal rider. And Calumet Fife, the Changer, was so thin that Gwen couldn't help wondering if a gust of wind would blow him away. She had to resist the urge to send him to the kitchen for a fattening up.

"I don't promise this will be easy," she said. "Some of you have been using your powers for work" – she nodded to the Jameson brothers – "while others haven't been using your powers at all. The French will have a great deal of training to use their powers for war. We need to catch up as quickly as we can."

"We *have* used our powers to fight," Harry said. He had a strong and oddly-familiar accent, although Gwen couldn't place it. "Together, we beat thugs down on the docks."

"That's true, Milady," O'Rourke said. "They make a formidable pair."

Gwen smiled at them. "But have you fought another magician?"

The brothers looked at each other, then shook their heads. Gwen wasn't surprised. The brothers had registered, probably shortly after they'd used their powers for the first time, then gone back to their lives on the docks. They would be sorely missed, Gwen was sure; they'd been able to unload boats faster than non-magicians, just by using their magic. But right now there was a different job for them.

"Very well," she said. "It's time you learnt how."

She waved a hand over the training ground. Someone had shelled out a great deal of money to purchase the land in land-poor Manhattan, then turn it into a walled garden rather than more tenement blocks. *She* would have preferred a training centre somewhere further inland, where the sorcerers could practice without being watched, but there was no time to move the facility into the hinterlands. Besides, if all hell *did* break loose, they might be better off close to the docks.

"None of us are going to go off the grass," she said, as she walked forward. She called on her magic and felt it billowing around her, ready to fight. "All you two have to do is defeat me."

Vernon leered. "And what do we get if we win?"

"You get to go into battle against the French without any further training," Gwen said, biting down the response that came to mind. No doubt Vernon had had something else in mind. "It would be a *very* impressive achievement."

O'Rourke cleared his throat. "And what do you want us to do, while you're skirmishing with them?"

"Watch and learn," Gwen said. She reached the centre of the lawn, then turned to face the two Movers. "Ready when you are."

Harry ran forward, magic billowing around him like a giant battering ram. Gwen was unwillingly impressed – he had a *lot* of power – but merely stepped to one side and Changed the grass below his feet into ice. It didn't last for more than a few seconds, yet it was more than enough to make him slip and fall to the ground. Vernon swore out loud, then lashed out at Gwen with his own power. Gwen allowed him to batter her through the air – her protections insulated her from the brunt of the blow – while she caught hold of his foot with her magic and yanked, hard. Vernon fell to the ground and landed hard.

"You hit her from that side," Harry shouted.

Gwen threw herself up into the air as the two Movers tried to crush her between them. It wasn't a bad thought, but they'd literally told her what they intended to do. Their magic collided, violently; they were thrown backwards by the force of the blow. Harry landed badly, banging his head into the ground; Vernon snarled and reached out with his magic once again, finally trying to grab her with his power. Gwen would have been more impressed if he'd tried to do that from the start.

"Got you," he snarled, as his power tightened around her. He *was* formidable, Gwen realised; if she'd been limited to one power herself, she might well have lost. "You …"

She lifted her hand and generated a blinding flash of light. The power crushing her vanished in an instant as Vernon stumbled backwards, rubbing his suddenly blind eyes. It would take several seconds for his eyesight to recover, far too long. Gwen dropped to the ground, summoned a fireball and held it up in the air.

"I think I win," she said. "You didn't do badly" – she added in a grudging tone of voice – "but you're not used to thinking on your feet."

"I think you win too," Harry said. He was rubbing the back of his head. Gwen was relieved to see there didn't seem to be any permanent damage. "Vernon?"

"She blinded me," Vernon stammered. He sounded as though he was torn between panic and rage. "The bitch *blinded* me!"

"Your eyesight will recover," Gwen told him, biting down the urge to reprimand him for his insult. She hoped he'd get over it and start treating her as someone he could learn from, rather than a potential enemy. There were already too many enemies on the wrong side of the fence. "And when it does, you'll know not to fall for the same trick twice."

"I never thought of that," O'Rourke observed. He didn't sound angry, merely surprised. "I should have thought of that."

Gwen gave him a sidelong look. "What did you *do* with your magic?"

"Charting waters," O'Rourke said. "And guiding boats in and out of the harbour at night."

Gwen looked at Wayne, who nodded. "Blazers will learn from me," he said, firmly. "We'll go down to the shooting range and start working on our offensive range."

O'Rourke looked dubious, but followed Wayne and the others. Gwen watched them go, then turned to Fife. The sole Changer looked nervous ... Gwen seriously thought about just letting him go, even though she had a feeling she might need him. A trained Changer would be invaluable, but even an unskilled one would be useful.

"Sit with your brother until his eyesight is back," she ordered Harry, who nodded. "Mr. Fife, come with me."

"Yes, Milady," Fife said.

Gwen felt a sudden flicker of *Déjà Vu* as they walked into the shielded area. "What do you *do* with your magic, Mr. Fife?"

"Very little, My Lady," Fife said. She was certain, very certain, that he was lying. "I merely registered shortly after I changed something for the first time."

"Very good," Gwen said. She hoped Lord Mycroft would release a handful of trained magicians soon. Even a couple would make it easier to train the Americans. "Watch this."

She picked up a stone, charged it with energy and threw it over the blast wall. It exploded, seconds later. Gwen smiled, remembering her first experiences with such magic, then picked up another stone and passed it to Fife. He took it, turning it over and over in his hands as he eyed it doubtfully.

"Charge it with magic, then hurl it over the blast wall as soon as you stop," Gwen told him, carefully. If he was lying about how he used his magic, what *else* was he lying about? Had she scooped up a Son of Liberty – or a criminal? "Don't hold on to it after you stop."

"I made things explode before," Fife said. He studied the rock for a long moment, then allowed his power to flow. "I never mastered the timing."

"No one has," Gwen said. She'd driven herself dotty trying, back in Cavendish Hall, but even the most experienced Changers couldn't predict when the makeshift grenades would go off. An impact might set them off ... or they might explode an hour or two later, when nearby watchers no longer took the threat seriously. "All you really want is something that will explode on cue."

Fife nodded, then hurled the rock over the blast wall. Gwen heard it hit the ground on the far side, but there was no explosion. She counted up to forty before it finally exploded, with enough violence to shake the ground. Fife gave her a long look and she nodded, pleased. At least he'd mastered the first lesson without a major effort.

"I'll be working with you, one on one," she told him, shortly. She'd have to arrange a chaperone too ... she gritted her teeth in annoyance. Irene and Raechel had too much else to do, while Arielle Franklin-Rochester was too young. Gwen couldn't see her uncle agreeing to allow her to visit Sorcerers' Hall. "Until then, keep practicing with the rocks ..."

She paused as a thought struck her. "When you get hungry," she added, "tell the cooks you want something to eat. They'll always have something ready for us."

"Thank you, My Lady," Fife said.

Gwen smiled at him, then walked back to where Harry and Vernon were sitting. Vernon seemed to have recovered, but there was an evil look in his teary eyes that boded ill for the future. Gwen met his gaze challengingly – she'd met enough obnoxious men to know that showing weakness was a mistake – and silently dared him to do something. Harry prodded Vernon in the chest before he could do anything stupid. Gwen was almost relieved. At least one of the brothers had some common sense.

"On your feet," she said. "You have some practicing to do."

Her sense of dismay grew stronger over the next hour. The brothers were *strong*, but dangerously untrained. Their magic was surprisingly delicate at handling large objects, yet they were clumsy with small items and neither of them had ever thought to fly. It was odd – surely, they should have been capable of realising the potentials inherent in their powers – but they hadn't. Losing their grip on Earth seemed to scare them.

"You'll need to practice harder," she said, after the fourth apple was ripped apart by Vernon, the debris dropping to the grass. "Using a lighter touch will make your life easier."

"It isn't something you need down at the docks," Vernon muttered. "Really."

They stopped for lunch – thankfully, the cooks had produced an enormous meal – and then went back to work. Gwen left Wayne supervising the two Movers – and teaching them how to shield themselves against magic – while she checked on the Blazers. None of them had anything like the level of skill she'd come to expect at Cavendish Hall, although O'Rourke had come up with a trick of his own. Gwen had never realised that it was possible to create a light source visible only to the magician who cast it, but O'Rourke had definitely made it work. She made a mental note to work on the trick herself – it might be very useful – then hurried back to the Movers. Neither Harry nor Vernon seemed to be capable of holding a shield in place for very long.

"I would have thought you'd be able to protect yourselves," she said. Were they holding back deliberately? "How did you fight on the docks?"

"We didn't need a shield for more than a few seconds," Harry explained. Beside him, Vernon merely grunted. "There was no need to hold it in place for long."

"You'll have to learn," Gwen said, unable to keep the tart note from her voice. She rubbed her forehead, cursing under her breath. Were there no other magicians, registered or not, in New York? Messengers had been sent to other cities, but she knew it would be a while before any other registered magicians could arrive. "The French will target you specifically."

She watched them go back to practicing, then glanced at Wayne. He didn't look pleased.

"This isn't going to work," he said, very quietly. "They have too much to unlearn."

Gwen winced, inwardly. She'd had things to unlearn too, although not as much as she might have feared. Her powers were far more versatile than any of her new recruits. But *they* had been using their powers – she heard another explosion from the direction of the blast wall and wondered if Fife was getting bored – without the training they needed. They weren't blank slates …

"There's no choice," she said. She had no idea how many magicians were on the French side of the border, massing near New Orleans, but she would bet her entire fortune that the French had sent a formidable force. If they couldn't take London, they'd try to take America. "We have to make it work."

"It won't be easy," Wayne said. "The brothers don't like you and …"

If only I'd been born a man, Gwen thought, savagely. Master Thomas could have cowed them both into submission with a raised eyebrow. *She* could flatten them every day and she'd *still* have to watch her back. *Bastards!*

She closed her eyes for a long moment, reaching out with her senses. There was no trace of Fife, somewhat to her surprise, but she had no trouble picking out the other magicians. The Movers were still practicing; the Blazers were slacking off and …

Her eyes snapped open. There was another magician nearby. They were being watched!

Wayne frowned. "My Lady?"

Gwen ignored him, looking around even as she probed with her senses. Had the other magician realised he'd been seen? She looked up towards the nearest tenement block, hunting desperately for the watcher. And then she saw him, lying on the roof … watching them. He could have been there for hours!

"Get them into the hall," she ordered. Hopefully, they'd listen to Wayne. He was a man, after all. "I'm going hunting."

She wrapped her magic around her and threw herself into the air.

Chapter Seventeen

he ignored Wayne's shout of surprise, behind her, as she hurled herself up towards the tenement block. The watcher was already scrambling to his feet, a dark-clad man wearing a cloak that reminded her of a monk's garb. His face was hidden completely behind a mask, his hands wrapped in dark gloves. He ran backwards, out of sight, as Gwen reached the top of the building, casually dropping down a level on the other side of the block. Gwen dropped down to the rooftop and ran after him, wrapping her power around her …

The rooftop edge disintegrated. Gwen jumped upwards, alarmed, as bricks and dust launched themselves at her. A Mover, part of her mind noted, as she threw herself upwards rather than try to fend off the pieces of debris. The enemy, whoever he was, had less power than the brothers, but rather more skill. His power threw the pieces of debris up after her as she drifted over the edge of the rooftop. Below her, the masked man crouched on a metal staircase.

"Stop," Gwen snapped. "Stop in the name of …"

The pieces of debris slammed into her shield. She grunted, pushing them away from her with an effort, then swore as his magic caught hold of her and disrupted her hold on the air. Gwen dropped, sharply, grabbing hold of the metal as she passed to keep herself from falling to the ground. She snatched a fireball out of the air and threw it at him. It struck his shields and disintegrated, sending a wave of heat fanning through the air. She raised her hand to create a flash of light, but he looked away just in time.

He must have been watching from the start, she thought. *And he saw what I did to Vernon.*

Rage filled her. Frenchman or treasonous American, he had no *right* to watch her sorcerers slowly learning the ropes. She reached out and *ripped* at the staircase, pulling it away from the wall and sending him plummeting towards the ground. He caught himself in midair – Gwen cursed inwardly as she realised the newcomer could fly – then launched himself back upwards as she pelted him with debris and fireballs, his magic crumbling the remainder of the staircase. Gwen tossed herself back up into the air and landed on what was left of the roof, feeling her magic curling around her. Her opponent landed on the nearest building and tossed her a jaunty salute, then jumped to the next building. And then the next.

He wasn't flying, Gwen realised as she gave chase, even though he shouldn't have any problem taking to the air. She warned herself to be careful – Jack had lured her into a trap through allowing her to think she was running him down – but it looked as though her opponent was merely toying with her, rather than trying to fight or run. She hesitated, considering her options. Some of the nastier tricks she could do would inflict a great deal of harm on the city …

"Stop," Gwen said, lacing her voice with Charm. "No more magic."

His legs quivered, but otherwise he showed no reaction to the Charm. Instead, he lifted his hand and sent a wave of powerful magic at her, knocking her back and over the far side of the rooftop. Gwen caught herself and flew around the building, hoping to catch him by surprise, but when she popped up onto the rooftop he was nowhere to be seen. She landed carefully, looking around for his hiding place, yet she saw nothing. Another metal staircase was clearly visible on the far side of the rooftop, leading down into a dark alleyway. Gwen braced herself, then dived down and landed neatly on the pavement. But there was still no sign of her mystery opponent.

Clever, she thought, ruefully.

She sniffed the air and instantly regretted it – the alleyway smelt worse than a London alleyway – but kept looking around anyway. There was nothing to be seen, save for a handful of metal dustbins and a pile of rags on the ground. A clattering noise caught her attention, but when she span around it turned out to be nothing more than a cat, clambering onto one of the dustbins. She eyed the cat suspiciously for a long moment, then told herself not to be silly. Werewolves were one thing, but no magician could turn into a cat!

Impressive, she thought. She'd been bested – and *that* didn't happen very often, certainly not by a single Mover. But he had to be *very* well trained, perhaps even trained to face her personally. His resistance to Charm had been strikingly powerful. *Very impressive indeed.*

She walked to the end of the alleyway, straining her senses for even the tiniest flicker of her enemy's presence and scowled as she peered out onto the street. It was crammed; horses and carriages making their way up and down the street, pedestrians walking, newsboys shouting out something about an exclusive. Hardly any of them paid attention to Gwen ... and there was no sign of her enemy. He'd slipped into the crowds and vanished. She looked up, just to make sure he wasn't clinging to the nearest building, but saw nothing.

"Damn," she said.

She turned and walked back into the alleyway, trying to make her way back to the Sorcerers' Hall. New York was *oppressive* at ground level, the buildings looming over her and making her feel small. London had plenty of tenement blocks too, but they were a *little* more spread out, even in places where the landlords worked hard to extract every last penny from their tenants. The shadows rose and fell around her, her imagination filling in too many possibilities for what could be lurking in the darkness. She caught sight of a man lying on the ground, his hand clutching a bottle and braced herself, before realising that it was just a drunk sleeping it off. Shaking her head, she walked onwards. Had she really gone *that* far from Sorcerers' Hall? Or had she taken a wrong turning ...?

The building came into view, just as she was considering taking to the air again. A gilded carriage was parked outside, guarded by a pair of men in army uniforms. They'd forsaken ceremonial garb, Gwen noted, as if they expected to go into battle at any time. *That* was not a reassuring sign. They eyed her doubtfully as she approached – God alone knew what they made of her – and then relaxed, slightly, as they recognised her.

"Lady Gwen," one said. "His Excellency is inside, waiting for you."

Gwen blinked. The Viceroy had come to Sorcerers' Hall? As informal as the Americas were, she rather doubted it. Normally, a politician would send a request to visit – which, of course, would not be denied. Just walking into her territory without permission was an insult and Viceroy Rochester hadn't struck her as the kind of man who would offer insult, not without due cause. He had too many problems keeping the snake pit of politics in line without insulting his allies from England.

"Thank you," she said, tartly. Now the thrill of the chase had worn off, she wanted a bath, a cup of tea and a quiet sit down. She had the nasty feeling she wasn't going to get any of them. "I'll see him inside, shall I?"

The mystery resolved itself as she stepped into the waiting room. Bruce Rochester, the Viceroy's son, sat in the chamber, reading a newspaper and drinking a cup of tea. Gwen wondered why she hadn't considered the possibility, then remembered that she rarely dealt with the sons of powerful men. Lord Mycroft had no children, as far as she knew, and neither had Master Thomas. Although, admittedly, she'd often wondered if *Jack* had been Master Thomas's son. He was definitely in the right age bracket.

"Your Excellency," Gwen said. As the Viceroy's son, Bruce, was entitled to the honorific as long as his father held the title. "What brings you to Sorcerers' Hall?"

Bruce rose to his feet and bowed, formally. "My father requests your immediate presence, Lady Gwen," he said. "I have a carriage waiting outside."

Gwen thought fast. Rochester wouldn't have sent his *son*, of all people, to deliver a message unless it was so sensitive it couldn't be shared outside the family. But if all he wanted was for Gwen to attend upon him ... she shook her head. She was too tired to make sense of American politics, not now. Maybe she didn't have time for a bath – the message was clearly urgent – but at least she could splash some water on her face and have a quick word with Wayne.

"I'll be along in a moment," she said. "I just have to use the facilities."

The mischievous devil in her wanted to see his reaction, but Bruce showed no hint of any response to her words. He'd grown up at the centre of politics, she reminded herself as she headed for the door. Learning to conceal his emotions and verbally dissemble would have been hammered into him from the moment he could walk. She walked up the stairs, washed her face hastily and glanced into the mirror. Her face still looked tired, but at least she looked more composed.

She sent one of the servants to summon Wayne, then headed down into the office. A handful of files lay on the desk, reminding her that she had to read them at some point; she scowled as she realised she would have to do rather more paperwork than she liked to do, just to keep her files in order. But then, when was she supposed to find the time? There just weren't enough hours in the day to train the sorcerers, let alone fill out their paperwork …

"My Lady," Wayne said. "The blighter got away?"

"I'm afraid so," Gwen said. She hoped he wouldn't hold it against her, but it was probably a forlorn hope. Maybe she *should* have risked something nastier than Charm. "He's a Mover of great skill, I think. Much better than either of the brothers."

Wayne frowned. "Better than you?"

"He has more awareness of his talent," Gwen said, reluctantly. Any single-talent magician would be more familiar with the strengths and weaknesses of his power than one who had access to *all* the talents. "And he has a great deal of raw power too."

She cursed under her breath. The rogue was a complete unknown. If he dumped his cloak and mask in the nearest dustbin, he could just stride off, leaving her none the wiser. Or maybe he'd just hopped into a passing carriage and threatened the driver to take him halfway across the city. In that case, there was probably a dead cabbie somewhere in the city, murdered after he had outlived his usefulness. And someone with that sort of raw power could easily get into the

Viceregal Palace and assassinate the Viceroy ...

"I've been summoned to the Palace," she said, instead. "Keep them training, as much as you can. I have a feeling it's bad news."

"Yes, My Lady," Wayne said.

Gwen watched him leave the office, then picked up her cane and hurried back to the waiting room. Bruce was reading one of the books the hall's former inhabitants had left behind, a tacky romance featuring handsome aristocratic men, beautiful aristocratic girls and almost as many social mishaps and misunderstandings as happened in real life. Men might sneer at how the women in the books treated the question of marriage as a matter of life or death, but to them it *was* a matter of life or death. The wrong husband would doom them to a hellish existence they would be fortunate indeed to escape.

"My Lady," Bruce said. "Shall we go?"

"Of course," Gwen said.

She allowed him to lead her to the carriage, thinking rapidly. The French, whatever their other flaws, didn't tend to take the risk of assassinating British politicians. There would be certain retaliation, after all; Britain might survive losing a king or even a dynasty, but would the Bourbons feel the same way? The only thing that held France and Spain together, save for mutual hatred of the British, was the House of Bourbon. If King Louis and his heir were to die, what would happen to their empire?

But the Americans – if the rogue was an American – might think differently. Viceroy Rochester wasn't a *king*. If he died, London would have to send out a new Viceroy, one who would have to learn the ropes under a great deal of pressure. He'd make mistakes, Gwen thought; offend the wrong people, alienate his natural allies ... the Sons of Liberty might make great gains if they murdered the Viceroy. And, at the same time, they'd also weaken the defences of British North America. The French might gain control of the colonies without a major struggle.

"I was surprised to hear that you weren't in the hall," Bruce said, as the carriage jolted into motion. "Why did you leave?"

"I'll explain that to your father," Gwen said. What *was* she supposed to do about the rogue magician? He was very definitely powerful and experienced enough to break into the Viceregal Palace and assassinate the Viceroy, but she didn't have the manpower to provide additional bodyguards. "It's a long story."

She looked him in the eye. "Why the sudden summons?"

"I don't know," Bruce said. He shrugged in a manner David had been fond of using before their father beat it out of him. "Father ordered me to go to the hall and bring you back to the palace."

"Something must have happened," Gwen said. She felt a cold pit of fear deep in her chest; a rogue magician, one powerful enough to evade her, and now an urgent summons. It augured badly for the future. "Did he say *nothing*?"

"He was sending out other messengers too," Bruce said. "I don't *think* it's another ball."

Gwen felt her lips thin in irritation. Another ball? She was supposed to work with the Viceroy, but if he'd dragged her away from her duties so that she could attend another ball … she was going to give him a piece of her mind. Girl or not, she had a job to do and she was going to do it. But it was unlikely, she told herself firmly. The local aristocracy would complain, loudly, if the Viceroy held two balls in such quick succession. No one else would have a chance to host a ball for themselves.

"Tell me something," she said. "What do you *want* to do with your life?"

Bruce shrugged, indolently. "There's nothing I can do," he said, dryly. "I certainly can't hope to match my father."

That, Gwen knew, was probably true. Viceroyalties did not run in families. Spain had experimented with making the Viceroy of Mexico an hereditary post, only to discover that the viceroys had begun to think of themselves as kings, rather than the king's servants. Bruce would be a landed aristocrat, when his father died, but he would never be a Viceroy. He would never wield the autocratic powers of his father …

"You could join the army," she said, instead. His family would certainly be able to buy him a commission, although the Duke of India would probably insist on some training before Bruce tried to take command of a regiment. Too many wealthy incompetents bought their commissions and then tried to take command in the middle of a battle. "You could certainly carve out a name for yourself."

She smiled. "Or you could join the navy," she added. "You might just make captain before the end of the war."

Her smile grew wider. Captains – successful captains – were *stars*. Men admired them, women threw themselves at them, children wanted to grow up to *be* them. A captain like Lord Nelson commanded more respect than King George! There was something about a successful warship commander that spoke to the British seafaring soul. Maybe the introduction of ironclad warships would change that, but she doubted it. The navy was the core of Britain's greatness.

"Too much like hard work," Bruce said.

Gwen stared at him. "You just want to sit around and do nothing?"

"Why not?" Bruce asked. "What would I gain if I did anything else?"

Gwen pursed her lips. "Self-respect?"

Bruce merely snorted.

Gwen shook her head in disbelief. *She'd* spent the first eighteen years of her life wanting to do *something* with her magic, to make *something* of her life. Bruce was a young man in the prime of his life, with enough connections to ensure that he could enter almost any trade at a very high level, yet he wanted to do *nothing?* She'd known too many aristocratic young men who'd just wasted their lives, but this …? Bruce's children would be lucky if their father left them any lands, when he finally shuffled off the mortal coil.

But he can never live up to his father, she thought, feeling an unwilling stab of sympathy for the young man. *Any more than I can ever live up to mine – or Master Thomas.*

She leant back in her seat and watched as the carriage passed through the palace gates. A dozen soldiers were on duty, outside the gates; twenty more were inside, digging defences and building emplacements for heavy weaponry. She caught sight of a pair of repeating guns being placed inside a trench before the carriage clattered past and came to a halt, outside the main doors. Five more soldiers were standing guard, their weapons at the ready. It was clear that the Viceroy was expecting trouble.

Then we'd better go and see what it is, Gwen thought, as Bruce opened the door. *The invasion might have finally begun.*

Chapter Eighteen

ady Irene," Lady Summer said. "And Lady Raechel! It has been *far* too long."

Raechel kept her face impassive as the door closed behind them, despite feeling as though she'd been basted with sauce and thrown to the lions. Lady Summer might be their host, but she'd invited a dozen other society madams from New York to the party. Any hope of a private chat with their host had faded before they'd even entered the building.

"It is a great pleasure to see you in your natural habitat," Irene said, playing the middle-aged woman for all it was worth. "We barely had the chance to chat at the ball."

Raechel fought hard to keep her thoughts under control. Lady Summer had spent *hours* talking to Irene at the ball – and if she'd wanted to talk to Irene privately, she could have refrained from inviting so many witnesses. Besides, if this *was* Lady Summer's natural environment, she couldn't imagine why *anyone* would even *consider* marrying into her family. The woman was far too fond of expensive golden knick-knacks for her tastes. A dark-skinned maid poured the tea as Irene and Raechel sat down, then retreated through the door. Raechel wished, devoutly, that she could go with her.

And this is just the first party, she reminded herself, numbly. Her mother had taken her to a few, when she'd been younger, but she hadn't been expected to stay for very long. Even her aunt had known better than to force Raechel to attend for more than a couple of hours. *We have a dozen more to attend over the next two weeks.*

"My husband is quite interested in opening negotiations," Lady Summer continued, as she passed Irene a cup of tea.

"He feels there is something to be gained by a formal alliance."

"It would need to be confirmed by Raechel's guardians," Irene said, casually. It was almost as if Raechel wasn't there at all. "But they would be interested to hear your offer."

Raechel smiled, inwardly. Irene had made her research Lady Summer and what she'd turned up had not been inviting. The Summer family – or at least the American branch – was short on both money and common sense. Lady Summer's husband had massive debts and nothing to pay them with, save for selling off the thousands of slaves who worked his land. Given the near-certainty of a slave revolt when the French came over the borders, Raechel couldn't help thinking that his investment was worth less than nothing.

"Very good," Lady Summer said. She looked at Raechel. "My daughter and a handful of her friends are downstairs in the playroom, having their own party. Would you care to join them?"

Irene leant forward. "Are they chaperoned?"

"My daughter has strict orders not to allow any young man to join them," Lady Summer said, blithely. She didn't sound the type to suspect her daughter of anything more than mild disobedience. "My son is with his regiment and my husband is currently attending on the Viceroy."

Begging for money, Raechel thought, nastily.

"Then she may go," Irene said, grandly. "Raechel, you are not to leave this building without my permission."

Raechel scowled as she rose. She knew Irene was playing a role, she knew the discussions concerning her marriage would come to nothing ... but it still hurt to be so casually reminded of her formal status. Irene was right, she thought, as Lady Summer rang for the maid and ordered her to escort Raechel to the playroom. It would be so much easier if she gave up her former life and just created and discarded identities at need.

She followed the maid down the corridor and into the playroom. The name would have made her smile, under other circumstances; the room looked more like a cosy sitting room than a place for children to play. No doubt Lady

Summer still thought of her daughter as a child, even though she was two years older than Raechel or Gwen. Poor Alison Summer would have real problems getting married too, Raechel suspected. Her husband would be unwilling to take on his father-in-law's debts.

"Raechel," Jane called. "I was hoping you'd make it! How are you?"

"Fine, thank you," Raechel said. There was something about Jane's enthusiasm that made her smile. "Are you going to introduce me?"

"Of course," Jane said. She waved a hand at the four other girls in the room. "Alison Summer, our host; Rebecca Fielding, Georgina Blyton and Susan Falcon."

"Welcome," Alison said. She gave Raechel a slightly-strained smile. "Are you going to marry my brother?"

"I've never *met* your brother," Raechel said. If Peter Summer had been at the ball, she'd missed him. "But I don't think I'm going to marry your brother."

"How terrible," Jane said. She gave Raechel another brilliant smile. "But you can still be friends."

"We can try," Alison said. She rose. "Would you like some tea before we go out?"

Raechel blinked. "Go out? Go out where?"

"There's a meeting being held not too far away," Jane said. A funny tingle ran through Raechel's mind. "We thought you might like to attend."

"A meeting," Raechel repeated. "And we can attend without being caught?"

"They'll be in discussions for hours," Alison said, with the same blithe confidence her mother had shown. "Long enough for us to get there and get back."

"It's really just across the road," Rebecca said. "May will tell us if they're breaking up earlier."

Raechel felt the tingle for a second time and swore, inwardly. If Irene hadn't worked her so hard, forcing her to develop her mental shields, she would have missed it completely. A Talker! There was a mind-reader in the room. She kept her shields in place, hoping the illusion of a naïve young girl would be convincing. The probe didn't feel anything like as powerful as Irene's probes, but that didn't mean it wasn't dangerous. Irene had told her that a weak Charmer could actually be far more effective than a strong one.

"I would love to attend," she said, trying to project a mixture of excitement and trepidation into her shields. It would be believable, of course. Being caught out of bounds – and unchaperoned – would be disastrous for a London girl. "When are we going?"

"Now, unless you want some tea," Alison said. "We can take the time to make sure that the oldsters are blathering happily amongst themselves."

Raechel shook her head. "I don't think we should take any chances," she said. "Lady Irene might lose her temper and storm out."

Jane gave her a sympathetic look. "A harsh chaperone?"

"My uncle and aunt are depending on her," Raechel lied. But it was a believable lie. "And she's taken that to heart."

Her thoughts raced as the girls led her though a maze of corridors and out into the gardens. A chill was settling over the city – clouds were gathering overhead – but none of her companions seemed concerned as they strolled into the garden, down towards the far wall. Another mansion rose up on the other side ... she concentrated, trying to remember the map Irene had shown her. It was Lord Tarleton's mansion, if she recalled correctly. And his son was very definitely a dissident.

"I bet you can't do this in London," Jane said, as they reached a half-hidden door set in the brick wall. "Just pop through a door to visit your friend?"

"Not without an escort, no," Raechel said, trying to sound uncomfortable. It was easy enough. She was halfway to being convinced that *Jane* was the Talker. "And out in the countryside ... if you want to visit a friend, you need a horse and carriage."

She sighed, feeling a sudden stab of pain. Her parents had been decent, certainly better than Gwen's. She might have been a daughter, but they'd let her ride around the estate ... and even go into the countryside, if she had an escort. Going to London had seemed a treat until she'd had to move in with her aunt and uncle, whereupon it had turned into a prison.

There were just too many opportunities for scandal in London.

They passed through the door and hurried to the mansion, where a doorway gaped open invitingly. Alison led the way into the building and down a corridor, into a large room. At least four dozen young men were already there, standing in the room while a dozen other young women leant against the far wall. Oddly, at least in her experience, two of the men were setting out the teapots and jugs of water. She thought they were servants until she caught a glimpse of their clothes. No servant wore clothes made of such fine cloth.

And they're pouring the drinks, she thought, numbly. There was no alcohol in sight, as far as she could tell. She'd wondered if she'd wandered into another erotic club, but it looked rather more like a church meeting. *Will wonders never cease*?

"We have a guest today," a familiar voice said, as the doors were finally closed. She looked up to see Hamish Tarleton, standing on a chair. He sounded less snooty than before. "Please welcome Lady Raechel Slater-Standish."

Raechel blushed as a number of glances were thrown in her direction, although there was an undercurrent of ... *wariness* ... that hung in the air. The crowd didn't seem inclined to welcome her with open arms, even if they weren't inclined to reject her either. Raechel wondered, inwardly, just how much of the whole affair was being staged for her benefit ... had they *known* she was going to attend? If Alison had already known she was coming to her mansion, it would be easy enough for her to pass the word to Hamish Tarleton ...

Her blood ran cold. Whatever was going on, she realised, she'd walked headfirst into deadly danger. If she failed to convince the group that she wouldn't betray them, if they were serious about revolution instead of merely being rich kids playing games, they'd cut her throat instead of letting her leave peacefully. She'd seen too much – names, faces – to be allowed to run free. Imprisonment was the best she could expect.

"You know why we are here," Hamish said. "America hangs on a knife-edge. We are a large continent with a growing population, yet we are subject to laws made by men in London. They tell us that we have representation in Parliament, but our MPs are not numerous enough to stop the imposition of policies that hurt our lives, ruin our industries and blight our future. Why *should* we be subject to men in London?"

He lowered his voice. "Time is pressing," he added. "The French plan to invade – and invade soon. When they do, our social order will disintegrate. This is our chance – our one chance – to break free of *both* Britain and France! This is our one chance to seize the power our forefathers surrendered to London!"

Raechel listened, feeling cold, as Hamish continued. The Sons of Liberty were clearly far better organised than the Viceroy suspected, particularly if they included so many aristocratic children. But she could see their point, too. America would never reach its potential when its fate was decided in London, by men who had never been to the colonies. And too many of the American aristocrats had sold out to the British Crown.

"We must claim the rights of freemen," Hamish concluded. "And for that we must fight!"

"He's an impressive speaker," Jane said. She elbowed Raechel in the side as Hamish jumped off the chair and headed over to a pair of young men. "Don't you think?"

"He is," Raechel said. She didn't need to *pretend* to admire the speech. The idea of genuine rights for women was one calculated to appeal to her – and to the other aristocratic women in the room. If she'd been able to inherit her father's money from the moment he died, she wouldn't have had to live with her aunt and uncle. "Does he mean it?"

"He means every word," Hamish said.

Raechel jumped. She had been taught to be aware of her surroundings, but Hamish had sneaked up on them without her sensing his presence. Irene would probably have slapped her, if they'd been practicing, just to remind her of the dangers. Hamish merely smiled at her, his gaze open and friendly. It was a far cry from the toff she'd met at the ball.

"I'm glad to hear that," she said, feeling an odd twinge of disquiet. "Do you really intend to give the vote to everyone?"

"Of course," Hamish said. "I believe the original revolution failed because it *didn't* give the vote to everyone. It lost because it was not firmly rooted in equality."

And I can believe as much or as little of that as I like, Raechel thought, cynically. She could understand upper-class women doing what they could to assist the poor, even though Irene had poured scorn on the concept, but not simply giving up power. *Will you be selling out your allies after the revolution?*

She looked up at him. "You're the son of one of the wealthiest men in the colonies," she said, challengingly. "Why do you want to overthrow the current order?"

"My father tamely accepts rules intended to keep us in place," Hamish said. "I could have covered this *continent* in rail lines by now, if I had the freedom to build factories and design my own engines. But father ... he is too blinded by his title to see the problems."

He cleared his throat. "But that's a question for another day," he added. "Tell me about Lady Gwen."

Raechel tried not to tense as she felt the tingle at the back of her head, once again. And Jane was standing right there ...

"I only talked to her a handful of times during the voyage," she said, picking her words carefully. A direct lie would be harder to conceal. "She caught me kissing one of the ship's officers and told me off for it."

Hamish snickered. "And why should you not kiss whoever you liked?"

"She spent most of her time with Colonel Jackson," Raechel continued, trying to convince them that she had no reason to know anything interesting. The tingle was still there. "They played a great deal of chess, when they weren't walking the deck together."

"Chess," Jane said. She sounded oddly amused. "Were they lovers?"

"I think he might have been interested in her," Raechel said. She had never had the chance to ask. "But they were never truly alone together."

Hamish nodded, slowly. "Do you think she's a decent person?"

"I think so," Raechel said.

"And yet, the only thing that gives her power is her *power*," Jane said. There was a hint of bitterness in her tone. "An accident of birth makes her equal to the men. You understand that, don't you?"

Raechel nodded. It was easy to feel the same bitterness. To be born a woman was to be born property, first of one's father and then of one's husband. It might be wrapped up in all manner of fancy words and concepts, but it boiled down to being property. And even if she managed to remain unmarried long enough to inherit in her own right, she would still have far more limitations placed on her, just for having been born female. There were only a handful of exceptions …

And all of them have to pay for their freedom, she thought. *Gwen is isolated by her power; Queen Elizabeth could never marry and died alone …*

Raechel kept a tight lock on her emotions as they bombarded her with more questions, the tingle waxing and waning as Jane monitored her reactions. They wanted to know about her family, about the politics in Britain … thankfully, she knew there was no point in concealing anything about the former and she knew little of the latter. Hamish seemed particularly interested in why the Duke of India had resigned as Prime Minister, just to lead the army into battle one final time, but Raechel knew little of the situation.

"We'll talk soon," Hamish told her, finally. "Until then, don't say a word about this meeting."

"Of course not," Raechel agreed. It was easy to make herself sound like an idiot. "Irene would throw a fit."

"And you would pay the price," Jane giggled.

Raechel nodded, then wandered the room with Jane, splitting her attention between the bubbly girl and the other attendees. They weren't just aristocrats, she realised; there were merchants, sailors and militiamen. One young man was telling another – she just happened to overhear – about leaving the city tomorrow to join the army. It took her several moments to realise he meant a *secret* army. The Sons of Liberty were clearly preparing a Swing of their very own.

She cringed, inwardly, at the thought. The *last* Swing had

caused no end of damage, even though it had been cut short by the French. Now, with British forces in disarray and the French probing the borders, an uprising would be utterly disastrous. It had to be stopped, but how?

And you feel they have a point, she told herself. The chance to be equal, to face her uncle or her future husband as an equal, was not one to disdain. *You don't need magic to be powerful* ...

"Ah," Jane said. She caught Raechel's arm. "A messenger has arrived for your chaperone, I'm afraid. It seems that the Viceroy wishes you would dance attendance upon his son."

Raechel glared. "Does *everyone* want to marry me?"

"He probably wants to keep you out of an American match," Jane said, as they turned to hurry out the door. "*That* would set the cat among the politicians."

Jane smiled, rather thinly. "If you want to leave," she added, "we can help with that."

"Thank you," Raechel said. Irene needed to know what she'd discovered, as quickly as possible. "I may need it."

Chapter Nineteen

ady Gwen," Rochester said, as Bruce showed Gwen into the War Room. "Please, take a seat. I am expecting the others shortly."

He glanced at his son. "You took your time."

"Lady Gwen needed time to get ready," Bruce said. There was a hint of amusement in his tone. "I brought her as soon as I could."

Gwen shot him a nasty look. "I had to leave the hall on an urgent matter," she said. She didn't want to talk about a rogue magician in front of several onlookers. "He waited for me to return, then brought me straight here."

"Good," Rochester said. He pointed to the table. "Please, sit down."

Gwen nodded and sat down, suspecting she knew what she was about to hear. The War Room was effectively identical to the one she'd seen in Whitehall, right down to the giant maps mounted on the walls and smaller maps scattered over the wooden table. Colonel Jackson was seated at one end, next to General Paget; he shot her a mischievous smile that had her smiling back, despite the seriousness of the situation. A man she didn't know was seated next to General Paget, his eyes closed; another man, wearing a naval uniform, sat next to him. He *had* to be Admiral Parker, Gwen decided, the commander of the American squadron. The situation was looking more and more dire with every passing second.

Bruce sat down next to her, saying nothing. Gwen cast a sidelong glance at him – she wasn't sure why he was attending, even if he *was* the Viceroy's son – but it wasn't her job to throw him out of the room. His father prowled the room until Lord Tarleton and Lord Jackson entered, then snapped out a command to the servants to serve drinks and then leave. Gwen forced herself to wait patiently, studying the other attendees while she waited. Lord Tarleton seemed deeply worried, but Lord Jackson looked like a man with a toothache. She couldn't help wondering if Lord Jackson and Colonel Jackson were related, although she knew it was probably unlikely. Jackson was a very common name.

"Gentlemen," Rochester said. "The French have finally begun their invasion."

Gwen sat upright, feeling a jolt of alarm running through the room. They'd known it was coming – they'd *all* known it was coming – but it was still a shock. Even Bruce looked surprised, and worried, before his features slipped back into an indolent mask. The war had touched America before – French and British ships had clashed in nearby waters – but now the fighting had turned serious.

Rochester picked up one of the maps and held it out. "As of the last report, the French have moved eastwards from New Orleans and are now advancing slowly north, relying on the Alabama for transport and logistical support. They are making a handful of small thrusts into Florida, but their main advance seems to be aimed at Amherst. That makes a great deal of sense, unfortunately. Amherst is our major logistical hub in the region."

"That's nearly five hundred miles, as the crow flies," General Paget said. "Even with river transport for part of the trip, their logistics are going to be thoroughly unpleasant and they have to know it."

"The French are good at long marches," Colonel Jackson offered. "And besides, it isn't as if they have a shortage of either porters or supplies."

Gwen nodded, briskly. There were hundreds of thousands of slaves in the war zone. They'd side with the French, naturally, and afterwards they'd do everything in their power to work for a French victory, knowing what would happen to them if the French lost. If all they did was carry supplies from New Orleans to the front lines – and the French would probably have established depots far closer to the expected battles – they'd make a major contribution to French firepower and mobility.

"If they take Amherst," Lord Tarleton mused, "they'll make it harder for us to undo the damage."

"Forget Amherst," Lord Jackson snarled. "What about the slaves?"

"The early reports indicate that a number of plantations have been burnt," Rochester said, shortly. "I've sent orders to the border forces to put contingency plans into operation, but ..."

"But nothing," Jackson interrupted. "Do you have any idea what the slaves will do to the *women*!"

Rochester stared him down. "I am aware of what is at stake," he said, coldly. "But panic will get us nowhere."

"This is your fault," Jackson insisted. "If you'd sent extra soldiers to the borders ..."

"They might well have been killed," General Paget said. His voice was harsh, deliberately so. "The border between us and the French is *far* too long for us to build a wall, My Lord, not when everyone from fugitive slaves to Indian bands cross at will. Our plans were always predicated on slowing the French, rather than stopping them, until we got reinforcements in place. Leaving large garrisons dotted all over the landscape would have been asking for trouble. The French would have overwhelmed them, one by one."

"And now the slaves are on the loose," Jackson insisted. "Our infrastructure lies in tatters."

Gwen felt her patience snap. Reaching out, she slapped the table hard enough to sting. "I don't see any point in fighting over something that cannot be changed," she said. "The question is how much we can preserve while waiting for reinforcements to arrive."

"Well said, Lady Gwen," Rochester said. He cleared his throat meaningfully. "General?"

General Paget took the map. "As you know, we made the decision to limit our road and rail construction past Amherst because we thought they would make French logistics easier," he said. "Our contingency plans, therefore, call for the militia and ranger troops to slow the French as much as possible, while we assemble a defence line here" – he traced a line from Amherst to the coast – "and cut the French off by sea. The sheer size of the terrain works in our favour, particularly once they start to run short on supplies. They would be forced into making an attack on Amherst itself or starving to death."

"And the slaves would die with them," Lord Tarleton said.

"That isn't a good thing," Lord Jackson snapped. "I ..."

"Enough about the slaves," Rochester said. He didn't shout, but his tone was hard enough to make Lord Jackson shut up sharply. "They are no longer a concern."

That was probably true, Gwen reasoned. And once New York realised that Lord Jackson's human property had joined the French, *Lord Jackson* was no longer likely to be a concern either. His creditors would come sniffing around, demanding repayment of any outstanding debts, while he and his wife would become social pariahs. She'd seen it happen before, in London.

"Lady Gwen," Rochester said. "Are your sorcerers ready for battle?"

Gwen honestly didn't know if she should laugh or cry. She should have told him about the rogue immediately, not waited in the hopes of speaking to him privately ...

"No," she said, flatly. She'd have a chance to talk to him after the meeting. "I have one trained Blazer and that's it. The conscripts show promise, but they need a *lot* more training and practice before they can use their powers for combat."

"You don't have the time," Rochester said. "If the French are advancing towards Amherst, they'll have magicians with them."

Gwen nodded. The French would probably need magicians to break through the defences of Amherst, unless they wished to attack over the bodies of their own dead. Hell, getting enough artillery up to force the city to surrender wouldn't be easy either. The only hope of winning quickly was to use magicians, which meant she *needed* to be there. Fighting enemy magicians was her job.

"I understand, Your Excellency," she said. "When do you want us to leave?"

"I'm assembling a force of regulars and militiamen," General Paget said. "Thankfully, we had contingency plans to seize as much rolling stock as necessary, so getting our troops down south shouldn't be *that* hard. You'll be going with the first train."

Unless the French cut the lines, Gwen thought. They'd done it during the Battle of Dorking, seemingly convinced it would keep the Duke of India from moving his forces around the battlefield. *If that happens, we're going to be in some trouble.*

She leant forward. "What happens if the French cut the lines?"

"We have repair crews attached to the trains," General Paget said. "The French would have to do a great deal of damage to keep us from sending reinforcements south."

I hope you're right, Gwen thought.

Lord Tarleton coughed. "Is there any word from London?"

"Not as yet," Rochester said. "The French Channel Fleet took a beating during the invasion, but the Prime Minister is reluctant to release regular soldiers until the safety of Britain itself can be guaranteed."

"Press him for magicians," Gwen said, bluntly. She silently tipped her hat to the French planners. Poisoning the magicians in New York had worked out like a dream. "We are critically short of magicians."

And we have at least one rogue hanging around the city, she added, silently. *Who knows what he has in mind?*

She leant back in her chair as the gentlemen discussed the plan, going over the basic details piece by piece. It looked good, Gwen thought, given the limitations on their ability to project power, but she had few illusions. They might have to hope that the Royal Navy would capture enough French possessions to exchange for any surrendered territory to the south of Amherst, assuming anyone wanted it back. But then, the south was practically a breadbasket in its own right, as well as the premier source of cotton. The economists would want to recapture it if possible.

And that means prolonging the issue of slavery, she thought, coldly. *The slaves are needed to harvest the cotton ...*

"Lady Gwen," Rochester said. "Can you be ready to depart in two days?"

"As ready as we will ever be, Your Excellency," Gwen said, shortly. A year of training would be far better, but they'd be lucky if they had time to practice once they reached Amherst. "It'll have to do."

"Good," Rochester said. "Colonel Jackson will accompany you and the magicians, along with the first reinforcements for the city. Colonel, I will be discussing certain contingency plans with you later."

"Of course, Your Excellency," Colonel Jackson said.

"General, please see to the plans," Rochester said. "Admiral Parker, have your squadrons been informed?"

"Yes, Your Excellency," Admiral Parker said. "I have given orders for them to assemble near the Potomac, where they will prepare to raid French shipping and sweep the coast of Mexico. We can also prepare transports, either to reinforce the defence lines or to land troops on the shores of New Orleans. It should give the French a nasty surprise, particularly if their advance northwards stalls."

"Good," Rochester said.

"We're ignoring the elephant in the room," Gwen said, quietly. "What about the Sons of Liberty?"

"We'll talk about that afterwards," Rochester said. "Lord Tarleton, Lord Jackson, I want you both to work on presenting *confidence* to the world. I'll be addressing the House of Lords later in the day – I want you to make it clear to everyone that we have good reason to be confident, despite the French menace. The French have threatened our shores before, but we have beaten them. Always."

"Yes, Your Excellency," Lord Tarleton said.

Beside him, Lord Jackson merely snorted. But then, Gwen thought, he didn't have *reason* to be confident. Whoever won the war, Lord Jackson was likely to lose. His slaves would either go with the French or be brutally hunted down, after the war. There was no way a rebellious slave could be allowed to live.

"Lady Gwen, stay here," Rochester concluded. "Everyone else, you know what you have to do."

Gwen watched as the men left, save for Bruce. He stayed in his seat, waiting. That was odd, Gwen thought. It was possible he was serving as his father's assistant – nepotism was alive and well in London – although the impression he presented didn't suggest he was trusted with anything important. But that could be an illusion … Irene had told her, more than once, that she'd known some very clever men who'd made a career out of looking like idiots. No one had taken them seriously until it had been far too late.

"There's another concern I didn't want to mention to the others," Rochester added, once the door was firmly closed. "General Kingsley was murdered, the night before the offensive began. The identity of the murderer remains unknown, but there are hints it might well have been one of his American subordinates."

"Damn," Gwen said. "If that's true …"

"The militia is unreliable," Rochester said.

"Maybe not," Gwen said, clinging to a wisp of hope. "If I were the French commander, I'd be trying to drive a wedge between the British and the Americans. Murdering a British officer and blaming it on the Americans would definitely make both sides reluctant to trust one another."

"We don't know," Rochester said. "I'd prefer to give Colonel Jackson a field promotion and put him in command, but that won't go down well with any of the America hands. They'd claim Jackson was another Braddock and they'd be right."

Gwen frowned. "Braddock?"

Surprisingly, it was Bruce who answered. "He was a British officer who took command of allied forces in North America, 1755, only to lead them to a disastrous defeat," he said, slowly. "Even *Washington* considered him a brave man, but dangerously ignorant of the realities of North American warfare."

"That's correct," Rochester said.

He sighed. "Lady Gwen, watch your back very carefully," he added. "I'll be sending Paget down to take command as soon as possible, but right now I have too many problems to spare him."

"I will," Gwen said. She sucked in her breath. "You also have another problem."

Rochester sighed, again. "What?"

"There's at least one rogue magician running around New York," Gwen said. "A Mover, a very well trained and *experienced* Mover."

"God damn it!" Rochester swore. "Are you sure?"

"He damaged several buildings during our brief confrontation," Gwen said, swiftly outlining what had happened. "Whoever he was, Your Excellency, he's good."

Bruce glanced at her. "Better than you?"

"He's probably had more time to practice with his lone talent," Gwen said. She didn't want to admit weakness, least of all to a young man she was starting to dislike, but there was no point in covering up the truth. "He certainly knew how to use his power to best advantage in a fight – he knew how to fight, he knew how to split his attention …"

"Isn't that a female skill?"

"He was very definitely a man," Gwen said, fighting down her irritation. "And powerful enough to be a real threat."

She looked at Rochester. "He might try to kill you, Your Excellency."

Bruce spluttered with shock. "He … he would never *dare*! This palace is heavily guarded!"

"He's a Mover," Gwen said. She had to fight the urge to reach out with her power and hold him upside down. "He can just smash his way through most of the defences."

"You can't stay here," Rochester said. He took a long breath. "If he comes for me, he comes for me."

"You can't die," Gwen insisted. "Your Excellency …"

"And we can't lose Amherst either," Rochester said. His voice was very firm. "Whoever this magician is, whatever he wants, it changes nothing. We have to stop the French from breaking into the heartlands or we'll lose most of the empire. If that means leaving me without a proper bodyguard … well, I'll take the risk."

"*Father*," Bruce said.

Gwen felt a flicker of vindictive glee, mixed with guilt and shame. Bruce didn't seem to care much for his father, but the prospect of losing him had to sting. Part of her wanted to enjoy his sudden horror; the rest of her was horrified with herself for revelling in someone's pain. Maybe Bruce only needed reality to give him a slap across the face.

"It has to be done," Rochester said. "You will accompany Lady Gwen to Amherst as my personal representative."

And get him out of the way if the rogue does come calling,

Gwen thought. Bruce looked to be in reasonable shape – he hadn't let himself go, like so many indolent aristocrats – but he was no match for a Mover. The rogue would tear him apart, probably without ever noticing what he'd done. *At least something of the Viceroy's family would survive.*

"If that is your wish, father," Bruce said, finally.

"It is," Rochester said. "Lady Gwen will take care of you, I think. Do what she says."

Gwen would have expected horror, if a boy her own age was told to obey her. But Bruce showed no visible reaction. She wondered, absently, if he was stunned by the prospect of his father being brutally murdered … or of facing the French himself. He would be brave, she was sure, but she doubted he had any real experience …

There was a knock on the door. Rochester rose to his feet. "Come!"

Gwen turned, just in time to see Irene and Raechel being ushered into the room. She stared, astonished. The Viceroy knew who they were, of course, but no one else was supposed to realise there was more than a casual connection between the three of them. Three weeks onboard a ship wouldn't automatically have made them close friends.

"As far as anyone knows, I invited them here to discuss a match between Raechel and my son," the Viceroy said, answering her unspoken question. "There is much to discuss."

"More than you know," Irene said. She sounded tired and worn. "Your Excellency, we have a vitally important report to make to you."

Chapter Twenty

s a child, Raechel had heard her father talking about meetings – some formal, some held over glasses of port – that had decided the future of the empire itself. She'd always wanted to be there, to have her voice heard as the great and the good debated what to do ... but now she *was* in a high-level meeting, and she was scared. It wasn't *she* who would be making the final decisions, such as they were, yet she thought she understood the implications. A mistake at this level would be catastrophic.

She outlined what she'd discovered as Irene had taught her, holding nothing back. Gwen's face betrayed her surprise, while both Viceroy Rochester and his son remained impassive as she listed the handful of names and faces she knew. Jane, Hamish ... the Viceroy showed a hint of surprise at the latter, but otherwise seemed unmoved. He must have suspected the younger generation for a long time, part of Raechel's mind noted. Hamish's dissatisfaction with the *status quo* would hardly be unknown to him. If his father hadn't been so important ...

"Clever of them," the Viceroy noted, when Raechel had finished. "Hiding in plain sight."

"Arrest them," Gwen urged. "If they're building an army they have to be stopped *now*."

"We don't know *everyone* involved in the conspiracy," the Viceroy pointed out. "If we arrest the people we *do* know, we might well trigger an uprising before we had a chance to interrogate the prisoners and identify the remaining Sons. Even if we did ..."

He sucked in his breath. "The militia is unreliable," he

added. "I'd bet good money that the Sons obtained their weapons from the militia in the first place. If we declare martial law and put troops on the streets, we might find that we were merely reinforcing the Sons."

"Use the regulars," Gwen said.

"The regulars are needed in Amherst," the Viceroy snapped. "Whichever way we jump, Lady Gwen, we're going to take a beating."

"Maybe not," Irene said. Her voice was very composed. "The Sons clearly aren't ready to move, Your Excellency. If they were, they wouldn't be risking exposure by recruiting more soldiers and assistants from New York. They may well have only a few thousand men under their banner."

"They'd want to ensure they could trust their recruits too," Gwen added. "Vetting them all, even with the aid of a Talker, could take months."

She looked down at the map. "The French might well be involved too," she warned. "They certainly played a major role in assisting the Swing. Maybe that was just a warm-up for *this*."

"An uprising on the streets of New York, if it succeeded, would tear the colonies apart," the Viceroy said. "And with the French pressing up from the south ... at best, we'd be refighting the revolution at the worst possible time. Losing the naval bases along the coastline alone would cripple our ability to hold territory and mount counterattacks."

"Which may well be what the French have in mind," Gwen said. "And they'd have the added advantage of ensuring the Sons take the brunt of the fighting. Losing their army would make it harder for the Sons to resist French rule."

Raechel looked at her. "You think the French want to rule America?"

Gwen shrugged. "America has great promise," she said. "And whoever controls the continent is going to be in a very strong position for future expansion. The French may be hoping that we and the Sons destroy each other."

She looked back at the Viceroy. "Does this make a difference to the original plan?"

"No," the Viceroy said. "You have to accompany the army to Amherst."

"Yes, Your Excellency," Gwen said.

Raechel swallowed. She'd known that Gwen had no hesitation in flying into danger, but the thought of losing her only real friend was terrifying. Gwen ... was one of the few people she could talk to, even if she *was* the Royal Sorceress. And yet, if there were good reasons for Gwen to go south, she'd go south.

"We also need to root out the Sons," Irene said. "Raechel, I propose that you accept Jane's offer of escape from" – her lips quirked – "my clutches."

The Viceroy frowned. "You'd think she'd be more useful to them in New York."

"I don't think so, Your Excellency," Irene said. "Raechel is a wealthy heiress, but she has no access to that money until she turns twenty-five – unless, of course, she gets married while she's over here. And if she did, her husband might not be friendly to the Sons. It's amazing how sudden wealth can change a man's character. Right now, she isn't even a pawn on the gaming board."

"True," Gwen agreed, reluctantly.

Raechel cursed under her breath. Irene was right, of course. Wealthy or not, as long as she had no access to her wealth no one would pay any attention to her. Even her suitors would be more interested in pleasing Irene than herself. Absently, she wondered just how many quiet offers of future favours had been made to Irene, while she'd been at the meeting. A chaperone stood to gain a great deal from organising a wedding to suit herself.

And then it hit her. She was going to go underground. She was going to leave the comforts and safety of New York and go ... where? She was going to be in a place where the slightest slip would get her killed, or worse. And Irene, her mentor, was going to be miles away, at best. She might have no way to slip out and send a message to New York ...

She fought to control her emotions, refusing to allow herself to slip, even as her heartbeat thundered so loudly that she was sure the entire room could hear it. As dangerous as the prospect of going undercover was, it was also her chance to prove herself. She could convince everyone, once and for all, that she was more than just a pretty face – and a name, with a sizable legacy attached. No one would ever be able to dismiss her again.

"Raechel," Gwen said. It took Raechel a moment to realise she'd missed part of the conversation. "Raechel, do you want to do this?"

Raechel looked down at her pale hands. On one hand, it was her duty; *someone* needed to infiltrate the Sons of Liberty and she was in the best place to get into their system. But on the other hand ... she'd faced danger before, in Russia, yet this was worse. Irene had told her what could happen to spies, who got caught. The Sons wouldn't hesitate to cut her throat if they saw her as a potential threat ...

"Yes," she said, firmly. "I do."

"We'll stage an incident," Irene said, briskly. "Something that will give you a motive to escape. Jane will, I'm sure, be willing to help you."

"She said as much," Raechel said.

The Viceroy coughed. "Why?"

Raechel winced. He was right. If she'd had access to her money, the Sons would have good reason to want to help, but right now ... she was useless. A man, at least, might make another soldier, someone to carry weapons and fight for the cause. But what good was *she* when her experience of life outside England was so limited? The whole affair might come to an end when Jane refused to help her ...

"Because they're *young*," Gwen said. Raechel glanced at her in surprise. "Hamish Tarleton is in his early twenties, I believe, Jane isn't any older than Raechel or me. By freeing Raechel from her chaperone, they're striking a blow against a social structure they have come to hate."

"I hope you're right," the Viceroy said.

He rose to his feet. "You may make use of one of the meeting rooms, if you wish," he said, flatly. "I have a speech to write."

Gwen nodded. "Raechel, we'll talk privately, if you don't mind."

Raechel glanced at Irene, then nodded. Bruce led them down the corridor to a small chamber, then bowed once and retreated. Raechel couldn't help noticing that Gwen's eyes followed him until he was out of sight, her expression unreadable. It was unlikely Gwen was *interested* in him, she told herself, but Bruce *was* the Viceroy's son. She needed to stay on reasonably good terms with him, at least as long as his father was in office.

"I'll wait outside," Irene said. "Call me when you're ready to discuss the plan."

Raechel nodded, then followed Gwen into the room. It was smaller than she'd realised, barely large enough for a couple of armchairs and a drinks cabinet. She eyed the bottles hopefully, remembering pleasant days at the club when she'd experimented with fancy liqueurs from France, then reminded herself – rather firmly – that drinking herself silly was a very bad idea. Gwen took one of the armchairs and motioned to the other, inviting Raechel to sit. Raechel nodded and sat down.

Gwen looked older, Raechel noted, although she wasn't quite sure why she had that impression. Her blonde hair had grown a little longer since they'd first met – her lips twitched as she recalled her aunt's sardonic remarks about young unmarried girls who cut their hair too short – and her eyes were as bright as ever, but there was something in the way she held herself that suggested she was tired. She hadn't had any real chance for a break, Raechel recalled; she'd come back from Russia and plunged straight into war. Even the voyage hadn't really been relaxing for her …

"You don't have to do this," Gwen said. "If you don't want to go, you don't have to."

"I *need* to do it," Raechel said. "This is my only chance to prove myself."

Gwen's lips quirked into a humourless smile. "There were plenty of times in my life when I wanted men to think of me as more than a foolish female," she said. "And half the time I did it by acting foolishly."

"This isn't foolish," Raechel said. "Gwen, if the Sons launch an uprising now, British North America is *finished*."

"You won't have any magic," Gwen warned. "If you get caught …"

"I know the risks," Raechel said. Some of Irene's stories had been dark enough to nearly turn her hair white. "Do you have any better plan?"

"No," Gwen said. "But if Jane's a Talker, the rogue magician I encountered today might be a Son too. And you can't count on the Sons following the rules."

"I know," Raechel said, frostily. She'd had quite enough of her family treating her as a delicate little flower. She wasn't going to take it from Gwen too … although, if she was forced to be honest, she hadn't made exactly the best impression when they'd first met. "Can I ask a different question?"

"Of course," Gwen said.

Raechel hesitated, trying to get her thoughts in order. "Are you sure we're on the right side?"

Gwen's eyes hardened. "Explain yourself!"

"They talked about equal rights for everyone," Raechel said. She tapped the space between her breasts meaningfully. "You only have power because of your magic – and because you're unique. I don't have any power at all, because I was born female. If I'd had a brother, he would be spending the family inheritance right now. How many women were sent into exile, over here, for doing something that would be feted if it had been done by a man?"

There was a long, chilling pause. "I think I understand, finally, how Master Thomas must have felt," Gwen said. She sounded irked by the realisation. "I asked him the same question."

"And he said?"

"He said that anarchists want to tear down the system," Gwen said. "They don't realise that they need to put something in its place. Even during the civil wars, Parliament had an alternate governing structure … maybe that's why Parliament won."

She sucked in her breath. "Anyone can point out problems, Raechel," she added. "And I agree with you. It isn't fair that a woman can be punished for something that isn't considered a crime if done by a man. But actually *tackling* those problems is a great deal harder. Jack had no plan for creating a government of his own. I wonder if the Sons of Liberty have a plan themselves.

"And if they don't, they might as well give the colonies to the French."

"They wouldn't want that," Raechel protested.

"I'm pretty sure the Highlanders didn't want to have their clans broken up and their lands confiscated, when they rose in support of the Young Pretender," Gwen snapped. Her voice grew louder. "That didn't stop it from happening! They launched an uprising without the weapons or popular support they needed to actually win. Getting all the way to Derby was a minor miracle in its own right, but it cost them *everything*.

"They're *young*; young and idealistic. Half of them don't have the slightest idea what it takes to run the government. And I'd bet that many of their supporters are so poor and desperate that they have nowhere else to go. But that doesn't mean they're in the right! I won't say the empire is perfect, because it isn't, yet it's a damn sight better than living under the French king."

"And you're the one who wants to have servants treated like people," Raechel said, before she could stop herself. "The Sons might do it."

"Or they might create a tyranny of their own," Gwen warned. "There's no government structure in place for them, not now. Building one in the middle of a war won't be easy."

She met Raechel's eyes. "I understand how you feel," she said, her voice softening. "But the Sons cannot be allowed to doom us all."

Raechel lowered her gaze. "Is it wrong to be idealistic?"

"No," Gwen said. "But it *is* wrong to be so idealistic that it blinds you to reality."

She sighed. "Maybe the Viceroy will make concessions," she added. "But right now, we have to regard the Sons as a potential threat, an enemy within. Anything you can dig up will be very helpful."

"I understand," Raechel said, reluctantly. "And I know my duty."

Gwen met her eyes. "It's never easy to force the head to rule the heart," she admitted. "But the head *must* rule."

Raechel scowled as Gwen reached out with her magic and opened the door, inviting Irene into the room. Men had been saying that women were ruled by their emotions since time out of mind, insisting that women were ill-fitted for government because they couldn't think logically. But, in her experience, men were ruled by their emotions too. It was just a different set of emotions, emotions that could be just as destructive to men as they were to women. Very few people could think logically and reasonably on a consistent basis.

And even when they do, she thought, recalling Irene's words, *they may be reasoning from false assumptions*.

"I wish you luck," Gwen said. She rose. "I'll see you afterwards, I hope. Right now, I have to get back to the hall."

"We'll see each other after the war," Raechel promised. "And I won't let you down."

She watched Gwen leave, then looked at Irene. "I'm ready."

"Very good," Irene said. "Do you think Jane had any reason to suspect you?"

"She would have thrown me out, if she had," Raechel said. She *hoped* that was the case. "I kept my thoughts under careful control."

"Lady Campbell was offering me a small fortune for your hand in marriage," Irene said, wryly. "Her son is in dire need of a wife."

Raechel had to think for a long moment. Lady Campbell's husband was an industrialist, if she recalled correctly, one who might well have overextended himself. She couldn't remember anything about the son. He hadn't danced with her at the ball, unless he'd been so unmemorable she'd forgotten him. It was quite possible.

"Lord Campbell is a staunch loyalist and his son was educated in England," Irene continued, seemingly unaware of Raechel's thoughts. "He is unlikely to have anything to do with the Sons of Liberty. In any case, Lord Campbell still makes his decisions for him."

"Poor man," Raechel said, sarcastically. "I would feel sorrier for him if every woman didn't have the same problem."

"Quite," Irene agreed. "Lady Campbell has good reason to want to bribe me, naturally. I shall inform her that I have not only accepted her offer, but have talked your guardians into accepting it too. You will be *officially* informed of this in a small party, which we shall hold in three days or so. At this point, you'll throw a fit and escape."

She stopped, waiting.

Raechel thought fast. "And the Sons would have good reason to want to take me in," she said, finally. Irene *liked* it when she used her brain, unlike her aunt and uncle. "They won't want the match to go ahead."

"Of course not," Irene said. She gave Raechel a mischievous smile. "Your family's resources would end up in the hands of a known loyalist. It gives them some incentive to hide you."

"Good plan," Raechel said.

Her blood was suddenly very cold. If Irene had been a *genuine* unscrupulous chaperone, she could sell Raechel to the highest bidder and no one would give a damn. Her guardians would have no reason to think that anything was wrong, not if Irene was telling them how wonderful Raechel's new family was. They'd sign the papers in London without ever meeting their new kin.

"It happens," Irene said, quietly. "More often than you might think, too."

Raechel felt her temper flare. "Stop reading my mind!"

"I'm not the mind-reader you need to worry about," Irene told her, sharply. Her voice hardened as she rose. "And if Jane gets one *hint* that this is all a put-up job, *you* will wind up dead!"

Chapter Twenty-One

ou're joking!"

"I wish I was," Gwen said. She'd called Wayne into her office as soon as she returned to the hall. "The French have launched their invasion, they're probing north towards Amherst and we have to be in place to join the defenders."

"We're not ready, My Lady," Wayne said. He still sounded stunned. Apart from her, he was the only British combat sorcerer in America – and he'd had a *year* of training before winning his badge. "We're nowhere *near* ready."

"I know," Gwen said. "But His Excellency hasn't offered us a choice."

She scowled at the map, hanging from the wall. It was a minimum of five days from New York to Amherst, unless the lines were cut so badly they couldn't be repaired on the fly – and if *that* happened, she had no idea how long it would take them to reach their destination or if they would arrive in time to make a difference. Indeed, given just how badly the demands of war had snarled up Britain's far more developed railway lines, she rather suspected it would be a *long* time before the reinforcements reached Amherst.

"We're meant to be leaving in two days," she said. "We'll do as much training as we can in that time, then practice as best we can on the trains."

"It won't be enough," Wayne said. "My Lady, this is not a reliable force."

"I know," Gwen said. She assumed Lord Mycroft had read her messages, but even if he dispatched reinforcements instantly it would still be at least three weeks before they reached New York. Longer, perhaps, if they reached New

York at all. The French had an extremely good motive to attack convoys making their way across the Atlantic. "But it's the best we're going to get."

She scowled to herself. *Jane* was a Talker ... and there was a rogue magician out there, a magician with far better training than anyone else she'd met outside Cavendish Hall. If that magician was American, he should be fighting alongside her, not plotting an uprising at the worst possible time. She wondered, briefly, if she could get away with conscripting Jane before deciding it would be pointless. Talking was a useful skill, but not during a battle.

"The servants can close up the hall once we're gone," she added. She'd have to do something about the classified documents, knowing that no one could be trusted to protect them. There wasn't much for French spies to steal, but what there was could cause real problems in the wrong hands. "Hopefully, we'll come back to New York after the war and take possession."

"Yes, My Lady," Wayne said. His tone suggested he doubted it very much. "We may well be outmatched and outnumbered."

"Yes, we may," Gwen said. "But British forces have been outmatched and outnumbered before and still prevailed."

"Only by the Sikhs," Wayne warned her. "And the Sikhs would have won if they hadn't fallen prey to infighting at the worst possible time."

Just like us now, Gwen thought. *Infighting between the Viceroy and the Sons might give the French an easy victory.*

"But we still won," she said, out loud. "And the French may only have committed a handful of magicians to America. They needed to concentrate on invading Britain."

The next two days passed quickly, far too quickly. Gwen worked hard to train the magicians, showing Fife how to use his powers more creatively while pushing Harry and Vernon into expanding their abilities. Neither of them learnt how to fly, even though it was a fairly easy trick. Gwen had a private suspicion that they saw their powers as extensions of their fists, not something separate from the remainder of their bodies. They could pick her up and hurl her around the battlefield, but carrying themselves was beyond their abilities.

At least their punches are strong, she thought, after picking herself up from the grass. *They will be formidable if they're given enough time to train.*

She'd half-expected a delayed departure, but Colonel Jackson arrived on the selected date to inform her that the trains were ready. Gwen had already ensured that the seven magicians had an excellent dinner; she ordered Wayne to get them into the carriages while she gave the servants their final orders. She'd had to burn a number of papers, just to make sure they stayed out of enemy hands, but the remainder of the hall wouldn't help anyone, if it were to be captured. There had been no sign of the rogue magician, which worried her. Had he been a French spy? Or was he biding his time until Gwen left the city?

"You've done well," Jackson said, as she joined him in the final carriage. "I've seen much less promising material."

"It's the wages," Gwen said, cynically. She'd already paid the six conscripts more than enough money to have a decent life after the war, even if they never worked again. She had a feeling most of it would be spent on drink, but she didn't care as long as it happened after the war was over. "And they are not ready to face trained magicians."

Jackson rapped on the panelling, ordering the driver to start moving, then looked at her. "I *have* seen less promising material," he assured her. "They may have their problems, but they'll do better than some of the others I've seen."

"I hope you're right," Gwen said. Normally, she had little to do with selection. The RSC took almost every magician who applied, although not all of them passed the final tests and became sorcerers. "I don't even know if half of them are loyal!"

"There's a lot of that going around," Jackson said. "My ... *very* ... distant relative is in deep ... ah ... trouble."

Gwen smiled. "How bad is it?"

Jackson shrugged. "The French clearly had a working plan to destroy most of the plantations," he said. "Many slaves have already revolted or fled; the remainder have been marched away from the plantations or simply massacred. Hundreds of plantations and minor farmsteads are on fire. It will take generations to recover, if it ever does.

"As for the bulk of the French army, it is still proceeding slowly towards Amherst," he added, after a moment. "They *are* being slowed down by the pickets, so they may *just* starve to death before they arrive."

Gwen *looked* at him. "Do you believe that will happen?"

"I would be astonished," Jackson admitted. "The French are masters at supporting an army in the field, Lady Gwen, and there are plenty of foodstuffs in the vicinity. Thanks to the slave revolts, it will be hard for us to get *everything* out of their way before it's far too late."

"And so the French may be able to lay siege to the city, rather than trying to take it by storm," Gwen said.

"Precisely," Jackson said. "And with thousands of refugees already heading *into* the city, food supplies are likely to get short rather quickly."

Gwen shuddered. She'd seen people on the brink of starvation in Russia ... and she'd heard stories from the last bout of European warfare. More people had been killed by starvation or disease than in fighting, although countless peasants had been robbed, raped and murdered by one side or the other. Just burning a farm to the ground could condemn an entire community to die. Hundreds of thousands of starving people, crammed into a city ... it didn't bear thinking about.

The carriage rattled to a halt before she could think of something to say. Jackson opened the hatch, revealing a long steam train attached to a line of coaches that stretched off into the distance. Some were clearly passenger coaches, like the London-Brighton express that some of her sorcerers took every weekend; others were designed for cattle or freight. Hundreds of porters worked frantically, loading the freight trucks with supplies for the front, while sergeants barked orders, marching red-coated soldiers onto the trains. The scene looked as chaotic as anything she'd seen in London, before the Battle of Dorking.

Fewer trains, she thought. Bridging the river hadn't been *that* much of a challenge, after British engineers had bridged hundreds of coastal rivers in Britain, but America was just so much *bigger*. Some parts of the colonies had only one rail line, if they were lucky enough to have one in the first place.

And that means our logistics will get harder.

"We should have gone by sea," Jackson muttered, "but there are too many complications."

"French raiders," Gwen muttered back. She could have fought to defend the convoy, but the French probably knew what had happened to their first raiding force. It had been talked about endlessly in New York. "Or is there another problem?"

"Mines," Jackson said. "A warship hit one last night and went down with all hands. The French have been busy."

Gwen cursed under her breath as Wayne escorted the sorcerers to their carriage. The French had *definitely* been busy. They knew just how strong the Royal Navy was, so they were working hard to find ways to offset Britain's advantages. Ironclad warships, submarines, mines ... each new innovation changed the face of warfare, constantly giving Britain's admirals new problems to worry about. Even *basic* mines could do a great deal of damage if they scored a hit ... and if they didn't, they'd still give the admirals fits. The mere *threat* of a minefield would be enough to keep a mighty fleet out of action.

Jackson raised his voice. "You've all been assigned to Coach Two," he said. "There are beds and supplies inside, suitable for your ranks."

"Thank you," Gwen said. "Where will you be?"

"Coach One," Jackson said. "You are welcome to join me for dinner, if you like."

Gwen smiled, then turned to look at the coaches. It looked, very much, as though the army had commandeered a set of luxury coaches for the use of the senior staff. Gwen had ridden in a couple, after she'd become the Royal Sorceress, and she had to admit they were quite fancy, even though the lower-class passengers were packed in like cattle. She hoped that the small army of servants had been left behind, no matter how much the officers wanted to enjoy themselves on the trip. It wouldn't impress any of the common soldiers if their superiors rode in luxury.

And it won't impress the Duke of India either, she thought, as she followed Wayne into the coach. The sleeping berths were larger than she'd expected and the beds more comfortable, although each tiny compartment barely had enough room to swing a cat. *He was fond of insisting that officers should march, eat and sleep with the men.*

"There isn't anything to do here," Vernon protested, loudly. "Are we meant to sleep for five days?"

"Be grateful if you can," Wayne said, before Gwen could say a word. "When you go on campaign, sleep is a priceless luxury."

Gwen agreed, wholeheartedly. She'd slept in worse places, particularly during the trip to Russia, but the coaches would grow claustrophobic over the coming days. Wayne had packed a number of books, at her suggestion, yet she had no idea how many of her half-trained sorcerers could actually *read*. It wasn't a fashionable skill in far too many places. Perhaps they could spend some of the time actually *teaching* the magicians how to read. She'd helped Olivia, after all.

She felt a stab of guilt as she recalled how they'd slowly fallen out of that habit, as the paperwork and other demands of her office had mounted up. And then Olivia had been kidnapped ...

"Settle down here," Wayne added. "We'll see what else we can do on the trip, once we're on the way."

Gwen nodded, then hurried back to her tiny cabin. Someone had clearly put *some* thought into her requirements – she needed a private room – but she knew she'd go crazy if she had to spend an entire week in the compartment. Her bag was already on the bed, waiting for her, while the remainder of her supplies were being loaded towards the rear of the train. She had to smile at the thought of just what her mother would say, if she saw how little Gwen was actually taking to war. If she was going to stay at a friend's, for the night, Lady Mary took at least two trunks, crammed with clothes.

There's no room for dresses on a battlefield, Gwen thought. It was an amusing idea – she'd seen far too many newspaper drawings of her defeating the French, wearing a ballroom gown – but any halfway decent dress would be in rags before the battle was done. *And the clothes I wear can be worn time and time again without needing a wash.*

Her lips quirked at the thought of what her mother would say to *that*, then she looked up as she heard another carriage canter up to the open door. Bruce Rochester jumped out, landing with surprising agility for someone so indolent, and waved cheerfully to her. Gwen felt a flicker of irritation, which she rapidly suppressed. It was easy to understand why the Viceroy wanted his son out of the city, but did *she* have to take him? She was not a nanny.

And he wouldn't listen to me if I was, she added, coldly. David had been a right little terror to his governess, if Lady Mary was to be believed. Gwen had problems accepting it – her brother had always struck her as a bit of a stuffed shirt – but he *had* been a young man once upon a time. *Bruce might rebel against me just because he can.*

Shaking her head, she watched as Bruce stepped into the coach. His two servants – who wouldn't be joining him in his cabin, she rather suspected – were unloading several trunks, each one seemingly heavy. Gwen rolled her eyes in irritation – Bruce seemed intent on carrying as much clothing as Lady Mary – and intercepted him before he could walk into the main compartment. Wayne had started a game of cards to keep the other magicians occupied.

"We need to talk," she snapped. Behind him, his servants were carrying his trunks towards the rear of the train. *"Now."*

Bruce blinked at her, owlishly. She wondered, in a fit of dark amusement, if he were hungover. She knew more than she wanted to know about the late night habits of young men, particularly if they were leaving the city and going to war the following morning. No doubt Bruce had spent the evening with a prostitute, if he hadn't been able to convince one of the aristocratic girls to sleep with him. Telling her that he was off to war would probably be enough, Gwen suspected. She knew sorcerers who'd got young women into trouble through using that exact line.

She pulled him into the next compartment, cursing the requirements of decency under her breath. There was little true privacy on the train – and even if there had been, being alone with him would have been used against her at some later date. But she needed to talk with him privately or else it would just cause more problems.

"I don't know what your father thinks you can do here," she said, pitching her voice as low as she could. "We're going to war. Do you do anything remotely warlike?"

"I shoot," Bruce said. He sounded mildly offended by her words. "I'm quite a good shot."

"Glad to hear it," Gwen said. Some of the best British snipers were aristocrats who had been shooting birds since they were very young, although that hadn't saved them from gruesome fates when they were overrun and captured by enemy soldiers. "You'll have your chance to take pot-shots at French soldiers soon."

She drew in her breath, wondering if she dared try to Charm him. It would make life so much easier, but the Viceroy would explode with rage when – if – he found out. After what she'd already done, to Major Shaw, it would destroy her career …

"Understand this," she said. "I am in charge of the sorcerers. You are just an observer, nothing more. If you try to interfere with my duties, I will tie you up and feed you bread and water until I can ship you back to your father. If I hear one word about you meddling in any way, I'll throw you to the French personally. Stay out of the way!"

"I can always stay here," Bruce said. He didn't seem particularly concerned by her threats, she noted. He probably thought they were empty. "Father wouldn't mind, I am sure."

"I'm not," Gwen said. She glared at him, willing the young fool to understand. "There's a rogue magician on the loose, you idiot! He could kill you as easily as you could stamp on a spider."

"I can defend myself," Bruce said. His hand dropped to his belt, revealing a fancy pistol half-hidden in the frills. "I'm armed …"

"And a Mover could deflect the bullets with ease." Gwen said. She resisted the urge, barely, to shake him with her magic, just to show him what a Mover could do. "There will be no further warnings. If you cause me any problems, you'll spend the rest of the trip in irons."

She glared at him one final time, then turned and strode back to her cabin as a whistle blew loudly. The train lurched to life seconds later, dull shudders running through the coach as the engine started to haul the convoy out of the station.

Gwen felt a thrill of excitement, mixed with fear. They were finally on their way south …

And when we get there, she thought, *we might find that we have arrived too late*.

Chapter Twenty-Two

aechel felt sick.

She stood naked in front of the mirror, recalling everything Irene had said over the last four days. If she were exposed as a spy, she would be unlikely to survive. Irene had gone into graphic detail of *precisely* what she could expect, from a quick death to slow torture and rape, perhaps even brainwashing. If the Sons of Liberty had a Charmer, as well as a Mover and a Talker, Raechel might find herself twisted into their servant. The agreements that protected prisoners of war, such as they were, didn't apply to spies.

Irene had already sent out the invitations, she knew. Society madams like Lady Sofia had probably already guessed what they meant, particularly as Irene – in Raechel's name – had declined a number of invitations over the last two days. If it had been real, she knew, the countdown to the end of her unmarried life would have already begun. Instead, she felt sick with worry and fear. Irene could play a role effortlessly, on stage, but Raechel wasn't so sure she herself could be a rebel for weeks or months without slipping.

"That's because you are a noblewoman," Irene had said, when she'd admitted her fears to her mentor. "You're not really *acting*."

She studied her body for a long moment. Irene's little exercises had expanded her muscles, although she was nowhere near as muscular as the washerwoman who cleaned their clothes or the cook who produced their food. She'd shaved everywhere below the neck, choosing to run the risk of being branded a scarlet woman, and washed herself thoroughly. Bracing herself, she opened the wardrobe and pulled out her costume. The dress looked no different from any of the countless others she had worn, over the years, but it had been carefully tailored to allow her to move freely. She pulled on her underwear, remembering all the times that she'd allowed a man to reach under her clothes and into her privates, then donned the dress and checked her appearance in the mirror. The blue dress looked a little odd, set against her hair, but Irene had assured her that unfamiliarity was good. If she got too comfortable, all hell was likely to break loose.

And concentrate on keeping the mental layers in place, she reminded herself. It was odd – she had to both believe her own lies and at the same time recognise that they *were* lies – but she thought she understood it. Getting caught up in one's role was a very definite advantage when building a mental shield. *Jane cannot be allowed to see below the illusions.*

There was a knock at the door. Raechel allowed herself a little twirl, admiring how the material shimmered around her, then turned and opened the door. Irene was standing there, her face impassive. The long dress she wore was designed to suggest both wealth and power, she'd insisted, although it was surprisingly understated. Raechel couldn't help thinking that it was the kind of dress that would be worn by a middleman, but she had a feeling that was the point. Irene *was* a middleman as far as her marriage was concerned.

"You look decent," Irene said, finally. "This is pretty much your last chance to back out."

"I'm doing it," Raechel said. Why did everyone seem intent on giving her chances to change her mind? She knew the dangers – her heart was thumping madly, no matter how hard she tried to calm herself – but she'd accepted them. "It isn't as if I'm *going* to be engaged to Bryon Campbell, is it?"

"We could always claim it was just a small tea party," Irene said, wryly.

She met Raechel's eyes for a long moment, testing her shields one final time. Raechel held them firmly in place, concentrating on projecting the impression she wanted – needed – to be seen. Irene nodded slowly, then turned and led the way down the stairs. The servants had spent the entire morning getting the parlour ready for the party, piling up enough cakes and teapots to give Lady Sofia a heart attack. Raechel felt oddly calm, as she sat down and rested her hands in her lap. The die was quite definitely cast.

"I'll follow you as soon as I can," Irene said. "But remember everything I told you. Do *not* assume there will be any help when you need it."

Raechel nodded.

There was a loud knock at the door. The maid opened it, her voice echoing down the corridor. Raechel heard Lady Sofia bossing the maid around, long before she stepped into the parlour and kissed Irene on both cheeks. She was followed by a young girl Raechel didn't recognise, a girl who had to be no older than ten. Raechel couldn't help thinking that she was surprisingly young to be introduced to the *ton*.

"My sister's child, sent up from Philadelphia," Lady Sofia said, by way of introduction. "I'm showing the poor girl around New York while we wait for news."

Raechel hid her amusement with an effort. The French were still hundreds of miles from Amherst, let alone Philadelphia. Sending the poor girl to New York was rather like tossing her into the fire, when she wasn't even in the frying pan! It hadn't escaped her notice, either, that Lady Sofia had neglected to *introduce* the girl. Clearly, her sister had married beneath her and Lady Sofia had never forgiven it.

She pushed the thought aside as several other guests arrived in quick succession. Lady Summer, with her daughter; Lady Campbell, looking pleased; Lady Seymour, followed by Jane and two younger girls who made a beeline for the pastry table. Jane met Raechel's eyes, briefly; Raechel felt, yet again, a faint tingle at the back of her mind. She allowed her tension to rise, very briefly, as Lady Summer was shown into the room. The heavyset woman might have been a loyalist, but she fitted in well. But then, most of the older generation were loyalists.

And Jane will have felt my tension, Raechel thought, as the maids began to serve tea. *She knows what it must mean.*

"My husband has gone to war," Lady Ford said. "I'm quite worried about him."

"There's no reason to worry," Lady Summer said. "The

French may have caused a great deal of damage, but they will be driven back to New Orleans with ease, once the redcoats get there."

Raechel concealed her amusement with an effort as the conversation flowed backwards and forwards. The women all seemed strikingly complacent, even though they had to have seen the troops surrounding the Viceregal Palace and warships prowling in the waters below Manhattan. None of them seemed to seriously believe that the French could reach New York, even though the British redcoats had had no trouble storming the city from the waters and putting an end to the revolution. She could only hope that they were right.

And Jane is just sitting here, listening, she thought, grimly. *Anything these ladies know, the Sons of Liberty will know too.*

"I have an announcement to make," Irene said. Her calm statement caused silence to fall like a thunderclap. They'd *all* known the true purpose of this tea party, whatever else might be discussed before reaching the *real* business. "As you know, my charge" – she nodded at Raechel – "came here to find a suitable husband."

Raechel froze. It was easy to pretend to feel fear. She knew how she would have felt if everything had been *real*. This was the moment when she was passed from one family to the other, as if she was nothing more than property. Jane gave her a sharp glance as the older women smiled, their kind expressions hiding their rapid calculations. Whoever married Raechel would have access to the Slater fortune, as well as ties to several of the most prominent families in England. It would shift the balance of power in the *ton*.

"A number of offers have been made," Irene continued, drawing the moment out as long as possible. "I sent messages home to her guardians, outlining the very best of the offers, as well as *my* impressions of the whole affair. They have finally consented to allow her to accept one of those offers."

Raechel forced herself to keep feeling fear, as well as a nameless dread. She didn't even know *who* had been making offers, let alone which offer had been accepted. A boy her age, or a year or two either way ... or a gentleman so old she could be his granddaughter? It was quite possible …

"It gives me great pleasure to say that Raechel Slater-Standish will marry Bryon Campbell," Irene concluded. "The engagement will be formally announced later today and, after a suitable contract has been drawn up, the date of the wedding will be set."

"No," Raechel said. It was terrifyingly easy to lose herself in the pretence. Panic bubbled along the edges of her mind, tearing at her rationality. "He's too old! I won't marry him!"

Lady Campbell coughed, loudly. "I beg your pardon?"

"I won't marry him," Raechel stammered. Bryon Campbell was ten years her senior. That might not have been a problem – she could have been engaged to a man older than her father or uncle – but who in their right mind would want Lady Campbell as a mother-in-law? "I don't even know him."

"Young lady," Irene said, warningly. "You are making a scene!"

"I *won't* marry him," Raechel repeated. She rose. "I won't!"

"The decision has been made," Irene told her. She played her role well. "And your guardians have already given their consent."

"They just want my money," Raechel shouted. Tears – real tears – were streaming down her face. "They just want …"

Irene rose in one smooth motion, caught her arm and span her around, landing a sharp smack on Raechel's bottom. Raechel yelped, in pain and shock that was only half-feigned. No one would have batted an eyelash if Irene had beaten her, but doing it in public was unusual. It was a tacit admission that she couldn't keep the younger girl under control.

"Go up to your room," she ordered, holding Raechel's wrist tight enough to hurt. It was easy to feel apprehension, after hearing the same thing from her aunt far too many times. "I expect you to be ready when I come."

Raechel fled, blasting thoughts of shame and fear – and grim determination – into the ether. If Jane was anything like as capable as Irene, she might have been leaning *away* from Raechel, her senses overwhelmed by the torrent of emotion. But she'd pick up on Raechel's desire to flee, to just get *away* from her chaperone. And after the announcement of who Raechel would marry, she'd have a very good motive to help.

"I apologise for my charge's behaviour," Irene said, her voice carrying along the corridor as Raechel kept moving. "Please rest assured that she *will* be marrying Bryon Campbell."

Maybe not, Raechel thought. Instead of running upstairs, she grabbed her cloak and made her way to the back door. *They might think I'd be a bad influence on the poor boy.*

She smirked at the thought, then sobered. There was a *lot* of money at stake, after all, as well as a great deal of influence. She doubted Bryon would be given any more of a choice than she had herself, if the match had been real. But then, he had far more options to enjoy life than his wife would … pushing the thought aside, she hurried out of the backdoor and past a handful of coaches. If everything went according to plan, Irene would have dismissed the younger girls – including Jane – while keeping the adults in the parlour. Jane should be able to slip out very quickly …

Too many moving parts in this plan, Raechel told herself, as she hastily rebuilt her mental layers. Jane *had* to believe she was running from an arranged marriage – and even though she might have *wanted* to believe it, she would still be careful. *And it could all fall apart if I say the wrong thing at the wrong time.*

She glanced from carriage to carriage, silently praying that nothing would go wrong, then stopped outside the Seymour carriage. The coat of arms on the side was easy to recognise; Irene had told her, only partly in jest, that men would spend fortunes just to have the right to claim a coat of arms for themselves. She passed the coachman a shilling, explained she was travelling home with Jane and climbed into the vehicle. The driver would have made more of a fuss, she was sure, if there had been anything worth stealing in the cab.

It was nearly ten minutes before the door opened, revealing Jane. Her eyes widened slightly as she saw Raechel, but she made no move to have her thrown out of the carriage. Instead, she nodded shortly and called out a command to the driver, before sitting down, facing Raechel. The carriage rocked to life, heading away from the building. Raechel couldn't help a twinge of regret and fear, which she forced down savagely. She was committed.

"So," Jane said. She sounded serious, all of a sudden. "You don't want to marry Bryon, do you?"

"No," Raechel said. She felt the tingle again and concentrated on her mental layers, silently grateful that Irene had made her work so hard on building her defences. "He's not who I want to marry. I don't want to marry anyone."

She met Jane's eyes, pleadingly. "And you said you could help."

"We can, yes," Jane said. "Do you have any access to your legacy?"

"No," Raechel said, truthfully. The Sons gained, didn't they, from keeping her money out of loyalist hands? "We have some money in the funds, but I have no access to it. Irene" – she projected a mixture of irritation and fear – "kept the key solidly in her name. I won't have any money of my own until I turn twenty-five."

Jane thought for a moment. "And you're prepared to commit yourself to run?"

"I won't marry a man I don't want," Raechel said. "And I don't care what I have to do to avoid it."

"There's a place you can go," Jane said. She lowered her voice. "You'll be a long way from your ... *chaperone*. But you will have to work. There are no free lunches here."

"I understand," Raechel said.

Jane smirked. "I would be surprised if you did," she said. "You might want to go back to your chaperone in a hurry."

The carriage lurched to a stop. "If you want to go back, now's your last chance," Jane warned. "There won't be any going back afterwards for quite some time."

"I can't go back," Raechel said. "Irene will kill me."

"She won't kill you," Jane said. There was a faint hint of amusement in her voice. "I imagine you'll have some trouble sitting down for a while, but you have to be alive to make your wedding vows. Lady Campbell offered her a thousand pounds to make the match."

Raechel barely needed to fake the hot flash of anger. A thousand pounds was a staggering sum, one Lady Campbell clearly expected to be repaid from Raechel's legacy. The older lady hadn't given a damn about Raechel's feelings …

"I'm coming," she said. "Where do we go?"

"In here," Jane said. She opened the door. They had parked outside a darkened building, its windows covered with wooden planks. "And I suggest you say nothing until we are finished."

Raechel nodded, then followed Jane out of the carriage and through a door. Inside, two men were sitting at a table, playing cards. Several others were lying on the floor, snoring loudly; Raechel couldn't help noticing that they all had weapons within easy reach. Jane nodded to the players and hurried Raechel up a flight of stairs, into a smaller room. A wardrobe stood open in front of them, crammed with all manner of clothes. Raechel felt a flash of *Déjà Vu*, remembering Irene's cabinet back in London. The Sons clearly followed the same logic as British Intelligence.

"Get undressed," Jane ordered. "Remove *everything*, and I mean *everything*."

"But …"

"Do as I say," Jane ordered.

Raechel glanced at the door, then removed her dress. She hesitated over the underclothes until Jane cleared her throat loudly. It was easy to summon the embarrassment she'd felt, back when Irene had ordered her to undress too. Jane looked her up and down, then passed her a dark outfit. Raechel stared at it, but Jane was remorseless. By the time she was dressed, she looked like a low-class girl. Even her hair had been tied up in a tight bun and hidden under a cap.

"Very good," Jane said. "And, more importantly, you won't look out of place on the docks."

Raechel shifted, uncomfortably, as Jane examined every last inch of her. The outfit was icky – there was a faint smell of fish surrounding it – and itchy, but she knew she had no choice. If she looked like this, no search party from the upper region of New York was going to spot her. No one was going to pay any attention to her until the sun started to go down.

"The men will escort you to the ship," Jane added. "They'll give you basic tasks to do, once you're away from New York. You shouldn't have any problem with them or the other recruits until you reach the camp. They'll tell you what to do there."

She clapped Raechel on the shoulder. "Don't worry," she said, as Raechel projected unease and concern at her. "You'll be fine. And your *dear* chaperone will end up looking *very* bad indeed."

"Yeah," Raechel said. "She'll never pick up my trail."

And she hoped to hell, as Jane led her back down the stairs, that she was wrong.

Chapter Twenty-Three

 was expecting more trouble," Jackson said.

Gwen nodded in agreement. The trip had grown from five days to nine, not entirely to her surprise, but there had been no contact with the French. She'd found herself relaxing more than was safe, chatting to Jackson when she wasn't helping the magicians master their powers. Bruce had spent most of the time in the cabin, chatting to his two servants. Gwen was mildly surprised he hadn't tried to talk to her or Jackson, but she wasn't about to look a gift horse in the mouth.

She watched, grimly, as the train started the final descent towards Amherst. The American countryside had been wilder than anything she'd seen in Britain, patchwork habitations springing up in the midst of untamed countryside, but now the signs of war were all around them. Burnt-out farmsteads, looted cropland; they drove past a burning farmhouse without slowing for a moment. Hundreds of refugees were fleeing, some heading south to the city in search of protection, which she feared would be elusive, others heading north, following the train tracks to safety. She caught sight of a band of former slaves, laughing as they drank wine straight from the bottle, as their former plantation burned around them. Gwen could only hope that their masters had escaped before it was too late.

"We'll be fighting them soon," Jackson predicted. "Once the French arrive, they'll hand out weapons and point them at Amherst."

Gwen nodded. It made sense, a cold brutal sense. The French might have every reason to expend as many of the former slaves as possible, if only to keep from having to feed and house them in the coming years. And every bullet that struck a slave was one that couldn't strike a French soldier. The French had a far larger army than the British, but much of it was in Europe. There was no way of knowing just how reliable their forces in Mexico actually were.

As long as they hold together long enough to fight us, it won't matter, she thought. There had been rebellions in Latin America for years, she'd heard, but the French had managed to put them down before they snowballed out of control. *And many of their people have good reason to hate us.*

She pushed the thought aside as the train started to slow to a halt. Amherst rose up in front of them, an ugly city composed of stone buildings, wooden huts and large warehouses. It had been intended as nothing more than a logistics hub, she recalled, but it had mushroomed out of control. The former commander had started work on extending the defensive lines before his death, she saw, yet the defences looked incomplete. Refugees were everywhere, sitting around, their eyes flickering from side to side nervously. Even the railway station wasn't clear, she saw, as the train finally stopped. Hundreds of men and women crowded the platforms, hoping desperately for a chance to board a train that would take them to safety.

"Those idiots are blocking the way," Jackson swore. He rose and grabbed his jacket. "Keep your sorcerers back, Lady Gwen. I'll take out the guards to clear a path."

Gwen nodded, shortly. She had no idea how close the French were to the city, but keeping the redcoats cooped up on the train was asking for trouble. Jackson hurried out of the door, jumping down to the platform and running to the first troop car. The refugees called out to him as he ran, Gwen saw, but he ignored them. Gwen wasn't sure if she should be impressed or disturbed.

"Clear the platforms," Jackson bellowed, in the distance. Gwen heard the sound of soldiers swarming out of their car. "Clear the platforms!"

"Not a good sight, My Lady," Wayne said, very quietly. "Whoever's in command of the city has lost control."

"General Kingsley was murdered," Gwen said. The

refugees were moving now, helped along by blows from the leading soldiers. There would be complaints, she knew, but right now they hardly mattered. "I'm not sure who's in command right now."

She turned as she heard Bruce emerging from his cabin. Somehow, he managed to look dapper despite having spent the last week on the train. Gwen was almost envious; *she* needed a hot bath, a proper rest and a change of clothes. She'd expected many more complaints from the young fop too, but Bruce had kept his mouth closed. Perhaps she'd actually managed to intimidate him into silence. *That* would be a first.

"Lady Gwen," he said, as a middle-aged woman ran past the window, screaming very unladylike words. "What is happening outside?"

"They're clearing the station so they can deploy the troops," Gwen said, curtly. "And then I imagine we will be moving to City Hall."

A handful of sergeants came into view, carefully directing the soldiers off the train and down to the barracks. Gwen eyed the porters doubtfully as they appeared, wondering just how many of them could be trusted. Half of them were black, their faces carefully impassive. A single spark in the wrong place could trigger a holocaust. She made a mental note to see if the refugees couldn't be turned into porters, then allowed Wayne to lead the way off the train and onto the platform. It was even more chaotic than she'd feared. The stench of so many unwashed humans in such close proximity greeted her as they hurried towards the exit. Even with the sergeants pushing people around, it was still dreadfully crowded.

"Lady Gwen," Jackson called. "Can you ask your Movers to stay and help with the unpacking? The rest of us will have to go to City Hall."

"Understood," Gwen said.

"I'll stay with them," Wayne said. He tipped her a jaunty salute. "Try and pick up what I can while helping, too."

Gwen nodded, then led the rest of the magicians out of the station. Outside, it was even *more* chaotic. People were everywhere, some sitting against the side of warehouses, others stroking guns as they watched the crowds warily. There were no horses or hansom cabs in sight, even though the stink of horse manure was omnipresent. Jackson and his escort rapidly gave up any thought of finding carriages and started striking out towards the City Hall, clearing the way through force of personality. Gwen followed, gamely resisting the urge to take to the air and fly. It wouldn't be fair if she was the *only* person who could escape the crush.

The crowds seemed to grow worse as they made their way into the centre of the city, where the buildings were stronger and designed to last. Countless buildings looked like armed camps, guards watching them carefully; there were only a handful of women in view and almost all of them carried pistols. The roads had long since turned into muddy tracks, despite a valiant attempt to pave them. There were just too many people in the city.

It won't be long until they start to starve, she thought. General Kingsley had been given orders to build up a stockpile of food, but with so many mouths to feed it was unlikely the stockpile would last very long. *And what happens to us then?*

She couldn't help a flash of relief as City Hall finally came in sight, surrounded by a company of redcoats in full uniform. Jackson muttered a curse – Gwen rather suspected she hadn't been meant to hear it – and led the way towards the building. Thankfully, there weren't so many refugees in front of City Hall, even though the muddy ground would have made an ideal place to pitch a few dozen tents. The guns mounted outside the building might have had something to do with it, she thought. *She* wouldn't have cared to sleep under their sights.

"Sergeant, deploy the men outside," Jackson ordered. "Lady Gwen, please stay with me."

Gwen told her remaining magicians to stay with the sergeant, then followed Jackson into City Hall. It was cooler than she'd expected – she hadn't really registered the heat until it was gone – but no cleaner. Muddy footsteps ran in and out of the building, suggesting that even the mayor couldn't get his home cleaned. No doubt the concept of putting refugees to work hadn't occurred to anyone. A young officer met them as they approached the office, his face grey and covered with dark stubble. He actually looked *relieved* to see Jackson.

"Lieutenant Travis, 3rd Americans," he said, saluting. His uniform looked untidy, as if he'd stopped caring about his appearance. "I just heard you'd arrived."

Jackson eyed him for a long moment. "A *lieutenant* is in command of the defence?"

"General Kingsley is dead, sir," Travis insisted. His gaze flickered over Gwen, then back to Jackson. "The militia leaders have been unable to work together."

"Send messages ordering them to meet with me in one hour," Jackson said, curtly. "I'll want a *full* briefing after I speak to the mayor."

"The deputy mayor," Travis said. "His Honour decided the demands of his office required him to go north to drum up reinforcements personally."

"You mean he fled for his life," Jackson said. "Send the messages, Travis. I'll speak to the deputy mayor now."

Gwen gritted her teeth as she followed Jackson into the mayor's office. The deputy mayor reminded her of David, right down to the gold-rimmed spectacles and the hangdog expression her brother had worn after discovering that *someone* had messed with his paperwork. A large glass bottle sat on his desk. It took Gwen a moment to realise he had to have been drinking it straight from the bottle. *David* would never have done *that*.

"Colonel," the Deputy Mayor said. Judging from his accent, Gwen decided, he was American born and bred. "Welcome to Amherst. I wish we could put on a better greeting."

"I saw more than enough, Mayor Talbot," Jackson said. He reached into his jacket and produced an envelope. "By order of His Excellency Viceroy Rochester, martial law is hereby declared over Amherst and the surrounding environs. I am to assume command of the defences, superseding all previous arrangements. If you want to register any objections, you may do so and they will be relayed to His Excellency."

Talbot blinked. "I'm not the mayor …"

"Your predecessor appears to have deserted his post," Jackson said, firmly. "Accordingly, I am appointing you to his position, where you will serve as my civil liaison. Afterwards, I imagine you'll be able to keep the title. My report will make it clear that you stayed when your superior fled."

"Yes, Colonel," Talbot said. He looked at Gwen, frowning as if he couldn't quite see past the male guise. "Everything seems hopeless ..."

"*Everything* seems hopeless at first," Jackson said. "Now tell me, just what has happened in this city since the war began?"

Talbot sighed. "All hell broke loose shortly after the first French horsemen were reported on the wrong side of the border," he said. "The Mayor – the *former* Mayor – sent out warnings to the homesteads, telling them to lock up their slaves. It was too late: hundreds of farmsteads were burnt to the ground, their owners murdered or forced to flee. General Kingsley raised volunteers for the militia and set to work improving the defences, while sending out horsemen to scatter and harass the former slaves. And then he was murdered.

"We lost control of much of the city shortly afterwards. Lieutenant Travis was the senior officer ..."

Gwen frowned. "He was?"

"A redcoat is always superior to a colonial," Jackson commented.

"That can't have gone down well," Gwen muttered. Hadn't similar concerns been raised about Jackson himself? "What happened?"

"Half the militia officers hate the other half," Talbot explained. "Without General Kingsley, a man they respected even if they didn't love, they started scrabbling amongst themselves; Lieutenant Travis was quite unable to bring them to heel. My predecessor fled shortly afterwards, claiming he was going to send reinforcements."

"He hadn't arrived in New York by the time we left," Jackson said.

"The streets aren't safe," Talbot added. "Parts of the city are sealed off from the remainder, Colonel. There're laws against hoarding, but everyone who has any food is keeping it to themselves. I have a strong guard on the warehouses and yet it doesn't stop pilfering …"

He shook his head. "And the Sons of Liberty are popping up everywhere," he added. "I heard of a man who was telling everyone that the crisis was Britain's fault …"

"Then the sooner we get the situation under control, the better," Jackson said, firmly. "I have enough troops to impose martial law, I think. You can make the announcement once we have them in place."

He smiled. "Chin up, Mr. Mayor," he added. "It may seem bad, but it *will* get better."

"I hope you're right," Talbot said. He cleared his throat. "Do you intend to turn City Hall into your base?"

"For the moment," Jackson said. "But we may have to move, later. The French will know *precisely* where City Hall is."

He turned and strode out of the room. Gwen followed him, wondering just what kind of nightmare she'd wandered into. It was like Russia, only worse. There, they'd been trapped in a palace while the undead roamed Moscow's streets. Here …

"One hell of a problem," Jackson said. He sounded energised, Gwen noted, rather than unsure of himself. He was practically rubbing his hands together with glee. "Can you and your sorcerers base yourselves in City Hall?"

"I imagine so," Gwen said. She had a feeling that getting a hot bath wouldn't be easy. "And then what?"

"It depends on how the militia react," Jackson said. "That young fool can stay here too …"

He stopped. "What happened to him?"

Gwen blinked. "We left Bruce Rochester at the station," she said, slowly. She wasn't quite sure what had happened to him. "I … I … don't know."

"Let's hope he has the sense to stay close to the redcoats," Jackson grunted. He looked up at the sound of running footsteps. "Ah, Lieutenant Travis."

"Sir," Travis said. "The militia leaders are assembled in Room Four."

"That was quick," Gwen said.

Travis stared, as if he hadn't quite realised she was female.

"They knew you'd arrived, My Lady," he said, finally. He sounded as though he wanted to ask a thousand questions, but didn't quite dare. It occurred to Gwen, suddenly, that he might not know who she was, or what she could do. "They were already on their way to City Hall."

"Then let us go talk to them," Jackson said.

He smiled thinly, then motioned for Travis to lead them to the meeting room. Gwen followed, bracing herself as best she could. She'd met several militia commanders in Britain and they'd been a very mixed bag, ranging from ex-soldiers with genuine experience to aristocrats who wanted to play at being military officers. They tended to wear fancy uniforms and get their men killed, from what she'd heard. And they'd often been consumed with petty rivalries.

The Americans looked *slightly* more promising, she had to admit, as she stepped into the room. Seven men, wearing drab brown uniforms rather than redcoats; they certainly didn't *look* as though they spent all their funds on fancy uniforms rather than weapons. But they'd have their own problems too, she knew. Militia leaders – particularly the men who *founded* the regiments – received payments in line with the number of men under their command. It was quite likely that they spent far too much time trying to lure militiamen away from their rivals.

Not an uncommon problem, she reminded herself. *It happens in Britain too.*

"Gentlemen," Jackson said. "I am Colonel Jackson. By order of the Viceroy, I am taking command of the defences and declaring martial law. You – and your regiments – are now under my command."

He went on before any of them could say a word. "This city is in trouble," he added. "It won't be long before the French arrive, having made their way up from New Orleans despite the best efforts of our skirmishers. If this city falls, the linchpin of our southern defences falls with it. Our menfolk will be killed, our women will be ravished and our children taken by the French. I have no intention of letting this city fall.

"By the time they arrive, I intend to turn Amherst into a fortress. We will put the refugees to work, piling up the defences and preparing surprises for the French. We will train the regiments until they are ready to fight to the last, once the French try to break the defences and storm the city. We will send out raiding parties to forage every last *scrap* of food from the surrounding countryside, denying it to the French even as we use it to keep our people alive. And when they come to take the city, we will give them a bloody nose they will never forget."

He paused. "We must hang together, gentlemen," he concluded, "or we shall most definitely hang separately."

Gwen tried to work out what they were thinking, but they were all skilled at keeping their expressions under control. The French wouldn't be merciful, not once they took the city, but did they realise that? Who knew *what* the French were saying to the Americans?

"The Sons say otherwise," a prune-faced officer said. "The Sons say we can live with the French."

"The Sons are wrong," Jackson said. "And the Sons had better keep their heads down, or they will be beheaded as traitors."

He took a long breath. "Make no mistake," he warned. "Those who side with the French are not just betraying their oath to King George, but the colonies themselves. And I will *not* tolerate it for a second."

And let us hope, Gwen thought grimly, *that we don't wind up fighting a civil war as well.*

Chapter Twenty-Four

ll up," a voice shouted. "Come on!"

Raechel jumped to her feet, along with several other female recruits. The barge contained over fifty recruits, from what she'd managed to overhear, but most of them were men. She'd been torn between relief and frustration when she'd discovered that the females were kept in a different section, trapped in semi-darkness for several days. Irene had taught her a few tricks for keeping track of time, even without a watch or being able to see the sun, but she had to admit she'd failed. She wasn't remotely sure just how long they'd been on the barge.

She blinked rapidly, as Irene had taught her, when she came out into the sunlight. The barge was tied up at a small jetty, a pathway leading up into the woodlands and out of sight. She glanced back at the river, but saw nothing, not even another barge making its way up into the hinterlands or down towards New York. The towering buildings she'd admired when the ship had sailed into harbour were nowhere in sight. She had no idea just how far they'd come from New York, but she was certain it was quite some distance.

There are canals and rivers everywhere, she reminded herself, as she followed the other women down the gangplank and onto the jetty. A couple of houses were within view, but little else. *We could be anywhere within two hundred miles of New York.*

She sucked in her breath, suddenly feeling very alone. The male recruits were already heading up the path, escorted by a handful of older men carrying weapons; the females, it seemed, had to wait for a short period. It struck her, suddenly, that there might be *anything* in the undergrowth.

Britain had foxes and wild dogs – and other animals, where they weren't hunted down by farmers – but America might have lions and tigers and bears! The armed guards might be there to protect the recruits, rather than keep them prisoner.

"This way," a voice called. She looked up to see a young man, wearing a blue shirt and trousers. "Come along, now. We don't have all day."

Raechel nodded and followed him up the path. It was steeper than she'd realised, weaving backwards and forwards so often that she rapidly lost track of where she was going, or the direction back to the barge. The trees closed in, making it impossible to see in either direction. Despite all the walking and riding she'd done in Britain, before her parents had died, she found it hard going, although she wasn't one of the women who stumbled back to the rear. Their escort didn't seem inclined to shout or curse at the women, merely waiting patiently as the stragglers caught up with them. Perhaps keeping them apart from the men had been a mercy, Raechel reasoned, as they kept moving. It stopped them looking weak under male eyes.

She studied her fellows as covertly as she could, although it was impossible to be *certain* of anything. Three of them looked to be working women – she could see scars on their hands and they didn't seem to be having any trouble keeping up with their escort – while the remainder looked no older than herself. She wondered, absently, if they were *all* on the run from arranged marriages, then dismissed the thought. Their clothes suggested they were lower class, which probably meant they thought the Sons would make the world better. But then, from what Irene had said, the lower classes lived permanently on the brink anyway.

They have nothing to lose, she thought, as the pathway widened suddenly. *And it makes them dangerous enemies.*

She sucked in her breath as she saw the stockade, surrounding a number of wooden buildings, each one large enough to hold a number of pigs and cows. A handful of guards were clearly visible, watching carefully as the women filed through the gate. Inside, Raechel saw a number of men running around the giant buildings, carrying weapons and chanting in unison as they moved. Others were marching towards a firing range ... she counted, quickly, and realised there were over a hundred men in view. She'd wondered if the Sons were exaggerating the size of their army, but evidently not. Even if this was the *only* camp, they might have over a thousand armed men who could be hurled into the battle for New York at a moment's notice.

And we must be too far from civilised territory for friendly ears to hear the sound of gunshots, she thought, as she heard the gunners open fire. It was far from uncommon to hear gunshots in the English countryside, but vast numbers of shots would definitely raise eyebrows. The Sons, it seemed, could fire off thousands of bullets without anyone being any the wiser. *How far am I from New York?*

The women were marched straight into one of the buildings, which turned out to be a small barracks. There were no beds, just blankets on the hard earthen ground; buckets of water and chamberpots instead of running water and toilets. Raechel felt a flicker of dismay, which she forced herself to bury as deep as possible. Running water was uncommon outside cities, she knew; they were too far from New York to have a reliable water supply. She just hoped the Sons had made certain to boil the water before handing it out.

"Please remain in this building until you are called," their escort said. His voice was polite, but there was a hint of firmness in his voice that made it clear that it was not a request. "You will be interviewed before you are given work to do."

One of the younger girls coughed. "Work?"

"Of course," the escort said. "You didn't think you were coming out here for a holiday, did you?"

He smirked as several of the women snickered. "You have to work for your freedom," he added, darkly. "Someone will tell you the rules, after you have been interviewed. Until then, stay in this building. Take a nap, if you like. You'll need the rest."

Raechel watched him leave, then wandered over to the water and splashed a little on her face and hands. Her clothes were thoroughly rank and uncomfortable after several days – however long it had been – without a change, but she doubted she'd be able to wash in the camp. Several of the older women had taken the escort's advice and gone to sleep; the younger women either chatted in low voices or sat down, looking torn between excitement and terror. Raechel felt a flicker of sympathy, remembering just how her world had turned upside down in Russia. They'd been dragged out of their familiar world too.

It was nearly an hour, she thought, before the escort returned and called out her name. She rose and followed him out of the building, down towards a smaller building to the rear of the camp. Most of the men were out of sight, but she could hear someone shouting, just as she'd heard sergeants shouting to their men on the streets of London. Her blood ran cold at the evidence the Sons were *definitely* building an army, probably with help and support from rogue militiamen. And if there were rogue magicians too …

"You coped well with the trip," the escort said. He stopped outside the smaller building and turned to face her. "We were expecting you to crack."

"Better to escape than be forced into an unwanted marriage," Raechel said. She *had* experienced worse, in Russia, although hardly anyone in America knew about *that* little adventure. "I just want to get away."

"And so you have," the escort said. He opened the door, then smiled. "Tell the truth – the whole truth – and you have nothing to fear."

That will be a first, Raechel thought.

She smiled wanly as she entered the office. It was smaller than she'd expected, illuminated by a pair of oil-filled lanterns hanging from the ceiling. Two men sat at a wooden desk; a middle-aged woman leant against the far wall, watching her with dark brown eyes. One of the men was badly scarred, like a soldier; the other looked rather like an inoffensive bank clerk. The woman might have been pretty, if she hadn't had a scar of her own running from her left eye down to her jaw. It looked as if someone had decided to deliberately mutilate her.

"Lady Raechel Slater-Standish," the clerk-like man said. "I am Adam. Welcome to Camp Ten."

Raechel nodded. Camp *Ten*? Were there nine other camps

– at least – or was it a deliberate attempt to make it seem as though the Sons were bigger than they were? There was no way to know, but so far from civilisation – she'd been told – there were entire towns that weren't on any of the official maps. It was a constant nagging sore in the hinterlands.

"We have a number of questions for you," Adam continued. "Please answer them as completely as possible. If we catch you lying to us, for any reason, the consequences will be unpleasant."

"I understand," Raechel said. Her mouth was suddenly very dry. She couldn't feel the presence of a Talker, but that didn't mean there wasn't one. "What do you want to know?"

Adam leant forward. "Why do you want to join us?"

"I want to escape being married off against my will," Raechel said, keeping her mental shields firmly in place. It would be more convincing, she thought, than an instant conversion to their ideology. But it would be better to admit to at least *some* attraction. "And because I was told you treated women as equals."

"We do," the soldier said. "But we don't treat you as delicate little flowers too."

"I'm not delicate," Raechel insisted. "My guardians just think I can't handle my own affairs."

"I'd say you could handle yourself pretty well," Adam said. His lips quirked in wry amusement. "What can you do?"

Raechel gathered herself. "I can read and write," she said. "I can ride a horse, shoot a rifle … what do you need?"

Adam ignored the question. "Your uncle is a powerful politician, is he not?"

"Yes," Raechel said. How much did they know about Russia? "He is – he *was* – a special envoy for the Duke of India. I believe he intends to continue in that role under Lord Liverpool."

"And yet he sent you over here," Adam said. "Was there a reason for that?"

"Officially, he wants me to find a good match among the American aristocracy," Raechel said, bluntly. "His idea of what makes a good match is different from mine."

"And unofficially?"

"My behaviour in London was getting a little out of his

control," Raechel admitted. It was true, from a certain point of view. "My aunt was having ... *problems* ... and it was decided that it would be better if I was sent to America *before* something happened that he couldn't keep from the rest of the *ton*."

Adam nodded. "What do you make of the current British government?"

Raechel blinked in surprise. "How do you mean?"

"Your uncle is a government minister," Adam said. "Did you not meet any of his fellows personally?"

"Not for long," Raechel said. It was true enough. Her uncle might have wanted to display her in front of prospective husbands, but his fellow government ministers were almost all married already. "I didn't get invited to their meetings."

Adam shrugged, then launched another series of questions at her. Raechel found herself sweating as she struggled to answer them, wondering just how much he expected her to know about the British Government. Neither Lord Liverpool nor the Duke of India had exchanged more than a few words with her; she'd certainly never been invited to Whitehall to give her opinion on matters political. Politics was a purely male sphere, she'd learnt at a very early age. The only women who wielded any kind of political power, save for Gwen, did so from behind the scenes.

"That is frustrating," Adam said, when she explained the realities of life. "I understand you *met* the Royal Sorceress?"

"We were on the same ship," Raechel said. There was no point in trying to hide it, not when everyone who was anyone in New York would already know. "But we didn't chat that much."

Adam snickered. "She caught you with a sailor," he said. "Just how far along were you before she grabbed you?"

Raechel blushed. "We were kissing," she said. Jane must have made a full report. Irene had told her that a suspected spy might be quizzed several times by different people, just to see if there were discrepancies in her words. "We didn't have time to go any further."

The woman spoke for the first time. "Why did you even start kissing him?"

"I was bored and frustrated," Raechel lied. "My chaperone wanted me to remain in the cabin at all times, but I hated it. I just wanted to rebel."

"Understandable," Adam said. "What sort of person *is* the Royal Sorceress?"

"I can't say I know her that well," Raechel said. "She struck me as a fair-minded person, but ... we never really spoke."

She hadn't expected that answer to satisfy them and it didn't. Adam asked her a dozen more questions, despite her clear irritation. Raechel could feel her head starting to pound as he tried to draw more details from her, even though she had tried to make it clear that there were limits to her knowledge. By the time the conversation switched to her impressions of America, she was nursing a headache and wishing it would just come to an end.

"I dare say your chaperone will have problems finding you here," Adam said. "Given your ... connections ... we have decided that it will be better if you remain here, rather than training to fight or slipping further into the hinterland. There will be work for you to do, I'm afraid, and you *will* do it."

"Yes, sir," Raechel said. She needed time to think. Hopefully, whatever work she was given would be sufficiently mindless. "The escort mentioned rules."

Adam smiled, showing his teeth. "They're very basic," he said. "You'll be assigned a barracks; don't slip into another set of barracks without an invitation or invite anyone else into your barracks without the permission of the occupants. Don't try to leave the camp without permission. Don't fight, steal or cause trouble among the men."

Raechel frowned. "Trouble, sir?"

"There are twenty men in this camp for every woman," Adam said, flatly. "You may start a relationship with one of the men, if you wish, but you may not cause trouble by flirting with other men."

"I see," Raechel said.

"Meg will show you to your barracks," Adam finished. "We'll be talking again soon, I'm afraid."

"We will?"

"You were born in England and raised amongst the *ton*,"

Adam said. "You'll have quite a few details we need to know, locked away in your head. Meg?"

The woman stepped away from the wall. "Come with me," she said. "The female barracks is just outside."

Raechel followed her through the door and into a long single-storey building. There were beds, she was relieved to note, and private washrooms. A fire burnt merrily under the stove, heating water for washing. It wasn't the most civilised place she'd visited, but at least it was marginally liveable. And yet, she couldn't help wondering where the other women were. Learning to shoot? Or something rather less useful …?

"There are spare clothes in the rear cabinet, so take what you need from there," Meg instructed. "Washing clothes is a communal activity here, so put any dirty clothes in the basket. Do you know how to wash your own clothes?"

"No," Raechel said.

"You're going to have to learn," Meg said. "We do all of the washing in this camp; clothes, plates … you name it, we wash it."

Her face twisted suddenly. "I know where you came from, *Lady* Raechel," she added. "And I assure you that there are no servants here! No one is going to spoil you or do your work for you. You will make your own bed, you will prepare your own water to wash, you will cook, clean and do other chores I assign to you as part of your duties. If you fail to pull your weight, I will take steps. Do you understand me?"

"It's better than being married off," Raechel said.

Meg snorted. "You'll be the first noble bitch to think *that*," she sneered. She pointed to the scar on her face. "Do you know how I got this scar?"

Raechel shook her head.

"A young brat like you thought it would be funny to tell her father I stole from the family," Meg hissed. "Her father beat me, then took his knife to my face to brand me a thief before he threw me out onto the streets. One word out of you, one hint of reluctance to earn your keep and I will cut your pretty face until even the whores won't want you."

She glared at Raechel, then nodded to the washroom. "You're stinking," she added, in a tone that made Raechel flinch. She believed every word. "I'll be back in twenty minutes. Wash, dress and get ready to go out. You have potatoes to peel."

"I will," Raechel said.

Meg snorted rudely, then turned and stalked off. Raechel shuddered – somehow, she *knew* Meg had meant every word – and then turned to find her new clothes. Twenty minutes … it would have to be long enough. And if it wasn't …

I got into the camp, she told herself, firmly. *And now I have to survive long enough to find out what I need to know and get out again.*

Chapter Twenty-Five

ell done," Gwen said. "You caught all of the bullets."

She lowered the gun and smiled at Vernon, who eyed her darkly. Two days of practicing in Amherst had made him far better at shielding himself, although Gwen had the private suspicion that a better-trained Mover – like the rogue – would be able to stab a needle through Vernon's magic. But it was very definitely an improvement. Vernon shouldn't have any problems tearing through a force of Frenchmen, as long as they didn't have any magicians supporting them.

And if they do, she added privately, *matters may become rather sticky.*

"I knew you could do it," Harry said. He clapped his hands as Gwen reloaded the gun. "I don't think we *need* to go back to the docks."

"The docks were *safe*," Vernon muttered.

Gwen kept her expression under tight control. She wasn't sure if he was complaining for the sake of complaining or if he meant every word. The docks didn't normally include enemy soldiers shooting at the workers, yet a single accident could kill a man – or cripple him for life. Lucy had Healed a number of men who'd been raced to Cavendish Hall in time, but very few supervisors bothered to make the effort. Dockyard workers were cheap.

"And we're making far more here," Harry reminded him. "Just think of what you can buy when we get back home."

"Lady Gwen," a new voice called.

Gwen turned to see a messenger standing by the gate. There was no Sorcerers' Hall in Amherst – an oversight that perplexed her – so she'd taken over an abandoned townhouse that had belonged to one of the former mayor's cronies. She had no idea who the crony had been, but he'd fled Amherst before the mayor himself, taking his wife, children and slaves with him. Thankfully, the garden was large enough to give the magicians room to practice.

"I'm over here," she said, striding towards the gate. "What do you have for me?"

The messenger stood straighter. "Lieutenant Travis's compliments, Lady Gwen," he said, his voice stuttering slightly. Up close, he looked no older than fourteen. "He requests your immediate presence. I'm to escort you to his position."

Gwen nodded, slowly. Once he was no longer in overall command, Lieutenant Travis had blossomed. She had a feeling he'd be promoted in the very near future, if only to ensure that there were experienced officers on the ground. Most of the officers who'd accompanied Colonel Jackson were as unfamiliar with America as Jackson was himself.

"I'm on my way," she said.

She called for Wayne and told him to continue training, then motioned for the messenger to lead her to the horse and open carriage. Colonel Jackson had managed to clear most of the streets by opening abandoned houses and turning them over to the refugees – while conscripting male refugees to build barricades and dig trenches – but there were still dozens of people on the streets. Gwen wasn't too surprised to see a line of ladies of ill repute, plying their trade among the soldiers, militiamen and volunteers. Colonel Jackson had strictly limited the consumption of alcohol, pointing out that it would be needed to treat wounds, but he'd done nothing about prostitution. Trying, Gwen suspected, would merely have driven it underground.

And that would have made matters worse for the prostitutes, she thought, grimly. *What else can we do?*

She shook her head. Jackson had rounded up hundreds of women for emergency training in first aid – no one doubted that there would be a great many wounded, once the French finally attacked – but there was little else he could do. Indeed, he was working hard to get the children out of the city, shipping them up the rail lines to Philadelphia. God knew it was going to be a major headache, she was sure, reuniting the children with their parents after the war. But there was no choice. Children were simply more useless mouths to feed.

The carriage rattled to a halt. Lieutenant Travis was standing by the roadside, surrounded by a handful of redcoats. The soldiers looked as though they were *trying* to be discreet, although Gwen didn't know who they thought they were fooling. Men in red uniforms – Jackson insisted it was so the blood didn't show – tended to be far too obvious anywhere. She dropped down to the street and nodded to Lieutenant Travis.

"There's a Son hideout down the street," he said, quietly. Too quietly. Gwen could barely hear him. "The Colonel wants the bas … ah, pardon me … the *buggers* alive."

Gwen nodded, shortly. The Sons of Liberty had responded to Jackson's warnings with quiet defiance. Leaflets had been popping up everywhere, calling for Americans to refuse British orders and stay out of the fighting. Jackson had had every printer in town investigated for sedition, but none of them appeared guilty. No one had *any* idea where the leaflets were coming from. The best guess was that the Sons had a printer of their own working somewhere within the city.

"Then we go in fast and hard," she said, grimly. Travis coloured, slightly. "They may already know we're here."

Travis nodded and drew his sidearm. "I'll take the lead."

"I will," Gwen corrected him. She knew he ran the risk of losing face by allowing her to go first, but better for him to lose face than lose his life. Her magic provided a layer of protection he couldn't hope to match. "Deploy your men to cut off any escape, then follow behind me."

She walked down towards the house, carefully preparing her magic. The house appeared silent, but that proved nothing. There might well be another magician inside, confusing her senses. And even if there wasn't, thick stone walls would make it hard for her senses to pick up *anything*.

If Travis is wrong about this, she thought, *someone is going to get badly hurt.*

She braced herself, then reached out with her magic and

yanked the door right off its hinges, tossing it across the street. "Don't move," she shouted, projecting as much Charm as she could into her voice. If she was lucky, the Sons would be unable to move long enough for Travis and his men to grab them. "Don't …"

The entire front of the house disintegrated, sending a tidal wave of debris flying through the air and right into her protections. Gwen swore – she hadn't sensed the magic until it was far too late – and threw up a shield, covering herself and her escorts. Lieutenant Travis barked a command at a dark figure, standing just inside the building, but he ignored it. Gwen cursed again as the figure hurled himself into the air, landing neatly on the next building's rooftop and waving at her. It *had* to be the same magician she'd faced earlier.

Lieutenant Travis pointed his sidearm at the rogue and fired. Gwen was impressed with his skill – firing a handgun accurately was far from easy – but she could have told him it would be useless. The bullet pinged off the rogue's magic and fell harmlessly to the ground. Gwen gritted her teeth and send a wave of fire towards him, threatening to incinerate his perch. He struck a dramatic pose – she couldn't help being reminded of Jack – and launched himself back into the air, daring her to follow him. She pushed the flames up instead, but they merely sputtered along the edge of his protections.

"Give up," Gwen shouted at him, lacing her voice with Charm for the second time. "There's no way out."

The rogue laughed and pointed a finger towards the damaged house. Gwen's jaw dropped as he shot a pulse of magic into the house, then she instinctively threw out another shield. The house exploded, the force of the blast slamming into her shield and hurling her and Lieutenant Travis right across the road. She sensed the death of the soldier who'd escorted them, caught in the blast before she could shield him too. Shock held her frozen for a second, just long enough for the rogue to make a getaway. She hurled herself into the air, trying to catch sight of him, but saw nothing. He could have vanished in any direction …

A Master, she thought, numbly. She'd thought she was facing a Mover, but she'd just seen him use a second talent. A third too, perhaps; her Charm had been completely ineffectual on him. *He's a Master.*

She looked back at the pile of smoking rubble, all that remained of the house. It had to have been a powder store, she thought, despite her confusion and horror. He'd deliberately blown it up to keep them from recovering anything and using it to defend the city ...

And he's a Master, she thought. Her thoughts chased themselves round and round. She'd assumed, after Jack's death, that she was the lone surviving Master Magician. But she had clearly been wrong. *Dear God in Heaven. He's a Master.*

Lieutenant Travis came up behind her. "That ... could have gone better."

He didn't see it, Gwen realised. She wanted to shout at him, to make him understand, but she knew she couldn't take the risk. Very few people understood how magic worked, how each magician – save for the Masters – had only one talent. If she told him that ... *someone* ... a Son of Liberty, perhaps, had the same power as she did, what would he make of it?

"Yes, it could have," she said. She rather doubted the soldiers would be able to pull anything useful from the remains of the house, but they'd have to try. "I have to go back to City Hall."

"I'll assign you an escort," Lieutenant Travis said.

"Don't bother," Gwen said. "I'll be fine on my own."

She turned and walked off before he could muster an objection, thinking hard. The rogue had clearly been a young man, from the way he'd moved; he was probably not more than a few years older than her. *Jack* had been older by at least ten years ... had he trained another Master in France? Or had the rogue learnt from single-talent magicians instead? Was he American or French? Gwen had no illusions of just how quickly the Royal Sorcerers Corps would have embraced another Master, even one of humble origins. Fatheads like Major Shaw would not have hesitated to follow a *male* Master ...

Even an American, she thought, as she reached City Hall. *They'd be delighted to have a man back in command.*

She lifted her eyebrows as she was shown into Jackson's

office. Bruce was sitting in front of the desk, reporting on his latest attempt to build morale in the city by holding a number of small parties and balls. Gwen rather suspected that it was completely futile, but at least it kept Bruce out of her hair. Jackson seemed rather more interested than she would have expected, too. But then, *he* needed support from the Viceroy if he were to be confirmed as General Kingsley's permanent successor.

"We have a problem," she said, without preamble. "A big problem."

Jackson looked up. "Worse than the snipers harassing our foraging parties?"

"Yes," Gwen said, flatly. She didn't want to admit to losing the rogue for a second time, but she had no choice. "The enemy has a *very* competent magician at their disposal."

She outlined everything that had happened since she'd been summoned, explaining the difference between a normal magician and the rogue when Jackson seemed baffled by some of her terms. Bruce listened, not saying a word. Gwen was almost relieved. The last thing she wanted, right now, was to have to slap him down for upper-class idiocy.

"I see," Jackson said, when she had finished. "Are you sure it's the same magician?"

"I think so," Gwen said. "His magic ... *felt* ... identical. The cloak and outfit was identical too."

"And he followed us down here," Jackson said. "Or did he fly?"

"If he flew so far in such a short space of time ..."

Gwen shook her head. Flying from Cambridge to London had nearly killed her, back when the Swing was reaching its height. And *that* had been a mere sixty miles, more or less. If the rogue could go faster and further than her, she was in big trouble. Indeed, if the rogue was *that* much more powerful, she could expect an attack at any moment. Taking her off the board would be a valuable achievement in its own right.

Master Thomas didn't have problems flying to London, she thought, recalling how the older man had flown without effort. *But he had a secret advantage of his own.*

She glared down at her hands, cursing the old man under her breath. How many secrets had been lost because he'd never shared them with her, or written them down somewhere in his archive? Doctor Norwell worked hard to make her write down everything, but he'd clearly not done the same for Master Thomas. And who knew what the other Masters had been able to do? Jack might have had secrets of his own too.

"This is *not* good news," Jackson said. "We've lost hundreds, perhaps thousands, of weapons that were issued to the militia. A handful going on walkabout would be understandable, perhaps, but not *hundreds*. And a number of militia officers remain unaccounted for, too. If they've joined the Sons, Lady Gwen, the other officers may be unreliable."

"So we're exposed here," Gwen finished. "Holding the line may be impossible."

"Difficult, perhaps, but not impossible," Jackson snapped. "The French will have to storm the city, almost as soon as they arrive. It will be difficult for the Sons to launch a coup in all the confusion."

"Unless they launch the coup before the French arrive," Gwen said.

"The timing would be tricky," Jackson said. "They'd have to take the city and hold it, despite counterattacks."

"But there aren't any other significant British forces for a very long way," Gwen said. "If we lose Amherst ..."

Jackson glared at the map. "What are they thinking?"

He muttered a word Gwen was sure she wasn't meant to hear. "If they rise up against us, the French win the war," he said. "But the French won't give the Sons their liberty, not after the way they treated the anarchists in 1789. They called it a whiff of grapeshot, remember?"

Gwen nodded. It had been long before her birth, but she'd learnt about it from one of her more interesting tutors. The French monarchy – before the union with Spain – had suffered a brief crisis, with mobs coming out onto the streets. But King Louis had kept his nerve and greeted the mobs with cannon fire. No one was sure just how many people had died – Gwen had seen estimates ranging from a few hundred to millions – but it had been more than enough to slap the French anarchists down for years. And by the time they'd started to raise their heads again, the government had not only united with the Spanish, but established a far more capable domestic intelligence service. There had been no anarchist attacks in France for decades.

"The Sons will be destroyed, after conveniently doing the dirty work of destroying the colonial government," Jackson said. "It isn't as if the French don't have people who want to live here" – he waved a hand towards the distant plantations – "and rule in their stead. The Sons will never get the freedom they want."

"They may even claim they were doing the British government a favour," Gwen added. "The anarchists threaten everything."

"No one would believe that," Bruce said. "It's … *madness*."

"Never underestimate just how many foolish things people can believe," Gwen said, rather crossly. The cartoons of her turning her enemies into frogs or pigs would have been amusing, if they hadn't made it harder for her to *talk* to people. And she couldn't turn a man into a pig, although some of them were definitely halfway there. "The French won't really care who believes them, as long as they have a rationale for occupying the colonies after the war."

"True," Jackson said. "Lady Gwen, we will be relying on you to hunt this rogue down. Put training in Wayne's hands and *find* the bastard!"

"I will," Gwen said. She wasn't looking forward to the fight, but now she knew what she was facing … she'd bet good money that the rogue had *never* faced another Master, while she'd faced two. But then, Master Thomas had beaten her handily. "I won't let you down."

She started at the loud rapping on the door.

"Come in," Jackson called.

A messenger entered, his face flushed. "Message for you, Your Grace," he said, passing it to Jackson. "Captain Vine says it's urgent."

"*Your Grace*," Jackson repeated. He took the envelope and unfolded it, slowly. "When did I get promoted?"

Gwen shook her head, too tired to feel amused. Jackson was minor nobility, *very* minor nobility. There was no way he *should* be addressed as 'Your Grace ...'

"Shit," Jackson swore. He seemed to have completely forgotten that he shouldn't be swearing in Gwen's presence. "That's not good."

Gwen felt a thrill of alarm. "*What's* not good?"

"It's a report from one of the scouting parties," Jackson said, grimly. "The French have attacked the railways and destroyed a great deal of the track, including one of the bridges. It won't be easy to repair."

"And until it is repaired," Gwen breathed, "we're trapped."

"Find that rogue," Jackson ordered. "And not a word to *anyone* about the railway lines."

It will leak, Gwen thought, as she headed for the door. The railway was their only link to the remainder of the colonies. Rumours would spread at terrifying speed. *And then all hell will break loose.*

Chapter Twenty-Six

ou appear to be a doing a good job," Meg said, reluctantly. Her gaze swept the pile of clean dishes and mugs, then wandered back to Raechel. "Barely."

Raechel groaned. She'd never realised just how hard the maids had to work until she'd tried some of their duties for herself. Washing dishes, even pewter and tin dishes rather than fine china, was boring, even sickening. But it was better than washing clothes. She'd learnt more in the last two days about disgusting male habits than she'd ever wanted to know.

"Thank you," she said, careful to keep her voice even. Meg was just waiting for her to make a mistake, she could tell. "Are there more coming?"

"There are things to clean every day," Meg said, dryly. Raechel felt her cheeks heat at her tone. "But for the moment, you can go get yourself something to eat."

Raechel nodded and hurried off to the dining hall before Meg could change her mind. The older woman seemed determined to work her until her hands were worn down to the bone, even though Raechel hadn't uttered a word of complaint. When she wasn't cleaning dishes – or clothes – she was peeling potatoes, boiling water or catching a handful of desperately needed hours of sleep. If she ever managed to get back to London, she promised herself, she was going to make damn sure the maids got a raise. And if her aunt dared to question her decision, Raechel would make sure she never saw a single penny of her father's fortune.

She pushed the thought aside as she stepped into the dining hall. The darkened room was crammed with tables and reeking of tobacco smoke, the men – and some of the women

– smoking heavily while they ate. There were dozens of men at the tables, sucking down bowls of stew before they went back to training; a handful of women, sitting with them, looked surprisingly dangerous for the fairer sex. Raechel couldn't help thinking that Irene would have liked them, if only for their skill at projecting an image. They wanted – needed – the men to take them seriously.

"Raechel," a voice called. "Come join us?"

Raechel smiled. John was a young man, one of the handful she'd seen in the recruitment centre in New York before they'd been transported to the barge. He was a tradesman by birth, he'd explained, but he hadn't been able to set up a shop of his own because of the government's regulations. Raechel was surprised the Sons had allowed him to train as a soldier – his skills would surely be of more use elsewhere – but men liked their pride. No doubt they'd offered John the chance to be something useful and he'd declined.

"Coming," she called back. "Just let me get some food."

She took a plate of stew and bread from the cooks – she hated to think what her aunt would have thought of the meal, although it was cheap and surprisingly tasty – and hurried over to John. The handful of young men with him smiled as she sat down, their gazes flickering over her breasts before looking away, hastily. Irene had warned her to expect everything from ribald commentary to outright groping, but the Sons had strict rules against any form of harassment. They were clearly serious about using women as well as men.

"It's been a while," John said. "What have you been doing with yourself?"

Two days, more or less, Raechel thought. *But I suppose I barely saw you on the barge.*

"Cooking and cleaning, mostly," she admitted. The Sons had promised firearms training for the women, but it was clear that their training was secondary. "And you?"

"I can now hit a target with a rifle," John said.

"Provided it's stuck to the muzzle," another young man said, quickly. "The trick is to keep up a steady volley of fire, not to try to *hit* something."

Raechel rather doubted her father, a keen sportsman, would have agreed, but she kept that thought to herself as the men argued cheerfully. John insisted he could actually shoot straight; two other men insisted that he didn't have a hope in hell of actually hitting anything unless it was at very close range. It wasn't the sort of discussion she wanted to hear, but she honestly didn't know how to change the subject. Men *always* liked talking about guns and shooting, in her experience. Some of the worst bores in the aristocracy talked of nothing else.

"So," another man said. "When do you think we'll go to New York?"

"When the boss says it's time," a third man said. He was older; Raechel rather suspected he was the training officer. "We don't want to tip our hand too early."

"Yeah," a fourth man said. "And we don't want to lose the chance of winning without fighting."

"Chancy," John said. "Do *you* think the Viceroy will give up without a fight?"

"I have no idea," the first man said. He looked at Raechel. "What do *you* think?"

Raechel flushed. "I don't know," she said. It was easy to push a hint of bitterness into her voice. "It isn't as if they told me *anything*."

She listened as the discussion raged backwards and forwards. John and many of the younger men were looking forward to the fight, enjoying the chance to prove themselves, while the older men were more pessimistic. Victory would come at a very high cost, if it came at all, and the fighting would devastate the colony. If the Viceroy – or his replacement – refused to surrender, he could bring reinforcements from Boston or one of the other garrisons to continue the fight. And the French, looming ominously in the background, might take advantage of the chaos.

"Rumour has it that the slaves have already revolted down south," one of the older men said, darkly. "Do you want those bastards up here?"

"Should send them all back home," John said. "They'll be taking our jobs after the war."

"And the Germans too," another man agreed. "You just can't trust them."

Raechel silently cursed the government under her breath.

There was something ... *honest* about the Sons, something that called to her even as she planned to betray them. Gwen had been right – the Sons had no plan or ability to govern, after the uprising – but she couldn't help liking them. If the government removed a few of the petty restrictions, allowing men like John to open their own shops, who knew what would happen? Even allowing official settlements in the lands beyond the line would be helpful ...

"It's time to get back to work," the older man said. "A pleasure, Miss Raechel, as always."

He rose. The other men followed him, dumping their empty dishes and spoons on the table by the door. Raechel had a feeling she'd see them again, once she went back to work. Meg *definitely* enjoyed making her do menial tasks, just looking for a chance to humiliate or hurt her. The fact Raechel hadn't uttered a word of complaint seemed to bother her more than any screaming fit.

Raechel allowed herself a smile, then listened to some of the other conversations as she finished her stew. The Sons seemed to be divided, something that had surprised her until she'd attended her first evening discussion. Older Sons talked about their ideals, younger Sons were encouraged to ask questions and hash matters out for themselves. Raechel had never seen anything like it, but she had to admit that the debates helped explain the ideology of the Sons and indoctrinate the newcomers.

But some of them want a war, she thought, *and some of them want to take their demands to the Viceroy himself.*

She sighed, inwardly. The demands weren't unreasonable – at least as far as she could tell – but she doubted the government would grant them. Showing weakness could be deadly, in politics. No one would call Lord Liverpool *weak* – she'd heard he was a stubborn reactionary – but he had enemies. A proposal to grant the Americans even modest concessions might be defeated in the Houses of Parliament. And *then* where would the Sons be?

Finishing her stew – making sure to use the remains of her bread to wipe the bowl clean – she rose and hurried out of the door, back to where she was sure Meg was waiting. The wretched woman seemed to have nothing better to do than torment her, even though she was technically responsible for the welfare of half the women in the camp. And yet, Raechel knew herself to be terrifyingly ignorant, compared to some of the others. In hindsight, it might have been better if she'd actually learnt to sew from her mother.

"Your Ladyship," Meg said sarcastically, as Raechel hurried into the barracks. "The boss wants to see you."

Raechel started. "Again?"

"Again," Meg confirmed. "Don't you have a prettier dress you can wear?"

Raechel resisted the urge to snap at her. Of *course* she didn't have any pretty dresses! The only clothes in the camp for women were basic skirts and shirts, the kind of shapeless outfit a farmwife or milkmaid might wear as she went to work. She'd managed to tighten her shirt around her chest, just to make the men more talkative, but otherwise it was nothing like the gowns she'd worn to countless balls. She reminded herself, firmly, that Meg was just trying to get a rise out of her and merely shook her head. She'd endured worse from her aunt.

Meg looked irked, but strode past Raechel, beckoning for her to follow. There were more men in the camp, Raechel noted; striding around as though they owned the place. She looked from man to man, but didn't see a single one who wasn't carrying a weapon. The Sons seemed to *insist* that everyone had to be armed at all times, a far cry from the normal laws in New York. But then, Raechel had to admit it might be necessary. The camp might be attacked at any moment.

"Raechel," Adam said, as she was escorted into his office. "How are you enjoying life in camp?"

"It's different," Raechel said. She wasn't quite sure what to make of Adam. Sitting behind his desk, he looked like a clerk – he certainly seemed to be in charge of the paperwork – but other officers, seemingly more dangerous, deferred to him. "I've never been anywhere quite like it."

Meg snorted. "She made a right dog's dinner out of the stew, sir," she said. "She's not used to doing *anything* for herself."

Raechel scowled, but resisted the urge to snap at the older

woman. It wasn't as if she was one of those girls who needed a maid to do *everything*. She could wash and dress herself with the best of them. But then, if she was being completely honestly, most aristocratic dresses were *designed* to require assistance to put on …

"I doubt anyone really cared, Meg," Adam said. "Did it get eaten?"

"Of course it did," Meg said. She shot Raechel a nasty look. "There's no wastage here!"

"Thank you," Adam said, shortly. "You may leave us."

Raechel expected Meg to snap at *him*, or at least to point out that he was acting more like an aristocrat than a Son of Liberty, but instead she merely nodded and retreated out the door, leaving Raechel alone with Adam. She felt an odd thrill of excitement, mixed with fear and trepidation. Being alone with a man – one she assumed to be unmarried – was a slap in the face to society's conventions … but, at the same time, she knew she was in his power. A scream wouldn't bring help …

Or perhaps it would, she thought. Meg had told her – and the other girls – that they had to scream, if they felt threatened by any of the men. *But it would be disastrous.*

"Have a seat," Adam said. "I have some more questions for you."

Raechel groaned, inwardly. Did Adam suspect? He'd asked her questions when she'd first arrived, perhaps hoping she'd trip up at some point. The other girls had bombarded her with questions too, mostly demanding to know what it was like to be an aristocrat. Had they been primed to ask questions that might blow her cover? Or was Adam playing at something else?

She sat down and glanced around the tiny office, trying not to meet his eyes. There was little elegance in the room, none of the gilt-edged furniture she recalled from her father's office, but it *did* look neat and tidy. Adam was *definitely* a clerk at heart, she decided; he'd organised the paperwork into something anyone could comprehend. And …

"I believe you met the Viceroy," Adam said. "What did you make of him?"

"I only met him once for more than a minute or two,"

Raechel said. "I was presented to him at the ball …"

"You were a debutante, I suppose," Adam said.

"I *came out* in London," Raechel said. "It was just a formal presentation to New York's social scene."

She winced as the memory caused her a pang of grief. Her mother had presented her to the *ton*, knowing her daughter's hand in marriage would be one of the most sought-after prizes in London. Queen Charlotte had been in attendance, too; Raechel had almost tripped over her own dress when she'd curtseyed to the Queen. And if she'd known that her mother would die, later that year, she would have been more appreciative of the chance to spend time with her. What she'd said, after the ball, had been unforgivable.

Adam shrugged. "And when the Viceroy wanted you to marry him?"

Raechel choked. "He wanted me to marry his *son*," she corrected. Viceroy Rochester was old enough to be her father. Indeed, he'd married young, but waited nearly a decade before fathering Bruce. *That* was odd, amongst the aristocracy. Every family needed a male heir and at least one spare before disaster fell. "I wouldn't have married *him*!"

"He's hardly likely to take your feelings into account," Adam pointed out. "Or is he?"

Raechel gathered herself. "My honest impression of him, sir, is that he is a little overwhelmed by competing problems," she said. "But he didn't bother to confide in me."

"A shame, that," Adam grunted. "Do you know anything of *use*?"

"I am a *girl*," Raechel said, tartly. What was Adam playing at? "Do you imagine I was meant for anything, but marrying and producing children?"

She felt another stab of … *something*. If she'd been a boy, she would have been involved in maintaining her father's estate from a very early age; she would have inherited, without any caveats, as soon as her father died. The Slater name would have opened doors at the very highest levels of society. She could have bought herself a commission, joined the civil service or even walked into Parliament. But for a girl … she was at her aunt's mercy for another six years. The prospect of being married off was all too real.

"Maybe," Adam said. "I understand you can read and write?"

He passed her a sheet of paper. "Read this."

Raechel took the piece of paper and scanned it, thoughtfully. The handwriting was awful, but she'd spent enough time parsing out her aunt's crabby writing to know how best to decipher it.

"Two men were arrested in Brooklyn for handing out warning notices," she read. "Franklyn has withdrawn from Theta."

"Very good," Adam said. Raechel glanced at him, but there didn't seem to be any mockery in his tone. "You'll be amazed at how few people here can read."

He passed her a pen and a sheet of paper. "Write down the following," he said. Raechel hastily dipped the pen in ink, then bent over the desk. "Franklyn is to meet George at Freedom Five. No further action is to be taken."

Raechel scribbled it down, word by word. She'd been taught to write in cursive, but she had a feeling it would be better, here, to write as simply as possible. Adam took the paper as soon as she had finished, reading it carefully. She wondered, absently, just who had taught *him* to read and write. There couldn't be *that* many differences between British and American writing, could there?

"Anyone can read that," he said, finally. "Very good."

"Oh," Raechel said. "How many people can *read*?"

Adam shrugged. "It isn't seen as a desirable skill in many places," he said. His lips curved into a smile. "It might give people *ideas*."

Raechel frowned. "And you don't try to teach them?"

"We do," Adam said. "But it takes time."

It made sense, Raechel supposed. She'd been taught to read by her tutors – she assumed Gwen had been homeschooled too – but she'd never heard of a maid learning to read. Irene had warned her that certain classes rarely had the chance to learn. Even a merchant's daughter might not learn more than basic arithmetic.

He smiled. "I need someone to assist me," he added. "Interested?"

Raechel blinked. "You want *me*?"

"We can't use you as a soldier," Adam pointed out. "And you *do* have skills that will be wasted, if you spend your time cooking and cleaning. You would make a very useful assistant."

And, Raechel asked herself, *what else do you want from me?*

It was a tempting offer, almost too good to be true. And that bothered her. Adam's logic was sound, too sound. He *needed* an assistant who could read and write ... and she'd see everything crossing his desk. And yet, why *her*? She was *new* to the Sons of Liberty ...

But she knew she couldn't let the offer pass. "I would be honoured," she said. If he wanted her personally, she'd just have to endure. "But what do you actually *do*?"

Adam gave her a toothy smile. "*Someone* has to organise everything," he said. "And *someone* has to make sure we have something to fight with, when all hell breaks loose."

Chapter Twenty-Seven

wen sat on the roof of City Hall, staring into the distance, as the sun slowly edged above the horizon and cast a shimmering light over Amherst. The city was quiet, but she knew it wouldn't remain that way for long. Jackson had imposed a curfew, warning that anyone caught on the streets after sunset would be arrested, yet it hadn't been enough to stop people from sneaking about. There just weren't enough redcoats – and militia – to enforce the curfew, not when panic was bubbling below the city's surface. The entire city was on edge. It wouldn't be long, she was sure, before there was an explosion.

Those damned rumours, she thought. *If I ever get my hands on the person spreading them ...*

She shook her head, knowing it would be pointless. There had been witnesses, of course, to her brief clash with the rogue magician. By now, everyone in Amherst believed that she'd been brutally thrashed to within an inch of her life by the rogue. They'd seen her patrolling with the other sorcerers, or flying over the city, yet they still believed she'd been beaten. Far too many of them wanted to believe it. And the news that they were cut off from the rest of America hadn't gone down well. The French might not *need* to storm the city to destroy it.

A plume of smoke rose to the west, marking yet another farmstead that had been destroyed by French horsemen or revolting slaves. Gwen sighed. The raids were becoming more frequent as the French army neared, even though it was still several days away. She hoped the farmers had survived – and, despite herself, that any survivors would head north, rather than trying to make it to Amherst. The city was bursting at the seams, despite the best efforts of the redcoats. Food supplies were already running low.

She rose to her feet, shaking her head. She'd spent four days searching for the rogue, either patrolling with the other sorcerers or wandering the streets alone, but she'd found nothing, save for more rumours. She liked to think that the rogue was as nervous about facing her as she was about facing him, yet she suspected the rogue was concentrating, instead, on making matters worse. A skilled magician would have no problems contaminating the water supplies, setting fire to food warehouses and a hundred other little tricks that would be devastatingly effective. She would sooner face him now, knowing she might lose, than leave him running around on his own …

… But he was nowhere to be found.

Gwen turned as she heard the hatch opening, behind her. Lieutenant Jansen stuck his head out, looking around until he saw her. He was a colonial officer, rather than a redcoat, but he'd managed to impress Colonel Jackson with his competence. Given the general run of things, Gwen had a suspicion that that proved he was actually a Son of Liberty. But the Sons had been quiet since their magician had been uncovered, as if they were biding their time and waiting for the French. It wasn't as if they needed to do anything until the French arrived.

"My Lady," Jansen said. "Colonel Jackson requests your presence."

"Very well," Gwen said. Jackson hadn't spoken to her since ordering her to leave the sorcerers with Wayne and search for the rogue. What did he want now? "I'm coming."

She dropped down the hatch behind him, relying on magic to land safely. Jansen looked impressed – he wasn't one of the officers who either viewed her as a weak and feeble woman or made the sign of the cross whenever they thought she wasn't looking – and led the way down to Jackson's office. City Hall had changed, since they'd first arrived; it bustled with life as Jackson rebuilt the civil service that had run the city. But everyone knew that it would be only a matter of time before the French arrived. God alone knew what would happen on that day.

"Colonel," she said, as she stepped into the office. A grim-faced man – Lieutenant Roscoe – was standing in front of the Colonel's desk. Jackson himself looked tired and worn. "You sent for me?"

"We just got a rider in from the east," Jackson said. "The French sent a raiding party to the Ingalls Homestead, one of the smaller settlements in the area. There's a good prospect of being able to catch the bastards if we act now."

Gwen nodded. The French horsemen wouldn't stand a chance if they ran into repeaters – she shuddered at the memory of what had happened to the Hussars – but as long as they did their best to avoid contact with the redcoats they could wreak havoc at will. Their horses gave them a mobility unmatched by the redcoats and, as long as they looted for supplies, they could keep going indefinitely. Each pinprick was minimal, but collectively they added up to a major disaster.

"There may be a magician – a Blazer – with them," Jackson added. "Lady Gwen, I want you to go with our horsemen. If you can catch that magician …"

"I understand," Gwen said. The rogue …? It was possible, but unlikely. The Sons of Liberty didn't really gain from burning out American homesteads, certainly not if they wanted allies instead of new enemies. And if the French ran into British horsemen, her presence would certainly tip the balance against them. "I'll just get my riding clothes and then I'll join you."

"Good luck," Jackson said. "We need a victory, Lady Gwen. We need one very badly."

Gwen nodded as she hurried down to her rooms. Her clothes felt grimy against her skin, but there was no time to wash. Instead, she tore off her shirt and trousers, replacing them with her riding outfit. Her mother would have had a fit if she'd seen Gwen in such clothes – they were tight in a number of places – but there was no choice. She knew how to ride, like most aristocrats, yet she knew the Hussars rode faster. Keeping up with them would be difficult.

I should fly, she told herself. *But that would just drain me before the battle.*

Jackson was right, she decided, as she met up with Lieutenant Roscoe and his hand-picked riders. The French would have problems evading British horsemen, allowing her a chance to get close to them. A horse was already waiting for her, its reins held by a young boy who gawked at her with worshipping eyes. Gwen would have been very surprised if he was older than ten, although that meant nothing. Outside the aristocracy, children were put to work almost as soon as they could walk.

The horse neighed uncomfortably as she scrambled into the saddle, but didn't try to throw her off. Horses had never liked her, Gwen recalled; her first instructor had told her that horses sometimes responded badly to magic. It had taken her longer – far longer – than David to get used to controlling the beasts and, even now, she was reluctant to ride on a horse's back. But there was no choice. She braced herself as Lieutenant Roscoe barked orders to his men, then spurred the horse into following him as he led the way down the road, through the gates and out into the countryside.

She might have enjoyed the ride, if she hadn't kept one wary eye on the horse at all times. He was a tempestuous beast, like many military horses, perfectly capable of kicking an infantryman in the face if he got too close. The countryside shifted with bewildering rapidity; tiny farmsteads, patches of forest, blue rivers flowing ever-east towards the sea, then more farmsteads. She couldn't help noticing that far too many of the farmsteads were burnt-out ruins, a handful of bodies lying where they'd fallen. No one had had time to return and give the corpses a proper burial.

The horse slowed with the remainder of the pack as they cantered down a dusty road, towards yet another plume of smoke billowing up towards the sky. Gwen tensed, readying her magic to strike down her foes, despite the ripple of complaint from the horse. It *definitely* didn't like magic. She wondered idly how a beast could sense magic, then dismissed the thought. There were plenty of humans who could sense magic, but do little else with it. She'd often wondered if it was a sign of an as yet undiscovered talent.

She shuddered as the homestead finally came into view. A handful of buildings, burning brightly; a dozen bodies, lying on the ground. She had to fight to keep her gorge from rising as she saw a young girl, her throat mercifully cut. They'd raped her before they'd killed her, she realised, along with her sister and her mother. The menfolk had been killed too, their bodies torn apart as if they'd been thrown to wild animals. Gwen hoped, inwardly, that they'd died before they'd seen what had happened to the women. If they met up again in the afterlife, they wouldn't know …

It wasn't the women's fault, she told herself. But she knew it wouldn't matter. They would be blamed for being raped. The simple fact that most men were stronger than women, that most women were taught to be subservient if not submissive, never seemed to occur to those who wanted to point fingers. A woman who admitted to being raped could expect to pay a price for it. *And it really wasn't her fault.*

"Magic," Lieutenant Roscoe said, quietly. "They burnt the homestead very quickly."

Gwen nodded in confirmation, silently relieved to have an excuse to look away from the bodies. The homestead had been built from wood, but it wouldn't have burnt *that* quickly without magic. There was definitely a Blazer with the party, unless the French had a Master Magician of their own. Now, she wouldn't have ruled out the possibility. She'd grown far too used to being unique before encountering the rogue.

There was the Saint of Grimsby, she reminded herself. *No one ever quite got to the bottom of her magic.*

"There's no one here, Lieutenant," one of the troopers called. He'd dismounted and inspected the half-destroyed buildings. "They're all dead."

Gwen winced, inwardly. A family had set up a home, miles from Amherst, in the hopes of finding a new life for themselves. And instead, they'd found death, a particularly horrific death. They hadn't deserved to die, she told herself. Judging from the angry comments the troopers were exchanging as they hunted for the French tracks, they evidently agreed.

"We should be able to run them down," Lieutenant Roscoe told her. "Coming?"

"Yes," Gwen said. Her magic pulsed under her skin, demanding escape. "I wouldn't miss it for the world."

She hunkered down in the saddle as the horsemen rode in pursuit. The French couldn't have been on the move for long, Gwen told herself; they'd needed time to … to … kill the men and violate the women, while destroying the remains of their life. She hadn't seen any chickens or pigs, she recalled; no doubt the French had snatched them up, intending to turn the beasts into dinner. A skilled hunter would have no trouble finding enough to eat in the countryside, she knew, but the French wouldn't want to waste time. And besides, it denied the British and Americans access to fresh eggs.

"Tally ho," Lieutenant Roscoe shouted, as the French came into view. Seven horsemen, carrying weapons … Gwen reached out with her senses, but she couldn't identify the magician at such a distance. "No quarter!"

Gwen half-expected the French to keep running, but instead they wheeled around and charged right at the British horsemen. For a long moment, her mind refused to accept what she was seeing. Did the French think they were going to tourney? It wasn't a game, when a horseman could be unseated one moment and rise to shake his enemy's hand the second. No one but an idiot would try to joust against rifle-armed men. She could see Lieutenant Roscoe and his men already priming their weapons. If the French wanted to joust, they'd accept the challenge …

She sensed the surge of magic an instant too late. A wave of force slammed into the horsemen, sending them flying in all directions. Gwen felt herself tossed into the air, her magic barely strong enough to keep her from landing badly. Lieutenant Roscoe's body flew past her, his head missing. The French had shattered the horsemen with a single blow … she shook off her shock – there would be time for panic later – and landed as best she could, ducking down in the hopes of avoiding notice. There wasn't just a Blazer with the French, there was a Mover. Perhaps more than one.

A howl split the air. She looked up, just in time to see a wolf-like monster hurl itself towards her, blood dripping from its jaws. Its disturbingly-human eyes fixed on her, glowing with a mixture of bloodlust and carnal desire. A werewolf … an *insane* werewolf. Gwen had heard stories of werewolves who couldn't control themselves, who became fell beasts with the intelligence of men. Lord Mycroft's brother had killed one in Dartmoor …

She threw up a shield as the beast neared, knocking it back. The werewolf would have been the rapist, she was sure. An insane werewolf would have all the lusts of men without any of the restraints. His comrades would have problems keeping him under control, too. He'd need to be knocked down regularly, convinced time and time again that his superiors were unassailable. Gwen wouldn't have risked using an insane werewolf as a weapon unless she had no other choice – and even then, she would have planned his murder as soon as the job was done. Giving a werewolf a taste for human flesh could be disastrous.

The beast roared and lunged again. Gwen braced herself, then blasted him with fire. The werewolf staggered backwards, howling in pain, but it was far too late. His fur caught fire, followed by his flesh and blood. She stumbled back as the beast went up in flames, his final howl splitting the air. And then he was dead …

A wave of magic washed towards her. She threw herself into the air, hastily surveying her enemies. Two of them were definitely Movers – she could sense the magic boiling around them – while a third was a Blazer, judging by the fireball he'd hurled after her. The other three were standing back, doing nothing. Were they magicians? Or were their talents useless on the field of battle? One of them might be a Talker …

She pushed the thought aside as the Movers slapped at her, their joint blow stronger than any she could generate herself. The punch knocked her over and over – she reached out with her own magic, caught hold of the Blazer and threw him into the air, wondering if any of his comrades would try to rescue him. Somewhat to her surprise, they did; one of them caught the Blazer before he could fall, while the other drove a needle of power into her shield, threatening to punch right through. Gwen cursed and allowed herself to fall to the ground, gathering her power around her as she picked up a rock. Infusing it with power, she hurled it back towards the Movers. They jumped apart, hastily, as the rock exploded with staggering violence.

They know how to work together, she thought. She'd tested herself against Merlin more than once, but Sir James and his men had been holding back. So had she. None of them had really wanted to kill anyone. *Jack must have trained them* ...

Another punch slammed into her shield from above, as if she was being slapped down by a giant hand. Gwen hastily reshaped her shield, but she knew it was just a matter of time before one Mover held her in place while the other formed a needle and tore her shield to shreds. Bracing herself, she hastily Changed the ground below her feet to dust and threw it at them, moving out from under her own protections as soon as there was enough room to move. They wouldn't expect her to do that, would they? It would be suicide if they saw what she was doing before it was too late ...

Flames exploded in front of her, burning her skin. She yelped in pain – she'd forgotten the Blazer – and threw a fireball back at him, aiming right for his exposed head. The Blazer caught fire and exploded, his entire body bursting into a towering inferno. Gwen stared, surprised. She'd seen Blazers die before, but none of them had gone up in flames ...

A force grabbed onto her, picked her up and slammed her into the ground. Gwen barely had the time to shield herself before a second force started to crawl over her body, holding her firmly in place. Her magic seemed drained, somehow; it took all she had to keep the Movers from crushing her to death. They walked forward, their eyes fixed on her. Behind them, their comrades brought up the rear.

Gwen opened her mouth, hoping to Charm them, but she could barely breathe. Her power seemed to have deserted her ... it had been an ambush, she realised. The French had been so scared of her that they'd set a trap and she'd walked right into it. She tried to look submissive, but she knew it was futile. Keeping her prisoner would be difficult, perhaps impossible, and the French had to know it.

"Kill her," one said.

I'm sorry, Gwen thought, unsure just who she was addressing. Colonel Jackson? Lord Mycroft. Her parents? *I* ...

"No," a new voice said. A fireball struck one of the Frenchmen, burning through his clothes and incinerating his body. "You will *not* kill her."

Chapter Twenty-Eight

wen stared.

The rogue was standing there, wearing a mask that covered the upper half of his face and a black cloak that shimmered around his body. He seemed completely composed, even though he was facing at least two magicians who'd hammered Gwen into the ground and two more Frenchmen who might have powers of their own. Flames danced over his hands, showing off his power. Gwen wasn't sure if she should admire his nerve or point out the dangers of accidentally setting his clothes on fire.

"Kill him," one of the Frenchmen finally snarled. "I ..."

The rogue lifted his hands, throwing a wave of force at the Frenchmen, Gwen felt the power holding her down snap out of existence as the Movers hastily moved to defend themselves; she stumbled to her feet, trying to get out of the line of fire. She had no idea why the rogue – she was *sure* it was the same magician – had moved to defend her, but she knew better than to look a gift horse in the mouth. At least the French would be equally confused.

She cursed under her breath as one of the other Frenchmen revealed himself to be another Blazer, shooting a hail of fireballs at the rogue. The rogue responded by tearing up the ground and throwing it at the Blazer, then hurrying over to shield Gwen as the Movers pushed back hard. He caught Gwen's arm ... and she felt a sudden surge of energy, as if she was drawing a little from him. His eyes were so blue ...

He smiled back at her, just before a force punch slammed into his protections. The Movers looked furious at being denied their prize, Gwen saw; they were hammering at the rogue's protections as if they were determined to crush *both* magicians. Her power surged within her and she lashed out, throwing both of them into the air. The rogue laughed and joined her, their magic blurring together into a single unbeatable wave.

"Stop," the final Frenchman said. Charm echoed on the air, powerful enough to make almost anyone stop in their tracks. Gwen and the rogue *laughed* at him. "Stop fighting and ..."

Gwen wasn't sure who took the lead, but their powers reached out and ripped the Charmer's head off his shoulders. His body hit the ground, blood pooling in the mud, as they hurled his head at the Movers. The Frenchmen ignored it, concentrating on hammering away at their joint protections while the Blazer threw fireball after fireball, but they might as well have been trying to tear an iron wall apart with their bare hands. Gwen was no longer certain where she ended and the rogue began, but it hardly mattered. United, they were so much greater than the sum of their parts.

Power surged within them, slapping the two Frenchmen apart. The Blazer's eyes widened with fear as he realised he was in deep trouble, but he kept fighting even as the air hardened around him. His body disintegrated as they crushed it into a bloody pulp, snuffing his life out once and for all. Gwen almost giggled, despite a voice at the back of her head telling her she should be careful. The power was so strong that it sucked at her thoughts, making it harder to think clearly. Why hadn't she known this was possible? She'd never felt such a strong connection with Jack or Master Thomas ...

Why? her own thoughts answered her. *You never saw either of them as equals.*

The Frenchmen broke and ran. Gwen and the rogue reached out, caught hold and pulled them back. A Frenchman tore at the nearby trees, yanking them out of the ground and hurling the shattered fragments of wood towards the two Masters, but it was pointless; the trees disintegrated into dust as soon as they slammed into the joint shield. One of the Movers ran forward, shaping his power into a needle ...

... But it was suddenly the easiest thing in the world to hold the shield. Gwen felt the Mover's power break on hers

– theirs – just before the rogue lashed out. The Mover stopped dead, then crumpled to the ground, blood leaking from his ears. They'd torn his brain apart from the inside. The final Frenchman threw himself up into the air in a desperate attempt to escape, one he *had* to know would be futile. They tore his power apart and watched him fall to the ground, then caught him a second before the impact would have killed him.

"Tell us who sent you," they said together. Gwen wasn't sure which of them wanted to know, but it didn't matter. "And why?"

The Mover knelt, his hands twitching uselessly. "Kill the sorceress bitch," he said. His voice was completely flat, as if his free will had collapsed completely. "Kill her before ..."

He fell to the side.

"Dead," the rogue said. Gwen suddenly realised he hadn't let go of her hand, but she made no move to pull free. "He couldn't tell it."

He turned to look at her. Gwen felt a sudden surge of passion and desire, far more than she'd felt before, even when Sir Charles had kissed her for the very first time. She wanted him ... and knew he felt the same way too. Their joined powers were pulling them together ... it was suddenly the easiest thing in the world to take a step forward and kiss him, their lips melding together until they were practically one. He wrapped his arms around her as the kiss deepened, running down the small of her back until he was stroking the top of her buttocks, every touch inflaming her still further.

She knew, at the back of her mind, that she should push him away, but she didn't *want* to push him away. The growing desire within her wouldn't let her stop. His hands were slipping into her trousers, pushing them down to her knees; her hands, guided by ... *something* ... were undoing his belt, removing his trousers. She glanced down as she stepped out of her own trousers, then let him push her gently to the ground. Their magic billowed around them as his hands stroked her breasts; she gasped in surprise as she felt his maleness pressing against her legs. There was a sudden stab of pain as he entered her, followed by a tidal wave of pleasure. She wrapped her legs around him, pulling him deeper into her as they rolled over and over. The same thought – the warning that she was going too far – resurfaced, but she ignored it. She couldn't stop. They were *alive*!

His maleness started to throb inside her, triggering off a surge of pleasure that had her throwing caution to the winds and crying out in delight. She hadn't known – she'd never known – just how wonderful it could be. If she'd known … she kissed him as he spent himself, her hands reaching up to cup his head and tear at the mask. It came off, revealing …

She stared, shocked again. "Bruce?"

The Viceroy's son stared back at her, pulling back instinctively. It dawned on Gwen just *what* they'd been doing. They'd made love. No, worse than that. She'd given up her maidenhood to him! And he was … he was the rogue. She was suddenly very aware that she was lying on the dirty ground, her bare bottom pressed into the mud and a man, naked from the waist down, lying on top of her. And he was …

"You're the rogue," she said, numbly. In hindsight, the clues had been right in front of her … and she'd dismissed them, without bothering to seriously consider the matter. Bruce had been nearby, when she'd first seen the rogue, and he'd come with her to Amherst, along with the rogue. "You're a Son."

"Quite literally," Bruce said. He gave her a goofy grin. "I …"

Gwen bucked her legs, torn between embarrassment, anger and horror. She'd slept with the enemy! Worse than that, she'd run the very real risk of getting pregnant. Bruce rolled off her, allowing her to sit up. There was a tiny trace of blood between her legs, as Lucy had warned her would happen when she surrendered her maidenhead. Her womanhood felt … odd, humming with contentment and, at the same time, warning her that she should not do it again for a while. She needed time to grow accustomed to what she'd done.

And she wanted to do it again. God help her, she wanted to do it again.

"You were there when we talked about the rogue," she accused. Anger was better than shame or humiliation. She looked around for her trousers and underpants, then swore as she realised they were over by the dead bodies. "You must have been laughing your head off at us."

"You accused me of wanting to kill my father," Bruce pointed out. He didn't seem bothered by being naked. "Do you think *that* pleased me?"

It took Gwen a moment to recall what she'd said. "It's a testament to the power of your aristocratic idiot act," she said, finally. "I never suspected you for a second."

Bruce preened. "What now?"

Gwen fought down the urge to smack him. Instead, she crossed her legs, concealing her secrets as best she could. It was futile – he'd just been inside her – but no one had seen her naked since she'd been a child. Even the maids had barely dared to enter her room, knowing that she was cursed with magic. No doubt they'd expected her to turn them into toads if they disturbed her sleep.

She met his eyes. "Why did you save my life?"

Bruce said nothing for a long moment. "Do *you* believe the French will betray us?"

"I think it's very likely," Gwen said, tartly. She gestured in the direction of the dead bodies, the soldiers and the settlers. "Do you think they'll go to war just to give you their freedom?"

Her mouth dropped open as a thought struck her. "Raechel. You knew. You knew all along!"

Bruce held up his hands, placatingly. "Your friend is in no real danger," he assured her. "I just thought it might be better to have a spy we knew about, rather than one we didn't."

Gwen shook her head in disbelief. She'd nearly been killed, then she'd been saved by a presumed enemy, then she'd lost her maidenhead ... and then she'd discovered that the Sons had been one step ahead of them all along. Bruce ... she'd never suspected him, standing right beside the most powerful man in the colonies. No wonder the Sons had been so confident that they could come and go as they pleased, even taking the risk of liberating Raechel from Irene. They'd known about every raid that might have exposed their secrets.

She swallowed, hard. No matter what they'd done together, they were still enemies. And she was in no state for a fight. She thought he would be just as drained, but it was impossible to be sure.

"Bruce," she said, quietly. "Why are you doing this?"

She half-expected a flippant answer, but Bruce did her the honour of taking the question seriously. "My mother was American," he said. "Her family were New York gentry, but they were very definitely American. Many of them ... many of them had made their peace with the Crown after the revolution failed; others chafed under the rules and regulations imposed by the government. There was no true freedom in New York. Many others ..."

He sucked in a breath. "The aristocrats who coddled up to my father were not true men," he added. "They would have dismissed my father in a heartbeat if they'd felt they could get away with it. The ... they thought of themselves as clever, but all they were doing was fighting over a diminishing pie. They weren't allowing anyone to compete with them on even terms. The same was true of the women – they might have been aristocrats, but they were trapped in gilded cages. And they were bringing more and more slaves and indentured servants to the colonies ...

"It took me far too long to realise that eventually they'd destroy themselves."

"Like the aristocracy in Britain nearly did," Gwen said.

"Exactly," Bruce said. "We want representation, the right to choose our own governments and officials. It isn't much, but ..."

"But you didn't get it," Gwen finished. "And now you've built an army, an army that will tear the colonies apart, only to run the risk of handing them to the French instead."

"We want to build a new world," Bruce said. He waved a hand in the air. "There can be something new and better here, Gwen. Aren't you tempted?"

"Tempted?"

"You only have power in Britain because you have powerful magic," Bruce pointed out. "I think you know it. But here, you could be a power in your own right."

Gwen shifted uncomfortably. Raechel had been tempted

... and, if she were forced to be honest, she'd have to admit that she was tempted too. God alone knew how many bright young women had been forced into becoming dull little dolls by their parents, while their brothers were given ranks and positions to which they were wholly unsuited. And Irene was one of the smartest people Gwen had met, but she was forever held down by factors beyond her control.

She met his eyes. "Do you expect me to betray my oaths?"

"No," Bruce said. "But I think you do have to ask yourself just what is likely to happen if the current situation continues."

Gwen hesitated. "There is something you need to know," she said. "And I'm going to drop my shields to allow you to read my emotions, just so you know I'm telling the truth."

Bruce's eyebrows crawled upwards, but he said nothing. Gwen carefully dismantled her shields, suddenly feeling naked – again – in front of him. She'd never needed to pretend to be something she wasn't, unlike Irene and Raechel. No one would be surprised if she had the power to shield her thoughts. But now she needed him to believe every word.

She took a moment to gather her thoughts, then began. "Whitehall *knows* the current situation is unsustainable," she said. "They are prepared to cede most of your demands, in exchange for your wholehearted support for the war. You could have your own united parliament as soon as next year, if you worked for it. There would be no need to overthrow the government and set up your own, while fighting a civil war!"

Bruce stared at her. It crossed her mind, suddenly, that he might not have very good control over some of his talents. God knew *she* didn't and she had a feeling she'd actually been playing with her magic for longer than him. Maybe he *couldn't* read her emotions, let alone her thoughts. How much did he know about his talents?

"I see," Bruce said, finally. "Are you serious?"

"Yes," Gwen said. "Bruce, I can ask your father to implement the contingency plan now!"

"I'd have to speak to the others," Bruce said. "Not all of them would believe you."

Gwen took a breath. "You have to know that time is running out," she said. "The French are approaching Amherst. If the Sons rise up against the redcoats, they're going to be branded traitors once and for all. There will be no hope of establishing a peaceful ... readjustment of power. Either the Crown crushes you as traitors or you take power by force, only to lose it to the French. Time is not on your side."

She hesitated, then rose and stalked towards the remains of her trousers. Her legs felt wobbly, but she refused to let herself fall over. Her trousers were caked in mud and her underclothes were torn; gritting her teeth, she pulled them back on and did her best to remove the mud. God alone knew what she was going to tell Jackson, when she finally made it back to Amherst. If she told him half the truth, he'd have a fit ...

And if I told him what we did together, she thought, *he'd have a heart attack.*

The horses were dead, she discovered; she wasn't really surprised. Lieutenant Roscoe and his men looked to have been torn apart, too. She wanted to bury them, but there was no time to waste. The only thing she could do was make her way back to Amherst and hope Jackson could send out a burial party before it was too late. She forced herself to check Lieutenant Roscoe's body for anything that might help the French, then took his pistol and remaining ammunition. It might be useful on the trek back to the city.

"I will have to speak to the others," Bruce said. He pulled on his own pants, then held out a hand. "But for what it's worth, I will help you get back before I go on to find them."

Gwen nodded. She doubted anyone in Amherst knew that Bruce had slipped out of City Hall, let alone shadowed Gwen and Lieutenant Roscoe to their fateful meeting. Did he even have a cover story for his servants, if he failed to return?

"I meant to ask," she said, as they started to walk. "How did you keep your powers secret from your father?"

Bruce made no pretence of being surprised by the question. "My uncle was the only one who knew," he said. Gwen guessed that something unfortunate had happened, just as had happened to her. "And he warned me to keep them secret until I knew what I wanted to do with them. Father never knew."

He gave her a sidelong look. "But he's going to know now, isn't he?"

"It depends on you," Gwen said. "Time is *really* not on your side."

Chapter Twenty-Nine

they fell into a companionable silence as they made their slow way towards Amherst, something which suited Gwen more than she cared to admit. Her world had turned upside down, no matter how much she might have wanted to deny it. She'd been wrong about Bruce, wrong – perhaps – about the Sons … and she'd surrendered her maidenhead. She couldn't help feeling strangely uncertain about the whole affair. If her mother had found out …

She cursed silently, wondering what was *normal*. Her mother had told her nothing of what passed between husband and wife, while the handful of books she'd managed to obtain on the subject had been demonstrably inaccurate when it came to female bodies. Lucy had been a little more explicit – it had been she who'd demonstrated the link between periods and the reproductive cycle – but even *she* hadn't gone into too much detail. Some of the younger girls had spoken of feeling attraction, even desire, towards men. Raechel had gone further, much further than Gwen …

I should ask her, Gwen thought. It wouldn't be easy, not after she'd told Raechel off for risking everything for a wild thrill, but she didn't know who else she could ask. Irene? *She might know what happened.*

She glanced at Bruce, feeling an odd string of emotions. She'd kissed Jack and Sir Charles, but neither of them had made her feel so … *strange*. Her emotions were a bizarre mixture of delight, relief, contentment and alarm, rapidly shading to panic. She'd fought beside Jack and Master Thomas, but she'd never felt so … so *lustful* afterwards. She felt a hot flash of shame as she realised just what she'd done, combined with a strange sense of freedom. The conventions of polite society no longer bothered her as much as they had.

Did our shared magic draw us together, she asked herself, *or were we attracted to each other right from the start?*

There was no way to know. It was rare for magicians to marry other magicians – but then, before Gwen there had only been a handful of registered female magicians. Were Blazers attracted to other Blazers? Movers to other Movers? Irene had admitted, once, that Talkers were often drawn to other Talkers, although their relationships rarely lasted. There was something about being so *open* with one's partner which made maintaining the relationship impossible. Gwen looked at Bruce, wondering what he was thinking. Could their ... whatever it was ... survive if he knew everything about her?

"I should have brought a horse," Bruce said, as the skies darkened. "It's going to rain."

Gwen looked at him. "You flew, I assume?"

Bruce nodded, wordlessly.

"You're good," Gwen admitted. "Who taught you?"

"There was a pair of magicians, a Blazer and a Mover, who fled the uprising in London," Bruce said. It took Gwen a moment to realise he meant the Unrest, Jack's first attempt at rebellion, rather than the Swing. "They made their way to the colonies, where they joined the Sons."

Gwen nodded, slowly. "What about the other talents?"

"I'm much less good with them," Bruce said. "Jane tried to teach me how to monitor emotions and thoughts, but I could never master it."

"It isn't easy," Gwen said. "Healing?"

Bruce shook his head. Gwen felt an odd flicker of relief. It had taken her nearly a *year* to make *any* progress with Healing, even with Lucy as a guide. She wasn't surprised that Bruce had managed to master Moving and Blazing, but having him outdo her with the other talents would have been ... irritating. Jack had been better than her, of course, yet he'd had at least a decade of training before he betrayed Master Thomas. And Master Thomas hadn't known that there *were* Healers ...

The skies opened. Rain plunged from the heavens. Gwen

drew on her magic to shield herself, then kept walking. She wasn't sure *quite* how far they were from Amherst, but she knew there was no point in wishing for a horse. Flying herself could be dangerous in the rain, she'd learnt through bitter experience. Bruce didn't seem bothered by the rain, even when it soaked his clothes clean through. Gwen wasn't sure if he was showing off or merely unconcerned. He'd have to change, probably in a hiding place within the city, before he slipped back to City Hall.

Bruce caught her arm as they finally reached the road. "Amherst is just down there," he said, softly. "I need to sneak in a different way."

Gwen nodded. It would be difficult to explain Bruce's presence, if they ran into a mounted patrol. "I'll see you tonight," she said, instead. "Are you going to talk to the Sons?"

"Yeah," Bruce said. "But I don't know what they'll say."

Gwen hesitated, unsure what *she* wanted to say. Raechel probably knew *precisely* what to say to a man, after making love to him. But there had been no time to think and plan ...

"We need to talk, later," she said. She was going to be dreadfully embarrassed talking to him, after everything they'd done, but there was no choice. "I don't ..."

Her voice trailed off. Bruce had her over a barrel and knew it. The merest *hint* that she'd slept with him would destroy her career, if it reached Britain. Her cheeks stung with sudden embarrassment. No one gave a damn about male sorcerers who slept with whores outside wedlock, but her? Her position would become untenable.

"We will," Bruce promised. He met her eyes. "Whatever happens, Lady Gwen, what we did back there" – he waved a hand back in the direction they'd come – "will not pass my lips."

He gave her a brief kiss, then turned and hurried into the distance. Gwen watched him go, feeling oddly unsure of herself. She *believed* Bruce meant every word, but ... what they'd done might have had consequences. Gritting her teeth, she looked down at her muddy clothes and started to walk. There would be time to think about the scale of the disaster later, if all hell broke loose. Right now, she had to get back to the city.

The rainfall came to an end as she crested the ridge and walked down towards the outer edge of the defences, careful to keep her hands in view. Colonel Jackson had mounted snipers along the walls, men who'd been hunters in civilian life. The defences themselves were constantly expanding, growing larger and larger as the workers added more and more refinements. Gwen hoped – prayed – that the French didn't have too many magicians with their army. If they had to take Amherst by storm, it would cost them dearly.

"Lady Gwen," the guard said. He stared at her in astonishment. "What happened?"

Gwen bit down on a sarcastic answer. "I need to go to City Hall," she said, instead. She needed to wash and change before she met Colonel Jackson, if only to keep from trailing mud throughout his office. "Send a runner; inform the Colonel that the remainder of the party is dead and I will report to him, after I've had a bath."

The guard nodded. Gwen walked past him and whistled to a coachman, who jumped down and helped her into the carriage. She took a moment to centre herself as the coach rattled to life, the driver cracking the whip enthusiastically. How did Bruce intend to enter the city and sneak back into City Hall? His servants must be Sons themselves, ready to cover for him if necessary. Gwen couldn't help a flicker of admiration, mixed with concern. If the Viceroy had missed his son's true nature, what *else* had he missed?

She jumped out of the carriage at City Hall and hurried up the rear steps to her suite. She'd wanted to stay near the other sorcerers, but Jackson had insisted on her taking the quarters that had belonged to the former mayor's daughter. For once, Gwen was almost relieved as she hurried through the door, the serving maid staring at her in absolute disbelief. She *had* to look a mess.

"Pour cold water into the bathtub, then leave me," Gwen ordered curtly. Maids were supposed to be discreet, but she hadn't hired *this* maid. If there was one thing she'd learnt from her adventure in Russia, it was that maids – and other servants – talked. "If the colonel sends a messenger, inform him that I will be along shortly."

The maid nodded and hurried to obey. Gwen removed her shoes – they'd have to be cleaned, along with the rest of her outfit – and then glanced in the mirror. She looked worse than she'd dared imagine, her trousers and shirt torn and ruined. The maid would probably need to throw them out, rather than try to repair them. She stepped into the bathroom and dismissed the maid, who looked surprised at Gwen's choice of water. But it was quicker for her to heat the water using magic than wait for the maid to carry buckets of warm water from the kitchen.

She undressed as soon as the maid had gone, closing the door firmly behind her, then studied her naked body in the mirror. There were marks everywhere, bruises from the brief confrontation mingling with red marks where Bruce had held her. Her lips looked swollen, although the swelling was clearly going down. She made a mental note to use an illusion to hide the swelling, then heated the water and climbed into the bath. After the long walk back to the city, the warm water felt like heaven.

A chill ran down her spine as she considered the possible consequences. What if Bruce had got her pregnant? It was possible ... and she might not know for months. Her periods had always been irregular, something she'd assumed was connected to her magic. It would take several months for her to be sure they'd stopped completely, by which time the baby would be well on the way to being born. What was she meant to do then? Her mother had aborted a child, once. All of a sudden, Gwen understood perfectly how her mother had felt.

Lucy could abort the child, she thought, *but ...*

She stared down at her flat stomach, cursing herself for a fool. Ending an unborn child's life was a sin, in and of itself. She'd sinned, but that didn't give her the right to commit *another* sin just to cover the first one up. And who knew what the child of two such powerful magicians would be like? It was her *duty* to find new magicians. She couldn't abort the child without breaking her oath.

I might have to marry him, she thought. She flushed. Part of her body liked that idea, liked it very much. But she didn't know him *that* well; hell, his *father* didn't know him that well. It was possible, she supposed, that she could find another prospective husband, but that would be awkward. There would be no way to hide the suspicious timing. *By the time I know I'm pregnant, it will be too late to pretend it happened on the wedding night.*

Gwen climbed out of the bath and stumbled into the bedroom. She looked at the bed wistfully, then hastily dressed and hurried back down the stairs to Jackson's office. He was standing in front of the map, looking grim. Someone – one of the scouts, Gwen assumed – had updated the map, warning of French troops approaching the city. It wouldn't be long before they were in a position to storm the defences.

"Lady Gwen," Jackson said. He turned to face her, his face pale. "What *happened*?"

"The French laid a trap for me," Gwen said. She sat down, rather quickly. "Their raiding party was completely composed of magicians. The others were killed … and I was only saved by the rogue."

Jackson stared. "The rogue *saved* you?"

Gwen nodded. She hated to admit that she'd needed help – it was always seen as a sign of feminine weakness, as if men didn't need help themselves – but there was no choice.

"We spoke afterwards," she said. There was no way she could tell Jackson *everything* they'd done. "He … he has been having doubts about the French."

"Smart man," Jackson said. "Who is he?"

"I need to keep that to myself, for the moment," Gwen said. She didn't want to lie to him outright, not when Bruce might reveal himself soon. "He said he would talk to the other Sons and then get back to us."

"He may have to move quickly," Jackson said. He didn't sound pleased, but merely nodded to the map. "The French will be on us in two days, perhaps sooner."

"They may have hoped to catch me first," Gwen said. She would have been surprised if there *wasn't* a spy or two in Amherst. "They came very close to killing me outright."

"That may mean they don't have any other magicians with them," Jackson mused.

Gwen shrugged. It was tempting to believe that he was right, but she knew better than to take it for granted.

Certainly, if *she* had to kill a Master Magician, she would have used overwhelming numbers … if she'd had them. But the French might think differently. Their team had worked together to catch Gwen and had almost won. They *would* have won if Bruce hadn't shown up.

And he never told me why he was out there, she thought. In hindsight, it was the one question she should have asked. *Was he shadowing us from the start?*

"I need to borrow your Talker," she said, instead. "And then I really need to rest."

"He's in the next room," Jackson said. He nodded towards the door. "Good luck."

"Stop the search for the Sons," Gwen said, rising. "Right now, we might as well try to make a gesture of good will."

She tested her mental shields carefully before stepping into the next room, even though a Communications Talker was unlikely to be able to read her mind. The young man sitting at a chair, his eyes unfocused, would have had a better job if he'd been a mind-reader, but there was no point in taking chances. Blackmail was a very real threat to a young woman in her position. She remembered Augustus Howell all too well.

"Lady Gwen," the Talker said. He sounded vague, as if half his mind was permanently occupied with some greater matter. There was no sense that he was trying to invade her thoughts. "Who would you like to contact?"

"Viceroy Rochester," Gwen said, sitting down. "Tell his Talker that it's urgent – and secret."

She forced herself to wait as the Talker began to mumble to himself. It might take some time before Rochester and his Talker were together, in private. He might be holding another ball, hoping to convince New York that matters were under control, or he might be coping with yet another crisis. Irene would be there to help him, at least, Gwen thought. And Raechel …

She won't come to any harm, she thought. As embarrassing as the whole affair was, Raechel shouldn't be harmed. It would definitely serve as a learning experience for her, unless it turned nasty. *Bruce said she'd be safe …*

The Talker cleared his throat. "This is Rochester," he said.

"What can I do for you?"

"I was able to talk to one of the Sons," Gwen said. She outlined the *official* version of what had happened, careful to leave Bruce's name out of it. *He* could explain his double life to his father. "It's time to put the parliamentary contingency plan into effect."

There was a long pause. "There will be opposition in the House of Lords," Rochester said, finally. The Talker captured his inflections perfectly. "Not everyone will go along with it."

"The Sons are far better organised than we dared fear," Gwen said. She took a breath, then pressed on. "We have to compromise now or risk losing everything. The French will not hesitate to take advantage of a prolonged period of civil war in the colonies."

She sighed. "And there are other problems we need to solve," she added. "The industrial restrictions only make it harder for us to supply the colonies, when the colonies are cut off from the motherland. We might need to expand our industrial base."

"I understand," Rochester said. "I'll consult with London, then make a formal announcement."

And hope to hell no one tries to walk the promise back later, Gwen thought. Lord Mycroft and the Duke of India understood the value of keeping one's promises – and being *seen* to keep one's promises – but Lord Liverpool was a reactionary. *The Sons will not tolerate us betraying them ... and if the war is won, they won't have to worry about the French.*

"Thank you, Your Excellency," Gwen said. Word would get out quickly in New York, regardless of what Bruce said. The handful of aristocrats she'd met would have a chance to adjust before their world turned upside down. "If you don't mind, I'll speak to you later. I desperately need to sleep."

"I understand," Rochester said. "Goodnight, Lady Gwen."

The Talker closed his eyes for a long moment, breaking the connection. Gwen nodded her thanks, then hurried back up the stairs to her room. She heard Bruce's voice, echoing down from his suite, but resisted the urge to go to him and ask just what had happened. Had anyone realised he'd left

City Hall? *She* certainly hadn't paid much attention to his comings and goings …

I'll need to spend more time with him, whatever happens, she told herself. Another Master Magician … she *needed* him on her side. *And who knows? Maybe the horse will learn to sing.*

Shaking her head, she stepped into her quarters, locked and bolted the door, then walked over to the bed and lay down, without bothering to undress. Sleep claimed her seconds later, sending her plunging down into darkness. Her last thought was that everything else could wait.

Chapter Thirty

It was hard to be sure, but Raechel was starting to have the feeling that Adam *hadn't* selected her because of her clerical skills. Maybe she could read and write, yet she was fairly sure that the Sons of Liberty would have no difficulty finding men or women of unquestionable loyalty who might be just as capable as she. And yet, all of her darker suspicions had proven fruitless too. Adam didn't even seem inclined to stare at her, when they were alone together, let alone send his hands wandering into forbidden territory. There was something about his actions that didn't quite make sense.

She scowled down at the ledger, running her eyes down the numbers with practiced ease. It had never occurred to her that an underground group must have a budget, but the Sons of Liberty disposed of quite startling amounts of cash. Raechel had to admit that it made a certain amount of sense, yet the ledgers were surprisingly vague about where the money actually came *from*. She doubted most of the recruits could contribute much to the cause, even if they were still paid wages in New York. Maybe the Sons were stealing money to finance their operations.

Her eyes narrowed as she reached an odd entry in the ledger, then glanced back to check that she was right. The entry insisted that the Sons had purchased several hundred rifles – it didn't say from whom – but earlier entries suggested that it should have been cheaper. It wasn't as if there weren't thousands of rifles washing around the colonies, from pre-revolutionary weapons to militia equipment that had gone walkabout. Someone seemed to have taken the money for his own use.

She looked up at Adam, bent over his own book. He wasn't much, she had to admit, and yet he controlled the purse strings. All of a sudden, she understood why her uncle had played such a long game, trying to gain a high position in the Treasury. The man who controlled the cash flow was in a position to dispense patronage and steer policy without ever being clearly visible. Just how much control did Adam have over the Sons? Was she looking at the true leader, the man in the shadows?

Adam looked up. "Yes?"

"There's an entry here," Raechel stuttered. How the hell had he caught her staring at him? "I think someone's been stealing money?"

"Let me see," Adam said, rising. He paced over to her and took the ledger, scanning it with practiced ease. "Yes, this could be a problem. Well spotted."

Raechel frowned. "What are you going to do about it?"

Adam patted her on the back, awkwardly. "Check carefully to make sure it isn't an error," he said, putting the ledger on the desk. "The cost of weapons has gone up, recently. I …"

There was a sharp tap on the door. "It's unlocked," Adam called, stepping away from Raechel's desk. "Come in!"

The door opened. General Roosevelt – the soldier she'd met when she'd first entered the camp – entered, looking … odd. He held a piece of paper in his hand, which he passed to Adam. Raechel wanted to see it for herself, but Adam didn't show it to her. Instead, he dropped it in his pocket.

"It has to be a lie," he said, flatly.

"It came directly from Amherst," Roosevelt snapped. Raechel's eyes widened. *Gwen* had gone to Amherst. "And there are rumours in New York that confirm it!"

"That proves nothing," Adam insisted.

"He can hardly make a promise and then go back on it," Roosevelt insisted. "Really …"

"He's an aristocrat from a long line of aristocrats," Adam said. "I *assure* you that his forefathers could lie, cheat and steal with the best of them. Whatever promises he makes, even in front of the House of Lords, will be so watered down that they might as well not have been made. You know as well as I do just how many wealthy and powerful men have an interest in ensuring that things stay the same!"

"Except we would be taking a big risk if we struck, even if we won the first battles," Roosevelt reminded him. "I don't want to spend the rest of my life under the French!"

"Nor do I," Adam said. "But do you want to spend the rest of your life under the British?"

"The issue needs to be debated," Roosevelt said. "Here – and everywhere else."

Adam took a long breath, clearly controlling his temper. "And if this is a lie?"

"You are at liberty to speak out against the proposal, if you wish," Roosevelt said. "I think everyone has a right to be heard, do they not?"

"Fine," Adam snapped. "Assemble everyone, if you wish. We'll hold a full meeting after lunch. Let's see how it goes."

Roosevelt nodded, then turned and stalked out of the office, closing the door behind him with a loud thud. Raechel watched, nervously, as Adam paced the floor, muttering under his breath. She wanted to know what the paper said, but she didn't dare try to reach for it. Adam was one of the most placid men she'd ever met. If it was enough to make him angry, she didn't want to know what he would do if she tried to take the paper.

"Finish the job," he growled at her, finally. "And when you go for lunch, lock the door and remain in the hall afterwards."

"Yes, sir," Raechel said.

Adam gave her a sharp look, then strode out of the office. Raechel hesitated, then rose to her feet and hurried towards his desk. She was so rarely left alone that she knew she couldn't miss the opportunity, despite the risk. The papers on his desk were nothing more than intelligence reports – troop locations around New York, she saw – and, when she opened the drawers, she found a bag of unmarked gold coins. They weren't legal tender, technically, but they *were* gold. A person with the right connections would have no trouble turning them into money.

She closed the drawers hastily, then hurried back to her desk and pretended to continue with the ledger, thinking all the time. What *had* been on that piece of paper? And why had Adam reacted so badly, when Roosevelt had been hopeful? What – if anything – had happened in Amherst?

The dinner bell rang twenty minutes later. Adam hadn't returned, so Raechel locked the office door and headed for dinner. Everyone seemed to be crammed into the dining hall – it was standing room only – including a number of men and women she hadn't seen before, all of whom were carrying weapons. She caught sight of John, on the other side of the room, but the crowd was too large for her to get to him. Instead, she took a bowl of stew and ate quickly, wondering just what was going on. If only she had Irene's talents …

Someone rapped hard on a wooden block. Raechel turned, just in time to see Roosevelt clambering onto a table, looking remarkably sprightly for a man of his age. Adam was standing next to the table, his face an expressionless mask. Meg was standing nearby, her face twisted in distaste. She'd barely spoken a handful of words to Raechel since she'd gone to work for Adam.

Maybe I impressed her, Raechel thought. *Or maybe she thinks I have influence with him.*

She pushed the thought aside as Roosevelt cleared his throat. Silence fell at once, broken only by a handful of coughs and the sound of men eating in the rear of the room. It looked as though the entire camp had been assembled, although Raechel was sure that wasn't true. If nothing else, the guards and pickets couldn't be called in at such short notice. It would run the risk of leaving the camp undefended.

"There has been an interesting development at Amherst," Roosevelt said. His voice echoed around the room. "One of our magicians ended up having a friendly conversation with the Royal Sorceress, after discovering what the French did to a number of innocent American homesteaders. The discussion raised an interesting point. London is prepared to grant most of our demands in exchange for our service against the French.

"I had my doubts, as you will know," he continued, as a low murmuring swept the chamber. "But one of our sources within the Viceregal Palace confirmed that the Viceroy has contacted London, requesting permission to announce the formation of an American Parliament with universal suffrage. This parliament would assume most of the Viceroy's powers. As yet, as far as we know, London has not replied. However, from what the Royal Sorceress said, the groundwork has already been laid for conceding the point."

Raechel frowned. Just *what* had happened in Amherst? She knew enough about British politics – and American – to know that establishing a parliament wouldn't be easy. There were just too many vested interests involved, some of whom would be adamantly opposed to granting any concessions. Hell, the slaveowners alone would be a major headache. The last thing they wanted was a parliament that would free the slaves, then send them all back to Africa.

"We always knew that our plan had its dangers," Roosevelt said. "If we won, we might lose the colonies to the French; if we lost, we might *still* find ourselves under French domination, when the French swept the weakened redcoats aside and took possession of the coastline. We told ourselves that we had no choice, that we needed to gamble for our freedom. If this offer is genuine, however, there is no *need* to gamble. We could win what we want without needing to fight."

Raechel stared. Did he honestly intend to put it to a vote?

Roosevelt scrambled off the table. Adam clambered up and took his place.

"I will not mince words," he said. "The last revolution happened because the Crown would not deal fairly with us. We were denied the rights of Englishmen, the rights that were an established part of political tradition since King John was brought to heel, because it suited the Crown to deny us those rights. And now, ever since the revolution was crushed, we have had to endure a steady decline because the Crown saw us as beaten men. They have made no attempt to compromise with us, no attempt to do anything but divide and rule. And when has the Viceroy ever cared about our opinions?"

He wasn't a good speaker, Raechel noted. His voice was thin and reedy, with none of the inspiration that Roosevelt had mustered. But she had to admit that he made a very good point.

"This is not a genuine offer," he warned. "The Viceroy knows he is in trouble. He knows that we are strong and that we will grow stronger. He knows that we are just preparing to take his city from him, to kick him and his government all the way back to London. He knows ... and so he is taking the tactical step of pretending to concede our points, long enough for the war to be won. Mark my words. Once the war is over, the Viceroy will *laugh* at the thought of making concessions to us.

"There is nothing to be gained by even *trying* to talk to a known liar and dissembler," he finished. "We have a plan. Let us put that plan into action and win on our own terms."

Raechel watched as, one by one, a number of speakers rose to comment. Meg agreed, loudly, with Adam, telling the crowd that the aristocracy could never be trusted. Raechel hadn't heard that Britain and France had made promises, only to go back on them as soon as it was safe, yet it sounded far too like what had happened after the Swing. Maybe there were a few new MPs in Parliament, Meg pointed out, but what did it matter? Their powers were so sharply circumscribed that they might as well not have been there, for all the good they did.

And they're divided, she thought. Some of the speakers were in favour of accepting the Viceroy's offer, others seemed inclined to continue with the original plan ... and a number seemed to think they could do nothing, merely wait for developments. *Who knows which way they will jump?*

The debate seemed to grow louder and louder as the hours wore on. She watched as the crowd separated into smaller groups, arguing over the merits of the proposal, then breaking up and reforming into different groups. This was democracy in action? It looked as though everyone was having their say, but she had no idea how the Sons were ever going to get a consensus. She looked for Adam and saw him on the far side of the room, speaking quietly with a couple of older men. Roosevelt, by contrast, was surrounded by a throng of younger men.

Adam doesn't have any charisma, she thought. *He can talk people into something, one on one, but he can't sway a crowd.*

A whistle echoed in the air and the chatter slowly died away. "There are three options on the table," a man she didn't know said. He looked old enough to remember George Washington and the first rebellion, Raechel decided. The shock of white hair gave him a gravitas none of the younger men could match. "And we must decide, now, which one to follow.

"First, we accept the Viceroy's offer and commit ourselves to fighting alongside the redcoats," he continued. "Second, we decline the Viceroy's offer and proceed with our original plan. Third, we wait and see what happens. If the Viceroy moves ahead with his announcement, it will be harder for him to change his mind afterwards; if he doesn't, we can proceed with the original plan."

He cleared his throat. "You are all familiar with the procedure," he added, pointing to three open doors behind him. "If you don't want to vote, stay in the room."

The crowd rose and headed towards the doors. It was just like the House of Commons, Raechel thought; the Sons cast votes by walking through the doors, in single file. She hesitated, then headed straight for the first door. Maybe she didn't have a vote, but no one seemed inclined to stop her as she walked through and round the building. The crowd had gathered outside the doors, waiting. No one, Raechel realised, would be allowed to re-enter the building until the last of the votes were counted.

But these can't be all the Sons, she thought, as the doors were thrown open. Adam had told her there were over thirty other camps, each one with two or three hundred Sons. *What about the other camps?*

"We have voted to wait and see," the old man said, twenty minutes later. "It won with a considerable majority."

He dismissed the crowd, which slowly started to break up into a number of smaller groups as they headed back to their work. Raechel meandered to the office, unsure what she should be feeling. At least the Sons weren't launching an attack immediately. What had Gwen *said* to them? How had it been convincing enough to make the Sons reconsider their position?

"Raechel," a voice said, quietly.

Raechel looked up. A young man was standing next to her, carrying a rifle slung over his shoulder. There was something oddly effeminate about his face … she slammed her mental shields into place as she recognised Irene, then allowed the thought to dance outside her shields for Irene to read. The young man nodded – it was a very good disguise – and inclined his head towards a smaller building. Raechel hesitated, then followed Irene into a place she hoped wasn't under observation.

"I'm glad to see you again," she muttered, resisting the urge to give the older woman a hug as soon as they were alone. "How did you get up here?"

"Tracked a recruiting sergeant, then joined up," Irene said, curtly. "There were no special arrangements for me, let me tell you."

Raechel was impressed. Hiding her femininity on the barge must have been one hell of a challenge. She honestly wasn't sure how Irene had got away with it.

"How I got here is not a concern right now," Irene added. She met Raechel's eyes. Up close, even knowing the truth, the disguise was almost perfect. "I understand you're working for one of the leaders?"

"The organiser," Raechel said. She winced as she lowered her shields, allowing Irene to read her memories. "They're definitely planning an attack on New York."

"Assuming they can't come to terms with the government," Irene said. She scowled. "You need to get back to work, I think. There should be a chance to learn more, given where you are."

She paused. "And one other thing," she added. Her voice hardened. "Your boss – and most of the senior leaders – have some very solid mental shields. And the technique is not one I recognise."

"Maybe they developed it on their own," Raechel said. The Sons knew about Talkers, of course. *Someone* had to have taught Jane how to use her powers. "If we did it in Britain, the Americans should be able to do it too."

"At the cost of a great many people being tossed into bedlams," Irene said. "For every Talker who mastered his power, there were a dozen who went mad or killed themselves just to get the voices to shut up. If the Americans developed a technique of their own, I'd expect to see more signs."

She stepped backwards, her face darkening. "I'll meet up with you tonight, I think, and we can go for a pleasant walk."

Raechel flushed. She knew what everyone would think.

"Better that than the truth," Irene reminded her. "Watch your back."

Chapter Thirty-One

hey're coming," Jackson said.

Gwen nodded as she stood on the wall, peering into the distance. The French had finally shown themselves, two days after the brief and brutal fight near the homestead. She watched as their army slowly deployed; infantry moving forward while horsemen set up mounted patrols and a handful of artillery pieces took up firing positions. It looked as though the entire French army was surrounding Amherst, laying siege to the city. She knew, intellectually, that there couldn't be more than twenty thousand soldiers at most, but her mind refused to believe it.

"Plenty of former slaves too," Jackson added. "Porters, as I expected."

"Yes," Gwen said.

Her eyes narrowed. The black slaves were digging trenches of their own, readying French positions in case the defenders launched a sally. She knew it wasn't going to happen – Jackson didn't have the numbers, with or without the militia – but she supposed it kept the French from launching an immediate attack. Laying siege to Amherst would be cheaper than trying to storm the city, she knew, yet they needed those soldiers elsewhere. They'd committed a sizeable percentage of their ground troops to the invasion of British North America.

And the Admiral had a plan to launch a flanking attack on New Orleans, she thought. She knew little of what was happening beyond the city, now that the French had closed in. *If he manages to force a landing, the French will be the ones in trouble.*

She closed her eyes in pain. Bruce had been completely

invisible over the last two days, even skipping the communal meals that Jackson had insisted on holding. She would have been relieved at his absence, three days ago, but now she wanted to speak to him, to find out what had happened with the Sons. And yet, he'd been out of touch. She had no idea how he'd managed to avoid suspicion …

"They're sending in a man with a white flag," Jackson said. "I'll see him at the edge of the defences. I don't want him to see too much of the city."

Gwen nodded, then followed Jackson down the wall to where the Frenchman was being apprehended by a pair of horsemen and blindfolded. Jackson had told her, back before the rail lines had been cut, that it was customary to send a messenger to demand surrender, but that the messenger would also be a spy, scouting out weak points in the defences. The only way to keep him from seeing something important was to blindfold him. Gwen braced herself as the Frenchman was frogmarched over by the guards, then pushed roughly to the floor. Up close, he looked every inch an aristocrat. She couldn't read his rank from his expensive uniform.

"I am Colonel Jackson," Jackson said.

"My commanding officer wishes me to speak directly to General Paget," the Frenchman said, sternly. He sounded as if he'd been personally insulted. "Where is he?"

"I am the commanding officer," Jackson said. Gwen couldn't help noticing that the Frenchman hadn't demanded to speak to General *Kingsley*. Clearly, the French knew he was dead. "You can speak with me or no one."

The Frenchman coughed. "Very well," he said. "My commanding officer demands your immediate surrender. The garrison may march out with all the honours of war, after which they will be interned until they can be traded for a French garrison or returned to Britain after the war. If you refuse to surrender, there will be no further opportunities to do so."

Gwen kept her face impassive. The laws of war were quite clear. If a city surrendered before the defences were broken, the victor had a certain responsibility not to sack the city or mistreat the population. But if the city was taken by storm, the defences broken before anyone chose to surrender, the victor could do whatever it liked to the conquered population. The stories she'd heard from the fighting in Germany, as France tightened its grip on the German states, had been horrific.

"We will not surrender," Jackson said, flatly.

"Be very sure," the Frenchman snapped. "You have rats in your hold, *Colonel*."

"We will not surrender," Jackson repeated. "If you want this city, come and take it."

The Frenchman snorted. Jackson nodded to the guards, who dragged him back towards the edge of the defences, then looked at Gwen. She swallowed, knowing that she was about to face a far greater test of her abilities than she had in Russia, and nodded back. The sorcerers were already waiting, ready to rush to meet the French once they started to break through the walls. She looked around for Bruce, but saw no sign of him. All she saw were British redcoats and American militia manning the walls.

"They'll start shooting soon," Jackson said, as they strolled back into the city. "I'll see you afterwards, Lady Gwen."

"Likewise," Gwen said. "Good luck."

The French guns began to boom, seconds later. There weren't many, Gwen reminded herself as she drew her magic around her; thankfully, the French had had real problems getting their larger guns from New Orleans to Amherst. But, as the shells began to land in the city, they still caused damage. They didn't seem to be shooting at anything in particular, but it was impossible to be sure. A direct hit on Jackson's HQ would cause a dispute over command at the worst possible time.

"Lady Gwen," Wayne said. He stood with the other sorcerers, watching explosions flicker and flare all over the city. The noise of gunfire was growing louder. "Here we go."

Gwen looked past him, at the men she'd dragged all the way from New York. "The French can only thrust one army up here," she said. Jackson had said as much, after all; English raiders had been attacking the French shipping. "If we beat this army, we hold the line."

She studied them all, one by one. Harry and Vernon looked grimly determined, although Vernon looked as disgruntled as always. The three Blazers looked keen, ready to show off their powers; Fife looked as though he wasn't quite sure what he was doing in the midst of battle. Gwen silently promised herself to make sure they were all cared for, after the fighting had come to an end. None of them had volunteered to fight, after all.

"Do not let yourself be captured," Wayne warned. "If you can go out with your hands wrapped around a Frenchman's throat, you'll do fine."

He was right, Gwen knew. The French wouldn't let any of the sorcerers survive, particularly her. They'd slit her throat rather than run the risk of keeping her alive. Even the prospect of forcing her to bear sons was too dangerous to be tolerated …

"Good luck," she said. She could hear men shouting in the distance. The French were starting their charge. "Honour to us all."

***

Colonel Jackson had never thought very much of the slaves. He'd been taught, a long time ago, that it was better to die on one's feet than live on one's knees, a lesson that had stuck with him throughout his career. The slaves had seemed nothing more than dumb animals, shuffling around picking cotton and serving their masters. Jackson would sooner have died than serve as a slave, knowing his wife or daughters might be separated from him or forced to bed the master at any moment. But now, watching the former slaves advance, he had to admit they were brave. They'd just needed the opportunity.

"Hold your fire," he ordered, as the slaves advanced. The French were expending them carelessly, knowing that their bodies would absorb bullets that would otherwise strike trained soldiers. He wondered just how many of the slaves realised that they were going to die, then decided it probably didn't matter. "Hold your fire until I give the command."

Accuracy was a joke, he knew, in rifle volleys. It was the

sheer volume of bullets that counted, not accuracy. A commoner from London couldn't hope to match an aristocrat for shooting proficiency, but all of his snipers were watching for French officers. It wasn't entirely cricket to snipe the leaders – if nothing else, it set a bad precedent – yet he knew better than to dismiss the idea. He needed every advantage he could get.

"First line, fire," he snapped. The soldiers fired in unison, sending hundreds of former slaves tumbling to the ground. Others ran forward, seizing the opportunity to die like men, as shells started to slam down amongst the riflemen. "Second line, fire!"

The French didn't fall back. Bullets started to crack through the air above the trenches as a line of French troops came into view, advancing in skirmishing order. They didn't look *quite* ready for defended fortifications, he noted; their uniforms made them exceedingly good targets. But then, they had concentrated on marching all the way from New Orleans on shoestring logistics. Getting as far as they had was quite an impressive feat. His lips quirked into a smile as Frenchmen started to fall. They had come all this way to die.

A cheer ran through the lines, followed by curses as the shells fell with greater intensity, one striking an artillery position and triggering a fireball. Jackson was fairly sure the French couldn't have transported *many* shells and guns from New Orleans to Amherst – it would have made their logistics even worse – but they *needed* to win. If they lost the battle, they'd have to fall back in disarray.

He gritted his teeth as he saw a fireball hurtling from the French lines, twisting in the air and diving towards one of the cannons. The gun exploded a second later; Jackson saw a man screaming, his body wrapped in flames, running around before one of the sergeants performed a mercy kill. Sorcerers! There was at least one French sorcerer advancing with the infantry, directing his magic to clear the way. Jackson had hoped the best of the French magicians had died, after their attempt on Lady Gwen, but clearly there were at least one or two left. And he couldn't handle them.

"Send a message to Lady Gwen," he called, as the outer edge of the defences started to crumble. His men were already falling back, as planned; there was no point in trying to hold the line now that the French were close enough to hurl grenades into the trenches. "Tell her the enemy is at the gates!"

***

Vernon twisted his lip in disapproval as he followed Harry towards the sound of the guns, his magic billowing around him. He'd never liked the idea of fighting for the Crown; indeed, if it hadn't been for Harry, he would have deserted long before the unwanted deployment to Amherst. *To hell with the money*, he thought. There was nothing to be gained by fighting for king and country, save an early grave. But Harry had been insistent they stay, pointing out that they needed to learn more about their powers.

And he had a point, Vernon thought, reluctantly. It had never occurred to him to use his powers offensively, not as anything more than extensions of his fists. He could punch hard enough to stun Lady Gwen, but she could still worm her way into his shields. *It's worth every taunt about working for a slip of a girl to know how our powers work.*

He eyed Lady Gwen, wondering just when dislike had turned into grudging respect. The sorceress was no fisherwoman, no strong-minded dockyard lady with the mouth of a sailor and the arms of a navvy. No, she was a slip of a girl, a girl who would be broken overnight if she wound up on the docks. Vernon's own mother had been tough, tough enough to slap Vernon around when he'd acted up as a teenager. It was hard to imagine Lady Gwen having that sort of blunt strength …

The wall exploded in front of them, revealing five Frenchmen wrapped in power. Vernon felt a surge of hatred as he reached out, melding his power with his brother's. Harry laughed, then forced their power forward, slamming it directly into the French magicians. One was thrown backwards hard enough to kill him; the others stood their ground, holding the British attack at bay. Vernon gritted his teeth as the Blazers walked past him, then dropped the shield. The Blazers hurled fireballs right into the French position, forcing them to defend themselves ...

"Needles," Lady Gwen shouted.

Vernon nodded curtly – he was damned if he was saluting anyone – and reshaped his power, wincing at the effort involved. Why had it never occurred to him – or Harry – that the best way to break a bubble was to use a pin? It wasn't as if his sister hadn't used needles and thread to sew their clothes, back before their parents had died and she'd married another dockyard worker. The first Frenchman stumbled backwards as the needle sliced through his protections, then rammed into his chest; Vernon ducked, sharply, as the other Frenchmen lashed out. But it was too late. A blow slammed right into his chest, hurling him into the air and tossing him right across the city.

He fought desperately to fly. Lady Gwen said he should be able to fly, with his powers, but he'd never managed it. And then it was too late ... He tried to wrap his power around him, but the ground came up and ...

***

Gwen picked up a chunk of debris, infused it with power and hurled it right into the teeth of the French position. There were three remaining Movers, all clearly well trained. The only thing giving her and her sorcerers an advantage, she realised numbly, was that the Frenchmen weren't anything like as *powerful*. Their superiors had held them back, fearing to throw them into battle ...

The explosion shattered their unity, scattering them. Gwen's Blazers concentrated their fire on them, burning through their protections. The Frenchmen had no time to gather themselves before she flew forward, shaping her power into needles. Their shields snapped seconds later, allowing the Blazers to incinerate them. Gwen allowed herself a moment of relief, then hurled herself into the air. She *had* to know what was going on.

It didn't look good, she saw. There were burning buildings all over the city, while the French had forced their way through the first set of defence lines and were fighting their way into the city itself. Women and children were running for their lives, while their menfolk fought hard to stem the advance. Jackson had to be feeding his soldiers in piecemeal, Gwen reasoned; bleeding the French rather than trying to stop them. The only advantage the defenders seemed to have, now, was that the French gunners had stopped firing. She just hoped it meant that they were out of ammunition, rather than being concerned about hitting their own men as they plunged onwards.

She dropped down next to Wayne. Vernon and Fife were gone; Harry lay on the ground, his arm clearly broken. The Blazers were alive, but tired; Gwen didn't feel any better herself. If there were any more French magicians – or if Bruce intended to put a knife in her back – they'd have the perfect opportunity. She'd seen war before, yet this was different. An entire city was being systematically destroyed.

"Harry's arm is gone," Wayne reported. "There aren't any Healers here, Lady Gwen."

"I know," Gwen said. She reached out with her senses, trying to locate any other magicians, but felt nothing. The fighting was growing louder, pushing back towards their position. It wouldn't be long before they'd have to move. "I ..."

She swore as a line of French soldiers came into view, their weapons at the ready. Did they know who she was? Did it matter? She reached for the last of her power, feeling it crackling around her. There was no way she could surrender.

"Take them to Jackson," she ordered. The others would need time to catch their breath before the French made their final push. Even if the British won the fight, Amherst would take years to rebuild. "I'll hold them off."

She ignored Wayne's shout as she strode past him, feeling power crackling around her fingertips. There were hundreds of dead bodies within view ... she wondered, absently, if she could reanimate them. They hadn't been dead for long. But she knew the undead would get out of control with terrifying speed. She didn't dare take the risk. Instead, she held up her hands and lashed out with her magic. The Frenchmen, ordinary soldiers, didn't stand a chance ...

And yet they came, charging straight at her and firing madly. Gwen held on desperately, feeling her magic starting to weaken, as she tore them apart or burnt them to ashes. She caught sight of young faces − some white, some brown − their eyes screaming with horror as they fell to her magic. She heard thunderclaps in the distance, but she hardly cared. Blood trickled from her nose as she pushed her powers to the very limit …

And then they were gone.

Gwen stood there, unsure what had happened. She was surrounded by hundreds of bodies, but the French seemed to have retreated completely. The sound of shooting had faded away, as if the French were leaving the city. And then she saw a man wearing a very familiar cloak hanging in the air. He held out a hand, inviting her to join him.

"We thought you could use a hand," Bruce said, when she floated into the air. "As you can see, we took the French by surprise."

He smirked. "Saving your life is starting to be a habit."

"Don't expect it to happen again," Gwen said. She looked back at the city, still burning even though the fighting was coming to an end. "Now what?"

"I think that hangs on you," Bruce said. All of a sudden, she wanted to kiss him again, but she resisted the temptation. "Now what … indeed?"

Chapter Thirty-Two

ady Gwen," Jackson said. "I must protest …"

Gwen rubbed her tired eyes. "The Sons saved our lives, Colonel," she said. "And they helped us hold the line against the French."

"After discovering just what the French were prepared to do to ordinary Americans," Bruce put in. He was still wearing his mask, slanting his voice slightly to ensure Jackson didn't recognise him. "We are prepared to join the defence on a more permanent basis if the Viceroy keeps his promise."

Jackson looked flustered. "With all due respect, Mr. …?"

"I am America," Bruce announced, grandly.

Gwen managed – somehow – to resist the urge to elbow him, hard. "Wouldn't *Spartacus* be a better name?"

"Spartacus died, along with a lot of other fellows who *also* claimed to be Spartacus," Bruce said. "We didn't think that set a good precedent."

Jackson snorted. "Regardless, Mr. America, I do need to know who I'm dealing with."

"No, you don't," Bruce said. "Right now, my men will assist yours in harrying the French as they retreat. But we are not going to reveal ourselves openly just yet."

He turned and strode off, holding his head high. Jackson moved forward, as if he were going to give chase, then sighed and looked at Gwen. She hastily pasted a composed expression on her face, hoping he wouldn't ask too many questions. She didn't want to lie to him, but there were things she didn't want to tell him either.

"Can he be trusted?"

"I think we're offering him what he wants without a fight,"

Gwen said, flatly. Lord Mycroft had taught her that it was better to rely on someone's self-interest, rather than their ideals or good natures. Humans were selfish creatures. Bruce would cooperate because it was the easiest way to get what he wanted. "And besides, if he wanted to take Amherst, could we stop him?"

Jackson's face twisted, as if he'd bitten into something sour. Half of the redcoats were dead or wounded, while there was a big question mark over the American militia. She looked around the rubble, where there were dozens of militiamen openly fraternising with the Sons. For all she knew, the *original* plan had been to start an uprising and stab the redcoats in the back when the French attacked. It might explain why the French had risked so much charging at the defences. They'd expected help from inside the city.

"I don't like it, Lady Gwen," Jackson said, finally.

"It has to be endured," Gwen said. She felt the remaining reserves of magic inside her, then winced. It was unlikely she could perform any Healing for hours, if not days. Far too many of the wounded would be left to the mercy of army doctors. "The Viceroy said so."

"See to your men, Lady Gwen," Jackson said. "And pray that this doesn't explode in our faces."

Gwen nodded, then turned to walk back to City Hall. Countless men were fighting to save as much of the city as they could, throwing buckets of water on fires or tearing down buildings to keep the flames from spreading. Others were removing bodies, dragging them off towards the edge of the city. They'd have to be cremated, just to ensure that a rogue necromancer couldn't use them as weapons. She shuddered as she saw a man being carried past on a stretcher, his right arm missing. Even the strongest of Healers wouldn't be able to return what he'd lost.

City Hall itself was undamaged, even though a handful of shells had slammed into the building next to it. Gwen wondered, as she made her way through the door, just what the French had been aiming at, if it had been anything more than random devastation. Shellfire was never very accurate, even with a crack team of gunners. They might have planned to kill the commanding officers or they might just have been hoping for a lucky hit. There was no way to know.

"Lady Gwen," Wayne said, as she stepped into the room. "Vernon is dead; Fife is missing."

Gwen frowned. Harry sat on a chair, next to his brother's body. She'd thought she'd known what was going on, but she hadn't even seen him *die*. Vernon had never liked her – she'd feared he would desert long ago – yet he'd stayed and fought, at the cost of his own life. She silently promised herself that he'd get a medal, even if it was posthumous. It might mean something to his family.

She walked over to Harry, unsure what to say. An aristocrat would be insulted by the suggestion that he needed consolation, even though she knew better than to think they didn't care. Vernon had died bravely, but he'd *died*. Harry ... who knew how Harry felt? He'd been wounded, yet losing his brother had to hurt worse.

"I'm sorry," she said, finally. "He deserved better."

"He only stayed because I dragged him along," Harry said, quietly. "I saw too many French officers in New York, when their ships docked, to want them to take over. It was my fault he died."

"The French killed him," Gwen said. She *really* didn't know what to say. "You didn't kill him yourself."

"It feels as though I did," Harry said. "But right now, he's looking down at me and thinking I really should drink a toast in his honour."

Gwen nodded. "Was he married?"

"He had a girl he liked, but her family wasn't keen on the match," Harry said. He shook his head slowly. "They thought a shopkeeper would be a better match for her, a step up from the docks. And I think they were a little afraid of his magic too. The money he earned from working for you should have changed their minds, if he'd lived ..."

He shook his head. "Our mother died two years ago," he added. "There's no one but me to mourn him."

Gwen looked at Vernon's body. It would have to be cremated too, but she didn't have the heart to insist on it right away. She'd make *damn* sure he got that medal. It was *her* task, after all, to nominate people for the Merlin Cross ... and she was fairly sure that no one would raise any objection, after the battle. Besides, the cynical part of her mind noted, Vernon was safely dead. He could be turned into a hero without interference from the real man.

Wayne stepped up beside her. "I'll take Harry out drinking," he said, bluntly. "It will be the best thing for him, right now."

If anything is open, Gwen thought.

She shook her head at the thought. Amherst had had dozens of pubs and taverns, but she was sure they were all closed. But then, there were thousands of thirsty soldiers roaming around who wanted to celebrate their victory. *Someone* would probably have opened up and started overcharging for weak beer and rotgut by now.

"Take everyone out," she said. Harry was wounded, but she trusted Wayne to know Harry's limits. "We can pick up the rest of the pieces tomorrow."

She left the magicians behind and walked through the building to where the Talker was waiting. He'd lost his uniform, something that surprised her more than it should. The French would not have hesitated to kill him, if they took him alive. A man who could constantly feed New York intelligence was too dangerous to live. She wondered, absently, just how much he'd already sent, then sat down facing him.

"I need to relay a message to the Viceroy," she said. "A private message."

"Of course, My Lady," the Talker said. His eyes unfocused as he reached out with his mind, contacting his opposite number in New York. "Lady Gwen, this is the Viceroy."

Gwen lifted her eyebrows. *That* had been quick. But then, the Viceroy had known the battle was about to begin. He'd probably kept the Talker with him while going through his daily routine, if he hadn't decided to stay in the palace until the battle was over. Getting the news first might make a difference, politically …

"The battle was won," she said. She outlined everything that had happened, from the French demand for surrender to the arrival of the Sons, doing her best to keep the report both complete and concise. Experience had taught her that government ministers wanted to go over everything in exacting detail, but that could wait. "We now have a promise to keep."

There was a long pause. "Thank you, Lady Gwen," the Talker relayed, finally. "I shall consult with London, then contact you."

Gwen scowled, inwardly, as she rose. She hoped – prayed – that common sense ruled the day in London, although *that* would be unusual. Hundreds of redcoats had been killed in Amherst and the French advance blunted, badly. If the Sons wanted to start an uprising *without* having to worry about the French coming in and picking up the pieces, they'd never have a better chance. And they'd know it, too.

She checked Jackson's office, but he wasn't there. His aide told her that he was still at the defence lines, probably trying to rebuild them before the French launched another offensive against the city. Gwen doubted they *could* muster the force to attack for a second time, but she understood Jackson's concern. If nothing else, keeping the defences in shape would keep his men – and the Sons – busy. There would be no time for them to think about politics.

Outside, she stopped in shock as she saw a dozen men being dragged towards a makeshift gallows. Lieutenant Travis was supervising, his face twisted with hatred. Nine of them were black, probably escaped slaves; the remainder were clearly of mixed blood. The crowd were howling for their blood, demanding bloody retribution for their revolt. She stared in horror – the mixed-bloods wore French uniforms – and then started forward. Lieutenant Travis turned in astonishment as she approached.

"Lady Gwen," he said. He stopped dead. Gwen would have bet half her fortune that he'd been about to say something about an unsuitable sight for women, even though hangings were public spectacles in London. "I ..."

"Stop this at once," Gwen ordered, putting on her most imperious tone. "They're prisoners, not bandits."

Lieutenant Travis hesitated. "Lady Gwen ..."

"If you start killing prisoners, the other side will do the same," Gwen added, firmly. "Put them in the stockade and hold them, so we can trade for our prisoners if necessary.

But don't hang them like this."

She understood the desire for revenge, but the French would just retaliate and the entire war would descend into a series of atrocities and counter-atrocities. Warfare along the frontier was always barbaric – she'd heard of tribes that had scalped every last man, woman and child in settlements they'd attacked – yet that was no excuse for descending into savagery themselves.

"They're escaped slaves," someone shouted, from the safety of the crowd. "Put them down like dogs!"

There was a low murmur of agreement from the watchers. Gwen felt sweat trickling down her back as she stared back at them, unwilling to show weakness. She was right, she knew she was right and she was damned if she was backing down.

"And what happens," she asked, "once the French start doing it to us?"

Lieutenant Travis's face flickered through a bewildering series of emotions. She didn't really blame him. There was a crowd of people who wanted revenge, who might turn on the redcoats if the prisoners were treated decently, but – on the other hand – going against her might mean the end of his career.

"Take the prisoners to the stockade," he ordered, finally. "Colonel Jackson will decide their fate."

Gwen half-expected the crowd to do something stupid, but instead they slowly dispersed towards the taverns. She allowed herself a moment of relief, then turned back to City Hall and blinked in surprise as she saw Bruce, standing nearby. He looked every inch the aristocratic fop, but now she knew what hid under his face she could sense his magic. It made her wonder why she hadn't sensed it before.

"That was brave, My Lady," Bruce said. He *sounded* a fop too. It wasn't the mask that disguised him as much as his attitude. "I wouldn't have had the nerve."

"I'm sure you would have," Gwen said, as they walked into the building. "Where have you been?"

"Oh, around," Bruce said, vaguely. He looked around to make sure they were alone, then lowered his voice. "Making sure there's someone to take command of the troops once I go back to New York."

Gwen looked at him. "The agreement will hold?"

"For the moment," Bruce said. "It all hangs on my father now."

Gwen nodded, slowly. "London has already agreed, in principle, to an American Parliament," she said. "The only question is how best to set it up."

She sighed, inwardly. There were too many things they needed to talk about, but they would require privacy – and privacy wouldn't be easy to find. Even being in the hallways was risky, if someone noticed they were together. Rumours could start very easily and ... and, she had to admit, there would be some truth in them. Girls had been ruined completely for doing far less than she'd done with Bruce. And yet, there was a part of her that wanted to do it again.

"I'm sure father will come up with a solution," Bruce said. "He's good at that."

He winked at her. "There are some of us who believe that slavery is a great evil," he added, dryly. "And that the *reason* Washington and the others lost their war was because they embraced slavery."

Gwen had her doubts. It was true that Washington had had problems with black recruits – while his enemies had been quite happy to lure the slaves from the plantations with promises of freedom – but the British Empire *also* kept slaves. There was a substantial body of politicians – in both London and New York – who fought desperately to *keep* slavery, knowing their livelihoods depended on it. America was hardly the only place touched by the practice.

"One wins if one deserves to win," Bruce added. "And maybe the others didn't deserve to win."

"Or maybe your people just got unlucky," Gwen said. She'd read the history books, including Master Thomas's unpublished memoirs. General Howe had been a ditherer, either no general or desperately hoping that a peaceful settlement could be worked out. Who knew what would have happened if London hadn't been constantly urging him to keep moving? "You never had the chance to recover from your mistakes."

"And let us hope that *this* isn't a mistake," Bruce said. "I ..."

He broke off as a messenger came into view. "Lady Gwen,

Colonel Jackson requests your presence in his office," the messenger said. "Your Excellency, he would also like to see you."

"I'm sure he would," Bruce said, wryly. "And do you want to bet he isn't *in* the office?"

Gwen rolled her eyes as the messenger turned and hurried back down the corridor, then led the way towards Jackson's office. The Colonel *had* managed to get back quickly, she noted; someone must have sent an urgent message. Unless, of course, he didn't know what had happened outside City Hall. He might have been on his way back already.

"Lady Gwen," Jackson said, as they stepped into his office. "We've had a message from New York. You and Master Bruce are to return at once."

Gwen frowned. "I thought the rail line was broken."

"It is," Jackson confirmed. "You'll be riding on horseback to Ashley Bridge, where a train will be waiting for you. I assume you'll be able to fly both of you over the river?"

"Yes," Gwen confirmed. The Viceroy had summoned his son home too? Did he know more than Gwen thought? Or was he just keen to get his son back to New York? "When do you want us to depart?"

"Now," Jackson said. "The message insisted you were to leave at once."

Bruce coughed. "Colonel, Lady Gwen was just in a battle," he said. "She hasn't had time to sleep!"

"The orders are clear," Jackson said. He didn't sound pleased, Gwen noted. "Even with a single coach, Your Excellency, it's going to take at least five days to reach New York. You will *both* have plenty of time to sleep."

Unless we get attacked, Gwen thought. She was already dreading the ride. *Or if something else happens along the way.*

She cleared her throat. "Very well, Colonel," she said. "I'll have to take some of my clothes out of a trunk and dump them into a bag, but that shouldn't take long."

"I'll have the horses ready for you in an hour," Jackson said. "I assume you can ride?"

Gwen blinked in surprise, then understood. Jackson was insulting Bruce, subtly. It was rare, very rare, to encounter an aristocrat who couldn't ride, but Bruce's public persona might not be *able* to ride. Hell, if he had the same problems with horses as she had, he might well prefer to avoid riding where possible ...

"It shouldn't be too hard, Colonel," Bruce drawled. "How are we to return the horses to you?"

"The engineers will take them," Jackson said. He didn't show any visible reaction to Bruce's tone, but Gwen could sense his irritation. "I'll see you both back in New York."

Gwen nodded, fighting down the urge to break into giggles. Jackson wouldn't be pleased when he found out the truth, and he *would*. She hated to think about what would happen then ... but Jackson wasn't the worst problem. What would the Viceroy do when he learnt about his son's secret life? Children had been disowned, cut out of their families, for far lesser crimes.

"Thank you, Colonel," she said, instead. "I look forward to it."

Chapter Thirty-Three

hat we need," Bruce called to her, "is an airship."

Gwen couldn't disagree. The horse was galloping at full tilt, as if it were trying to get away from the sorceress mounted on its back. Beside her, Bruce seemed to be having similar problems in keeping his mount under control, even though he had his powers under a tight restraint.

"An airship would be burnt out of the sky the moment it got near a Blazer," she said, as they approached the river. The bridge, formerly a piece of magnificent engineering, was torn and broken, pieces of stone and metal sticking up out of the water. On both sides of the river, she could see teams of Royal Engineers hastily establishing a pontoon bridge. "And there aren't any in America."

"Hamish used to say we could build them for ourselves," Bruce said. He slowed to a canter, then came to a halt. "It wouldn't be too hard."

Gwen gave him a sharp look. America was vast, easily large enough to hide a secret airship construction facility. It wouldn't be hard to hide the airships themselves too, as long as they stayed beyond the line. Anyone who saw the craft might blame them on the French.

"And did you?"

"Not yet," Bruce said. "One of the engineers had a theory about a flying machine that didn't need a giant gasbag to fly. He was going to experiment with it after the war."

"He'll have his chance," Gwen said. A handful of soldiers appeared on the nearside of the bridge, watching them carefully. She pulled the horse to a halt, then slipped down to the ground. "Better let me do the talking."

"Lady Gwen," the leader said. "The train's on the far side."

"I understand," Gwen said. She passed the reins to the soldier with considerable relief, then watched as Bruce joined her. "Make sure the horses get back to Amherst."

"Yes, My Lady," the leader said.

Gwen suspected that Bruce wanted to fly under his own power, but they were being watched by too many eyes. She levitated them both over the river, which was easily wide enough to accommodate a few barges, if they could be steered up from the sea, and landed neatly on the far side. The train – a single locomotive connected to a passenger coach and work car – was already steaming, indicating that the driver and fireman had started preparations as soon as they had come into view. Gwen scrambled up into the cabin, dropped her bag in one of the bedrooms and then hurried into the dining compartment. Behind her, Bruce did the same.

"I forgot to buy a ticket," he said, as he sat down. "Do you think they'll kick us off the train?"

"Oh, probably," Gwen said, wryly. "Fare dodging isn't a harmless little prank, you know."

She smiled, rather tiredly, as the train began to move. It had been a *very* long day.

"I suppose not," Bruce agreed. He glanced from side to side. "Can we talk freely?"

Gwen closed her eyes, reaching out with her senses. "I don't think we've being watched," she said, after a moment. It struck her, suddenly, that they were alone in the coach. People would comment, if they knew. "And we do need to talk."

Bruce nodded, slowly. "I didn't ask for orders," he said, his voice suddenly very serious. "I made the decision to intervene on my own."

"I see," Gwen said, slowly. "What will the Sons say?"

"That rather depends on what happens," Bruce said. The train lurched suddenly, then started to pick up speed. "If we get what we want, I dare say everyone will be pleased; if we don't, they'll be very angry with me."

"Because the original plan was to work *with* the French," Gwen said. "Right?"

Bruce didn't bother to deny it. "Drowning men will clutch at any straws," he said. "And we were drowning."

"Not any longer," Gwen said.

"No, but that depends on London," Bruce said. He let out a long breath. "It was decided, when I took your words to the others, that we should wait and see what my father had to say before we committed ourselves. What I did will upset a great many of my allies."

"Even though the battle was won," Gwen said. She leant back in her chair, fighting down a sudden wave of exhaustion. "They're not going to be happy."

"It depends, like I said," Bruce said. "But you're right. They're not going to be happy."

Gwen met his eyes. "Why did you take the chance?"

Bruce looked embarrassed. "Because of you," he said. "The first time we met … I'd never met anyone like you before. The girls I met at my father's balls were boring, interested only in marriage. I didn't want to be tied down like that, Gwen. And then I saw you fighting for your life and I felt … *something*. I jumped into the fight before I could think better of it."

"Did our magic pull us together," Gwen asked, "or was it something else?"

"I don't know," Bruce said. "I like you. I … *enjoyed* … what we did together. And yet, I don't know if we could spend a lifetime together."

Gwen touched her stomach, lightly. "We might have to."

Bruce's eyes widened. "Are you …?"

"I don't know, yet," Gwen said. "The gentleman" – she saw him blush at the reference to her periods – "has not yet made his visit. If he doesn't show in a month or two, we may have a problem."

"My father is going to kill me," Bruce said. "Getting a young woman into trouble …"

He cleared his throat. "I will marry you," he said. "If you're pregnant, we can have a hasty wedding."

Gwen found herself torn between relief and horror. If she *was* pregnant, she needed to get married quickly, before the pregnancy started to show. And there was no doubt over who had fathered the child. She didn't *want* to have to raise a child alone, or force someone else to serve as the father. And yet his casual assumption that he would marry her grated. She hadn't spent the last year as the Royal Sorceress to give up her freedom so easily.

But there might be someone else to think of, she thought, wanly. *The child.*

"I don't know, not yet," she said. She would need to make *some* explanation to her parents, even though she was technically emancipated. Her father would explode with rage; her mother might be more understanding, but it wasn't something she could say in public. "The wedding might have to be organised *very* quickly."

Bruce frowned. "There's no way to check?"

"Not for some time," Gwen said. A Healer might be able to check, but she wasn't sure how long it took before her condition became obvious. "I don't know."

"It was my fault," Bruce said. "I should never have kissed you."

"I could have pushed you away," Gwen said. It was true. She could have shoved him back, but she hadn't. "Bruce ..."

Bruce leant forward. "Whatever happens," he said, "we'll face it together."

Gwen felt an odd warmth spreading through her body. She feared abandonment – or worse, the loss of her reputation and the stigma of being a single mother. Even if she wasn't pregnant, she might well lose everything if Bruce talked or if a future husband discovered she wasn't a virgin on their wedding night. But Bruce talked about staying with her, supporting her ... she couldn't help responding to that.

"You're the Royal Sorceress," Bruce added. "I don't think they can just dump you, can they?"

"I'm not sure," Gwen said. "They might want to put you in my place."

Bruce lifted his eyebrows. "Even though I'm – horror of horrors – *American*?"

"Half-American," Gwen said. She stuck out her tongue. "But I suppose being a Son would be enough to put *anyone* off giving you the job."

"I don't want the job," Bruce said. "Too much paperwork, I think."

Gwen nodded, curtly. "But it's quite rewarding too," she admitted. Bruce, at least, would have no trouble leading men into battle. "The Royal Sorcerers Corps could use you."

"But only if America gets its parliament," Bruce said, firmly. "I don't know what will happen if my father goes back on his word."

"They'll rebel," Gwen guessed.

"Probably," Bruce said. "And damn me for a traitor, while they're at it."

Gwen yawned. "I need to sleep," she said. She rose. She'd snatched a bite to eat before they'd left Amherst, but she still felt hungry. "Can you ask them to hold dinner until I wake?"

"I need sleep too," Bruce said. He rose and stretched. "And there are other things we can do."

He kissed her, gently. Gwen felt her tired body responding to him, demanding more and more; his hands started to stroke her back, reaching down to her trousers …

"Not too far," she said, pushing him back. She didn't mind kissing – and perhaps a few other things – but she wasn't ready to have sex with him again. "If I'm not pregnant, I don't want to take the risk, not yet."

She'd heard – from Lucy – that some men could get very nasty if they were rejected, but Bruce merely nodded. They kissed again, deeply, before she turned and stepped into her bedroom, feeling her lips tingling at the memory of his touch. She closed the door behind her, then stumbled into bed. Sleep claimed her almost at once.

"You have so many talents I don't have," Bruce commented, the following morning. He'd let her sleep all night, then taken some rations from the train crew. "I could never get the hang of Changing or Infusing."

"I'm not that good with either of them," Gwen admitted, picking at her food. The rations weren't very good, but they were edible and that was all she cared about. "Changing something isn't easy, not without a very good grasp on one's power."

"I didn't have a tutor," Bruce said. "And Charming never worked for me."

Gwen lifted her eyebrows. "How did you practice?"

"I had volunteers subject themselves to my power," Bruce said. "It never worked."

"Charm requires a subtle touch," Gwen told him. "The more power you use, the more obvious that you're using magic. It tends to annoy people."

She shuddered as she recalled Lord Blackburn. The man had been a monster, a Darwinist who believed that magicians were inherently superior to everyone else. And he'd been quite happy to use his powers to molest women ... he'd vanished, just after the Swing. She had no idea where he'd gone, but she hoped she never saw him again.

"I could get them to do what I said," Bruce mused, "but they never stayed under my control."

Gwen shook her head. "The best Charm works when the victim invents their own reasons to do as you want," she said. "It's harder to do anything to resist if they talk *themselves* into following orders."

She frowned. "Are there any Charmers among the Sons?"

"Not to my knowledge," Bruce said. "We have a number of magicians, but ... you know ... many magicians get killed here, as soon as they show themselves. I was surprised Harry and Vernon lived long enough for you to recruit them."

Gwen blinked. "You *know* them?"

"They refused the invitation to join," Bruce said. He shrugged. "I was *equally* surprised they didn't abandon you, after the call to war. They could have vanished completely, if they'd wished."

"You can ask Harry, afterwards," Gwen said. She felt another stab of guilt. "Vernon ... died."

"It happens," Bruce said. "Seventy of my men died in the battle, Gwen. I may have to account for each and every one of them, once we reach New York."

Gwen nodded. Given time, the British Crown could muster hundreds of thousands of soldiers – and the Franco-Spanish could muster *millions*, but the Sons had been far more limited in how they could recruit newcomers. Seventy dead was nothing, compared to the numbers of dead that had been piled up across Germany, yet it still had to hurt. Bruce definitely had a great deal to answer for.

She felt a sudden rush of affection that surprised her. No

one had ever done anything for *her*, not really. As a little girl, she'd known she would be married off; as an older girl, she'd known it was unlikely she'd ever be more than a burden to her family; as a magician, she'd known she'd only been recruited because she was unique ... and yet Bruce had risked everything, his life and his position, for her. Her mother and father had never shown her so much consideration as he had, in that one glorious moment.

And yet he's technically a traitor, her thoughts reminded her. *You cannot allow yourself to feel for him until you know the outcome.*

She shook her head, morbidly. There was no *technically* about it. Bruce was a traitor, even if his motives were better than Sir Charles's had been. His father might be able to convince London to forgive, but it would never be forgotten. Perhaps it would all work out for the best – the Sons would make powerful allies – yet there would be consequences ...

"Gwen?"

Gwen blinked. She'd been so lost in her own thoughts that she hadn't been listening to him.

"I'm sorry," she said, clearing her throat. "I was miles away."

"I was saying you should teach me how to Charm," Bruce said. "It's a very useful skill."

"It would need an unwary victim," Gwen said. She disliked using Charm, if it could be avoided. Lord Blackburn had inadvertently taught her what it was like to be on the receiving end. "Using it on someone who knows what to expect can be difficult."

"I need to learn," Bruce said. "How many talents are there that I have never mastered?"

"You were good at playing the fop," Gwen said. "Are you sure you didn't use Charm to convince people not to look behind the facade?"

"That's just play-acting," Bruce said. He smirked. "The trick is to be annoying, but not too annoying; blatant, but not too blatant. It helps that I really wasn't expected to do much of anything in New York."

"I suppose you were never offered a chance to shine," Gwen agreed. "Didn't your father try to offer you a commission?"

"New York Militia," Bruce said. He puffed out his chest. "A fancy uniform, a stipend and absolutely nothing to do. No one gave a damn if I attended training sessions or not."

"I always hated people like that," Gwen said, without thinking.

Bruce looked hurt. "Because we're lazy?"

"Because you got the rank and the uniform, but you did nothing with it," Gwen said. She remembered Major Shaw and shuddered. "And people like me were expected to stay at home, wear frilly dresses and let the men make all the decisions."

"I suppose," Bruce said.

"And there are plenty of careerists who would make better officers," Gwen added. "But rich men buy commissions and push the careerists back down."

"I could have been more," Bruce said. "But I didn't *want* to look too good."

Gwen looked him in the eye. "When – how – did you find out that you were a magician?"

Bruce frowned, then smiled. "I'll tell you my story if you tell me yours," he countered sweetly. "Deal?"

Gwen hesitated. She hadn't wanted to talk about her experience to anyone, even Master Thomas. Enough rumours had got out, despite her mother, to ensure that she was no longer considered a suitable marriage prospect for anyone of her station. But she *did* want to know Bruce's story. She didn't know the stories of *any* of the Master Magicians.

"Deal," she said.

"I used to spend a lot of time climbing trees," Bruce said. "Father never approved, said I'd fall and break my neck. Never stopped me, of course. One day, while father was in England, I slipped and fell. But I never hit the ground."

"You stopped yourself in midair," Gwen said, flatly.

"More or less," Bruce said. "My mother's family warned me to keep my abilities a secret, even from my father. And so I did."

He lifted his eyebrows. "And your story?"

Gwen closed her eyes. She wasn't sure she wanted to see his reaction. "I was seven," she said. "Mother was having one of her headaches and the nanny was visiting friends, so she banished me into the garden and ordered the maid to take care of me. The poor girl didn't have the slightest idea how to handle a child. There I was, throwing a tantrum, and she was desperately trying to get me to shut up. Everything she said just made me scream louder."

Bruce gave her an odd look. "And then?"

"I wanted sweets," Gwen said. "I must have used Charm, somehow; the maid stopped nagging me and ran to get sweets, a whole *pile* of sweets. She was shaking like a leaf, dropping them in front of me … she collapsed, moments afterwards. The gardener came running, but it was too late. They couldn't do anything for her. The last I heard, she was in a bedlam."

"A madhouse," Bruce said. "Couldn't you do anything?"

"I didn't know," Gwen said. "It wasn't until I overheard some of the other servants talking that I knew what had happened. They were all scared of me after that, Bruce. We couldn't keep servants for long, no matter how much we offered. They called me a monster, a devil-child. And there were times when I believed them."

"It wasn't your fault," Bruce said.

"I was a spoilt brat," Gwen said. She couldn't help feeling guilty. She hadn't known what she could do, but she'd been throwing a tantrum anyway. It wasn't as if the maid had any power over her. "And as my powers developed, I became worse."

"At least you grew up in a loving household," Bruce said. He reached out and took her hand, squeezing it gently. "Not everyone has *that* opportunity."

"I suppose," Gwen said. "But I still feel bad about it."

Chapter Thirty-Four

 want him dead," Adam snapped.

Raechel looked up, closing her eyes so she could hear better. Adam had taken Roosevelt into the next room, but he was speaking so loudly she could hear him through the wood. She knew that *something* had happened, from a report a messenger had given straight to Adam, yet she had no idea *what*. And she couldn't escape the feeling that it was something important.

She rose and pressed her ear against the wood, despite the risk. If she was caught spying on the two men, she'd be lucky not to be hanged at once. Adam would remember just how many documents had crossed her desk and insist on it, before she had a chance to report to anyone. She listened as hard as she could, but it was still hard to pick out the words.

"He did what he thought was right," Roosevelt was saying. He was deliberately pitching his voice low, as if he was trying to calm the older man. "And it may have worked out in our favour."

"At the cost of pissing off the French," Adam thundered. "Has it occurred to you that we *need* French support?"

Raechel felt her blood run cold. She hadn't been sure where some of the money came from, but she thought she knew now. Every last *franc* spent on the Sons of Liberty would be worth it, for the French, if the Sons rose up at the right time. The information she'd seen as it crossed her desk made it clear that the Sons had been planning multiple uprisings. Even if they were all put down, they would distract the redcoats from the *real* enemy.

"The *plan* was to rise up in the rear, when the French attacked Amherst," Adam added, sharply. "Doing nothing might have been survivable, but actually joining with the redcoats to resist the French? They're not going to ignore *that*!"

"The French are just as bad as the English," Roosevelt said. "At least this way we can count on English gratitude."

"We *can't* count on their gratitude," Adam insisted. He made a discernible effort to lower his voice. "We have betrayed one friend in hopes of winning over our enemies, revealing far too much about ourselves in the process. And it *happened* because that … that … *idiot* thought it would be a good idea to impress a girl!"

"A very well-connected girl," Roosevelt noted.

Raechel considered it as Adam fumed. Gwen? She couldn't think of anyone else who might be well-connected in Amherst. Just what had happened down south to convince the Sons that it might be worth standing aside, for a while? And what had … *someone* ... done to piss off the French?

"This is a deadly mistake," Adam repeated. "Need I remind you that we voted? And that the vote was for doing *nothing*? We have been pushed into joining the wrong side …"

"If the Viceroy keeps his word," Roosevelt pointed out, "it will not *be* the wrong side!"

Adam snorted. "And you expect the Viceroy to keep his word?"

"He's already started laying the groundwork, according to our spies in New York," Roosevelt said. "And they *have* had a taste of our power."

"Not enough to make them compliant," Adam hissed. "If the French want to screw us, General, all they have to do is forward our letters to the British and watch the chaos from a safe distance. We gave them our word."

"To hell with the French," Roosevelt said. "Do you expect *them* to keep their word?"

"Then we fight another revolution," Adam said. "The English *have* betrayed us …"

"The French have not had a chance," Roosevelt said.

"I *demand* that we take steps," Adam insisted. "The vote was taken!"

"And circumstances changed," Roosevelt said. He

sounded as though he was reaching the end of his tether. "If this goes badly wrong, we can and we will demand disciplinary measures. Our friend made a number of decisions that might well go badly wrong. But until then, we will cling to the promise of winning what we want without a fight."

"Bah," Adam said.

Raechel heard someone walking and hurried back to her desk, sitting down hastily before the door opened and Roosevelt strode across the office and out of the door. Adam followed him, his face dark with anger. *Something* had clearly happened, but what? Adam glowered at her as she looked at him, then sat down at his desk and poured himself a glass of rotgut. He didn't offer her any as he took a long swig.

"Raechel," he said, suddenly. "I have a job for you."

Raechel blinked in surprise. "Yes, sir?"

"Go find Ivan," Adam ordered. He still sounded angry, although it didn't seem to be directed at her. "Tell him I wish to speak with him, at once, and then go for a long lunch. Don't come back until two."

"Yes, sir," Raechel said. If she'd been genuinely working, she would have been delighted at the prospect of taking two whole hours off. Instead, she found herself wanting to know just what Adam and Ivan were going to say to one another. "Do you know where I can find him?"

"He's normally at the shooting range, this time of day," Adam said. "Try not to get shot when you speak to him."

Raechel bit down the sarcastic response that came to mind and rose, grabbing her cloak as she hurried for the door. Behind her, she heard Adam pouring another glass of rotgut. It bothered her, more than she cared to admit. She'd never seen him drinking anything stronger than water before.

The camp was teeming with activity, she noted, as she hurried towards the shooting range. A number of men sat in the stocks, punishment for violating one or more of the camp's handful of rules; she gave them a wide berth as she passed. They were lucky, she thought. Being trapped in the stocks was humiliating, but if they were in Britain they'd be ducking rotten fruit – or stones, if their crimes had been bad enough. A woman sat at the rear of the group, looking sullen. What had *she* done to wind up in the stocks?

She made her way hurriedly down to the shooting range, tasting the whiff of powder in the air. The Sons never stopped shooting from dawn till dusk, practicing their skills until they were almost as good as some of the huntsmen she'd known. Meg had made her practice with a small pistol, but Raechel had worked hard to hide the skills Irene had taught her. Enduring the woman's taunts about noblewomen had been easy, given what she knew. The only problem was getting her hands on a pistol …

A man stood outside the shooting range, looking grim. Raechel waved cheerfully to him as he approached, but he showed no inclination to relax. Either he wasn't impressed by a pretty girl or he'd been one of the watchers as a handful of guards were forced to run the gauntlet for falling asleep on duty. Raechel had found it a sickening spectacle, but she'd watched anyway, knowing she had to harden herself. Besides, the Sons were right. A guard who fell asleep on duty could be disastrous, if an attacker was sneaking up to the camp.

"I need to speak to Ivan," she said. "Can you ask him to come out to me?"

The guard nodded and turned to shout into the shooting range. A moment later, Ivan appeared; a tall, muscular man wearing a shirt and a pair of trousers that seemed too small for him, carrying a heavy rifle over his shoulder. Raechel had to fight down the urge to take a step backwards. Ivan looked harmless – or no more harmful than any of the other men in the camp – but there was something about him that alarmed her. She just couldn't put her finger on it.

His voice was cold and hard. "Yes?"

"Adam asks that you visit him, now," Raechel said. She didn't want to admit it, but he intimidated her. Her fingers itched for a pistol. "Please could you go see him?"

"Of course," Ivan said. There was an odd accent in his voice, one she'd never quite been able to place. She'd wondered if it was Russian, but none of the Russians she'd met had sounded like him. "It would be my pleasure."

He snapped a command to the guard, then strode off

towards Adam's office. Raechel followed, wondering if there would be a chance to spy on the meeting, but when the building came into view she saw a handful of men hanging around, seemingly doing nothing. Irene had shown her covert guards on the streets of London, men who looked ready to intervene if something happened. Adam, it seemed, followed the same principle himself.

She muttered a curse under her breath and headed for the dining hall. It was half-empty, but the tables that were filled were buzzing with conversation. She spotted John on the other side of the room, talking to Irene in her male guise; she picked up a bowl of potatoes, sausage and beans, then headed over to join them. John seemed far too pleased to see her for her own peace of mind.

"There's been an interesting development," Irene said. Really, if Raechel hadn't already known she was female, she wouldn't have had a clue from her voice. It was pitched perfectly. "John? You want to tell her?"

"The French attacked Amherst," John said. He sounded excited. "And we joined with the redcoats to repel them."

Raechel blinked. That ... *that* ... was what Adam was so mad about?

"The person on the spot took the decision," Irene said, quietly. Raechel hadn't felt Irene reading her mind, but she tightened her shields anyway. "The battle was won."

"That's good," Raechel said. "Isn't it?"

"Unless the redcoats turn on us, now the French have been beaten," John said. "They may recall the convoy that left New York."

It took Raechel a moment to put it together. From what she'd picked up in New York, the Viceroy's plan had been to land troops near New Orleans and capture the city, making it harder for the French to support their offensive into British North America. But if the French offensive had been blunted

...

They may fear what the Sons will do, she thought. *Or take advantage of the French being weakened by striking at the Sons.*

She ate her food slowly, listening to the ebb and flow of the chatter. Opinion seemed to be torn. No one actually *liked* the French, as far as she could tell, but very few liked the British either. And no one was particularly happy about how the decision had been made. The Sons took their voting seriously.

"Meet me outside in ten minutes," Irene hissed, as she rose. John had already headed back to his duties. "Please."

Raechel nodded, finished her dinner and headed out of the door. Irene was waiting in the same spot, her eyes half-closed as she leant against the wooden barracks. Raechel glanced from side to side, then stepped up close. If anyone saw them, they should assume they were kissing, rather than sharing secrets.

"Adam isn't pleased," she said.

"Something *very* odd happened at Amherst," Irene agreed. "I can generally tell when a story doesn't quite add up, Raechel, and something *really* doesn't add up here."

Raechel frowned. "Gwen was involved, somehow," she said. "But how?"

"We'll find out in New York," Irene said. "I need to slip out of the camp and vanish. Do you want to come with me?"

"I may find out something else we need to know," Raechel said, after a moment. She was tempted, but she was growing used to her double role. "It's far too early to leave now."

Irene nodded. "You know where you can find a compass? If you have to leave in a hurry, make sure you head eastwards. You should come across a road; follow it to the east until you reach a settlement. There are stagecoach inns in most of them, just buy yourself a ticket to New York. Don't second-guess yourself, just go…"

Raechel winced. "That doesn't sound like a good plan," she said.

"It isn't," Irene said. "But right now you don't have much of a choice."

She gave Raechel a brief hug, then turned and walked away. Raechel stared after her, feeling lost and alone. Getting out of the camp wouldn't be easy for her – Meg had taken pains to tell the new recruits that it was impossible to leave, without the correct password – but Irene would have no trouble reading it from the guard's mind. And even if she did get out, Raechel had no illusions about what awaited her on the far side. She might well die of exposure before she reached safety, if she wasn't hunted down and killed. Irene had incredible nerve to just make the walk on her own.

And now I need to see what else I can find out, she thought.

She pushed the thought aside as she headed slowly back towards Adam's office. The guards were still there. She glanced at the sun, silently calculating the time. It was, by her best guess, half past one. Shaking her head, she walked back to the barracks, wondering if she had time for a brief nap. It didn't look like it. Instead, she lay down on the bed and forced herself to relax. It wasn't long before Meg entered, looking annoyed.

"It's too early to be lying down," she snapped. "Why aren't you at work?"

"The boss said I wasn't to go back until two," Raechel said. She glanced at the clock on the wall, which insisted she had ten minutes left. "Why aren't *you* at work?"

"Don't get cheeky with me," Meg snapped. She looked as if she were about to slap Raechel, then thought better of it. "I have work to do here."

Raechel frowned, wondering just what Meg had to do in the female barracks. It wasn't as if she did *anything*, beyond issuing orders and snapping out commands. Raechel had a private suspicion that Meg didn't do anything at all, save for welcoming new recruits. It would certainly explain why she was always lurking around, ready to hand out punishment duties to anyone who messed up.

"I'll leave you to it," she said, drawing her cloak around her shoulders and heading for the door. She braced herself, half-expecting a slap, but Meg let her go unmolested. Maybe she thought Raechel would complain about her to Adam. "Have fun doing whatever you do."

The guards were gone, she noted as she walked back to the office, but the door was locked and bolted. She tapped on the door and waited, sure she could hear *someone* moving around inside the building. It was nearly five minutes, however, before she heard the sound of the bolts being drawn back, one by one, and the door opened. Adam was standing just inside, looking angry. His filing cabinets were a mess.

"You were in New York, I believe," he said, as he

beckoned her inside and closed the door firmly. "What did you make of the Viceroy?"

"He struck me as a little overwhelmed by his job," Raechel answered, before she could stop herself. What *should* she say? "He wasn't a bad person, but he had too many problems."

"I see," Adam said. "And what did you make of his son?"

"He's a fop," Raechel said. She'd danced with Bruce Rochester at the ball, once, but he hadn't made much of an impression on her. Indeed, he hadn't paid much attention to her at all. "I didn't think much of him."

"The Viceroy hasn't announced the formation of an American Parliament, not publicly," Adam told her. There was no doubt in his voice at all. "What do you make of that?"

Raechel hesitated. "My uncle always said it took time to lay the political groundwork for anything," she said, finally. The words came out of her mouth, one by one. "Giving the Americas a parliament would change things dramatically. The other politicians would not be pleased if they were surprised."

"I see," Adam said, again. His voice was oddly thoughtful. "You don't think he's planning to cheat us?"

"He wouldn't be laying the groundwork if he was," Raechel said. Despite her uncle's best efforts, she knew politics better than *that*. "The more people who know about it, the more people who adjust their plans to account for it, the more people who will be angry if the plans get cancelled at short notice. He means to keep the agreement, I think, but he needs to lay the groundwork first."

"Very good," Adam said. He stepped back from her – she hadn't realised he was so close – and turned to his desk, rooting through the piles of paperwork. "Pack yourself a bag, Raechel. Clothes ... and whatever else you need for a trip to New York."

Raechel tensed. "We're going to New York?"

"No, we're going to Moscow," Adam sneered. Luckily, his back was turned to her and he didn't see her flinch. "I was under the distant impression that you had a working brain, young lady."

"I'll be recognised in New York," Raechel protested, trying not to protest too much. It would be inconvenient if she talked her way *out* of the trip. She had a hunch that staying with Adam was *important*. "They'll see me ..."

"You'll be wearing a tatty dress," Adam told her, flatly. "They won't recognise you for a second. Now go, pack your bag. I expect you back here in less than an hour, as we have an appointment in New York City. No conversations along the way."

Raechel nodded and hurried to do as she was told.

Chapter Thirty-Five

I was expecting a band," Bruce said. He sounded slightly disappointed as they climbed off the train in New York. "Not ..."

He waved his hand at the station. It was almost empty, save for a handful of soldiers on guard duty and the ever-present porters. A hansom cab sat at the far end of the platform, driven by a man Gwen recognised from the Viceregal Palace. She could hear the sound of a newsboy shouting about an exclusive, and a great victory, in the distance, but otherwise the station was remarkably quiet.

She concealed her amusement with an effort. "Better for us to slip in unnoticed than have to pose in front of a band," she said. She'd never liked taking part in parades, even though the Royal Sorcerers Corps was supposed to march in unison through London every year for the King's birthday. "We need to talk to your father before we do anything else."

Bruce nodded and almost reached for her hand before he thought better of it. They'd been alone in the coach for most of the trip, spending the time chatting about their lives and getting to know one another better. Gwen had to admit she felt comfortable in his presence, a comfort she found far more reassuring than any sparks of passion. But they had to remember not to be indiscreet until they had told the Viceroy just what had happened. There were already far too many rumours flying around America.

But there are always rumours, she thought, as they walked towards the cab. The driver dropped to the ground and opened the hatch for them, allowing Bruce to help her into the vehicle. *This time, there might be some truth in them.*

The carriage rattled to life moments after the doors were

firmly closed. Gwen watched Bruce carefully, sensing his nervousness despite his best efforts to hide it. He was going to face his father, a man who had every reason to be angry with him, both for hiding his magic and for joining the Sons. She had no idea if Viceroy Rochester was disappointed in his son or not, but the poor man was in for a nasty fright. It would look *very* bad when the whole affair was reported to London.

They won't know what to do about it, Gwen thought. She almost took Bruce's hand herself, to offer what comfort she could, but she knew he'd reject it. Men didn't like admitting to emotional weakness. *Lord Mycroft is going to have a heart attack.*

"He's not going to be pleased to see me," Bruce said, quietly. "Even if we do have a working agreement ..."

His voice trailed off. Gwen nodded in understanding. *She* was technically emancipated, but her father's disapproval could make life very difficult for her; Bruce would have problems, in the future, if his father disowned him for his ... double life. But then, he *was* a powerful magician. She rather doubted he'd have problems finding employment, even if he *didn't* stay with the Sons. No doubt the French, the Ottomans or whatever government emerged from the Russian Civil War would be glad to have him. Jack had advanced the French magic programme by leaps and bounds.

And they managed to produce a great many magicians in a short space of time, Gwen thought. Now she had a moment to think about it, she was sure the French had deployed over fifty single-talent magicians to Britain and America. It was an impressive achievement, all the more so for having been done so quickly. *Jack must have taught them a great deal.*

The carriage came to a halt. Bruce opened the door and jumped down, calling for Gwen to follow him. They'd stopped outside the rear of the palace, as if they could avoid notice by sneaking in the back way. Gwen glanced around as they headed for the door, noting the large number of soldiers on patrol. The Viceroy was clearly worried for his safety, something that didn't surprise her in the slightest. He was, after all, the only thing keeping the American government together.

She picked up on Bruce's growing agitation as they walked through the door and up a long flight of stairs. The palace was the centre of American government as well as the Viceroy's residence, but it felt almost empty. Rochester had had plans, she reminded herself, to move as many of the civil servants elsewhere as possible. No doubt he'd taken advantage of the emergency situation to do just that, limiting the potential damage if the rogue magician attacked the palace. Killing the bureaucrats might do just as much damage as killing the Viceroy himself, if not more. Replacing the Viceroy would be easier.

"Lady Gwen," Viceroy Rochester said, as they stepped into his office. He was sitting at his desk, reading a letter. "Bruce. Welcome home."

"Thank you, Your Excellency," Gwen said. The Viceroy sounded tired, but she didn't blame him. God knew he would have been bombarded with demands for everything from more troops to government compensation for war damage. "It's good to be back in New York."

"The Royal Navy managed a landing near New Orleans, after a brutal battle with the French squadrons defending the river mouth," the Viceroy said. "As of last report, New Orleans was under siege and the French were screaming for reinforcements from Mexico. General Paget is confident that the city's defences can be reduced before reinforcements arrive."

"That's good," Gwen said. The French had gambled heavily by attacking Amherst, gambled and lost. "The entire French position east of the Mississippi might come undone."

"One would certainly hope so," the Viceroy said. He rang the bell on his desk. "Tea?"

Bruce swallowed. "Father," he said. "I – we – have something to tell you."

The Viceroy looked at him for a long moment. Gwen wondered if he already had some inkling of his son's activities. God knew *her* father had supervised David closely, even though he'd insisted Gwen's brother had to make his own mistakes. But then, her father hadn't been anything like as busy as the Viceroy. Bruce would have been left to his own devices for far too long.

"I understand that you worked out an agreement with the Sons," the Viceroy said. A maid arrived, carrying a tray of tea and cakes. She placed them on the table, then retreated as quietly as she'd come. "London has quietly approved the deal."

Gwen allowed herself a moment of relief. But Bruce wasn't finished.

"Father," he said. "I'm a Son."

The Viceroy stared at him in shock. He *hadn't* known, Gwen realised; he hadn't had a *clue* that his son had a double life. And now ... she watched, unsure what to say or do. The Viceroy was the head of his family. If he wanted to disown Bruce for rank treachery, it was well within his purview ...

"He's also a magician," she said, quickly. "And we're courting."

She disliked pouring tea – it was very much a feminine thing to do – but she made an exception and poured three cups while the Viceroy stared, glancing from her to Bruce and back again as if he didn't believe his ears. She wasn't sure *how* Bruce had managed to keep his powers hidden, when she'd been unable to keep hers under wraps for long, but he'd clearly managed it. And yet, a *male* magician would be feted, rather than hidden in the attic ...

"You're courting," the Viceroy managed, finally. Gwen couldn't help feeling amused that *that* was what he chose to focus on. "You intend to marry my son?"

"Yes," Gwen said, simply.

The Viceroy's mouth worked incoherently for a long moment. "And what," he asked, "do your parents think about this?"

"I'm effectively emancipated," Gwen reminded him. She passed him his cup of tea, then offered the second to Bruce. "But I don't think they would disapprove."

She watched as the Viceroy sipped his tea and took advantage of the pause to organise his thoughts. Bruce being a Son was a nasty shock, although he knew – thanks to Raechel and Irene – that there were quite a few Sons among the upper classes. And yet, a skilled politician could easily find a way to turn the whole affair to his advantage.

Rochester already had ties to the American nobility, through his dead wife. Now, he had ties to the Sons too. London wouldn't be amused, she knew, but Lord Mycroft would see the potential advantages in leaving Rochester in office.

And in our marriage, Gwen thought. *Blood ties to the Sons would be very helpful.*

"They might," Rochester said, finally. "I won't be Viceroy forever."

"I believe you will be rewarded with lands and a greater title," Gwen said. Viceroys were normally kicked up the social ladder, once they finished their term in office. Lady Mary would have no grounds to complain about Gwen's match. "And there is no questioning your connections in high office."

Rochester met her eyes. "And your superiors?"

Gwen took a breath. Love – or attraction – was all very well and good, but it wasn't the foundations of a good marriage. There had to be other advantages too, from huge tracts of land to titles and connections that might benefit both parties. And she'd spent the last five days reasoning it out with Bruce. They needed an excuse to marry quickly, if nothing else.

"Bruce is a very senior Son of Liberty," she said, "and the Sons will be very important in governing America. My superiors will be pleased at having such a strong connection, rooted in marriage. Our match will underline the new unity between Britain and America after the American Parliament is firmly established."

She took a breath. "And Bruce is a powerful magician," she added. "My superiors will be delighted to think of what our children might be like."

The Viceroy finished his tea, then leant forward. "You do realise that marriage is a *commitment*? That you and Bruce will be together until death do you part?"

"I do," Gwen said.

"I took the liberty of setting up rooms for you in the palace," the Viceroy said. "I suggest" – his voice hardened just enough to tell her that it wasn't a *suggestion* – "that you take the time to freshen up before dinner and compose messages to your parents. Bruce and I will need to have a long talk."

"I understand," Gwen said. She finished her tea, then rose. "I also need to compose a report on the battle."

"General Paget will be very interested, when he returns," the Viceroy said. He looked from her to Bruce. "In order to avoid scandal, when news of your courtship spreads, you will be chaperoned by Arielle. I trust this will not be a problem?"

"Arielle is discreet," Bruce said. "I don't think she will be spreading rumours."

"Irene will be happy to take over, once she returns," Gwen said. "And she will probably escort us back to London, if we have to get married there."

"Good," the Viceroy said. He rang the bell for the maid. "I need to have a long talk with my son."

Bruce didn't look happy, Gwen saw, but there was nothing she could do about it. If the Viceroy intended to give him the same talk as her father had given David, before his marriage, she doubted he was in for a very pleasant experience. Or perhaps he was going to demand to know just what Bruce had been thinking, when he'd joined the Sons. Or ... she knew the Viceroy's career would survive, after the Sons helped save Amherst from the French, but his reputation would be tarnished. His Son, after all, would have been a traitor if things had been different.

She smiled at Bruce, then allowed the maid to lead her through another maze of corridors until they reached a large suite. Inside, a handful of dresses had already been placed in the wardrobe, along with her spare sorcerer's outfit. She dismissed the maid, closed the door and walked over to the desk. Someone – she suspected the Viceroy – had already placed paper and ink on the table, along with a handful of dispatches from London. Lord Mycroft and Lord Liverpool already wanted answers.

Of course they do, she reminded herself. *I was out of contact for five days.*

She sat down and started to compose a reply, a bare-bones outline of what had happened since she'd arrived at Amherst. There was no way London would accept an outline without asking for more details – particularly the moment when she'd unmasked Bruce – but she had a feeling that could wait until she was back in London herself. Lord Mycroft would have no trouble filling in the blanks, when they talked face-to-face, yet she knew he'd keep the more sordid details to himself ...

Composing a message to her parents was harder, far harder. In truth, she'd always assumed she'd never marry. There had been no hope of a marriage agreement, once her powers had become common knowledge. No one had wanted to marry the Royal Sorceress – and, if they did, it would complicate her life beyond repair. Lady Mary, she suspected, had quietly assumed that her daughter would live and die a spinster. Now ... now she not only had to tell her parents she was getting married, but that she might be getting married in America, to a half-American who might be a traitor, depending on how one looked at it. Her mother was going to throw a fit.

Not because I'm getting married, she thought, *but because I might not be inviting her to the wedding.*

She smiled at the thought, even though she knew it was wrong of her. There were girls who'd found their weddings controlled, right down to the last detail, by their mothers. They had had no say at all in anything, from the wedding cake to the dress they'd wear when they walked down the aisle. Lady Mary would have done that, Gwen was sure, if she'd been a normal girl. God alone knew just how much of the family fortune would be spent on the dress alone. The thought of just getting married in America, without her parents, was very tempting. And yet, it all depended on how matters progressed. If she was pregnant ...

It was nearly an hour before she had something written out that satisfied her, although she knew it wouldn't satisfy her mother. But it would have to do. Bruce wasn't a *complete* unknown, after all, and the Rochester side of the family was a very old and honoured line. Lady Mary would be pleased by that, at least; the ties to the Franklins would probably please Gwen's father. And Lord Mycroft would probably have a quiet word with him, if he raised objections. The match's political advantages would not go unnoticed.

There was a knock on the door. "Come in!"

The door opened, revealing Bruce and Arielle. The latter looked excited, grinning from ear to ear, while Bruce looked as if he'd been torn apart and then put back together again. Gwen hoped – prayed – that his father hadn't asked *too* many questions, although she knew it was a futile hope. Her prospective father-in-law would have wanted to know everything, starting with how they'd started the courtship in the first place. She could only hope that Bruce hadn't been *too* detailed.

"Congratulations, Lady Gwen," Arielle said. She hitched up her dress, ran forward and gave Gwen a tight hug. "Welcome to the family!"

"We're not married yet," Gwen said, awkwardly. She hadn't given any thought to acquiring other relatives. "But we will be."

"I want to be one of the bridesmaids," Arielle said. She twirled on her feet, her dress fanning around her. "Can I be one of the bridesmaids?"

"It depends on where we get married," Bruce said. "Are you going to keep your side of the agreement?"

Arielle wagged her finger at him. "Don't do anything I wouldn't do," she said. "And don't do half the things I would do either."

She leant against the wall as Bruce beckoned Gwen to the other side of the room. If they spoke quietly, Arielle would have problems hearing them. Gwen made a mental note to practice Talking with him – they should be able to send messages to each other without opening their mouths – and followed him, keeping a wary eye on Arielle. The younger girl was doing a pretty good impression of someone who wasn't paying attention to them.

"Father was not pleased," Bruce said. "But I think he's relieved by how matters worked out in Amherst, and London has approved the idea of a Parliament, so he's not complaining too loudly."

"That's good," Gwen said. She felt somewhat relieved. Bruce had made it clear that the Sons wouldn't tolerate betrayal. "Is the Viceroy ready to make the announcement?"

"There will be a ball tomorrow night," Bruce said. "He'll be making the announcement there, once he's finished laying the groundwork. You and I are, of course, invited."

"I look forward to it," Gwen said. It was, she thought, the

first time in her life that she'd said that and actually *meant* it. Maybe it was different when one was courting. "And the other announcement?"

"He wants to hear from your parents first," Bruce said. He sighed. "Do you just want to run off and get married?"

Gwen smiled. "Don't tempt me," she said. "I have written them a message, but …"

She shook her head slowly. "And I need to speak to a lawyer too," she added. "My father won't be writing the marriage contract."

"Mine will," Bruce said. "Just keep the money separate and we should be fine."

Gwen nodded. "And a few other minor details too," she said. Some of them, she knew, would be regarded as objectionable. How many men wanted their wives to have political freedom? "But we can discuss those later."

"Of course," Bruce agreed. "Please let me know what your parents say."

Chapter Thirty-Six

I never realised the city smelt so bad," Raechel admitted, as the barge approached the docks. "It ... *stinks*."

Adam gave her a funny little smile. "That's the smell of humanity," he said. "You were in the countryside for weeks, breathing clean air and living in a camp where strict laws of sanitation were enforced. Here ... there's very little sanitation at all."

Raechel swallowed hard, trying to breathe through her mouth. The docks were filthy, covered in everything from discarded pieces of fish to guano. Adam had told her that this particular section of the docks was largely abandoned, worked only by the poorest of dockyard crews, and it looked as though he was right. She could see a handful of drunks leaning against the nearby warehouse, clutching bottles in their fists as they stared into nothingness, their faces prematurely aged by life. Irene had said that playing a drunk could be a very useful disguise, but it wasn't something she was in any hurry to try.

She scowled as the barge was hastily tied to the quay. The outfit she wore was quite bad enough; a loose shirt and a baggy pair of pants that were stained with something that smelt thoroughly unpleasant. She'd need a bath, she told herself, when they finally reached their destination, although she had the feeling she wasn't going to get one. Washing in the camp had been difficult enough, despite Meg's willingness to scrub anyone down who didn't pay enough attention to their personal hygiene, but in the city ...? She would be surprised if this part of New York had hot and cold running water.

"This way," Adam said, as he scrambled up the ladder. "Keep your eyes lowered as you follow me."

I look like a whore, Raechel thought. *Does he want me to act like one too?*

She pushed the thought aside as she followed him up the ladder, looking around with interest as she reached the top. The drunkards barely moved, as if they were so drunk that they no longer cared what was happening near them. On impulse, she glanced into the murky waters and saw a body drifting just below the surface. Her gorge rose as she remembered the undead stalking the streets of Moscow; she swallowed hard, forcing herself to look away. The poor bastard had died and no one cared enough to fish his body out of the water, let alone take it to be burnt.

The lower part of New York didn't get any more attractive as they moved through poverty-stricken streets. There was hardly anyone in view, save for a handful of listless youngsters and old men. She wondered, darkly, why the young lads didn't join the army, then decided it wasn't likely they'd want to risk their lives for the government. Some of them glanced at the small party, clearly trying to decide if it was worth attempting a robbery, then flinched back as they saw Ivan and his men. Raechel wasn't sure if she should be relieved or fearful that even young thugs had the wit to be scared of Ivan. Every time she saw the man, she was convinced he saw her as nothing more than a *thing*.

They stopped outside a tenement block in a slightly more refined area and waited while Adam dug a key out of his pocket. Inside, it was dark and cold; they tramped up two flights of stairs and into a small apartment. A young woman – it took Raechel a moment to recognise Jane – was standing in front of a fire, cooking a pot of stew. She hastily slammed her mental defences into place as Jane turned to face them.

"You're early," she said. She sounded surprised. "The stew is edible, but the bread isn't ready yet."

"We picked up speed on the last part of the voyage," Adam grunted, as he locked and bolted the door. Ivan and his men moved past him and into a smaller room, closing the door behind them. "Do you have a report?"

"My sources in the palace confirm that" – she glanced at

Raechel – "our mutual friend and his partner have returned," Jane said. "The Viceroy is planning to host a ball tonight where he will announce the formation of an American Parliament, after he finishes smoothing ruffled feathers. I didn't dare try to probe too closely, but it all *looks* genuine."

"I see," Adam said. He sounded displeased. "And is our ... *friend* ... compromised?"

"I didn't dare probe," Jane said. "But their body language suggests that they have become distinctly affectionate."

Raechel looked from one to the other. "Who?"

"Be quiet," Adam ordered. "Are you sure?"

"They respond to one another differently," Jane said. "I don't think they realised just how easily it can be seen, by someone who knows to look."

"So he's definitely compromised," Adam mused. "What did his father have to say?"

"Nothing, as far as I know," Jane said. "But I wasn't present for the conversation and nor were any of my sources."

"Understood," Adam said. "What time is the ball due to begin?"

"Six o'clock," Jane said. "But everyone is expected to be there by seven. That's when the Viceroy is planning to make his speech."

Raechel nodded to herself. There was normally a formal opening time for a ball, but it was generally understood that any important speeches would be later, just to ensure that half the *ton* could be fashionably late without missing anything. They'd all try to be at the ball for half past six, perhaps, giving them a chance to share a couple of dances before the Viceroy called for silence. And then, afterwards, there would be dinner, more dancing and a whole host of private meetings.

"Very well," Adam said.

He cleared his throat. "Raechel, take the stew to Ivan," he ordered. "Jane, I need to have a chat with you."

Raechel hesitated, then picked up the stew pot – Jane held out a tray – and carried it into the next room. Ivan and his men were inspecting a number of weapons, ranging from tiny pistols – Irene had called them assassin's pistols – to hunting rifles. She almost dropped the stew as she realised, to her horror, just what Adam had in mind. He'd claimed they were going to New York to support the Sons, but in reality he was planning to assassinate the Viceroy!

She put the stew down on the table, then hurried back into the first room. Adam was standing next to Jane, muttering in her ear. She looked at Raechel … and Raechel *knew*, with a sickening certainty, that Jane knew that she was a spy. And if Jane knew … she glanced at the door, only to recall that it was both locked and bolted. She was trapped.

"Sit down," Adam ordered. "Now."

There was power in his voice, too much power. Raechel's legs gave out and she dropped to the floor, staring at him in horror. A Charmer … a *very* powerful Charmer. She remembered just how much she'd told him, over the last few days, about her life in Britain and her observations in America. Had he been Charming her all the while, subtly pushing her to answer honestly? She felt sick, again. What else had he done to her?

"You're planning to assassinate the Viceroy," she said. Her mouth felt odd, as if she couldn't quite shape the words properly. "You want to destroy the agreement …"

Jane frowned. "What agreement?"

Understanding clicked. "You're working for the French," Raechel charged. "Aren't you?"

"We have an *agreement* with the French," Adam said. He sounded surprised by her deduction. "Now …"

Raechel cut him off before he could Charm her again. "No, you're *working* for the French," she said, dropping her shields just enough to let Jane see the truth in her mind. "You don't want the Crown and the Sons of Liberty to come to terms, you want them at war. And now you're planning to assassinate the Viceroy, just to make sure the Sons get the blame!"

"Adam," Jane said. She sounded worried. "Is this true?"

Adam turned and grabbed Jane's neck. Raechel could only watch in horror as he squeezed hard, slowly choking Jane's life out of her. Jane struggled, but Adam was far too strong. Raechel tried to move, desperate to do something, but Adam's commands held her in place, as firmly as if she'd been tied to a chair. Jane gasped, once, then her body fell to the ground like a sack of potatoes.

"A waste," Adam observed, idly. He kicked Jane's body, then looked at Raechel. "I would have had to dispose of her eventually, but I might have had a use for her beforehand."

Raechel stared at Jane's body, not trusting herself to speak. Jane … had been genuine, she thought, even though it was clear she'd been caught out at some point. Perhaps Adam had invited her into his office to keep an eye on her, making sure she wouldn't have the time to influence the other Sons. Jane … had risked herself to get Raechel away from an unwanted marriage … unless her cover had been blown before then. She knew she'd never know the truth.

"She was on your side," Raechel said, numbly. Casual violence had never been part of her life, even during the trip to Russia. To see someone killed so carelessly … she had to swallow again, just to keep herself from throwing up. "She was on your side and you killed her."

"She was a Son," Adam said, dryly. "As you deduced, my loyalties lie elsewhere."

"You're French," Raechel said. "You do a remarkable job of pretending to be American."

Adam gave her a pitying look. "Do you really think it's that hard?"

He shrugged. "Most of my cover is real, of course," he added. "That does help."

His voice hardened. "And a simple plan to ensure a civil war within British North America goes awry because a Son falls in love," he added. He smirked, although Raechel wasn't sure she got the joke. "The idiot ordered our forces to *assist* the redcoats, rather than attack their rear. Can you imagine such treachery?"

"Is it actually treachery," Raechel asked, "if one gets what one wants out of it?"

"Not for long," Adam said. He shrugged, a smile ghosting across his face. "I admit I didn't expect London to cave in so quickly. The invasion of England must have concentrated a few minds. But it won't matter. By tonight, the Viceroy will be dead and the civil war will be underway. There will be no peace."

"Because the Sons will get the blame," Raechel said.

"Of course," Adam agreed. "You will help us, of course."

His smile grew wider. "It will be a great story," he added. "The tragic heroine, escaping the Sons of Liberty, too late to save Viceroy Rochester from the assassin's bullet or blade. You will tell them how the Sons plan other uprisings, you will show them where to find the camps, sparking off a civil war in spite of yourself."

"I won't," Raechel said.

"Of course you will," Adam said. His voice was very casual. "You're a strong-minded woman, Lady Raechel, but you're *only* a woman and I am a skilled Charmer. I will Charm you to the point where you won't know truth from lies, where you will say *my* lies with utter conviction because you will believe every word. By the time the Charm wears off, and it will, it will be far too late to prevent the civil war. The redcoats will go after the Sons and the Sons will fight back and the true cause of the fighting will no longer matter."

"And so France will win the war," Raechel said. "It is a dishonourable way to win."

"Honour is a lie," Adam said, flatly. "The only true honour lies in victory."

Raechel glanced at the door, again, but there was no way out. If she tried to fight ... he was stronger than her, meaner than her and he might not even *need* to keep her alive. She could see his logic – her words would help to condemn the Sons – but after the assassination, the civil war might start anyway. Her only hope was to find a way to leave the room, after the assassins were gone ...

A hundred possible words ran through her head, but she knew they would be futile. She could have talked sense into Jane, she thought, yet Adam wouldn't be swayed by the voice of reason. He was French, not American; he'd set out to start the civil war and he'd come alarmingly close to success. The original plan had failed, but his second plan might work out better than he'd dared to dream. After the Battle of Amherst, *both* sides would be convinced that the other had betrayed them.

"I hate you," she said, finally.

Adam laughed. "Is that all you have to say?"

"Yes," Raechel said. "I hate you."

"I don't care," Adam said. "You're nothing more than a tool. You never *were* anything more than a tool. Your parents – and your guardians – were ready to sell you to the highest bidder, to make you the key to greater social status for themselves. British Intelligence used you as a tool to infiltrate the Sons, carelessly unaware that your cover was blown from the start. And now you're *my* tool, to be bent and reshaped into the form I desire."

Raechel looked down at the wooden floor, fighting to hold back tears. He had a point, she had to admit, despite herself. She knew her parents had loved her, but they *had* seen a girl-child as the key to making new connections for themselves, rather than carrying on the family name. Her aunt, too, had been more interested in her reputation than her happiness. But Gwen and Irene hadn't seen a tool. They'd been interested in her personally …

"Go to the devil," she managed.

"I'm sure I will," Adam said. Her entire body twitched as power flowed into his voice. "You cannot leave the apartment. You can use the facilities, if you wish, but you cannot leave the apartment."

Raechel felt her head spinning. She tried to fight the commands as they sunk into her mind, but she knew it was impossible. He had her under control; he could make her do anything, anything at all. And when he came back, he'd twist her into his agent, spreading his lies and starting the war …

"Stand up," Adam said. He smirked as she obeyed. "Stand against the wall and wait until we are gone."

Her body jerked, then did as it was told. Raechel scowled at him as she marched over to the wall, trying desperately to fight the commands. But it was impossible. She managed to turn around – there was a loophole in his commands – yet she couldn't leave the wall. Ivan entered, followed by his men. They were all carrying weapons, their eyes cold. Raechel *knew*, with absolute certainty, that they knew what they were going to do …

… And they didn't care.

"Have fun when we're gone," Adam said, cheerfully. She

had never hated anyone quite so much, in her entire life, as she hated him at that moment. "We'll see you when we get back."

He led the way out of the apartment, closing the door behind him. The compulsion holding her in place vanished as soon as the door closed; she staggered to the floor, dry-retching violently. Somehow, she managed to fight her way back to her feet and stumble over to the door, but no matter what she did, she couldn't step through the threshold. There was no way to leave the apartment. She glanced out of the windows, hoping there was a way to scramble down, but there was nothing. Even if her commands allowed her to climb out, getting down to the road safely would be impossible.

She refused to give up. Adam had promised her a fate worse than death – a fate worse than anything she might have *considered* a fate worse than death – and she refused to stay where she was, a lamb to the slaughter. She searched the rest of the apartment in a fit of desperation, but found nothing beyond a handful of supplies and a toilet that stank almost as badly as the docks. Revolted – she glanced at Jane, wondering how the girl had put up with the smell – she staggered back to the door. Nothing she did – not even trying to fall over the threshold – worked. She was trapped.

There has to be a way out, she told herself, as she peered into the darkened hallway. *But what?*

Gritting her teeth, she opened her mouth and screamed, as loudly as she could. The entire block couldn't belong to the Sons, could it? It was probably rented – one of the more common complaints among the Sons concerned New York landlords – and the other tenants might not be Sons. She heard a door opening above her, but she kept screaming until a young man – no older than herself – came down the stairs. He looked unpleasant, but he would have to do.

"Help me," she called, pitching her voice higher. Irene had told her it made men want to help. "Please!"

He caught her arm and pulled her over the threshold. The commands in her mind snapped, completely, as soon as she was out. She was free.

"What's the matter?" He asked, holding her tightly. "Why...?"

Raechel shook herself free, then ran down the stairs. She didn't hear him following her, but it wasn't a relief. If he looked into the apartment, he'd see Jane's body ... God alone knew what he'd do then. Somehow, she had the feeling that the locals weren't the sort of people to report a dead body, or do more with it than drop it into the street ...

But at least she was free, she told herself, as she reached the bottom. And she had to warn the Viceroy of what was coming his way.

Chapter Thirty-Seven

ell," Irene said. "You've had quite an interesting time, haven't you?"

Gwen nodded as she checked her appearance in the mirror. The green ballroom gown she'd borrowed from Lady Sofia hadn't fitted well at first, but the seamstress had gone to work and fitted it neatly to Gwen's taller form. Bruce was going to be there, after all; she wanted to look good for him, even though their engagement hadn't been officially announced. It was a new feeling for her, but she had to admit she rather liked it.

"Yes," she said, shortly. There was little point in trying to conceal anything from the older woman. "Fought a battle, won a battle, fell in love ..."

"Lost your virginity," Irene said. Gwen felt her eyes widen in surprise. "It's a good thing Jane isn't here, Gwen. Your emotions are all too recognisable."

Gwen swallowed a curse. She trusted Irene not to tell anyone, but Jane ...? Maybe Bruce could talk her into keeping her mouth shut. She was a Son, after all.

"Keep your shields in place, but don't lean towards Bruce when you're dancing," Irene added, warningly. "Your body language will betray you even if your thoughts don't."

She met Gwen's eyes. "Are you sure of him?"

"I think so," Gwen said. There were a number of questions she wanted to ask the more experienced woman, but she wasn't sure she dared. "We click."

"Marriage isn't just about romantic feelings," Irene reminded her. "And if you are pregnant, someone's going to count backwards on their fingers and realise the truth."

Gwen *looked* at her. "Can it be undone?"

"Of course not," Irene said. "But you have to be prepared for problems."

Gwen shrugged, then started to brush her hair. It was still shorter than was normal for an unmarried girl, but people would make allowances. She *was* the Royal Sorceress, after all, and long hair got in her way when she flew. The repetitive motion calmed her, despite the churning feeling in her stomach. Tonight, the Viceroy was going to announce the American Parliament ... and her engagement to Bruce.

"My parents gave their approval," she said. It had been nearly a day before her parents had replied to her message, long enough to make her think that Lord Mycroft had stuck his oar in somewhere. Her mother had noted that she wanted a formal ceremony in London, even if Gwen was legally married in New York, yet she'd raised no other objections. "And I don't care about anyone else."

She nodded to the papers on the table. "How does that sound for a draft?"

Irene picked up the papers and read them with practiced skill. "You're clearly not a legal expert," she said, dryly. "This is *far* too easy to understand."

Gwen snorted. "A terrible oversight."

She shook her head. David was the one with legal training, not her. She'd seen enough documents to take a guess at the form, but in the end she'd kept the marriage contract as blunt and basic as possible. Bruce would have most of the rights of a traditionalist husband, she'd determined, yet he would have no claim to her money and no right to object to her relationship with Olivia. Not that he'd raised any objections, when she'd mentioned her adopted daughter to him, but it was an issue that needed to be covered. And he wouldn't have any right to object to her work.

"You do realise that the final two clauses may well be illegal?" Irene asked. "I'd check those with a lawyer beforehand."

Gwen sighed. A man had the right to keep his wife in the home, if he wished, and treat her as nothing more than his property, but she was damned if she was accepting such treatment for herself. She was the Royal Sorceress, not some brainless piece of fluff who couldn't even get *dressed* without help. *And* she had a career, one she wasn't going to throw away because she was married. Bruce would just have to learn to live with it.

And he might want to join the corps himself, she thought, although she knew that was going to cause problems. *They'll be looking to him to overrule me.*

"It's astonishing what you can get away with if you try," she said. "If he signs the contract, doesn't it make the contract binding?"

"Depends," Irene said. She shrugged. "I don't think you can force someone to honour a contracted obligation to do something illegal. You'd probably end up wasting a great deal of money on lawyers, if the case went to court. If you *could* take it to court in the first place."

Gwen sighed. An emancipated woman *could* take a man to court, but a married woman was not emancipated by definition. A woman couldn't sue her husband, any more than the cow could sue the farmer. Reserving all the rights – and duties – of an emancipated woman to herself in the contract might be technically illegal, even though it was what she'd told him she wanted. But then, it wasn't as if she couldn't escape, if marrying Bruce proved to be the worst mistake of her life. She had more than enough power to vanish overseas ...

And some money hidden away in the funds, she thought. Master Thomas had been a paranoid man and, as far as she knew, she was the only person who knew that the money existed, let alone how to withdraw it. *I wouldn't be penniless if I had to run.*

"Make sure you get a lawyer to look at it," Irene said. "I dare say you could get an exemption from some ancient legalities, if you tried. Lord Mycroft would probably be happy to oblige."

"I will," Gwen said. At least she didn't need her father's approval for the marriage contract, although she knew she should probably run it past him before it was signed. "But I'll see what the lawyer has to say first."

There was a tap at the door. "Bruce," Irene muttered. "You want me to stay here?"

"I think you have to," Gwen said, crossly. The real answer

was *no*, but she knew there was no choice. The moment their engagement was announced, everyone would be looking at Bruce and her with gimlet eyes, trying to catch them out. Society dames *loved* embarrassing younger women, particularly ones who ranked higher than them. "We can't be alone together."

She raised her voice. "Come in!"

Bruce entered, followed by his cousin. "Gwen," he said. "And Lady Irene."

"Try not to do anything I would have to report to your father," Irene said, a hint of ice entering her tone. She hadn't been amused when she'd found out about Bruce, particularly after having been so close to him and picking up nothing. "Please."

Bruce nodded, then waited for Irene to lead Arielle to the other side of the room. "I heard the news," he said, quietly. "Your parents agreed?"

"Yes," Gwen said. "I'm afraid my mother does want a big wedding in London, even if we're married here beforehand. You'll have to come meet my father."

Bruce shuddered. "Is he going to hate me on sight?"

"Probably," Gwen said. "But I don't think he'll take out a shotgun and open fire."

She smiled at the thought, then sobered. There was no way to hide from the fact that they were in for a very rough ride, despite countless special circumstances. Normally, both sets of parents would have discussed the marriage prospects carefully, perhaps before the happy couple ever knew they were going to get married. Everything would be sorted out, definitely, before the outside world heard about it. But she'd practically presented the whole affair to Bruce's father – and her own parents – as a *fait accompli*. She couldn't blame them for being more than a little concerned.

"That's a relief," Bruce said. "Do you think I'll be welcome in England?"

"Once they hear about your heroism, probably," Gwen said. England hadn't exactly welcomed Benedict Arnold, but Bruce was hardly on the same level. "You'll be just like Lord Nelson, beating admirers off with sticks."

She nodded towards Arielle. "How's she taking it?"

"She still wants to be a bridesmaid," Bruce said. "I trust your parents won't object?"

"As long as she's in England," Gwen said. Traditionally, bridesmaids were drawn from the family or close friends of the bride, but she had no sisters and only a couple of distant cousins who had been too afraid of her magic to talk to her. No doubt there would be hundreds of applicants, if the wedding turned into a circus, yet Arielle would definitely be on the list. "I can make sure of it."

"Don't be too sure," Bruce said. "My father warned me that it might be a *political* wedding."

And that's what I told him, Gwen thought.

"There're thirty minutes until the ball is due to begin," she said, looking him up and down. He might have worn a nice suit, but it was crumpled, as if he were slipping back into his rich fop persona. "Are you planning to go like that?"

"I could," Bruce said. "Should I?"

"No," Gwen said. She poked a finger at him. "Wear something that *doesn't* make you look like a tramp."

Bruce smirked, then nodded. "Of course, My Lady," he said. "Your every wish is my command."

"A splendid attitude," Irene called. "Just make sure you stick to it."

"We could go flying tonight, afterwards," Bruce added, lowering his voice. "Leaving the palace won't be hard."

Gwen was tempted, more than she cared to admit, but she knew it wasn't possible. Irene would let her sneak out, she was sure, yet hers weren't the only pair of watchful eyes in the palace. Arielle wouldn't turn the other cheek and the maids ... she was morbidly sure they'd report any lapse on her part to their master, even if they thought she *could* turn them into frogs. She knew, all too well, that maids had eyes and minds. And Viceroy Rochester was not a bad master. They'd do more than the bare minimum for him.

"We'll have time together later," she promised, keeping her voice low. She *had* planned to take Bruce to Sorcerers' Hall, if only to show him the training rooms. "But now, we have to be careful."

"I know," Bruce said. He drew back from her, his eyes conveying disappointment mingled with determination. "I'll see you soon."

"We'll go down the stairs together," Gwen promised. She saw Irene walking towards them and sighed, inwardly. "*That* should start a few tongues wagging before the end of the dancing."

Irene cleared her throat. "Before you go, did you hear anything from Raechel?"

"I sent a message, asking ... asking one of the officers to send her back to New York," Bruce said. "As yet, there hasn't been a reply. But she isn't in any real danger."

***

Raechel ground her teeth in frustration as she looked up and down the street. She'd had the impression that she could just jump into a passing cab, but there wasn't a cab to be seen in either direction. She wasn't even sure where she *was*, relative to the Viceregal Palace. She'd looked at a map, back when she'd first arrived in New York, yet she hadn't memorised more than a bare outline. In truth, she wasn't entirely sure they were in *Manhattan*. Adam had been careful to keep her inside as the barge made its slow way down the river. He could easily have had them stop on the other side of the Hudson ...

She forced herself to think through it, recalling what little she *did* know. The main dockyards were to the lower end of Manhattan, to the east; logically, the Viceregal Palace was to the west, further into the city. But she wasn't sure which way was east or west ... and then she looked at the sun, sinking slowly towards the horizon. It sank in the west, if she recalled correctly, which meant the opposite direction was the east. Silently grateful she wasn't wearing a skirt, she started to run.

The streets weren't quite empty, she realised, as she ran as fast as she could. There was no traffic, but there were quite a few men on the streets. Some of them glanced at her running past, their faces either bemused or lustful. She did her best to ignore them as the sun vanished behind the tenements, hoping she could make it to the palace before it was too late. Manhattan wasn't *that* large, was it? Irene and she hadn't taken *that* long to explore parts of the island. But the further she ran, the harder it became to keep going and eventually she sagged to a stop, breathing heavily. Irene had made her exercise, but she hadn't kept up with it once they'd left London.

I should have kept running, she told herself, cursing her own foolishness. She could have taken a bottle of water or other supplies from the apartment, but she hadn't thought of it before she'd started to scream. *Irene would be so disappointed in me.*

The thought nagged at her mind as she forced herself to start moving again, as quickly as she could. She was a failure as a spy. Adam had known what she was from the moment she'd entered the camp, perhaps earlier. No, she hadn't fooled Jane at all. Irene had been so proud of her logic, so convinced that the Sons would *have* to take her ... and yet she'd been played for a fool. They'd *both* been played for a fool. Adam could have tied her up, or killed her as easily as he'd killed Jane, but he'd seen no harm in merely using his Charm to keep her under control. He just hadn't taken her seriously.

And he's probably already there, she thought, numbly. Adam had been gone for at least half an hour before she'd managed to escape – and he'd probably hired a horse-drawn carriage to get to the palace. *It might already be too late.*

Raechel gritted her teeth and ran harder, despite the growing stitch in her side. She *had* to get to the palace before it was too late. Adam could *not* be allowed to assassinate the Viceroy, no matter what else happened. He wouldn't have a chance to plant commands in her mind to turn her into an unwilling agent, yet the mere act alone might be enough to trigger the civil war. No matter what she said, to Gwen or anyone else, the war would destroy British America. And then the French would walk in and take over.

She heard a whistle and slowed to a walk as she saw a cabbie, stopping outside a tenement block. It was his home, she realised; there was a stable round the back for the horse and carriage. His shift had probably come to an end, but she needed him. A horse could get her there before Adam made his move. She stumbled over to the Cabbie as he fed the horse tiny pieces of sugar, stroking the beast's mane.

"I need help," Raechel gasped. She swallowed hard, forcing herself to speak normally. "I need you to drive me to the palace."

The cabbie looked her up and down, then leered. It struck her, suddenly, just what a sight she had to be, wearing tight clothes and sweating like a pig. She fought the urge to step backwards, hoping he would help her. There didn't seem to be many other options ..."

"Money?" He grunted, finally. "Do you have money?"

Raechel cursed. She had nothing ... in hindsight, she should have taken money as well as food and drink. But then, she hadn't seen any money ...

"You'll be paid when we get there," she said, knowing it wouldn't be enough to convince him. She didn't *look* like a respectable person. There was no way he'd believe she had any influence, let alone money. "The guards will have money."

The cabbie snorted. "That'll be the day," he said. He let go of the horse and unbuttoned his pants, allowing his manhood to escape. "You want a ride? Suck this first."

Raechel stared, feeling horror and a wave of burning rage, directed at him and her younger self. She'd thought she was being a brave rebel when she'd gone to the club, when she'd played with men ... she looked back on her younger self and wondered just why she'd been so foolish. There were far braver acts than crossing lines where her aunt couldn't see her ...

"Suck this and I'll take you wherever you like," the cabbie offered. He stroked his manhood, taunting her. She couldn't take her eyes off it as a plan formed in her mind. "I'll even take you to heaven and ..."

Raechel kicked him square in the groin. He doubled over, bellowing in pain, as she caught hold of the reins and pulled herself up onto the horse's back. She heard someone shouting behind her, but ignored it as she dug in her feet, forcing the horse forward. The shouting grew louder – it sounded female, making her wonder if she'd just got the cabbie into trouble with his wife – as she searched for the emergency release. She pulled it as soon as she found it, releasing the cab and sending it crashing behind her. The horse lunged forward, trying to throw her, but she kept it under control. She'd had nastier horses when she'd been a child.

And now all I have to do is keep heading east, she thought, as the shouting died away behind her. She felt a flicker of guilt, then reminded herself that the cabbie had tried to molest her instead of helping. *If I keep moving, I should reach the park – and the palace.*

It wasn't much of a plan, she admitted privately, but it was all she had.

Chapter Thirty-Eight

"You look stunning," Bruce whispered, as they met at the top of the stairs. "I can't believe no one was ever interested in you."

"They were frightened," Gwen admitted. *Bruce* wasn't scared, but then he had similar magic to hers. "They saw me as dangerous."

"Idiots," Bruce muttered. He held out a hand and she took it, delicately. "Shall we go?"

The announcer cleared his throat. "The Honourable Bruce Rochester and Lady Gwendolyn Crichton, Royal Sorceress," he said.

Gwen descended the staircase slowly, reminding herself not to orient herself on Bruce. It was far from uncommon for a young man to escort a young woman to a dance – the entire room would be their chaperone – but she didn't have a history of being invited to balls by *anyone*. There was no way to keep tongues from wagging, even though there were no clues to suggest that Bruce and she were doing anything more than scratching the surface of a relationship. She kept her face under tight control as the crowds – thinner than she recalled – turned to stare at them. The slightest misstep would keep the gossips gossiping for years to come.

The band struck up a merry tune as the next couple appeared at the top of the stairs. Bruce pulled her onto the dance floor, then led her around the room as the music grew louder. He was a better dancer than she'd thought, she realised; in hindsight, the first time they'd danced together he'd clearly been worried about concealing his abilities. She relaxed, slightly, as more and more couples appeared on the dance floor. There would be time to worry about politics later.

"We could dance in the air," Bruce suggested, so quietly no one else had a hope of hearing him over the music. "Or on the ceiling."

Gwen had to suppress the urge to do exactly as he suggested. It wouldn't cause any harm – she'd taken care to wear dark-coloured pantaloons under her gown – but it *would* cause comment, a great deal of comment. And while she would normally not have cared, she knew her mother – and Bruce's father – would care a great deal.

"It would be a bit too revealing," she whispered back. "I thought you were going to keep your powers a secret."

"Just for now," Bruce said. "It all depends on how matters shake themselves out."

Gwen nodded as they continued to dance, the room slowly filling up with the great and the good. She spotted Lord Tarleton and his son – the former heading for the Viceroy while the latter led a girl onto the dance floor – and wondered just what they'd said to one another, now the younger man's double life had been revealed. Viceroy Rochester had taken the news calmly, better than Gwen had dared hope, but she knew other families would not be so forgiving. She kept a wary eye out for Jane – the Talker was a potential headache – yet there was no sign of the young girl. Perhaps her family were keeping her at home until they knew how matters had settled down.

Poor girl, Gwen thought, feeling a stab of sympathy. A Talker would be a great boon to her family, but Jane had kept her abilities a secret. Her parents would not be pleased, if only because they'd be wondering just how many times she'd read their minds. *I'll have to look her up, after the dance, and see what I can do for her.*

The dances grew more complex as the evening wore on, but Bruce showed no sign of slowing down. Gwen had never had the time to master the more complicated dances, so she allowed Bruce to lead her through the motions as she kept an eye on the newcomers. There was an uneasy muttering in the air, something that worried her. The creation of an American Parliament would please the Sons – and everyone who had chafed under the Viceroy's rule – but it would also put a great many noses out of joint. People who had been winners under the old system would become losers under the new, if they failed to adapt in time.

"Lady Gwen," a gruff voice said, as the dance came to an end. "Can we have a word?"

Gwen blinked in surprise as she saw Lord Jackson, looking rather angry. It was clear he'd drunk quite a bit before coming to the ballroom. She had no trouble recognising the signs of drunkenness, or that Lord Jackson would be an angry drunk. Gritting her teeth, she nodded to Bruce and allowed Lord Jackson to lead her over to the wall. Bruce followed, keeping a steady distance. It was what a *normal* escort would have done.

I should have asked for a dance card, Gwen thought, although they didn't seem to be in fashion in America. *He could have marked me off for every dance.*

"This is quite intolerable," Lord Jackson said. He waved to a passing server without taking his eyes off Gwen. "The Viceroy proposes to end slavery!"

Gwen lifted her eyebrows. The *Sons* would want to end slavery, if Bruce was any guide, but she hadn't heard the Viceroy making any public statement for or against the slave trade. It was quite possible he'd been testing the waters, trying to see just how far he could go, yet she had no way to know for sure.

"I spent thousands of pounds on my slaves," Lord Jackson continued, without waiting for her to say a word. "The government cannot just *take* them from me!"

"The French already have," Bruce commented. "I rather doubt the government can legislate to force the French to return them."

Lord Jackson took a glass of wine from the server as he glared at Bruce. "Your father cannot steal my property!"

Bruce's expression hardened. Gwen spoke before Bruce could say something he would probably regret, later.

"The French have freed countless slaves in the south," she said, quietly. "And thousands more have escaped, running south to meet the French. They have tasted *freedom*! If they were somehow returned to you, would you want them back?"

She scowled, recalling how she'd been treated when she'd been posing as a maid. If she'd lived that life for years, then escaped ... there was no way she'd want to go back. A maid had few rights – she could have been beaten to within an inch of her life for spilling soup or speaking out of turn – and a slave had none. Even if the slaves were returned, there was no way they could be trusted. Leaving them with the French seemed the kindest option.

"They're my *property*," Lord Jackson insisted. "They're *mine!*"

"And now they are free," Bruce taunted. Gwen shot him a warning look. "Turn your back on them for a second and you might find a knife in it."

Gwen sighed. "The Viceroy is merely recognising a reality," she said. It was unpleasant, but she had no doubt that Lord Jackson could buy new slaves, if he had the funds. How much of his money had been tied up in the escaped slaves? "And that reality is that the slaves have made their escape. Let the French have them."

Lord Jackson's hand twitched sharply, as if he wanted to punch her or draw the sword at his belt. Gwen braced herself, readying her magic, but instead the older man merely turned and stalked away, his back ramrod straight. It was hard to feel any sympathy for a slaveowner, Gwen admitted privately, yet she knew that Lord Jackson was staring utter ruination in the face. If his family collapsed into debt, creditors howling at his door, the only thing he'd have left was his title. He'd have to try to find a wealthy woman to marry his son, just to keep the family alive.

"Charming fellow," Bruce muttered, sarcastically. "A week or two of being a slave himself would change his outlook, I think."

Gwen shrugged. Lord Jackson didn't regard members of the lower classes as *human*. It had been her own attitude, she had to admit, until Jack had rubbed her nose in the plight of the poor. And Lady Standish had treated her like a disposable girl ...

"Come on," she said. It wouldn't be long before the Viceroy's speech. "Let's mingle."

She kept her eyes and ears open as they moved around the room, speaking briefly with individuals and couples. Just about everyone had heard about the planned parliament, even though there hadn't been a formal announcement. The Viceroy had done a good job of laying the groundwork, Gwen admitted to herself. He'd sold the concept to the most powerful of the nobility by pointing out all the advantages that would accrue to them afterwards. Even with universal suffrage, the nobility would have an advantage for at least two generations. It was up to them to see what they made of it.

"After the war, we're going to be building airships," Hamish Tarleton said, when they met him and his partner. "I imagine we can sail through the air, over the mountains, and keep heading west. The Russians aren't going to pose much of a challenge when we reach their former borders in California and Alaska."

"Alaska declared independence," Bruce agreed. "We could always just swallow them up, or invite them to join."

Gwen smiled. Russian Alaska wasn't much, beyond a handful of settlements and a thriving fishing, hunting and trapping trade. Whoever won the civil war in Russia would have no trouble recovering the settlements, if the Alaskans didn't make an alliance of their own beforehand. Lord Mycroft was probably already plotting how best to take advantage of the whole affair, but she made a mental note to mention it to him anyway. If Britain blocked access to the Alaskan interior, there would be plenty of time to settle it without interference.

"The Indians launched another set of raids along the line," an older man she didn't recognise said. "Scalped a few dozen men and took a number of captives. We need to take steps to deal with them once and for all."

"It's the rogue settlers," another man insisted. "The Indians wouldn't be so much of a problem if they weren't buying arms from the settlers."

Bruce nudged her. "The French are probably supporting them instead," he muttered. "It gives us something else to worry about."

Gwen shrugged. Indians had been used in colonial warfare since the very first settlements, she'd heard; their unmatched mobility giving whoever managed to bribe them into assisting a considerable advantage. But they didn't make gunpowder weapons for themselves or anything else that might be used as trade goods. Lord Amherst and his successors had viewed them as barbarians; the French, again, took a more pragmatic approach. She had to admit it had worked in their favour.

She glanced towards the foot of the room, where the staff had established a small podium for the Viceroy. Bruce's father was slowly making his way towards it, now everyone who was anyone had arrived. He spoke briefly to a handful of late arrivals, but otherwise kept moving onwards. He'd made sure everyone knew the time of the speech, after all. Very few people would dare to be *too* late, even if they thought it was fashionable.

And so the world changes, Gwen thought.

She took Bruce's hand and squeezed it lightly, then let go. Bruce gave her a smile, one that seemed torn between hope and fear. He'd worked for America, but, at the same time, getting what he wanted would change everything. There was no guarantee that the Sons of Liberty would be elected into power. The voters might find the familiar more comfortable than setting sail to an uncertain destination.

"It'll be fine," Gwen muttered. "It isn't quite what you wanted, but slow change is better than violent twists."

"I know," Bruce muttered back. "But, whatever happens, father is never going to look at me in the same way again."

Gwen nodded in agreement as the Viceroy stepped up to the podium, his mere presence a call for silence. The crowd quietened, slowly turning to face him. He'd be a good speaker, Gwen was sure. Debate was taught in public schools, after all. But he'd *need* to be a good speaker to convince them not to oppose the new parliament. Lord Jackson wasn't the only person whose property would take a hit …

But they will have no choice, she thought. *And that has already been made clear to them.*

***

The streets grew more familiar – and wealthier – as Raechel cantered down them, heading constantly eastwards. There was very little traffic on the streets, but she recognised a number of buildings, including one of the large townhouses she'd visited while she'd been pretending to be looking for a husband. The Viceregal Palace was clearly visible in the distance, on the other side of the giant park. But the park itself was sealed, guarded by armed soldiers …

She cursed under her breath and steered the horse around the park, wondering just what idiot had designed New York. There was an order to the city she had to admire – there was none of the randomness of London – but, at the same time, it was awkward to get straight to the palace. Darkened alleyways promised danger; wider roads were crammed with people taking an evening stroll. A scent of anticipation hung in the air, a quiet awareness that things were going to change.

They're right, she thought, as she finally cleared the park and pushed the horse to canter towards the palace. *If Adam succeeds, things definitely will change.*

There was a crowd outside the palace, waiting. She flinched, half-expecting to see Adam and his men blocking her way, before she realised that the crowd was waiting for the Viceroy's speech. Was he planning to address the crowd? It wasn't typical, she thought, but very little was *typical* in the Americas. Or was the crowd just a cover for Adam? She couldn't see any sign of him, but that proved nothing. Adam could have disguised himself or merely assigned the crowd to one of his operatives.

She looked at the gates and frowned. A handful of redcoats, carrying rifles, stood in front of the small barricade, eying the crowd nervously. They were pushing far too close to the wall, she noted, but the redcoats clearly hadn't been allowed to close the gates. There would be carriages going in and out of the complex all night. She caught her breath as she cantered up to the gate, a redcoat stepping forward to block her way. His face was very pale.

"The French are going to attack," she gasped. She hadn't quite recovered from her earlier run, even though she'd been on horseback. It was hard, so hard, to speak clearly. "You have to warn the Viceroy!"

The redcoat frowned. "Who are you?"

"Lady Raechel Slater-Standish," Raechel said, without

thinking. "Open the gates!"

The redcoat stared at her in disbelief. She had to look a sight. Nothing less like Lady Raechel Slater-Standish could be imagined. She had no idea if he'd seen her before, but she'd been wearing a dress at the time, her face scrubbed clean and then carefully made-up to bring out her cheekbones. The redcoat had to believe she was lying through her teeth ... and if he believed she was impersonating an aristocrat, he had every right to drag her off to goal.

"Get off the horse," the redcoat ordered. He reached for her, clearly willing to drag her off the beast. "Now."

Raechel's thoughts raced. How could she convince him? She had nothing that indicated her true status, nothing that identified her as either a British agent or an aristocrat. If she asked to speak to Irene – or Lady Gwen – they'd laugh in her face. The redcoats, just by doing their damned duty, would allow the assassination attempt to go ahead.

Or was it malice? Adam would have needed help from inside the palace, just to get the assassins into the complex. *Jane* might have had an invitation, but she doubted *Adam* had one, let alone Ivan and his men. A redcoat could have provided the invitations or simply cleared them through the gates ... if they'd been posing as servants, hardly anyone would have questioned them once they were through the outer wall. All of a sudden, she didn't dare let the redcoat take her off the horse ...

Digging in her heels, she urged the horse forward. She had no idea if the horse could jump, but it managed to leap the barricade without problems and run towards the palace. A shot cracked out behind her, missing by a mile. At least the defenders would be alerted, she thought, as she pointed the horse towards the ballroom windows. The beast slowed as they approached the wall, its better instincts forcing it to fight her commands ...

"One last jump," she whispered, as the sound of running footsteps grew louder. People were shouting, spreading the alarm. Another gunshot cracked out behind her. She *heard* the bullet flying past her ear, pinging off the stone wall. "Please."

She closed her eyes, pressing her head against the horse, as the beast leapt right *through* the windows. Glass shattered around her – she gasped in pain as something cut into her skin – and they fell. The horse lurched violently under her as it hit the floor, bucking so violently that she was thrown off. People were screaming and scattering, women heading for the exits while men grabbed weapons or hurried towards her. She barely had a chance to collect her wits before strong arms grabbed her and pulled her to her feet. Resistance was useless.

"The French," she said, desperately. They *had* to believe her. She'd gone too far for anything else. "They're coming!"

All hell broke loose.

Chapter Thirty-Nine

wen stared.

The Viceroy had barely begun his speech when a young man – no, a young *woman* – had crashed a horse right through the windows and fallen to the ballroom floor. She grabbed for her power, holding it around her like a protective shroud, as the woman was thrown off the horse, landing badly on the ground. All around her, women were scattering back while men were advancing towards the newcomer. Gwen was so surprised that it took her a moment to recognise Raechel.

"The French," Raechel gasped. Two men were holding her, gripping her arms as though they thought she was a serious threat. "They're coming!"

Gwen turned, just in time to see a servant produce a pistol from a bag and open fire, targeting the Viceroy. She threw up a shield, deflecting the bullet into the ceiling, then picked up the Viceroy with her power and thrust him to the ground as Bruce hit the servant with a fireball. The man twisted, firing randomly in all directions; Gwen saw Lady Sofia fall to the ground, blood staining her dress, as one of the bullets struck her in the stomach. Bruce killed the man a second later, too late to save Lady Sofia. Other servants were producing their own weapons and opening fire.

"Get down," she shouted, launching a fireball at the nearest assassin. "Get down ..."

The entire building shook, violently. Gwen shielded herself as chunks of debris fell from the ceiling, realising that the assassins must have rigged up a bomb nearby. It hadn't been enough to destroy the building, but it would make it harder for the defenders to muster a response. She glanced around hastily for more targets, rapidly taking out two more of the armed servants. Another had been ploughed under and beaten to death by a pair of young men.

"For America," one of the assassins shouted, hurling a grenade towards the prone Viceroy. "For freedom!"

The grenade exploded. Gwen wrapped her power around it, just in time, directing the force from the explosion away from the crowd. The pieces of debris fell harmlessly to the floor a second later when she let go. Bruce let out a bellow of rage and threw himself towards the assassin, his power beating on the air and lashing out in fury. The assassin disintegrated into bloody chunks, his body scattered over the entire room. Another popped up as Gwen shielded the Viceroy, only to meet the same fate. Bruce would find it impossible to hide his true nature in future …

"Lady Gwen," a voice said. Two *more* assassins were approaching from the rear. "It is a *pleasure* to make your acquaintance."

Gwen reached out with her magic … and started, in shock, as her power slipped away from her. A Null, she realised, as the first man grabbed hold of her dress, a power-drainer. The assassins had clearly known who to expect, although they seemed to have been surprised by Bruce. Who *were* they? She slipped the dagger from her sleeve as the Null leered at her, then stabbed him in the chest. His power vanished as he bent double, allowing her to throw him and his friend right across the room and into the wall.

Never again, Gwen thought, as she checked on the Viceroy. He was alive, but he seemed to be in shock. It was funny how so many Nulls seemed to believe that taking her powers would render her helpless. Did they make the same mistake with male magicians? *That trick will not work twice.*

She looked up, even as she shielded the Viceroy with her magic. The floor was littered with bodies, some groaning in pain, others either playing dead or actually dead. She hoped – prayed – that casualties had been light, but she knew that far too many people had been hit. Outside, she could hear the sound of gunfire. The assassins, whoever they were, seemed to be engaging the redcoats …

Bruce, she thought, suddenly. *Where are you?*

***

In all his life, Bruce could never recall being quite so *angry*.

He'd issued orders, specific orders, that the Sons of Liberty were to wait for the new parliament, not put the plan to take New York into action. They'd always known the plan would be a gamble, even if the Royal Sorceress and a number of redcoat regiments were trapped to the south, in or near Amherst. And now they were getting what they wanted without a fight … rage boiled through him as he tore one of the assassins apart, looking around for their leader. It wasn't hard to guess just who was behind the attack.

Adam, he thought. It *had* to be Adam. No one else had been so violently insistent on sticking with the French alliance, even though the French were untrustworthy. And Adam had plenty of contacts in New York. He could easily organise an operational cell into attacking the palace, despite Bruce's orders. *Where are you?*

He searched, wishing he knew more about his other powers. *Gwen* had been trained by another Master, not a pair of single-talent magicians. She had advantages he lacked … it made him wonder, deep inside, just what would have happened if they'd clashed openly, each trying to kill the other. And, thanks to Adam, he might be about to find out. The attack on the palace had been carried out by Sons of Liberty, that much was unquestionable. His only hope of preventing a civil war lay with finding Adam. Where *was* the bastard?

A figure moved, pointing a pistol towards the foot of the room. Bruce lashed out, slamming Adam hard against the wall. He'd never dared use his powers openly in the palace – only a couple of his manservants were Sons of Liberty – and it felt odd to take the risk now, but he *needed* to take Adam alive. The wall started to crumble under the impact, pieces of brick and mortar hitting the floor as his power billowed out of control. Adam stared at him, his spectacles knocked from his eyes and hanging from one ear. Bruce yanked them away and threw them right down the hall.

"Adam," he snarled. He pushed, hard enough to keep the older man in place without risking his ribs. "*Why?*"

"Sleep," Adam said. His voice was suddenly *humming* with magic. "Sleep and dream of peace."

Bruce shook himself, violently. Gwen had been right. Charm had to be subtle to be devastatingly effective, certainly against a strong-willed enemy. And Adam was a Charmer ... no wonder so many people had trusted him, even though he was a damned paper-pusher instead of a fighter. He'd known everyone, controlling everything from money to the ebb and flow of intelligence. A French agent in that position could practically use the Sons as his very own weapon.

"Damn you," he growled. He heard the sound of ribs creaking and pulled back, slightly. "Why?"

"To start a war, of course," Adam said, dropping the Charm. "Do you believe there will be an American Parliament after this?"

Bruce risked a glance behind him. Dozens of bodies lay on the floor, blood seeping from open wounds. The assassins hadn't been very precise, part of his mind noted; they'd missed their target, but left dozens of others dead or wounded in his stead. And yet, so many dead or wounded, all among the great and the good, would shock public opinion on both sides of the Atlantic. It was just possible that Adam would get his civil war after all.

Gwen was bending over Bruce's father, her back to him. He felt a stab of regret, mixed with a love and tenderness he hadn't thought he could feel. None of the girls he'd met in New York had felt quite *right* for him, even Jane. They'd all felt like puppets in his hands. But Gwen was different. He'd never imagined a life with her, yet now he couldn't imagine a life without her. Maybe their shared powers had drawn them together, but it didn't matter. The thought of being separated from her was intolerable.

"Kill her," Adam said.

Bruce whirled. "Try to Charm me again," he hissed, "and I'll burn you to ash."

"No Charm," Adam said, as casually as if he were ordering dinner. "Just simple pragmatism, my friend."

"You're not my friend," Bruce snapped.

Adam shrugged. "The war will start, will it or not," he

said. "Once word gets out, the redcoats will turn on the Sons, hunting them down like dogs. That girl is a weapon, a weapon in the hands of your enemies. Kill her now or watch her turned against you."

Bruce stared at him in horror. The argument seemed logical, too logical. He checked and rechecked his logic, as Gwen had taught him, but found no objections, no hints that Adam might be Charming him towards a specific conclusion. If the Sons had to fight for their freedom anyway, after the carnage Adam had wrought, which side would Gwen take?

He shook his head, bitterly. Gwen had *always* put her duty first. She'd made that clear to him, back when she'd explained the advantages to both sides of sealing the agreement with a marriage. She might have strong feelings for him – she wouldn't have kissed and cuddled him during the long train ride without them – but she wouldn't let it interfere with her duties. And if they came to blows ..."

"Do it," Adam whispered. "Her back is turned. There's no risk."

Bruce swallowed. It had been his mother's side of the family that had turned him towards the Sons. America deserved better than to be held down by the British Crown for the rest of eternity. There was so much *potential* in the continent, for better or worse, so much growth for society once the British Crown lost its grip. He'd worked hard to develop his powers to serve the American cause, yet he'd known it would mean coming to blows – eventually – with his father. Gwen had offered him a way out ...

... And Adam might have slammed it closed.

"I hate you," he hissed.

Adam smiled, as if Bruce had said something funny.

"It matters not," he said. He didn't seem concerned, even though he had to know Bruce could kill him in an instant. "Kill her now, before she turns. You have no choice."

Bruce could imagine it. Gwen wouldn't be expecting an attack, not from him. He could take off her head before she even *knew* she was under attack, leaving her body to crumble on the floor while he ripped the palace apart. His father would die, buried under falling masonry, while Bruce flew back to the camp to rally the troops. There would be risings all over the colonies, as planned. But then the redcoats would counterattack. Sorcerers would arrive from Britain, trained and experienced enough to defeat him. The carnage would be unimaginable …

… And Gwen would be dead.

"There's always a choice," he said. His mother had told him so, back when he'd been a child, back before her death. "And there are always options."

He drew back his fist and slammed it into Adam's face. The Charmer rocked backwards, slamming his head into the wall before slumping, unconscious. Bruce punched him again, just to be sure, then let his body fall to the ground. It was funny just how small he looked, in that moment, so small and harmless. And yet, he might just have succeeded in sparking off a civil war. Bruce stared down at him for a long moment, then turned to Gwen. She was just rising to her feet.

"Your father is fine," she called. The sound of shooting from outside was fading away. "I didn't find any damage, but I put him to sleep for a while. It'll do him good."

Bruce nodded as he surveyed the room. A handful of people were climbing to their feet, looking rather shamefaced now the fighting had come to an end. Others, clearly wounded, were gasping for help. His eyes sought Raechel and found her, doing her best to bandage a man who'd been shot in the shoulder. He had no idea why Adam had brought her to New York – he couldn't think of any other explanation for her arrival – but he was glad he had. If she hadn't brought the warning, it was quite likely that his father would have been killed in the assassination attempt. And, in so many ways, he loved and admired his father.

And yet you were planning to betray him, his own thoughts reminded him. *One more thing you owe Gwen.*

"Raechel's wounded," Gwen said. "Can you help me take her up to my rooms?"

Bruce nodded. Help – servants and soldiers – was already flooding into the ballroom. He spoke briefly to one of the servants, telling him to get his father to *his* bedroom, then watched as Gwen levitated Raechel into the air. The younger girl didn't seem very happy with this treatment, but clearly didn't see any point in arguing. Bruce followed the two women, forcing himself to take one last look at the carnage before they walked up the stairs. He'd never liked Lady Sofia, or Lady Harrington, but neither of them had deserved to be killed so brutally. The *ton* was going to be in mourning for weeks.

Or maybe they'll all attend Lady Sofia's funeral, just to be sure she's dead, he thought, nastily. Lady Sofia had been respected, but very few people had actually *liked* her. She was just too loud and wealthy to be ignored. *The old hag knew too many secrets for anyone to be comfortable around her.*

"I'm fine," Raechel insisted, as they reached Gwen's rooms. "Really."

"You're bleeding," Gwen said. She placed Raechel on the bed, then gently touched the gash on her leg. "Let me Heal it."

Bruce watched, impressed, as the wound slowly closed. The Sons hadn't been able to find a Healer, even though they'd looked. Healers were rare. He'd tried to use that power himself, but he'd never managed to get it to work. In truth, he'd assumed it was a talent he didn't possess. But if Gwen could do it ...

"Sleep," Gwen ordered, firmly. "We'll chat tomorrow."

She walked into the next room, Bruce following her. "We need to talk."

"Yes," Bruce said. "Adam ... that man ... he wanted to start a civil war."

He stared at her, unsure how she'd react. He didn't want to fight her, not again, and yet Adam had had a point. Gwen was too dangerous to be allowed to live, if they *had* to fight a civil war. Had he been a fool to give up his best chance of killing her? But the thought of ending her life was unbearable.

"They were Sons, then," Gwen said. "Not Frenchmen."

"Adam was working for the French," Bruce said. He was sure of that, now. Adam had controlled the secret communications conduits to the French, after all. Who knew what *else* he might have been saying? He'd certainly had no shortage of money for the cause. "And I didn't recognise the assassins."

"Then we blame everything on the French," Gwen said. Her mouth twisted oddly, as if she was remembering something. "Adam was a traitor twice over, to the Crown and to the Sons; he tried to start a war to ensure the colonies would eventually fall into French hands. That should be sellable, I think."

Bruce eyed her. "Are you sure?"

"People will *want* to believe it," Gwen said. "Can you keep the rest of the Sons from doing anything stupid?"

"I think so," Bruce said. Adam wouldn't have been able to rope in *every* Son in New York, he thought, not without alerting him ahead of time. Even *Adam* hadn't known the identity of every last Son within the city. "But without the speech …"

"It can be given tomorrow," Gwen said, firmly. "As long as everything is blamed on the French, we should have time."

Bruce nodded, slowly. If Gwen was right, disaster could be averted and there would be no civil war. And even if she wasn't, they could keep a lid on everything long enough to smooth out the crisis. The Viceroy wasn't dead, after all. *That* would have made it impossible to talk London out of ordering quite draconian measures.

"Thank you," he said. He looked towards the window. "I have to go, if I'm to get to the camp quickly."

He hesitated, then caught her in his arms and kissed her as hard as he could. Gwen kissed him back, her power humming against his … for a moment, he wanted to forget everything and just make love to her. He could do it, too. She wanted it as much as he did …

… But there was no time. They couldn't delay.

"I love you," he said, drawing back. It was the first time he'd said it, to anyone. "I'll see you tomorrow."

Opening the window, he wrapped his power around him and hurled himself into the night.

***

Gwen watched Bruce fly into the dark sky, then touched her lips gently, savouring the sensation. She'd been tempted, more tempted than she wanted to admit. The link they shared was real, but she had her duty. And so did he. Turning, she walked back into the bedroom. Raechel, somehow, was not asleep.

"I'm sorry," she said, quietly. "I should have been quicker."

"You did fine," Gwen said. She patted Raechel's hand, gently. Irene would probably be a little more scathing, afterwards, but for the moment Raechel needed encouragement. "You saved us all."

"Thanks," Raechel said. "He ... he *Charmed* me. He wanted me to tell everyone that it was the Sons who killed the Viceroy."

"But you escaped," Gwen said. She'd wondered why Raechel had been left alive, but if someone had hoped she'd bear witness to the attack ... she shrugged artlessly, dismissing the thought. "And the Viceroy survived. I think you did very well indeed."

She kissed Raechel on the forehead, very gently, then rose. "Try to sleep," she urged, quietly. When Irene returned, she'd send her up to sit with Raechel. "I'll see you in the morning."

Chapter Forty

hey claim he didn't say a word before he died," Raechel said slowly, as she looked up at the gallows. Adam's body was swinging on a rope. "Is that true?"

"True enough," Irene said, dispassionately. "He *was* a strong and capable mentalist. There was little hope of extracting anything from him, even through torture."

Raechel shuddered. "And was he tortured?"

Irene waved a hand at the body. "Does he *look* tortured to you?"

"I don't know," Raechel said.

She shook her head. Adam had been bound and gagged, then marched to the gallows and hanged. She didn't know if he'd been offered the traditional last meal, but the trial had been the shortest formality on record. There wasn't a single person, British or American, who wanted to spare his life. Adam's name would be remembered longer than Benedict Arnold, for much the same reason. He'd been a traitor to everyone.

Irene snorted, then led the way back to their new house. No one had connected Raechel Slater-Standish with the crazed girl who'd fled the Sons, riding to bring a warning to the Viceroy and that was for the best. As far as the *ton* was concerned, Raechel had vanished; she'd probably taken up residence in a friend's house while exchanging letters with her guardians. Raechel hated the thought of not being given credit for her success, but she knew that her safety hinged on her remaining anonymous. She couldn't be an effective agent if *everyone* knew who she was.

"You did well, for your first mission," Irene said, once they were safely indoors. There were no servants in the new house. "The Sons knew who you were, which could have been fatal if things had gone differently, but you had no way to know it. Overall, you did well."

"Thank you," Raechel said, numbly. She didn't *feel* as though she'd done well. Yes, she'd made it into the enemy camp, but only because the enemy had chosen to let her in. "If I'd realised Adam had gone bad ..."

"People like him are very good at concealing their true natures," Irene said. "And it was you who stopped him. I don't think there's any good reason to blame yourself."

"I don't feel that way," Raechel admitted. "Is that wrong?"

"You're new to the game," Irene told her. She started to pace the room. "Like I said, under the circumstances, you did well."

"But I was tempted," Raechel said. "There was a bit of me that *wanted* to join them!"

"There always is," Irene said. "These groups wouldn't be half so dangerous if they didn't have an ideology that appealed to the poor, the dispossessed, the men and women yearning to be free. One cannot bury oneself in a larger group without feeling an attraction to that group."

She shrugged. "And the idea of being a free woman was tempting, no?"

"Yes," Raechel admitted. She wondered, briefly, what her aunt was plotting, in London. If, of course, she was out of the madhouse. "I've got six years to go before I can consider myself a free woman."

"You could give it up," Irene pointed out. "You'd be free then, would you not?"

Raechel frowned. The idea of just walking away, of leaving Raechel Slater-Standish behind and assuming a whole new identity, was tempting. It wasn't as if she had free access to her father's money anyway – and, with a little fiddling, she could make sure that no one else had access to it either. Irene could show her a whole new way to live, if she wished. Just selling some of her jewellery would be enough to ensure she could start a life well away from London – and her relatives. And there would be plenty of work for secret agents.

"I don't know," she admitted, finally. "It's all I have left of my family."

She cursed under her breath. If she'd been born a man, she wouldn't have to even *think* about the prospect of being married off to a fortune hunter. But instead ...

"Think about it," Irene said.

She cleared her throat. "We can't stay much longer in New York in any case, so I was thinking we'd explore some of the other cities before heading back to England," she added, thoughtfully. "My record as a chaperone is a little spotty" – Raechel had to laugh – "and so the Viceroy's niece will be accompanying Gwen and Bruce, now the replacement magicians have finally arrived. I don't *think* she'll get in their way."

Raechel smiled, rather wanly. She was pleased that Gwen had found someone, but at the same time she couldn't help feeling a little envious. Gwen had the power and clout to keep herself safe, if her husband turned nasty; hell, she could practically write her marriage contract to suit herself. Raechel didn't have that freedom, no matter what she did. She would concede most of her independence the moment she tied the knot.

"She probably won't," Raechel said. "Gwen could certainly talk her into leaving them alone for a few hours, every so often."

She smiled at the thought. She had the feeling that Arielle Franklin-Rochester would spend half of her time getting into trouble – she reminded Raechel far too much of herself – but that was someone else's problem. Gwen's mother would no doubt be happy to present her at court, for the start of the London season. And, as someone with ties to several different families, Arielle would be very sought after in London. Gwen would probably find herself warding off marriage proposals after her introduction.

"Probably," Irene agreed. She smiled. "And now we have some peace, I think it's time to do more practicing with your shields."

"My shields held," Raechel protested. Jane had known who she was, but she hadn't done it through reading Raechel's mind. "They did, really."

"You may meet a stronger talent next time," Irene said, firmly. She sat down, making eye contact as soon as she was facing Raechel. "Let us see how well your shields hold up."

Raechel sighed and gathered herself for the fight.

***

"It feels awfully strange to be leaving," Bruce said, quietly.

Gwen nodded, watching New York's towers slowly receding into the distance. The fast clipper would be uncomfortable, compared to Gwen's first ocean crossing, but the ship would be nearly uncatchable, unless the French got very lucky. And, with no less than *two* Master Magicians onboard, it was likely the French would consider it a stroke of very *bad* luck.

She wrapped an arm around him, knowing they were largely unobserved. Arielle was below decks, suffering from a nasty bout of seasickness, while the crew had other things to do rather than keep an eye on two of their passengers. The clipper would pick up speed as soon as she hit open water, seeking a fair-weather passage back to Britain. If Arielle thought the constant motion was bad so close to New York, she was in for a nasty shock soon.

But it's hard to be angry at her, Gwen reminded herself. *We could have been landed with an older chaperone.*

Bruce glanced at her. "Are you nervous?"

Gwen shrugged. "About facing my mother? That ... that could be bad."

"I meant about getting married," Bruce said. "Did you think we should have gotten married in New York?"

"My parents insisted on having a London wedding," Gwen said. She had the feeling that Lord Mycroft had pushed them to that conclusion, although there was no way to be sure until she got home. "Your father agreed with them."

"We could have gotten married in New York, even if it was just a private wedding," Bruce reminded her. "I don't think father would have stood in our way."

Gwen shrugged, again. Like it or not, their marriage was political, regardless of their feelings for one another. She had no doubt that the British Government was already laying the groundwork for the wedding, billing it as a sign of the newfound unity between Britain and America. Bruce was practically American royalty, insofar as it existed; he even had family ties to one of the most well-known American rebels. There would be no bigger wedding, certainly not one with more significance, until Princess Charlotte's children were married.

"I can wait," she said, although she wasn't sure if that were true. Her dreams mocked her, reminding her of everything they'd done together. She awoke, sometimes, utterly unsure if she'd been dreaming or not. "It does have to be done."

She felt her tummy, carefully. If there was a new life growing there, she couldn't tell. Lucy might be able to check, once they reached Britain … and then? She'd just have to insist on holding the wedding as quickly as possible. Luckily, Lord Liverpool and King George had ample reason to insist on it themselves. The ties between America and Britain had to be made as tight as possible before the new parliament came into existence.

"It does," Bruce said. He smiled at her. "Do you want to go flying around the mainmast?"

"I think the sailors wouldn't be pleased," Gwen said. "And besides, wouldn't that give away your powers?"

"Too many people saw me at the ball," Bruce admitted. He shook his head, slowly. "There might be no *formal* acknowledgement of my magic, but they know I am a magician."

And people will think I should have left him in America, Gwen thought. *Wayne is in charge now, and new magicians have arrived, but a Master would be far more useful.*

"Don't worry about it," Bruce added. "I couldn't have kept my powers a secret for much longer."

"They'll want you to take my job," Gwen said, only half in jest. "Or at least to learn how to fight."

"I wouldn't," Bruce said. "I hate doing paperwork."

Gwen laughed, then elbowed him. "Good," she said, sticking out her tongue impishly. "My career is saved."

She caught his arm before he could elbow her back, then held him, gently, as America slipped away in the distance, the last of the giant towers slowly vanishing beyond the horizon. And yet, she knew she'd be coming back. Bruce would want to return, she was sure, and the war was not yet over …

And there are many other places to go, she thought, as she leant into his embrace. *The whole world is waiting for us.*

***

"My career is doomed," Viceroy Rochester muttered to himself.

"Surely not, Your Excellency," his secretary said. "Everything has been placed in order. A potential disaster has been averted and the war is going well."

Rochester scowled at the younger man. "Leave me," he ordered. He wasn't in the mood to be flattered, even though there was a part of him that enjoyed the attention. "Have the maid send in tea."

"Of course, Your Excellency," the secretary said.

He bowed, then hurried out of the office. Rochester watched him go, thinking dark thoughts about young men who only saw the immediate results of their actions and never considered the long-term consequences. Yes, there *was* an agreement between the Crown and the Sons; yes, the war was going reasonably well. And yet, Rochester had no illusions. Too much had slipped past him, in the last year or so, for him to believe his term in office would be renewed. His son's magic, his son's allegiances …

The maid opened the door, her dark face frowning with worry. Rochester pointed at the table, motioning for her to leave the tray and then nodded at the door. The maid hurried out, clearly worried. A number of black men had been lynched since the news of the slave revolt had spread through New York, leaving the remainder terrified for their lives. It was yet another problem his successor would have to deal with.

He poured himself a cup of tea, then walked over to the window and drank it, slowly. There had been too many shocks, recently; he knew he needed a rest. But there were certain matters that could not be put aside any longer. He put the teacup down as soon as it was empty, then strode over to the desk. One of the drawers had a false bottom, where he kept some of his most sensitive documents. Opening it carefully, he removed a set of top secret contingency plans, reaching underneath to pick up an old envelope. In truth, he didn't really know why he'd kept it. It was a bitter memory he would have preferred to forget.

Closing the drawer, he sat back and held the envelope in his hands, remembering. He'd been old when he married his wife, old enough to be more interested in her social position than her body. Indeed, lust had never been a great part of his life. He'd certainly never patronised the brothels where so many of his fellows sowed their wild oats, or caught something unpleasant that killed them, if they couldn't work up the nerve to seek medical treatment before it was too late. It wasn't something that had ever bothered him. And he'd never really grasped that it *did* bother his wife. The best doctors in the land swore that women had no interest in sexual pleasures.

But that hadn't been true. And his wife had had an affair.

She'd confessed, of course, when her pregnancy became obvious. She was a married woman who had had almost no contact with her husband. Rochester hadn't needed to be a genius to deduce that his wife had had an affair. Indeed, part of him had almost been relieved. The thought of fathering a child had bothered him more and more, even though he wouldn't be the one carrying the baby. He'd acknowledged the child as his own, the moment the baby had been brought into the world, and thought no more of it.

But did *Gwen* know?

She was the Royal Sorceress. It wasn't beyond belief that she'd know that the Rochester line had never produced any magicians. She'd certainly look it up when she returned home, he thought, just to try and see where Bruce had come from. And she'd find nothing. But would she think to cross-reference Bruce's date of birth – and date of conception – with her former master's visit to the Americas? Would she realise that it had been *Master Thomas* who'd fathered Bruce?

And what would she say, if she did?

Rose's family had forced her to confess, fearing what

would happen if her husband found out that he'd been cuckolded. They'd clearly helped Bruce to conceal his powers too. A Master Magician, appearing in a magic-less line ... people would ask questions. Master Thomas might have returned, just to take his son. He'd been desperate for a heir long before he'd decided to train Lady Gwen. The family would not have survived the scandal.

There was no proof, of course, save for the envelope in his hand. Rose's confession, her plea for mercy. He could have killed her for sleeping with another man, directly or indirectly, or kept her a prisoner in his house, and it would have been perfectly legal. And yet, he'd been relieved. He didn't really care enough about the bloodline to want a son of his own. Master Thomas had probably never even *known* he had a son. He'd certainly made no attempt to investigate Bruce for potential powers ...

And Bruce himself didn't know the truth.

If it got out, now, there would be a scandal. Bruce's position in society would be destroyed, ending his marriage before it had almost begun. Rochester himself would be the laughing stock of the *ton*, just like poor William Hamilton. And who knew how Lady Gwen would react? *Her* family would certainly not be pleased.

Rochester rose and walked towards the fire, holding the letter in one hand. In truth, he wasn't sure why he'd kept it. He'd liked his wife, he'd been affectionate towards his wife, but he had never really loved her. Perhaps if he had, he would have been angrier at proof of her adultery. Instead, they'd shared parenthood together until she died, leaving him with a lone son who wasn't really his. But he was proud of the man Bruce had become.

He stood in front of the fire for a long moment, gazing into the flames. There was no way to escape the sense that he wasn't long for the world, that his aging body wouldn't last much longer, that one day the flames would burn him as surely as they burnt wood and coal. But his death wouldn't be for a while yet ...

Goodbye, he thought, taking one last look at his wife's handwriting. He didn't care to reread the letter. He'd read it too many times over the last few days. *And farewell.*

Quite calmly, he dropped the letter into the fire and watched it burn.

He would take the secret with him to the grave.

The End

Background:

British North America

The destruction of George Washington's army in the Battle of Brooklyn effectively concluded the American Rebellion, although it was a further two years before combat operations finally came to an end. General Howe's occupation of every major American settlement, the absence of help from France, the treachery of Benedict Arnold and the flight of much of the remaining Continental Congress ensured that further large-scale resistance was rapidly and cheaply suppressed. A grateful George III and Lord North appointed the Brothers Howe (General William Howe, 5th Viscount Howe; Admiral Richard Howe, 1st Earl Howe) as joint Viceroys of the Americas, with orders to bring the whole matter to a speedy conclusion.

Once firmly lodged in command, General Howe handled the problem of the Americans with a combination of tact and firmness. Never one to believe that British and Americans were separate, his attitude was one of a loving but firm father. The small fry – individual soldiers who had served in Washington's army – were released on their pledge not to take up arms against the British Crown. Larger fish – including the captured congressmen – received more individual attention. George Washington and a number of others were hanged; Benjamin Franklin was dispatched to Britain, where he spent the rest of his life in Cambridge University in reasonable comfort. (Arnold, not the most popular person in America *or* Britain, was quietly reassigned to the East Indies, where he died some years later.) Howe was determined to avoid large-scale reprisals and worked hard to keep the bulk of the American population reasonably happy with his rule.

Matters were helped by the outbreak of (yet another) war with France and Spain. British troops (and American militias) helped to capture large swathes of Franco-Spanish territory, as well as pushing the borders of explored territory further north. The Indian problem – a constant headache along the frontiers – was solved by constant raids, forcing the Indians south-west into Franco-Spanish territory. Quebec, which half-heartedly rebelled against British rule, suffered from mass expulsions; the population was largely transported to Louisiana (perversely, this gave the Franco-Spanish enough of a population to stiffen the defences of their territory).

The end of the war saw the redesign of the local government. Each of the fourteen colonies (Quebec was counted as a colony, although its population remained low for decades) was to have a local parliament, which would serve as local government. The parliaments would be responsible for raising militia – to secure the borders – and maintaining the road network, to enable additional troops to be rushed around the continent if necessary. Central government would be vested in the Viceregal Government and American House of Lords, under the Viceroy (a political appointee from Britain). Wealthy Americans would be eligible for the peerage; indeed, the tendency for wealthy Americans to marry British aristocrats and claim peerages was a constant – but minor – scandal between 1804-1832.

Voting rights were, however, strongly restricted. Originally, voting was the province of white men who owned land; later, as American merchants gained in political power, voting rights were extended to everyone who had more than a certain amount of money in the funds (the banks). Surprisingly, a number of women claimed the right to vote long before the Trouser Brigade movement spread into the Americas. However, the limitations on voting threatened to cause political unrest as the elites were more interested in securing their own power than expanding the base of their support.

A further problem was caused by the expansion of slavery. Black slaves imported from Africa had no rights and, by 1830, the slave-owners were so firmly established in the halls of power that attempts to ban the slave trade (or mistreatment of slaves) in both Britain and America failed spectacularly. This caused considerable unrest among poorer whites, who suspected that the slaves were a security risk (slavery had been banned in Franco-Spanish territory, one of many measures intended to bind the overseas territories more firmly to the Franco-Spanish Empire) and feared that slave labour would be used to push them out of work. Limitations on American-based factories (much resented in many quarters) only made matters worse.

The American population responded to this in several different ways. Large numbers of freeholders started to head west, beyond the borderline, and establish their own settlements beyond government control. (The government quietly assisted this in some cases, as the settlers were seen as better allies than the Indians.) The interior of America became a semi-lawless patchwork of settlements; some impinging on the government's attention, particularly during the ill-fated Whiskey Rebellion of 1797, others having very little contact with mainstream society.

Others, however, started to join increasingly radical political parties. While the defeat of the American Revolution had quelled the desire for full independence, the Swing in Britain and (yet another) threatened war with France fuelled the desire for change. An American version of the Whigs started to claim seats within the various parliaments, but a more underground movement – the Sons of Liberty – started to demand attention. Their demands – equal voting rights, an end to the slave trade and a united American Parliament – were outrageous, as far as the American Tories were concerned. The Sons of Liberty were forced even further underground by a government crackdown as the threatened war grew closer.

Elsewhen Press

an independent publisher specialising in Speculative Fiction

Visit the Elsewhen Press website at elsewhen.press for the latest information on all of our titles, authors and events; to read our blog; find out where to buy our books and ebooks; or to place an order.

Bookworm

Elaine, an inexperienced witch in Golden City, has her life turned upside down when she triggers a magical trap to end up with all the knowledge in the Great Library stuffed inside her head. Avoiding the Inquisition she tries to understand what has happened to her. But she is a pawn in the dark plans of one who wants the Grand Sorcerer's power.

Bookworm won the Gold Award in the Adult Fiction category of the 2013 Wishing Shelf Independent Book Awards.

ISBN: 9781908168320 (epub, kindle) / 9781908168221 (368pp, paperback)

Visit bit.ly/Bookworm-Nuttall

Bookworm II – The Very Ugly Duckling

Not every ugly duckling becomes a swan ...

In the wake of the disastrous attack on the Golden City, Lady Light Spinner has become Grand Sorceress and Elaine, the Bookworm, has been settling into her positions as Head Librarian and Privy Councillor.   But any hope of vanishing into her books is negated when a new magician of staggering power appears in the city, one whose abilities seem to defy the known laws of magic.

ISBN: 9781908168382 (epub, kindle) / 9781908168283 (432pp, paperback)

Visit bit.ly/Bookworm2-Nuttall

Bookworm III – The Best Laid Plans

Elaine and Johan prepare to leave Golden City, with Daria and Cass, to search for the Witch-King. But Elaine is arrested on the orders of a new Emperor, puppet of the Witch-King. She must escape and destroy him. Privy Councillors and Heads of the Great Houses have bowed to the Emperor. Only Elaine and her friends can prevent an all-out war.

ISBN: 9781908168764 (epub, kindle) / 9781908168665 (400pp, paperback)

Visit bit.ly/Bookworm3

Bookworm IV – Full Circle

Until now the Witch-King had remained hidden as a lich. But Elaine was intent on his destruction. Bonded to the unknowingly powerful Johan, she was the only other magician who understood the deeper layers of magic. As they slowly made their way towards the catacombs in Ida where his lich was hiding, he had to rely on the new Emperor to stop them.

ISBN: 9781908168948 (epub, kindle) / 9781908168849 (416pp, paperback)

Visit bit.ly/Bookworm4

Existence is Elsewhen

Twenty stories from twenty great authors
including
John Gribbin
Rhys Hughes
Christopher G. Nuttall
Douglas Thompson

The title *Existence is Elsewhen* paraphrases the last sentence of André Breton's 1924 *Manifesto of Surrealism*, perfectly summing up the intent behind this anthology of stories from a wonderful collection of authors. Different worlds... different times. It's what Elsewhen Press has been about since we launched our first title in 2011.

Here, we present twenty science fiction stories for you to enjoy. We are delighted that headlining this collection is the fantastic **John Gribbin,** with a worrying vision of medical research in the near future. Future global healthcare is the theme of **J A Christy's** story; while the ultimate in spare part surgery is where **Dave Weaver** takes us. **Edwin Hayward's** search for a renewable protein source turns out to be digital; and **Tanya Reimer's** story with characters we think we know gives us pause for thought about another food we take for granted. Evolution is examined too, with **Andy McKell's** chilling tale of what states could become if genetics are used to drive policy. Similarly, **Robin Moran's** story explores the societal impact of an undesirable evolutionary trend; while **Douglas Thompson** provides a truly surreal warning of an impending disaster that will reverse evolution, with dire consequences.

On a lighter note, we have satire from **Steve Harrison** discovering who really owns the Earth (and why); and **Ira Nayman,** who uses the surreal alternative realities of his *Transdimensional Authority* series as the setting for a detective story mash-up of Agatha Christie and Dashiel Hammett. Pursuing the crime-solving theme, **Peter Wolfe** explores life, and death, on a space station; while **Stefan Jackson** follows a police investigation into some bizarre cold-blooded murders in a cyberpunk future. Going into the past, albeit an 1831 set in the alternate Britain of his *Royal Sorceress* series, **Christopher G. Nuttall** reports on an investigation into a girl with strange powers.

Strange powers in the present-day is the theme for **Tej Turner,** who tells a poignant tale of how extra-sensory perception makes it easier for a husband to bear his dying wife's last few days. Difficult decisions are the theme of **Chloe Skye's** heart-rending story exploring personal sacrifice. Relationships aren't always so close, as **Susan Oke's** tale demonstrates, when sibling rivalry is taken to the limit. Relationships are the backdrop to **Peter R. Ellis's** story where a spectacular mid-winter event on a newly-colonised distant planet involves a Madonna and Child. Coming right back to Earth and in what feels like an almost imminent future, **Siobhan McVeigh** tells a cautionary tale for anyone thinking of using technology to deflect the blame for their actions. Building on the remarkable setting of Pera from her *LiGa* series, and developing Pera's legendary *Book of Shadow*, **Sanem Ozdural** spins the creation myth of the first light tree in a lyrical and poetic song. Also exploring language, the master of fantastika and absurdism, **Rhys Hughes,** extrapolates the way in which language changes over time, with an entertaining result.

ISBN: 9781908168955 (epub, kindle) / ISBN: 9781908168856 (320pp paperback)

Visit bit.ly/ExistenceIsElsewhen

TimeStorm
Steve Harrison

In 1795 a convict ship leaves England for New South Wales in Australia. Nearing its destination, it encounters a savage storm but, miraculously, the battered ship stays afloat and limps into Sydney Harbour. The convicts rebel, overpower the crew and make their escape, destroying the ship in the process. Fleeing the sinking vessel with only the clothes on their backs, the survivors struggle ashore.

Among the escaped convicts, seething resentments fuel an appetite for brutal revenge against their former captors, while the crew attempts to track down and kill or recapture the escapees. However, it soon becomes apparent that both convicts and crew have more to concern them than shipwreck and a ruthless fight for survival; they have arrived in Sydney in 2017.

TimeStorm is a thrilling epic adventure story of revenge, survival and honour. In the literary footsteps of Hornblower, comes Lieutenant Christopher 'Kit' Blaney, an old-fashioned hero, a man of honour, duty and principle. But dragged into the 21st century… literally.

A great fan of the grand seafaring adventure fiction of CS Forester, Patrick O'Brien and Alexander Kent and modern action thriller writers like Lee Child, Steve Harrison combines several genres in his fast-paced debut novel as a group of desperate men from the 1700s clash in modern-day Sydney.

ISBN: 9781908168542 (epub, kindle) / ISBN: 9781908168443 (368pp paperback)

Visit bit.ly/TimeStorm

Jacey's Kingdom
Dave Weaver

Jacey's Kingdom is an enthralling tale that revolves around a startlingly desperate reality: Jacey Jackson, a talented student destined for Cambridge, collapses with a brain tumour while sitting her final history exam at school. In her mind she struggles through a quasi-historical sixth century dreamscape whilst the surgeons fight to save her life.

Jacey is helped by a stranger called George, who finds himself trapped in her nightmare after a terrible car accident. There are quests, battles, and a love story ahead of them, before we find out if Jacey will awake from her coma or perish on the operating table. And who, or what, is George? In this book, Dave Weaver questions our perception of reality and the redemptive power of dreams; are our experiences of fear, conflict, friendship and love any less real or meaningful when they take place in the mind rather than the 'real' physical world?

ISBN: 9781908168313 (epub, kindle) / ISBN: 9781908168214 (272pp paperback)

Visit bit.ly/JaceysKingdom

GHOSTS ON THE PRAIRIES
A SACRED LAND STORY
TANYA REIMER

Some things are worth a fight. Strong words that Antoine's father drilled into him. After his father mysteriously vanishes one night, Antoine must find another income or he risks losing the Sacred Land that his father swore to protect.

On a well-paying ranch, Antoine meets Emma, a victim of underground slavery. Fighting for her freedom costs him his home, his sister, his best friend, and puts in question all of his values. If he succeeds, will she and her son fit into his world?

The prairies of 1916-19 come alive with bootleggers, slavery, fools in sheets, haunting spirits, shifty tunnel runners, and even exploding churches. *Ghosts on the Prairies* is alternative history suspense incorporating the paranormal and infused with romance.

ISBN: 9781908168535 (epub, kindle) / ISBN: 9781908168436 (356pp paperback)

Visit bit.ly/GhostsPrairies

CAN'T DREAM WITHOUT YOU
FROM THE DARK CHRONICLES

TANYA REIMER

Legends say, tens of thousands of years ago Whisperers were banished from the heavens, torn in half, and dumped on the mortal realm. Over the years, they earned magic from demons, left themselves Notebooks with hints and, by pairing up with human souls, eventually found their other halves. Humbled, they discovered the true purpose of life and many were worthy of returning to the heavens. But others were not.

Steve isn't a normal boy. He plays with demons, his soul travels to a dream realm at night using mystical butterflies, and soon he'll earn the power to raise the dead. In a haunting ritual performed by his father, Steve's soul is linked to Julia, an innocent. To protect her, Steve haunts her dreams, but it has the opposite effect and now he can't dream without her.

ISBN: 9781908168924 (epub, kindle) / ISBN: 9781908168825 (288pp paperback)

Visit bit.ly/CantDream

LiGa series
Sanem Ozdural

A thought-provoking series of books in an essentially contemporary setting, with elements of both science fiction and fantasy.

LiGa™
Book I

Literary science fiction, LiGa™ tells of a game in which the players are, literally, gambling with their lives. In the near-future a secretive organisation has developed technology to transfer the regenerative power of a body's cells from one person to another, conferring extended or even indefinite life expectancy. As a means of controlling who benefits from the technology, access is obtained by winning a tournament of chess or bridge to which only a select few are invited. At its core, the game is a test of a person's integrity, ability and resilience. Sanem's novel provides a fascinating insight into the motivation both of those characters who win and thus have the possibility of virtual immortality and of those who will effectively lose some of their life expectancy.

ISBN: 9781908168160 (epub, kindle)
ISBN: 9781908168061 (400pp paperback)

Visit bit.ly/BookLiGa

THE DARK SHALL DO WHAT LIGHT CANNOT
Book II

We find out more about the organisation behind LiGa as we travel with some of them to Pera, a place which lies beyond the Light Veil on the other side of reality. There are light trees there that eat sunlight and bear fruit that, in turn, lights up and energises (literally) the community of Pera. There are light birds that glitter in the night because they have eaten the seed of the lightberry. The House of Light and Dark, which is the domain of the Sun and her brother, Twilight, welcomes all creatures living in Pera. But in the midst of all the glitter, laughter and the songs, it must be remembered that the lightberry is poisonous to the non-Pera born, and the Land is afraid when the Sun retreats, for it is then that Twilight walks the streets...

ISBN: 9781908168740 (epub, kindle)
ISBN: 9781908168641 (400pp paperback)

Visit bit.ly/Darkshalldo

THE RHYMER
an Heredyssey
DOUGLAS THOMPSON

The Rhymer, an Heredyssey defies classification in any one literary genre. A satire on contemporary society, particularly the art world, it is also a comic-poetic meditation on the nature of life, death and morality.

A mysterious tramp wanders from town to town, taking a new name and identity from whoever he encounters first. Apparently amnesiac or even brain-damaged, Nadith Learmot nonetheless has other means to access the past and perhaps even the future: upon his chest a dial, down his sleeves wires that he can connect to the walls of old buildings from which he believes he can read their ghosts like imprints on tape. Haunting him constantly is the resemblance he apparently bears to his supposed brother, a successful artist called Zenir. Setting out to pursue Zenir and denounce or blackmail him out of spite, in his travels around the satellite towns and suburbs surrounding a city called Urbis, Nadith finds he is always two steps behind a figure as enigmatic and polyfaceted as himself. But through second hand snippets of news he increasingly learns of how his brother's fortunes are waning, while his own, to his surprise, are on the rise. Along the way, he encounters unexpected clues to his own true identity, how he came to lose his memory and acquire his strange 'contraption'. When Nadith finally catches up with Zenir, what will they make of each other?

Told entirely in the first person in a rhythmic stream of lyricism, Nadith's story reads like Shakespeare on acid, leaving the reader to guess at the truth that lies behind his madness. Is Nadith a mental health patient or a conman? ... Or as he himself comes to believe, the reincarnation of the thirteenth century Scottish seer True Thomas The Rhymer, a man who never lied nor died but disappeared one day to return to the realm of the faeries who had first given him his clairvoyant gifts?

Douglas Thompson's short stories have appeared in a wide range of magazines and anthologies. He won the Grolsch/Herald Question of Style Award in 1989 and second prize in the Neil Gunn Writing Competition in 2007. His first book, *Ultrameta*, published in 2009, was nominated for the Edge Hill Prize, and shortlisted for the BFS Best Newcomer Award. Since then he has published more novels, including *Entanglement* published by Elsewhen Press. *The Rhymer* is his eighth novel.

ISBN: 9781908168511 (epub, kindle)
ISBN: 9781908168412 (192pp paperback)

Visit bit.ly/TheRhymer-Heredyssey

Evil Above the Stars
by Peter R. Ellis

This thrilling fantasy series appeals to readers, of all ages, of fantasy or science fiction, especially fans of JRR Tolkien and Stephen Donaldson. If old theories are correct until a new idea comes along, does the universe change with our perception of it? Were the ideas embodied in alchemy ever right? What realities were the basis of Celtic mythology?

Volume 1: Seventh Child

September Weekes discovers a stone that takes her to *Gwlad*, where she is hailed as the one with the power to defend them against the evil known as the Malevolence. September meets the leader and bearers of metals linked to the seven 'planets' that give them special powers to resist the elemental manifestations of the Malevolence. She returns home, but a fortnight later, is drawn back to find that two years have passed and there have been more attacks. She must help defend *Gwlad* against the Malevolence.

ISBN: 9781908168702 (epub, kindle) / ISBN: 9781908168603 (256pp paperback)

Volume 2: The Power of Seven

September with the Council of *Gwlad* must plan the defence of the Land. The time of the next Conjunction will soon be at hand. The planets, the Sun and the Moon will all be together in the sky. At that point the protection of the heavenly bodies will be at its weakest and *Gwlad* will be more dependent than ever on September. But now it seems that she must defeat Malice, the guiding force behind the Malevolence, if she is to save the Land and all its people. Will she be strong enough; and, if not, to whom can she turn for help?

ISBN: 9781908168719 (epub, kindle) / ISBN: 9781908168610 (288pp paperback)

Volume 3: Unity of Seven

September is back home and it is still the night of her birthday, despite having spent over three months in *Gwlad* battling the Malevolence. Back to facing the bullies at school she worries about the people of *Gwlad*. She must discover a way to return to the universe of *Gwlad* and the answer seems to lie in her family history. The five *Cludydds* before September and her mother were her ancestors. The clues take her on a journey in time and space which reveals that while in great danger she is also the key to the survival of all the universes. September must overcome her own fears, accept an extraordinary future and, once again, face the evil above the stars.

ISBN: 9781908168917 (epub, kindle) / ISBN: 9781908168818 (256pp paperback)

Visit bit.ly/EvilAbove

THE MANDIGO TRILOGY
BY ANDERS REEMARK

MANDIGO
AND THE HELLHOUNDS

When eight-year old Mandigo finds a baby on a raft in a river, he saves it but, when he tries to carry it back to his village, he is stopped by a large stag. The stag forces Mandigo to take the baby deep into the forest, and soon other animals join the curious trio…

Thus begin the adventures of Mandigo, a boy who spends his days toiling in his father's mill in the mediaeval village of Oakhill. Little does he know that his life until this moment has all been one big lie. When the cataclysmic event known as the Storm wreaked havoc across the world many years before, it changed the landscape and released violent magical forces.

By his twelfth birthday, Mandigo has discovered that he has become the unwitting focus of those magical forces. He must quickly learn how to deal with them in order to save not only his own soul, but also the lives of everyone he loves.

The problem is that the Hellhounds are already on to him…

Anders Reemark was born in 1980 in Denmark. After highschool and business school, Anders was employed by Danske Bank, where he still works. Anders and his wife and four-year-old daughter currently reside in a suburb of Copenhagen together with a cat called Mouse(!)

Always an avid reader, Anders got into writing when reading aloud to his daughter. She always wanted more stories, and he discovered that he had a storytelling gift of his own. He began to write his stories down, and *Mandigo and the Hellhounds* is his first novel.

Anders' first novel, *Mandigo and the Hellhounds*, the first book in the *Mandigo* trilogy, was originally published in Danish (as *Mandigo og Helvedeshundene*) by Lars Stender e-books in 2015. Keen to see the story reach a wider audience it has been translated into other languages and is published in English by Elsewhen Press.

ISBN: 9781908168139 (epub, kindle) / ISBN: 9781908168030 (288pp paperback)

Visit bit.ly/MandigoHellhounds

THOMAS SILENT

or

Why there are no more mermaids

BEN GRIBBIN

When widower Angelo found a small baby on the beach twelve years ago, he decided to bring him up as his own son. A sign around the baby's neck said 'THOMAS SILENT", so that was the name he was given. Apart from other people's curiosity about his name, Tom's life so far had been happy and uneventful. When he wasn't at school Tom would help Angelo run the café in his beachside shack. One sunday morning Tom was in the café on his own when a tall, thin, old man called Phillimore came in to escape from the rain. He showed Tom seven bright blue-green stones that he claimed came from a mermaid's necklace. When Tom held one of the stones he could almost feel the rise and fall of the ocean. Phillimore left and Tom thought no more about the stones or the strange old man until Angelo died and the café shack was closed.

Six months later when Tom visits the deserted shack, he finds an envelope from Angelo and discovers what else had been found with the baby on the beach. Tom's simple life suddenly becomes a mysterious adventure that starts with a magical night-time swim to the shore of a strange land. He meets Coralie, a girl hiding in the caves on the beach with Phillimore. The people of the land are held captive to the will of an evil tyrant whose power comes from more of the blue-green stones, which he has been hoarding in the city of Murmur. Tom realises that he, Thomas Silent, is the only one who can defeat the tyrant and save the people of Murmur. But first he must understand the power of the sea-stones and discover his true self.

This delightful tale of real mermaids and mermen will enthrall any teenager who knows that they are special and have a great destiny waiting for them. Those of us who have left teenage years behind will equally relate to Tom's personal journey. We have all looked out from a beach and wondered what is over the sea, but so very few of us find out like Tom.

ISBN: 9781908168931 (epub, kindle) / ISBN: 9781908168832 (144pp paperback)

Visit bit.ly/ThomasSilent

About the author

hristopher G. Nuttall has been planning sci-fi books since he learnt to read. Born and raised in Edinburgh, Chris created an alternate history website and eventually graduated to writing full-sized novels. Studying history independently allowed him to develop worlds that hung together and provided a base for storytelling. After graduating from university, Chris started writing full-time. As an indie author he has self-published a number of novels, but this is his ninth fantasy to be published by Elsewhen Press, and the fourth in the Royal Sorceress series about Lady Gwendolyn Crichton. The first was *The Royal Sorceress*, followed by *The Great Game* and then *Necropolis*. Chris is currently living in Edinburgh with his wife, muse, and critic Aisha and their son.